Four

R E CARR

♡ R E Carr
Thanks for being
my fanged Yoda

ISBN: 1515099520
ISBN 13: 9781515099529

To the person in my life who left too soon—
The one who showed me my demons when she tried to drive them out.
Only shadows let you truly see the light, so from darkness let this tale bring some
sunshine—
Just not when any vampires are around.

1

"Well, it's not every day that you give your resume to a vampire, now is it?" Georgia asked with a wink as she leaned over her desk. Across the mahogany the applicant's eyes widened ever so slightly.

The interviewer smiled. "Oh, come on, sweetie, what else do you call a boss who works every night and drains his competition dry?" she asked.

The interviewee shrugged. "I don't know . . . a very successful real estate magnate?" she asked weakly. "I've handled some tough executives before, though. My last boss was in publishing, and she had me on call twenty-four seven."

Georgia read over the beautifully embossed life story of one Elizabeth Shaw one more time, careful to take note of her extensive experience spanning over nearly a decade. The interviewee wore an impeccable black suit and stunk of high-end cologne, with nary a single frosted strand out of place from her little blonde bun.

"We're still reviewing candidates, but I'll let you know," Georgia said while rising to shake Ms. Shaw's hand.

"If you need any more references—" the frosty blonde offered.

Georgia smiled again. "Don't worry, you have amazing qualifications. Any sane boss would be thrilled to have you as his assistant," she offered.

As soon as the candidate slipped out of the room, Georgia promptly tossed the resume into the already full bin. "It's a crying shame this one isn't sane, sweetie," she muttered before sliding around to the door and yelling out, "Next!"

Only one candidate remained perched on the sofa in the waiting room of Lambley, DeMarco, and Young, LLC—a slip of a college grad in a cute flowery top and pleated skirt. She stared up at Georgia with big brown eyes and a hopeful smile. "Ms. Sutherland?" she asked.

"Call me Georgia, sweetie. Everyone around here does," Georgia said as she reached out to shake the young girl's hand. As she led the next victim into her office, Georgia managed to make out the edge of some colored ink just peeking out from under a flouncy cuff.

"I'm Gail Filipovic," the interviewee offered. "The agency said I was supposed to say that Steve sent me, but I don't really know what that means."

"Oh, Steve sent you, did he?" Georgia said as her eyebrow immediately shot up. "I guess this afternoon hasn't been a bust after all."

Gail smiled as big as she could as she took in the swish office tucked into the back corner of a fifth floor of a downtown Boston high-rise. Her gaze darted between the wall of stately leather-bound tomes on one side and the old-school wood paneling on the other. The center of the space was filled by a claw-foot mahogany executive desk. Only the large dual monitor backs on the right side of the desk broke up the time-lapse Old World scene, and in the midst of all this traditional luxury, one Georgia Sutherland eased back into the towering leather chair, her eyes sparkling under a layer of thick eyeliner and golden fringe. The interviewer cracked her knuckles, showing off the red-white-and-blue nail polish that coordinated with her Union Jack T-shirt.

Across the table Gail plopped into her chair and fumbled with a well-worn leather messenger bag. Georgia watched the poor girl yank out a printout and try to smooth the corners before handing the flimsy piece of paper over.

Georgia scanned the Times New Roman font and ragged indents, along with the standard bullets of an out-of-the-box word processor template. Instead of reading the objective section or checking for a degree, Georgia zeroed in on Gail's unpainted, well-filed nails and clunky, comfort-driven footwear. Under one cuff was clearly a tattoo, and the other wrist sparkled with a silver chain with a caduceus printed charm.

"So you want to be a high-end personal assistant?" Georgia asked the girl wearing little flower stud earrings and a tortoiseshell plastic barrette.

"I really just want a job," Gail confessed. "My recruiter said it was a long shot, but that I should try to, um, branch out in this economy."

Georgia dropped the resume and her elbows on the desk before cradling her chin on the back of her hands and taking in the skimpy little sentences that described Miss Filipovic. "So you took care of day-to-day needs of a few wealthy older men . . . a Guido . . . Anderson? Oh, and this guy was named Rocco . . . Smith?" she asked the girl sinking into the guest chair. "What kind of business were they in?"

Gail's eyes darted to the left. "I guess you could say it was a family business," she said with a little laugh. "They did do some shipping though—like the executives here, right?"

Georgia smiled again, "You actually looked up what we do here?"

"I tried to do a little homework. I saw some references to global specialty transport and speculative real estate when I googled you all," Gail said. "I mean there wasn't very much, but then again most of the guys I've worked for were a little hazy with the business details too."

"You googled us?" Georgia asked. "That was your homework?"

Gail slumped a bit more. She ended up gnawing on a knuckle as she took the time to take in the woman behind the desk. Georgia Sutherland kept alternating between reading the resume and monitoring the screens on her phone and desktop. Her business attire consisted of a T-shirt under a white dinner jacket, skinny jeans, and stilettos. She occasionally flicked at the hacked-off ends of her hair as she tried to conjure the next talking point out of thin air.

Finally Gail managed to choke out, "I was in private nursing mostly."

"So that is how you assisted all these generically named fellows who worked for *family* businesses?" Georgia asked.

"I mostly worked for a specific Italian and Eastern European clientele, yes," Gail said. "But I always knew better than to ask too many questions or to really hope for a reference."

4 R E C A R R

"And you were hoping to find a different career path?" Georgia asked.

"My last boss referred me to the agency shortly before . . . before he passed, and he thought that I'd be a good fit, that they could place some-one like me," the interviewee said nervously, now checking the corners of the room. "Please don't be a bust," she whispered under her breath.

"You do realize that this is a live-in position, right? My boss is excep-tionally particular," Georgia said. "I've got to know that if you take my place, that he's taken good care of."

"So I'm interviewing for your old job?" Gail asked. "Did you get a promotion?"

Georgia sighed. "Something like that."

Her eyes lit up as a new document opened up on one of the screens. "So you went to nursing school and have taken care of two guys that died while under your watch and under rather suspicious circumstances—"

"To be fair Mr. Anderson did die of a heart attack . . . after the drive-by shooting," Gail said.

"Look, sweetie, I know what it's like to have employers with secrets," Georgia said. "And I know that you used to work for the Scribano family in New York, and I know exactly why your auntie sent you up here to start fresh, so don't worry about hiding anything, OK?"

"Oh my God, do you work for the FBI?" Gail squeaked as she hopped from her seat. "Mom warned me that they'd come looking after I cashed that check in DC—"

Georgia shook her head. "No, I don't work for the FBI. My boss just happens to be very well-connected, and, trust me, you are by far the most qualified applicant I've seen all day, Miss Filipovic."

"Really? I mean, you know who I really used to work for and that's OK?" Gail asked now, eyeing Georgia's hands to make sure that they stayed clearly visible and on the desktop.

"Indeed, my boss has had to use Viktor Scribano on a credit applica-tion before. They go way back," Georgia said with a smile.

"Oh, is he in a family business too?" Gail asked.

"Very different family," Georgia reassured her.

"I should have known something was up when I got an interview that didn't involve adult diapers," Gail said, chewing on her lip. "Did my folks set this up?"

Georgia shook her head. "Look, you know how it goes when there are groups that want to keep their true nature secret. It's rare that you can really get out completely once you start, but within any secretive group, there are always *different* levels of involvement and commitment, if you know what I mean?"

Gail took a deep breath. "Is it safe to talk if we're in this room?" she asked weakly.

"Want to walk and interview?" Georgia asked.

"Sure!"

The pair ended up exiting the swanky office building in record time and grabbing a quick coffee before continuing into the relative expanse of the Boston Common on a fine late spring afternoon. Once surrounded only by squirrels, Gail finally opened up again. "Were we under surveillance?" she asked.

"Don't think so, but you can never be too careful," Georgia said with a wink. She took a sip of her latte and let the sun pour onto her face for a moment. "Sorry, just been a while since I've had a nice afternoon outside."

"You know, it's funny. I know the men I worked for weren't the nicest people on the planet, but to me they were just old guys who needed help." Gail said and sighed. "I helped them, and now I fear every interview is a potential racketeering bust."

Georgia smiled. "Sometimes even bad people need good help."

"What kind of job is this really?" Gail asked. "I couldn't find much on Lambley, DeMarco, and Young, LLC, but it did seem like it would fit in with my former bosses' type of operation and the phone number always went to voice mail."

"So you called *and* googled?" Georgia asked slyly.

"If I had gotten to a second interview, I would have called my dad and asked his associates to check it out too," Gail said, returning the grin. "And trust me, they are very thorough when it comes to my safety."

"I'm sure they are," Georgia said as she checked her phone once more. "Hang on a sec." After a furious rain of texts, she finally had to make a call. "I'm on the interview right now . . . Yes, she's fine . . . Stop interrupting . . . Top drawer for shirts, your shoes are already laid out . . . Supper's made and in the fridge . . . There's a new box of straws in the cabinet over the microwave." She hung up after a quick "buh-bye."

"Was that—?"

"Mr. Lambley," Georgia finished. "I swear, some days he wouldn't know how to get out of bed without me."

"So he's needy?"

"He keeps a live-in personal assistant. What do you think?"

"Is he, you know, disabled?" Gail asked.

"No, but he's certainly special needs."

The pair walked for a bit more along the path until Gail broke the silence once more. "So as his assistant, you like—?"

"Take care of any day-to-day emergencies, answer his mail, run errands, do the shopping, and all that," Georgia said.

"Seems a little vague," Gail muttered between sips of her own coffee.

"Well, it's really a job that I can only fully describe once you agree to take it, sweetie," Georgia said.

"And why would I just do that?" Gail asked.

"Because you've been a nurse for mobsters since you graduated, and your mom balances the books for a Serbian drug cartel—not to mention the fact that you're running an assumed name and have about twelve dollars to your name. So unless you want to pick up work spoon-feeding the grandpa of a local Ukrainian hacker, this post is about the best one the agency is going to find for you."

"How—?" Gail squeaked.

"Echelon Employment Agency specializes in finding work for those with issues. They set up these sorts of deals all the time, along with their normal clientele. To keep up appearances, they sneak real candidates, like you, among a bunch of entitled hipster graduates who think that an MBA will make everyone fall all over them. They sent me pretty much everything about you, and I'm pretty sure that you'd be perfectly awesome taking my place, even if you've never worked in these exact circles before."

"So you know everything about me, and I'm just supposed to take this job?" Gail asked. "I mean, are you supposed to intimidate me or something, and I'm just going to fall over?"

"Oh puh-leeze," Georgia said with an exaggerated wave of her hand. "I was just going to show you the starting salary. That's what won me over."

It was Gail's turn to raise a brow. "Seriously?" she asked. "I mean, how much could it possibly—?" Her jaw dropped as Georgia showed off an image on her phone.

"Did you forget a decimal point?" Gail squeaked.

"You know how life can be really funny sometimes?" Georgia asked. "You sometimes find yourself in a situation so utterly ridiculous that you know somehow that once you accept it, that anything is possible? Well, I'm about to offer you that very same situation."

"Oh my God, your boss is some billionaire perv, isn't he?" Gail asked as she looked at the number again.

"Nope, he's just a vampire."

"A—a—" Gail stammered. She darted quickly to a nearby bench and planted her butt firmly on the weathered wood so that she could shake her head thoroughly a few times and take it in. She started to burst out laughing but stopped as she noticed just how serious Georgia's face had become. "A—a—?"

"Vampire," Georgia finished as she settled down beside her.

"Now you're just getting ridiculous." Gail laughed. "How can you even say that without a touch of irony in your voice?"

"A year of practice," Georgia said with a little shrug. "I used to think it was crazy too, but after a while, you just sort of get used to it."

Gail cocked her head and studied her interviewer for a solid minute. Nothing changed on Georgia's face no matter how far forward the brunette leaned in. "Are we talking like bizarre sex-cult blood drinker, then?" she asked.

Georgia shook her head.

"For real?" Gail offered.

"The salary is totally real. I'm looking to retire in Fiji this month at age twenty-nine," Georgia said in all earnestness. "Like I said, sometimes you get to a point where it's so insane that it has to be true, and you make that choice. You can walk away right now, and I guarantee you won't even think about this in a day or so. You'll have some white wine, tweet about it, maybe tell your cat, and it will be all over."

"How did you know I have a cat?" Gail muttered incredulously.

Georgia smiled again and continued with, "Or you can just run with it and have the craziest and most rewarding job you'll ever imagine."

"Do you think we could start with the white wine?" Gail asked weakly.

2

Although Klondike Bar never filled up completely until after the Boston theater crowds let out, Gail found herself squished against the retro chic wallpaper as a bachelorette party muscled its way toward the neon temple to all things alcoholic. She blinked as the mix of super-cold AC and super-warmed perfume mix assaulted her eyes. She slipped past a blonde in pink and tried to pick up a specific face in the lighting specifically designed to make everyone's specific flaws fade into a hazy shadow. Somewhere among the young businessmen fishing and the gals congregating for spritzers, Gail needed to find one woman in a pixie cut.

Something moved to the right. The young Serbian applicant quickly glanced at the mirror behind the vast array of vodka but couldn't see anything clearly.

"Excuse me," a soft voice said next to her. An arm in a slick gray suit passed in front of her, and she could see a really well-groomed head of raven-black hair, but the man in swanky threads slipped into the crowd before she could get any more details.

"Let's all cheer the future Mrs. Witherspoon!" one of the bachelorettes cried as the waiters tried to settle the group into a booth.

Once more Gail's eyes darted to the mirror. A pair of bright blue eyes surrounded by glam makeup flashed in the neon. She turned to see the back of the gray suit slip by. Before the disparity could quite register, a familiar voice piped up over the blaring dance music, "Gail!"

Tucked among white leather booths full of dozens of people all trying to look perfectly generically unique in their suits and cocktail dresses, one Georgia Sutherland lorded over the scene in a suit and tie of her own, having somehow managed to change into a tux in the less than two hours since she last met her potential replacement in the Common.

"I feel underdressed," Gail said as she eased into the banquette..

Georgia tugged at each cuff and straightened her tie. "It's actually part of the job. Mr. Lambley hates the smell of the dry cleaners. He's got a fund-raiser this weekend, and he prefers his tux broken in. A little lipstick on the collar only adds to the effect."

"You have to wear—" Gail was interrupted by a waiter setting a neon green concoction in a martini glass onto the table.

"It's an open tab. Get what you want," Georgia offered.

"What?" Gail asked as the music swelled into a hook. As the other person in a black jacket and white shirt waited patiently at the table, she finally took the hint and ordered a rum and Coke.

"Is this really the best place to talk?" Gail asked again as the song continued.

Georgia took a slow savoring sip of her dayglow beverage. "The best part about bars is that no one really listens to what is said, even if you're supposed to be talking to that person, right?"

Gail leaned in. "Is it always this loud?"

Georgia kept looking past the brunette until she could give a slight nod to the bartender. As the waiter returned with a glass full of fizzy booze and an umbrella, Georgia rose to her feet.

"We can go to the back now. Grab your drink," she said quickly.

Both girls darted to the back side of the U-shaped bar, past the magic zone where the girls who thought themselves most worthy jockeyed for prime stools with a clear view of the entrance—places with the added bonus of an occasional glimpse of just what sort of vehicle their potential prey left with the valet as the door opened.

Gail paused as a living, breathing wall of human flesh stepped between the pair and a velvet rope, but Georgia didn't even skip a beat. The bouncer slipped effortlessly to the left, sweeping the entrance free just long enough for the women to disappear under a VIP sign.

Unlike the outer holding area, this section of the bar kept the volume at a decent level, and the neon and mirrors gave way to plush sofas and rich velvet drapes. In one corner a blonde in sunglasses and a miniscule black number lounged over the arm of her settee. Gail could barely make out a single arm in gray silk, the rest of the man attached remained doggedly obscured behind a divider curtain. The suggestive smile and constant giggling of the blonde, however, painted a pretty clear picture of just how well he must have filled out the rest of his outfit.

A faint smell of smoke wafted from the blonde's corner. Both Gail and Georgia wrinkled their noses at the same time. "I thought you couldn't—" Gail said as they took over another table.

"Couldn't isn't a word used much around here," Georgia noted as she once more checked her phone. "Always on duty," she sighed as she had to take a minute to type furiously on her screen. As the little device lit up Georgia's face, Gail could just make out a touch of red in the corner of her otherwise flawless eyes. The interviewee decided to focus on her beverage as best she could until Georgia's rapid-fire thumbs finally came to a rest.

The blonde plopped her phone unceremoniously on her lap and chucked back the better part of the martini. "So, you decided to come back?" Georgia asked. "I had a good feeling about you."

Gail looked off to the corner with the blonde. "So are there, you know—?"

Georgia nodded.

"Over there?" she asked, nodding slightly toward the couple in the corner.

"First day, and you can already pick one out," Georgia said, beaming with pride. "Actually, once you notice one, it gets easy. It's kinda like once you notice the arrows hidden in the FedEx logo. Once you find it, you just can't not see it, right?"

"There's an arrow in the FedEx logo?" Gail asked.

"Don't worry, there's time," Georgia reassured her. "The one in the gray is a shy one. You won't find him unless he wants to be found."

Gail leaned in and said as loudly as she dared, "He didn't have a reflection."

Georgia laughed. "Of course he didn't." She pulled up her phone and took a quick snap of the other group. The blonde blew a kiss their way. Gail gasped as Georgia showed her a picture of an empty seat.

"No reflection, no photos. Hell, they can't even open the doors at the supermarket. I listened to some of the science suckers try to explain it once, but it was exceptionally dull and I tuned the details out."

"The blonde—"

"Yeah, that's Minnie. Don't worry, you're not her type," Georgia dismissed. "You ever seen that movie *Predator*? Eighties classic . . . got Arnie in it?"

Gail shook her head.

Georgia let out a little sigh. "Shame, it's one of my favorites. Anyway, apparently our vampire friends are just like the aliens in that movie, only *slightly* less ugly. Go ahead, try your phone if you don't believe me."

Gail pulled out her own phone, hands shaking. Sure enough, she too ended up with an empty sofa in her viewfinder. As she peeked over the tiny plastic shield, Minnie lowered her glasses to reveal bright red eyes. The interviewee responded by gulping down the rest of her drink. "It wasn't a trick," she squeaked.

"I've found that dealing with this situation really requires the Band-Aid approach. It's a lot easier to take if you just rip it off without warning," Georgia said. She motioned to the shadows, and within minutes a fresh rum and Coke was slipped in front of the obviously paler Gail.

"No reflection," the little Serbian girl croaked.

"Nope."

"Sunlight?"

"It doesn't set them on fire, but they will burn badly without protection."

"Bats?"

"Can communicate with them but not turn into them."

"Stake through the heart?"

"Allergic to wood."

"Immortal?"

"As far as I've seen.

"And they—?" Gail gulped and pointed to her neck.

"Oh yeah, we are pretty much walking lunch boxes to little miss blondie. Well, we would be if we weren't American. She thinks all of us taste like mass-produced junk food and subsidized GMO corn," Georgia said, tipping her drink toward the now-interested flaxen bombshell.

Gail let out all her breath at once, furrowed her brows, and stared at the empty sofa shot still filling up the screen of her phone. Georgia gently patted her on the shoulder. "It's rather a lot to take in, isn't it?"

Gail nodded furiously.

"Believe me, there is nothing they do that can't be overcome with a little common sense and a well-funded bank account. Trust me."

Gail continued to stare at her phone.

"Alcohol helps too," Georgia continued.

The phone just sat in her lap.

"If it makes you feel better, I sat in an old man's bathroom for two hours when I first figured it out," Georgia offered.

"This . . . is . . . insane," Gail finally choked out. She sniffed her drink suspiciously.

"I thought I had lost it too, but if you can just keep an open mind here, I think you can handle it," the interviewer reassured her. "Vampires are just like the mob. They do a few questionable things, but if you follow their rules, they don't bother you. They also tend to be secretive and have accents."

Blondie finally rose from her perch and drifted over to the living, breathing table. "Georgie, you brought a friend," the blonde purred in a ridiculously thick Austrian accent. "She seems so sweet."

Georgia casually slipped her finger under her collar and lifted a chain up over her tie. Instead of a crucifix, a house key plopped onto her chest. "Minnie, how is your brother doing tonight?"

"Oh, you know how he is," she said, easing back a step. "So, this one is with you?"

Georgia nodded slowly. "You know, Geoffrey keeps a reserve keg on tap here. I'm sure he wouldn't mind sharing. Now if you wouldn't mind, Minnie, I'm trying to do a little business."

"They have kegs?" Gail asked as the blonde slunk away in a huff.

"It's a slang term for a live goat. Many of the Eurofangs prefer imported livestock," Georgia said matter-of-factly. She giggled as Gail's eyes widened. "It's the twenty-first century. They can't just eat random people. It would be all over the Internet faster than the latest celebrity muff shot."

"Live goat," Gail said, quickly eyeing the door.

"Goats, pigs, horses . . . you name it. You would be absolutely shocked about the cows hidden in Harvard," Georgia said knowingly. "They feed off blood, preferably very fresh, but it doesn't matter as long as it's a mammal."

"So they don't have to, um, you know?" she asked, once more pointing to her neck.

"We're the lobster, really," Georgia confessed. "You see, the truth is that most of them are very picky, pickier than any toddler or entitled socialite. Every person is unique and thus hard to predict flavor-wise, so most of them prefer a simpler diet that's easier to control. The older ones, though, they don't want anything but human, and it's tricky to take care of them while upholding certain standards."

"Do you have to, you know?" Gail asked.

"You'd be amazed how many blood banks have a back door, if you know what I mean," Georgia said. "I have a friend that I've transitioned from stealing pharmaceuticals to plasma. At least this way, he's actually saving some lives. Oh, I'm starting to get kitten face again. You're still in shock, aren't you?"

Georgia was answered by the sounds of a straw slurping the bottom of the glass again. Gail nodded toward the waiter in the corner this time.

"How can you be so nonchalant about all this?" Gail asked.

"You mean besides the appletinis?"

"Yeah! I mean, is this what is going to happen to me?"

"Maybe. I'm not the only assistant out there and I'm sure everyone handles it a little differently, but yeah, we all get used to it at some point. It's a job."

"And someone just grabbed your resume and swept you off to a bar one night, and poof, you ended up super vampire secretary?"

"We prefer the term undead assistant, but no, my story didn't start with a resume. Mine started with a mix-up over a Craig's List ad and my roommate's sex life," Georgia said.

"Oh, now this I've got to hear," Gail said as she started on round three.

3

A little more than one year before happy hour at Klondike Bar, Georgia Sutherland found herself cursing at auto-formatting options as she tried her best to get her education bullet points to line up with the section she had copied in for previous work experience.

"Stop tabbing over," she growled as once more "university" rolled over to the next line. Across the room a pair of bold purple-and-white-striped knee-highs flicked over the edge of the sofa while their owner giggled continuously under a leopard-print velour blanket.

"Oh, yes! I want you to tell me I'm a bad girl. Why else would you have to spank me?" the girl under the covers chirped as Georgia continued to fight with margins.

"Alice, what did I tell you about using your inside voice?" Georgia snapped as she distinctly picked up three different euphemisms for male genitalia in a single minute span. Georgia slapped her forehead with her palm as she realized she had added herself as a "throbbing member of the National Honors Society" near the bottom of the page. After making the corrections, she quickly tabbed over to her e-mail to look for the daily update of Boston-area real estate. The lowest-priced studio within walking distance still made her cringe.

"New job, new apartment, new life," she hissed before stomping across the living room and into the repurposed closet that served as a kitchen/ entry hall to their two-bedroom urban paradise.

"Mmm, keep talking, sugar daddy," the voice continued as Georgia checked by the mail pile for something. After she rummaged over each counter and the disaster zone otherwise called a dinette set, she finally saw a black plastic object encased in a case with little skulls and hearts.

"If her phone is here—" Georgia mused.

"Oh, I'll tell you where my hand is," the voice moaned.

"Alice!" Georgia barked. "You have my phone again, don't you?"

"Gotta go," Georgia's roommate said as the cover went flying off the couch and joined its distant cousins of dirty socks and unidentified sweat-shirt visitors. The girl under the covers deftly tugged her T-shirt down with one hand while the other gingerly set the phone down between a pizza box and the remote.

"Boundaries, Alice," Georgia snapped as she picked up her cell. "Do I need to get any sort of cleaning product?"

Alice raised three fingers. "Scout's honor, it's clean. I'm not sure I can say the same on the other end. Paul was definitely making squidgy noises."

Georgia took a deep breath. "T . . . M . . . I . . ." she sighed. "You ran out of minutes again, didn't you? You're the one with the job, so could you please get something with an unlimited plan?"

Alice broke into hysterical laughter, her mouth full of braces click-ing against her lip ring. "You want me to pay for one of those rip-off contracts? Look, I can't afford to keep us in this life of luxury if we don't tighten our belts a little."

"Last week I had someone called Dirt Rat asking me if I could suck his cock while humming the '1812 Overture,' Alice. That's not exactly the kind of call I'm expecting midday."

"Oh, he's harmless, and not bad-looking either," Alice dismissed.

"I was shopping with my mom!" Georgia snapped.

"Well, if you were shopping for underwear again, I'm sure you could have worked that in—"

"Alice! I don't want to have to keep screening my calls for perverts, OK? I'm supposed to get callbacks for jobs, and I never know what I'm going to hear—and why, in the name of all things holy, would a man want to hear the '1812 Overture' while getting a blow job?" Georgia ranted.

Alice grinned like a Cheshire cat under her mop of orange and pink hair. "You kept him on the line, didn't you? You dirty little minx!"

"Only for a minute while my mom was getting a latte, but that's beside the point—"

"Well, you haven't gotten laid for months. That's probably why your job search is going so bad too. Frustration never leads to anything positive in the workplace. That's what I always say."

"No, you don't, and how would you even know what I'm up to?" Georgia protested.

"Because the only one raiding the condom drawer is me," Alice noted. "You also only shave your legs halfway up, and you're constantly wearing a ponytail. The signs say that you are either married or not getting any. Hmm, don't see a ring, do you?" Alice asked, prancing toward the closet-like kitchen. "Hey, are you going shopping this weekend, because the Chinese in here smells like pizza—"

"Alice, please!" Georgia barked. She took a few deep breaths and flipped her ponytail back over her shoulder. As she felt fuzzy elastic, her face fell. "I'm wearing a scrunchie every day, aren't I?"

Alice walked over and placed a hand on each of her roommate's shoulders. As she nodded gravely, Georgia stared right past her to the pile of dirty dishes overflowing the sink and the bills stuck to the fridge.

"You know what you need?" Alice said, trying to maneuver her metal-studded face squarely into the sight lines of her roommate.

"I need a job," Georgia said.

"True," Alice agreed. "But you need something even more, hun."

"I'm not calling back Dirt Rat if that's what you're going to suggest next."

"Oh, hell no, I'm not giving you one of my good ones!" Alice said. "What you need is a makeover."

Georgia took in her roommate's Wicked Witch of the West beach attire, gaudy makeup, and spectacularly unnatural hair color. "I need to finish my resume," Georgia countered. "I should be working on the important stuff."

"Didn't your agency tell you all about making a good first impression? Georgie, you're going all jeans and T-shirt on me today. Next comes rocky road and sweatpants, and soon in a year or two, I'm going to have to sell you off to reality TV to pay the bills. Give yourself a little pick-me-up from the outside in!"

Georgia scoffed. "I have interview clothes from my mom—"

Alice pointed to the ponytail. Georgia rolled her eyes in return. "There is more to getting a job than a haircut," she said as she broke away to go back to the computer.

"Georgie, I hate to be the bearer of bad news—"

"But you will anyway," Georgia muttered as she pulled up her resume again.

"Your resume isn't going to wow anyone, no matter what you do. If I were you—"

"But you're not," Georgia interjected.

"I'd go for getting your feet in the door with good hair and a low-cut blouse," Alice finished.

"Wow, and here I was thinking we were in the twenty-first century." Georgia sighed.

"Your last job was selling doughnuts—just saying."

"High-end pastries," Georgia defended. She turned back to the document that was supposed to define her life to this point. After a few minutes of good solid staring, she smacked her palm with her forehead. "You're right, I managed to get fired from a doughnut shop," she admitted slowly.

Alice once more wrapped her arms around her stressed-out roomie. As she rubbed her friend's shoulders, she offered up, "At least they were obnoxious hipster doughnuts."

"What does that have to even do with anything?" Georgia asked.

"On the bright side, we've lost about five pounds each since you stopped working there," Alice offered. As Georgia laughed, Alice rested her chin on top of her friend's head and stared at the lines of retail employment filling up the screen. "Hey, I know I'm a terrible roommate, but—"

"You're not that bad," Georgia admitted.

"I'm the one who steals your phone for kinky Internet-based hookups, Georgie. I also may have lent your toothbrush to Paul once or twice—"

"Oh my god, Alice!" Georgia snapped as she broke away from her friend. "You didn't—"

"I got you a new one, silly. Like I said, I'm a terrible roommate, but you're the only person on the planet patient enough to put up with me, so let me help you out this time."

"Does it involve kinky phone sex gigs?" Georgia asked.

"My aunt said something about needing a weekend receptionist at her firm. It's not glamorous, but nothing gets you a job around here quite like nepotism."

"Wouldn't I have to be related to her for it to be nepotism?" Georgia asked with a raised brow.

Alice flopped back on the couch. "This is what gets you into trouble, my friend. You simply don't know how to communicate without using sarcasm," she teased. "So, should I give her office manager your number?"

"Nothing weird, right?" Georgia asked.

"She does, like, real estate. Just because I'm a freak doesn't mean my whole family is," Alice said with a little laugh. "I think she needs someone to answer the phone and collect paperwork while she's off at the Cape all weekend. I doubt it pays six figures, but it would save asking for one more check from Daddy."

"You know, you are a terrible roomie, Alice, but you're still a pretty kick-ass best friend." Georgia sighed. She saved her current resume and hopped over to the couch. As the back of her head pressed against the cushion, she furrowed her brows together.

"You know what?" Georgia asked.

Alice grabbed the remote and eased next to her friend. "What?" she asked as her eyes glazed over to find something on the television.

"I'll go get that haircut . . ."

"It seemed so innocuous at the time," Georgia said as she once more focused on the girl back in the present. "But you know, there are some times where just the smallest thing can start a chain reaction that throws your whole life into a tailspin."

"Like going on an interview?" Gail offered.

Georgia began playing with the hacked-off ends of her hair. After a moment she twirled the loose strands behind her ear. "She was right, you know. I had gone totally into pity-party mode."

"Over losing a job selling doughnuts?"

"I kinda had a thing for the assistant manager there. When I found out he was shoving his cream filling elsewhere, I may have said a few things I regretted—very loudly and very publicly," Georgia said. "Bottom line, I was one hot mess living in a two-bedroom in Allston."

"And you got a haircut that changed everything?" Gail asked.

"Like I said, it's the little things sometimes. Alice was right. I needed to snap out of it, so I went to Newbury Street and blew the better part of my food budget getting prettied up. Nothing quite makes you feel better than looking a bit better and having a message on your phone that your interview is all set."

"So her aunt was the vampire?" Gail asked, confused.

Georgia cringed a bit. "Remember how I was saying that Alice liked to borrow my phone whenever she ran out of minutes?" she said with a little laugh. "I did mention that for a reason . . ."

"You said take it all off. I'm a man of my word."

Georgia opened her eyes and stared back at a decided lack of hair. All of her long dark blonde locks were piled on the linoleum, leaving only boyish remains to frame her shocked face. She turned from side to side, admiring the neat lines around her now decidedly visible ears.

"Wow," she said.

"You like?" the hairdresser asked again.

"It's just so different . . ." She trailed off as she felt vibrations from under the salon apron. She pulled out her phone to read the text she'd been waiting all morning to read: "Interview on at two," with the address following in the next line.

"This is the start of something great," Georgia said.

"Well, you look fabulous. You'll knock them dead," her stylist proclaimed proudly before brushing away the stray hairs from her neck.

She took a deep breath as the layers were peeled away. New hair and a new top had her beaming at her reflection. She curled her lip back to check for any remnants from lunch and did a final check for any snags in the hose.

"Telling you, you're fabulous," the stylist reassured her again.

Georgia made sure to leave an extra twenty for a tip before stepping out into the sun. Her phone buzzed again from the same number.

"Don't forget your references," it cautioned.

Georgia checked her bag again. A folder kept her resume copies safely tucked away from a thorough collection of emergency lipstick, deodorant, feminine products, and breath mints.

"I've got this," Georgia said as she started toward the subway. "Bye-bye, retail hell."

She didn't dare drown out the noise on the T with headphones, not with her brand-new perfectly coiffed locks. Instead she focused on staying in the far back, keeping a sharp eye out for any potential stains that might mar her new ivory top. A kid with a bright red slushie nearly gave her a heart attack as they shuddered their way out of Back Bay and into the stops on the way to the wealthy suburb of Brookline, Massachusetts.

She smiled as she noticed at least one guy eyeing her hemline. She stood a little taller until the sway of the trolley car nearly sent her plowing into a fake wood-paneled wall.

Her stop was near the end of the line, in the midst of trendy restaurants and expensive brownstones. She took in the vista of parking spots full of luxury cars rather than taxicabs, and breathed deep to take in a heady mix of fresh air and Thai food.

She set out toward the main thoroughfare of shops and little offices, always keeping a lookout for her cross street. As she rounded past a little jewelry store and a burrito joint, the businesses rapidly faded into row upon row of high-end residences.

"This can't be right," she said as she found herself in front of number 122. She checked her phone again.

Number 122 fit in with all the other houses on the street, a stately little red brick building with beautiful bow windows, shaded by a lovely old tree. Big planters of bright red begonias marked either side of the outer glass door, while little concrete bunny statues peeked from behind the bars on the first-floor windows.

Georgia eased into the vestibule, her heels clicking on dirty black and white tiles. A row of old bronze postboxes lined the wall to her left, but only one of them had a name card tucked into a slot: "Lambley, Apt 1."

"Of course," Georgia muttered as she saw all the blank spaces. She peeked at the inner door, but could see just some stairs in the darkened hallway. "Excuse me?" she called out, but no one answered. She checked the ground around the postboxes and the wall next to the door, but only found a single doorbell.

She looked at her phone—one forty-five. She paced around the entrance one more time and triple-checked the number placard over the main door. Finally she opened up her last text and pressed the link to call the number. It kept ringing and ringing.

"Don't panic," she cautioned herself. She quickly flicked through her phone, checking desperately that the address was in Brookline and not some other suburb. Her phone buzzed.

"Are you here?"

"Yes," she texted back.

A moment later she could hear a door open from within. She tugged her cuffs and made absolute last-minute adjustments as footsteps came closer and closer. She raised a brow when she could just make out a distinctly male silhouette in the glass.

"That's not your aunt, Alice," she muttered under her breath as the door opened.

Instead, the door opened to reveal a bespectacled man in a three-piece suit, the kind of suit that didn't come off of a warehouse rack. He raised a brow as he stood face-to-face with a girl in sensible pumps and a pencil skirt. "You're here about the position?" he asked, his voice smooth and deep, like one of those voices that read off movie trailers or tried to sell single malt scotch. It was definitely tinged by some sort of European accent, but in her jitters, poor Georgia couldn't quite fathom exactly where it was from.

For a moment Georgia tried to speak, but she simply had to just stop and appreciate a chiseled jaw and dark wavy hair that somehow managed to look completely controlled yet untamed at the same time. "Hi, I'm Georgia Sutherland, Alice's friend," she said, extending her hand.

The stranger's eyebrow remained arched over his glasses, which had darkened into sunglasses the moment he stepped into the hallway. "You're Alice's . . . friend? Not quite what I was expecting."

Georgia breathed a sigh of relief. "Yeah, we're nothing alike. I'm at the right place, thank god. I thought I'd gotten lost. Is this one of your properties?"

"Mine?" the stranger asked. "No, it's owned by Mr. Lambley's estate. I'm just here for business. He's waiting for you inside."

"Is Alice's aunt . . .? I mean, is Ms. Stafford here too?" Georgia asked.

"Not today. This is your interview. You're here about being the secretary, right?"

"Yes, I'm here about the weekend job. Alice said—"

"I'm sure you'll do fine," he said, moving to the side and propping the door open. "Mr. Lambley doesn't like to be kept waiting."

"Well, it's a good thing I came early then," Georgia snapped. She winced as she heard the tone of her words. "I mean—"

"Upstairs, first door on your right," he said brusquely.

"Was I supposed to get your name?" Georgia asked as the stranger walked out without another word. "Whatever," she said before heading up the stairs.

Unlike the cheery outer facade, the interior décor consisted of dingy sepia-toned wallpaper and hardwood desperately in need of fresh stain and polish. Georgia wrinkled her nose as she passed a rather fragrant corner. She could see a small pile of mousetraps behind the banister. She stopped just shy of the first door on the right.

"Hello?" she asked. "Mr. Lambley?"

"Are you the girl here about the job?" a pleasant enough voice replied.

"Yes, I'm Georgia. I thought I was meeting Ms. Stafford today, though."

"Ms. Stafford, eh? Well, she's not in here. Come on in so we can get started."

Georgia stayed outside of the door. "You know, I'm pretty sure that I'm supposed to be meeting Alice's aunt, so I'll just be going," she said quickly. As she took her first step back down, however, she heard the front door slam shut.

She pulled out her phone and slid one finger across to unlock it. She peered back down the stairs, but no one was there.

"Don't go, Georgia. I thought you were here about a job," the same kindly voice said from the first room on the right.

"Something is just wrong," she muttered. As soon as the words left her lips, she gulped and pressed a hand to her stomach. Her eyes widened in horror as her previously perfectly functioning cell phone went suddenly and inexplicably black. "Oh no, no, no," she hissed as she pressed every button in a vain attempt to bring it to life again.

"Georgia?" the voice asked again. "Is something the matter?"

She took stock of her options. Mr. Lambley remained only a voice. The guy in the high-end threads seemed to have vanished into thin air, and the front door was shut. She looked once more to the flickering light in the doorframe. "Not worth it," she declared as she hustled back down the stairs.

The front door, however, had made a different decision. No matter how hard she wrenched the knob, it refused to turn. "Oh, hell no," she declared as it refused to budge. Undaunted she sped past the base of the stairs and looked for another door, all the while trying to get her phone to come back to life.

She quickly found another bright red exit sign just down the first-floor hall. "Thank you, fire code," she declared as she shoved down the latch. The button gave way limply under pressure, but the door refused to budge. She shoved all her weight against the wood, but all she ended up doing was leaving a dirt stain on her sleeve.

"Is there something wrong, my dear? Are you playing hard to get?" That same damnably sweet old man voice called again, "Georgia?"

"Look, I don't know what's going on here, but your door is broken. If you don't let me out, I'm calling the cops!" she snapped.

"And how are you going to do that with no reception, little girl?" the voice taunted. "Don't worry. I don't . . . bite, unless you ask me to."

Georgia took a deep breath and reached into her purse. She carefully wrapped her fingers around her keys and pushed the sharp edge of one of them between her knuckles. Next she eased out of her heels and took a slow deliberate pace up the stairs.

"Why are the doors locked, Mr. Lambley? It is Mr. Lambley, right?" she asked as she inched toward the one open door.

"There's nothing to be afraid of," the voice reassured her.

"I'm locked in a strange apartment building by some creepy stranger, and I'm being taunted by an old man who knows exactly when my cell phone decided to act up—"

"Wait, did you say creepy?" the voice asked abruptly.

"Yeah, the guy in the suit. He had a totally douchetastic, creepy vibe going on—"

"Gray suit? Brown hair? He read as creepy to you?" Mr. Lambley interrupted again.

"Yeah, he totally put me off once he started talking, and I'm really getting the same feeling about you, so could we stop playing games and you just let me out of here before anyone does anything stupid?" Georgia warned.

"But I don't understand. Stefano never fails me. Tell me, Georgia, are you perhaps a lesbian? Did you respond to the wrong advertisement?"

"I was here about the weekend receptionist position!" Georgia snapped.

"Well, I wanted a dirty little secretary. I thought you were here to replace Alice," Mr. Lambley said.

"Hold on—a dirty secretary?" Georgia asked. "You were expecting Alice? Oh, crap, you're one of her . . . friends, aren't you?"

"Oh, I've never met her before, but she seemed ever so charming responding to my advertisement. When you arrived I just assumed that you worked with her or that it was going to be something like a two-for-one special."

"I wanted to answer phones for a real estate agency, Mr. Lambley. There has been a terrible mistake, and while I'm not sure exactly what sort of kinky hoedown you were planning here, it certainly wasn't supposed to involve me."

"This is terribly unfortunate," he sighed. "Could we maybe just talk for a moment?"

"We're talking now," Georgia said.

"I mean face-to-face? Everything is so impersonal now with the Internet and the chat and cell phone stuff," Mr. Lambley lamented from his room.

"That depends," Georgia said. "Are you wearing clothes?"

"Oh yes, indeed!"

She kept her keys ready in one hand and held her purse in her fist as she slowly inched toward Mr. Lambley's weak little voice. Sure enough, the room was a bedroom, complete with an oversize four-poster bed, fireplace, shag rug, and enough candles going to put a Catholic mass to shame. As she crossed the threshold, she picked up the distinctive scratch of a needle hitting vinyl. Sure enough, a second later the sultry sounds of a saxophone filled the air.

"Is that Kenny G?" she asked. Something danced just past the corner of her vision. Instinctively she flattened against the doorjamb and put up her improvised weapons.

"Please don't be frightened. You are perfectly safe, I swear," the voice said again.

Finally she could pinpoint the location to an armchair facing the fireplace that, even though it was daytime and April, was still roaring and crackling at full blast. It was one of those stereotypically Hollywood gothic red velvet chairs with claw feet and a back just high enough to obscure the person sitting in it. Only an arm could be seen, hanging limply over the arm, with fingers lazily twirling in time with the oppressive sounds drifting from near the mantle.

"Nothing about this situation reads as safe. Sorry, man," Georgia said, still maintaining her defensive stance. "Contrary to whatever impression you may have gotten from my roommate, I am not into this sort of thing. Hey, you said you wanted to talk face-to-face. Right now all I'm getting is the back of a chair."

"You aren't calming down," the voice said. The genuinely confused tone in his voice made Georgia lower her guard for barely a second.

"We're not going over this again, Mr. Lambley. You have me locked in a kinky gothic love nest with smooth jazz playing, so you really can't expect me to be any calmer than this. Now are we going to diffuse this situation, or am I going to have to break a window and cause a scene? It's a really busy street out there."

"Nothing fazes you, does it, Miss Sutherland?" he asked softly. "How remarkable."

"You have five seconds, Mr. Lambley," Georgia warned.

He pushed slowly up from the chair. Something creaked louder than the smooth jazz as a mop of shockingly ginger hair drifted into view. It seemed more like a bird's nest than human hair, scraggly and whorled around a central bare spot.

He turned slowly and flipped his mane like a would-be romance cover model and revealed not one but two distinct chins and a rather girlish little mouth. That same perky pout curled into a coy smile as frightfully bright green eyes positively lit up as he took in the girl making fisticuffs in his doorway.

"Wow," both of them mouthed at the same time. Each of them seemed focused on the pleasantly jiggly chest area of the other.

"Some things are actually worse than I imagined," Georgia said as she found herself staring at a portly little man in a green smoking jacket and silken yoga pants. He smiled sheepishly and wiggled his stubbly little fingers all at once, showing off an impressive array of golden bling, while at the same time wiggling his feet in a pair of fuzzy slippers. However, all of his clothing paled in comparison to just how ghastly the skin peeking out from every cuff and collar and mat of ginger fur was in the firelight.

"You may call me Geoffrey," he said, this time smiling wide enough to reveal that his incisors were blackened and very pointy. He lunged.

Georgia reacted on instinct, popping a left hook right into her would-be attacker's cheek. He yowled and stumbled backward, his slipper catching on the edge of the rug. Georgia didn't wait to see the results of the crash and instead ran across the hall. This door actually yielded as she turned the knob, and she quickly found herself in a dingy little bathroom. She locked the door and shoved everything not bolted down—from the over-the-toilet shelves to the plunger—against the exit.

"What the hell are you?" she screamed through the wall.

"You can see the fangs too?" Geoffrey asked incredulously. "How can you see the fangs?"

"Because you showed them to me!" Georgia said. She once more fumbled with her phone, but to no avail. "What are you, some kind of freak?"

"Freak? Well, that's rather rude," he said.

"You lunged at me!" Georgia said. She managed to angle the shelves perfectly to form a wedge between the sill and the toilet. Once sure of her barricade, she turned her attention to the window over the tub, but much to her chagrin, it was purely decorative and barred from the outside too.

"You weren't supposed to see the fangs yet. Sorry about that. Usually, you know, the miasma works. This has never happened to me before," he said apologetically.

Georgia started rummaging through the medicine chest, but could only come up with a can of air freshener and a wash cloth that was wadded in such a way that she didn't dare grab it. The door shuddered slightly, but the jerry-rigged étagère held firm.

"I'm terribly sorry if I frightened you," he said. "Please come out."

"I thought you said you didn't bite!" Georgia snapped as she started looking for a weapon among the paltry supply of cleaning products under the sink.

"I said I don't bite unless you want me to. You were supposed to want it!" he said. "The miasma was supposed to work!"

"Well, it didn't, and what the hell is miasma?" she snapped.

"It's the seductive aroma of the vampire," Geoffrey said. "It makes women weak in the knees."

"Yeah, well, I'm not really swooning over here. Is it some sort of cheap cologne?"

"No, it's the aura of a natural-born predator," Geoffrey stammered. "You do get what I am, don't you?"

"A very strange old man who thinks he's a vampire?" Georgia offered.

"Wait? What?" Geoffrey cried. "I am a vampire!"

"That's ridiculous, and yet it strangely makes sense," Georgia said. "But that doesn't change the fact that vampires aren't real, so we're back to square one."

"But you saw my fangs," Geoffrey cried. "And I can only guess by your initial reaction that you saw my true countenance and pallor."

Georgia hopped into the bathtub and clutched her knees to her chest. As she rocked back and forth against the cold porcelain, she slowed her breath and closed her eyes, taking in the past few minutes as best she could.

"Georgia?" Geoffrey asked. When she didn't immediately answer, the door suddenly banged again.

"Hey!" she snapped back. "I've got a lighter and some hairspray in here, and I'm not afraid to use it," she bluffed.

"You can't stay in there forever," Geoffrey warned.

"You just watch me, Geoff!" she snapped back.

Thus the standoff began as Georgia made herself comfortable in the bathtub while her stalker paced just outside the door. Occasionally the knob would wiggle or the wood panel would creak, but mostly the afternoon consisted of eerie stillness and quiet. As the sun started to grow longer through the window, Georgia took the time to try taking the battery out of her phone and replacing it, but it still stubbornly refused to boot up.

"Your trinket won't work around me," Georgia heard from outside her sanctuary.

"Really? How'd you break my phone?"

"It's my power," he said proudly.

"Your power? Because you're a—"

"Vampire," Geoffrey finished. "It's true. I spent years and years being mocked for only being able to shift subtle currents with my mind. Now, though, everyone needs a cell phone silenced or a computer fried. I guess you could say I'm a late bloomer."

"So you have the vampiric power of screwing up a cell phone? I guess you can't turn into a big cloud of mist and ooze under the door to get me then?"

"Mist? Ooze? Is that really a power you think we have?" Geoff asked. "Is that in one of the movies?"

"Yeah, it was in one of them, I think," Georgia said. "Vampires can turn into wolves, bats, mist, all that."

"Well, we most certainly can't!" Geoffrey said huffily. "But we don't need to sleep or eat for days on end. Can you say the same?"

"I'm still good in here." She sighed. "But you must be getting pretty hungry, though, since you obviously went all blood crazy and lunged for me soooooooooooo desperately."

"I was not desperate!" Geoff cried. "You were just so scrumptious. I got ahead of myself."

"Did you actually just call me scrumptious?" Georgia asked.

"Well, yes. I guess I did."

Georgia stood up and carefully approached the door. She pressed her hand against the wood and took comfort in just how thick and steady the old paneling remained.

"You're a real vampire, Mr. Lambley?" she asked. "And you were going to trap and eat my roommate?"

At first there was no response, but after a few minutes, she could hear the floor outside creak. A defeated voice mumbled, "I had the advertisements placed online."

"Kinky sex ads? Don't you think that draws attention?"

"No one really looks at those, do they?" he asked.

"Well, I'm sure they will once people turn up dead," Georgia said.

"Dead?" Geoffrey gasped. "Oh heaven's no! I wouldn't even dream of it. All I want is a little fun and a light snack."

"Really?" Georgia asked.

"Of course!" he said. "It's a win-win situation. I bring in girls who want to be seduced by a vampire. We share pure pleasure, and I get what I need to survive. I only take a few sips, and then they can return unharmed and we're both sated. What's the harm in that?"

"You get sweet vampire sex from girls like Alice?" Georgia asked in disbelief.

There was another moment of silence. "Well, normally I have the benefit of the miasma. It just doesn't seem to work on you for some reason. They see what they want to see."

"And I see a man who doesn't get lucky very often," Georgia said flatly.

"I panicked!" Geoffrey said suddenly. "I didn't know what to do, so the old reflexes kicked in."

"Wait, were you going to kill me?" Georgia asked.

"I didn't kill you," he defended weakly. "Please understand it's nothing personal. You're the first one of *those* people I've ever come across."

"Do I even want to know what *those* people are?" Georgia asked.

"So, are you like a vampire slayer or something?" Gail interrupted, wide-eyed as she worked on her third alcohol-infused cola. Next to her, Georgia nearly inhaled her own drink as she fought a fit of laughter.

"No, not a slayer or anything like that," she said, eyeing the blonde across the room.

"But how are you immune to the miasma stuff?" Gail whispered. "What's the secret?"

Georgia leaned over and gave an exaggerated look to her left and right. "The secret is . . ." she hissed in Gail's ear. The applicant held her breath as she waited. "The secret . . . is . . ." Georgia taunted. "Hang on, I'm hungry."

Georgia flagged down a waiter and whispered something in his ear. Meanwhile Gail flopped against her seat and kicked her legs furiously in anticipation.

"Is it like a secret technique?" Gail asked earnestly.

"Oh yes, there are monasteries in Tibet that have spent centuries learning how to battle the weapons of the vampire," Georgia said.

"Really?" Gail gasped.

Georgia shook her head. "No," she replied flatly. "Listen, Geoffrey . . . Well, let's just say he wasn't at the top of his game that day. I spent over two hours locked in his bathroom."

"And you still ended up working for him?" Gail asked incredulously.

Georgia nodded. The waiter returned with a tray packed with various dips and a basket of multicolored corn chips. She waved over the array. "Help yourself, please. There is no way I can finish the Arriba Sampler by myself."

Gail took a swipe at the pico de gallo. "Mmm, that's good," she said.

Georgia's face fell a little. She bypassed the bright red and green bowl and instead plunged her chip in a bowl of queso. "You'd be amazed what a little bit of chips and dip can tell about a person," Georgia noted. "Anyway, what was I saying?"

"You were in a bathroom for two hours," Gail prompted.

"Oh yeah," Georgia said. "Yeah, it's funny what can happen after you're just sort of left terrified, on a toilet, for the better part of an afternoon . . ."

"So, are you going to ever come out?" Geoffrey asked after one more shove against the beleaguered door.

"Nope!" Georgia called back. "I'm getting rather comfy in here. I just read through your two-year-old copy of *Sports Illustrated*. I don't have the heart to tell them that the prediction about the World Series was totally wrong."

"You really feel no desire at all for me?" Geoffrey asked. "Like nothing?"

"Not one iota," Georgia confirmed. As she sat on the toilet with her head buried in her hands, however, a faint and rather disturbing sound drifted from the hall. "Wait, are you crying?" she asked.

"No!" Geoffrey sniffled. "What do you care, anyway? You're one of *those* people. Did Stefano get you on purpose? Did he bring you here to taunt me?"

"I don't know this Stefano, but you said he was the creepy guy downstairs, right? He didn't give me the best first impression either, you know."

"Was he pale to you too?" Geoffrey asked, still sounding stuffy.

"I didn't really notice. He was just, you know, off to me."

"And I disgusted you, didn't I?" Mr. Lambley asked. "Please, I'm over two hundred years old, I can handle the truth."

"Well, you weren't what I'd call classically handsome," Georgia confessed. "And your outfit was both distracting and disturbing."

"You're sugarcoating your words," he sighed. "I'm a toad."

"I didn't see any warts or slime," Georgia said. "But you are really pale, you know that, don't you?"

"I've never had the most potent aroma, you know, but I could get by," he said. "As long as I could get a little time before the girl actually saw me—"

"You might want to start with a little bronzer," Georgia offered.

"Oh, some of us use makeup, but do you know how hard it is to not look ridiculous when you can't even see yourself in the mirror?" Geoffrey lamented.

"I guess I could see where that would be difficult—"

"Oh, Georgia, I'm such a failure, an utter, utter failure," Geoffrey sobbed. Georgia remained frozen in utter slack-jawed silence as the vampire in the hall carried on whimpering and sniffling like a soap opera diva.

"It started so long ago. I just lost my mojo," he blathered. "There just came a time when I couldn't get the fangs to even come out."

"Well, I saw your fangs," Georgia offered weakly.

She heard a clatter outside the door. "These black ones? They're fake!" he bawled, now sounding mush-mouthed. "I was hoping if I could get you good and scared that it would be like the good old days when I could chase a flapper down a dark alley and have my way with her. Oh, it was so wonderful when the hemlines started rising and the standards lowered after the Great War."

"You're kind of oversharing here, Mr. Lambley, but if it feels good to let it out—"

"They call me Toothless Geoff!" Mr. Lambley wailed. "Me, the Scourge of Essex . . . the Wolf of Wembley! Now I'm just this sad old sack of dust who can't even bite the single most beautiful woman he's seen in fifty years."

"Oh, come on now, it can't be that bad—"

"I've been eating blended rats!" he sobbed. "Do you know what a blended rat is? It's literally a rodent shoved in a blender."

Georgia pulled out her phone one last time and slammed it against her leg in a vain attempt to bring it to life. As it remained frustratingly black and the sky looked darker and darker, she eased off the john and crept closer to the door.

"But what about all your advertisements?" Georgia offered.

"Your friend Alice was the only one who ever responded," Geoffrey sniffled. "Tell me truly, do you think she would have had me?"

Georgia took a deep breath. "Um, probably not."

He responded by breaking out into another round of violent sobs. Finally, reluctantly, Georgia shoved her full body weight against the étagère and dislodged the jam. Sure enough when she opened the door, Mr. Lambley was collapsed in a puddle of pink-streaked tears and holding a pair of pointy dentures in his shaking hands.

"You're free to go, Miss Sutherland," he whimpered. "Just promise me you will never speak of this to anyone."

Georgia eased down next to him and gingerly wrapped an arm around his surprisingly narrow shoulders. "Honestly, who is going to believe that I spent my afternoon in a bathroom hiding from a sobbing vampire? I'm looking for a job, not a one-way ticket into an asylum."

The old vampire collapsed against her chest, sobbing anew. She cringed as she patted his back and muttered, "There, there."

"You should go," he choked out.

She eased away from him. "Do you really think that I'm the prettiest girl you've seen in fifty years?" she asked as she headed for the stairs.

"Sixty," he said softly. He pulled out a brass house key and offered it to her.

"I can really go?" she asked.

"First, I will invite you to stay," Mr. Lambley said, sniffling once more.

Georgia pulled back and eyed him suspiciously. "Let's not get into that crap again—" she started.

"Oh no!" he said quickly. "It's just that my kind have certain unquestionable rules. The law of hospitality dictates that no vampire may cause harm to any person welcomed into his home, nor may vampires enter a home where they are not welcomed."

"So there is truth to that whole vampires-have-to-be-invited-to-come-in thing?" Georgia asked incredulously.

"Hollywood did get a few things almost right," Geoffrey confessed. "So I am offering you this key to my home. So long as you accept it, you are safe from me."

Georgia grabbed the key from him. "It's that simple?" she asked.

"Well, technically you would have to stay here for me to grant full protection, to accept my hospitality," Geoffrey said. "I assume that you'll throw it away as soon as you are out of sight, but at least for these few moments, I can keep you safe."

"Keep me safe?"

"Stefano may still be near," Geoffrey warned. "He's from a very traditional family, very German, if you know what I mean. If he were to figure out that you know . . . that we didn't . . . well, let's just say he might get a little bitey."

"So, I accept your invitation to live here and receive your hospitality," Georgia said slowly while checking the vampire's face for any more clues as to exactly what she needed to do. "*But* I can still leave right now, as long as I do my best to forget this ever happened?"

"I admit it's playing with the rules a little, but it's probably for the best," Geoffrey said sadly. "Now you should go."

"I should."

The two of them stared at each other in the hall. She finally noticed the frayed and stained edges of his cuffs and a little rusty stain on his lapel that very clearly had gray fur still matted in it.

"Yeah, I'm gonna go," Georgia said quickly as she hustled for the door. The key slipped right into the lock, and for the first time in the afternoon, she was free. She eyed her reflection in the glass of the outer door and quickly smoothed her top and tried her best to look presentable. As she stared at her now-disheveled do, it became obvious that there was no corresponding image of Geoffrey in the glass. She looked over her shoulder, and sure enough, the hunched little mess of a man was indeed right behind her.

"You are a vampire," she whispered.

He waved his hand in a flourish worthy of a Vegas illusionist. A moment later her phone screen flickered with new life. She looked down once to see the welcome message, and by the time she looked back up, the squirrely little bloodsucker had vanished into the shadows of his hollow brownstone.

She hustled out the door and into the crowded streets of Brookline. It occurred to her as she stumbled onto the concrete that her heels were still somewhere in the vampire's den. Still, she continued a few more feet until a very bright neon palm tree sign caught her eye. Not a half block from the vampire's abode was a Caribbean restaurant that was bypassed by most of the post-work crowd, who were hunting swankier take-out options. Just beneath said palm tree sign was a little handwritten note offering up the house specials. Georgia broke out into hysterical laughter.

She walked straight to the counter and plopped her wallet down. "I'll take a number two and the blood-sausage special to go. Actually, make that two sausage specials."

4

"It started with takeout?" Gail asked incredulously. "And they can actually eat blood sausage?"

"It's basically the vampire equivalent of popcorn or rice cakes, but yes, they can eat cooked blood or meat," Georgia said as she paused to pick at more chips and cheese dip. "You just have to liquefy it first."

Gail set her chip back in the basket. Georgia continued to blissfully scoop up some guacamole. "Half the job is meal planning," she said. "You aren't grossed out by raw meat or a little blood?"

"Meat . . . no . . . liquefied meat . . . a little," Gail confessed. "And you know this blood. It's not, um—"

"Human?"

Gail nodded.

"At times, but it's not like you're going to be asked to kidnap people and shove them in a closet to be human juice boxes. I would get you in touch with some of my medical suppliers. You would be amazed what a little creativity and leverage over a phlebotomist can get you in this town. We'll get to that, though. You should probably focus on the first real rule of dealing with vampires."

"And that is?"

"You need to know their rules."

"But I'm still imagining liquefied meat," Gail said while fixating on the little red pool of tomato juice left in the salsa bowl.

"It's easy to get focused on the gory details. Yes, part of the job may involve scrubbing goat guts up after a wild kegger, but the day-to-day isn't so dramatic. Mr. Lambley likes a Morcilla Mojito every holiday with an extra wedge of lime and insists on a live chicken on Sundays. Don't worry; we have a supplier out of Super 88 who just makes the delivery without question. Asian markets are brilliant for finding whatever you need."

"I never thought about that," Gail said.

"Yes, you can get liter bags of pig's blood surprisingly cheap," Georgia said. "Pretty much every ethnic butcher in town knows me as the blood sausage queen of Boston. I even had to write a blog entry on it."

"Oh, I guess you'd have to explain why you always needed a bunch of blood," Gail said.

Meanwhile Georgia tapped away at her phone until she managed to pull up a picture of herself in a head scarf and bright white apron proudly showing off a plate full of dark brown sausages on a bed of glistening roasted beets. The tagline read "Bloody Good Recipe."

"I got some stalkers from this," Georgia said. "Also one person commented that it tasted like disgusting, overworked dog crap, and I've always wondered just how he knew exactly what that tasted like. Anyway, I digress. Did you need another drink?"

Gail nodded.

"Just remember that if you take this job, you will be surrounded by a whole bunch of creatures that regard you as little more than this plate of tasty sausages. They may look human. Some of them even act human, but never make the mistake of humanizing them, Gail," Georgia warned. "I'm lucky, their perfume doesn't work on me, but they all have different powers that I can't do a damn thing to stop. You need to understand how they think and how they work if you want this job."

"And they have rules?" Gail asked.

"Four to be exact," Georgia said. "If you know the four rules, then you never have to be afraid of a vampire ever again."

"Four?" Gail asked, making a bit of a face. "That just seems like an odd and arbitrary number, doesn't it?"

Georgia looked off toward the blonde's table. "A friend of mine once said that four was the number of death, so it's only appropriate that their kind had exactly four laws." She quickly took another drink to cover up the catch in her voice. "Vampires are a persnickety lot. Why would they stop at three rules or stretch it out to Ten Commandments anyway?"

Gail shrugged and starting sipping on another tasty beverage. "So one rule is that they have to be invited in, right?" she asked.

"It's actually rule number three," Georgia noted. "But it's the rule that saved me for a while."

"And rule number one?" Gail asked.

Georgia put down her drink and continued, "Of course, I asked that too . . ."

Georgia perched uneasily on a musty wingback chair as her strange new companion paced back and forth in front of his now snuffed fireplace. She leaned toward him and asked again, "So, what's the first rule I need to know?"

Geoffrey continued to chew on his lip. Although he claimed to be toothless, he somehow managed to crack open the inside of one corner, causing a distracting feather line of red against his icy white skin.

"Well, the first rule doesn't really apply to you, but to us it's the most important of all the rules," the vampire noted as his pace increased. He kept gesturing wildly to the corners of the room as if he was searching for something to say or for confirmation from a shadow.

"Is someone else here, Mr. Lambley?" Georgia asked as she squinted to see anything in the corner.

"No, I guess not," he said. "I suppose I've been alone so long that I started talking to myself. I'm not entirely certain that you're real, Miss Sutherland."

She held out her arm and pinched it. "I feel pretty real to me," she said with a little smile. "I've been wondering if I'm actually awake. After all, I am talking to a vampire in Brookline."

Geoffrey paused to ponder the concept. He then let out a very sad little laugh. "Please, if you were dreaming of a vampire, why would he look like me?" he asked.

"Good point, and if you were dreaming of a girl to end up in your clutches, why would she be as hard to get as me?" she countered.

"I guess this is all too strange not to be real," Geoffrey mused. "I'm just not usually the one to get the woman alone in my house, and I suppose my age is showing."

"I'm guessing your mother would not approve?" Georgia laughed.

"My human mother?" The vampire mused, "Actually I think she'd be rather thrilled for me. She did worry ever so much that I would have no real prospects. At the time I had an older brother, and I was never considered much of a catch, I must confess. My brother was far more of a Lambley than I ever wanted to be, but that is a story for another time, Miss Sutherland. We live in the present and thus should be focused on such."

"Well, I don't often get to talk to someone who's seen the nineteenth century, so excuse me if I keep you digressing," Georgia said. "Did you want me to blend you another sausage? Your cup looks empty."

Geoffrey waved his hand. "Oh no, it's richer than I'm used to, and it has garlic in it—" he said quickly.

"Oh my god, I didn't even think!" Georgia cried. "Garlic and vampires don't really mix."

"Actually, I've always had a strange fondness for it," Geoffrey confessed. "Stefano always called me a cat who craves milk for that."

"So it makes you sick but you like it anyway?" Georgia asked.

"Exactly! You are a clever girl," he exclaimed. "I even have garlic bread dipped in a bowl of pig's blood on my deathday. Something about garlic just makes me feel positively tipsy, but most of my kind want to vomit at the mere smell of it."

"So, you're special," she said. "Eww, the salad they gave me has cilantro in the dressing. I can't stand it."

"Oh, can you add it to my next sausage shake then? It's one of my favorites, and I never get it," Geoffrey said, positively giggling.

"I thought you guys could only drink blood," Georgia muttered as she dumped the remainder of her Styrofoam container onto his remaining sausage.

"Can your kind only eat broccoli and oatmeal?" he countered. "Vegetables to me are like candy to you. It's terrible for me, but I love it anyway. I need blood to live, but it's the variety that gives me pleasure. I remember I once drank from a young girl from Barbados who I thought tasted just like rum and mangoes . . ." He trailed off as he watched his companion's face tighten. "I do feed off your kind, Miss Sutherland, but I've never killed anyone. I don't think it's right."

"Well, I'm glad you have standards," she said softly.

"You should know that the first rule of being a vampire is that life is sacred," Geoffrey said. "Our law of kinship dictates that no vampire can kill another. We are honor-bound to protect life, and there are even families that have extended that to humans—"

"Your family included?"

Mr. Lambley nodded vehemently. "My vampire parents taught me from the day I was turned that humans exist to give us life, to kill them is a sacrilege. I think that may have come from my prime sire's Hindu upbringing, but I'm not sure. Still, the English clans have always been more concerned about your kind than other families."

"So, no killing at all? That's admirable, but you are eating a dead animal."

"I have to, to live," he said. "And despite what some of the more elitist families think, I do think there is a difference between a pig and a human. Killing isn't just wrong, it's messy, you know. If bunches of people turn up dead in a single city, it's news and attention. Attention is the bane of our kind. In fact, that is rule number two!"

"Attention is bad is actually a rule?" Georgia asked

"No, the second law is the law of secrecy!" Geoffrey cried. He stopped to look at the fireplace. "Are you cold? Should I put on the fire again?"

"Nope, still not cold," she said. "Are you getting hyper again?"

"I just never know what your kind want. I don't have to worry about my temperature, but your kind seems to need a certain range to be comfortable."

"What my kind really needs is to stop being called 'your kind,'" Georgia sighed. "My name is Georgia, try it out."

"But, Miss Sutherland—"

"Georgia," she ordered. "Just like the state."

"Georgia." He rolled the word around in his mouth like an old wad of gum. "What was I even saying?"

"About the fireplace or the super-important law of secrecy that vampires seem to love so much?"

"The second law," he sighed. "And if I am to call you Georgia, then you must certainly call me Geoffrey, though if others of my kind are around, especially the older ones, you'd want to refer to me as Mr. Lambley."

"OK, Geoff," Georgia said, now smiling again. "So, you like secrets."

"We have to keep our existence a secret," he said with a fervent nod. "Can you imagine what would happen if the world was to learn that humans weren't the top of the food chain, so to speak?"

Georgia furrowed her brow. "Yeah, I can see where that might get awkward."

"There have been leaks to be sure. After all, there are too many of you to not have a few notice that we exist, but the beauty of looking so much like you is that we can disguise ourselves right under your noses—"

"And as long as vampires seem like ridiculous fiction—" Georgia continued.

"Then you refuse to see us. After all, vampires *are* ridiculous!" Geoffrey finished with a gleeful laugh.

"Especially when you are teen angst sparkling mumblers who stalk the most emo girl in the room!" Georgia laughed.

Geoffrey rolled his eyes and snorted, "Sparkling? What are we, a beverage? Still, sometimes the folklore and the stories get too close."

Georgia started giggling uncontrollably as she looked at her can of soda. "So if you don't sparkle, what has Hollywood gotten right?" Georgia asked.

"Hollywood," Geoffrey snorted. "You should ask Stefano. He's the one who likes all those movies. Hours and hours, he likes to talk about them. Oh, most of it is close. We don't like sun, we drink blood, and we don't die. Pretty much everything else is wrong somehow."

"You're pale and have an accent," Georgia added.

"You have an accent to me, you know," the vampire sighed. "And you are currently under my protection, never forget that."

Georgia got quiet, so quiet that they could both hear her stomach gurgle from the carbonation. She looked at the filthy hearth, the melted-down candles and the tattered rugs. Then she noticed the old-style mousetraps in the corners.

"Did I sound threatening?" Geoffrey gasped.

She shook her head, and the vampire's shoulders fell a bit. He too took in the general state of disrepair. Finally he shuffled to his feet and wandered off to a bookcase, where he pulled out a rather old-looking volume clad in brown cloth.

"It's a first edition *Oliver Twist*," he said. "I always loved this story. It's from 1838, and it looks newer than most of this house."

"You really need help, don't you?" she asked.

Geoffrey nodded. "As long as you take my hospitality, you will be protected," he said. "The third law is what allows us to keep certain humans safe."

Georgia smacked her forehead with her palm. "You've pretty much just told me everything about vampires. You've broken rule number two."

"Indeed," he said as he shelved his book carefully among a neat row of other tomes. "And I can't make you forget."

"Look, you might be immortal, but I'm not, so let's stop beating around the bush. You wouldn't tell me all of this unless you had an angle. What do you really want?"

"Rule number four: a vampire's oath is his bond. Once we make a promise, we are honor-bound to keep it," Geoffrey said.

"What?" she asked, staring right at the vampire for the first time in a while.

"We can make unbreakable contracts," he said quickly. "If we break them, our lives are forfeit. For ages we've used them to take on human retainers to help us in our times of need. After all, we can't truly hide among humanity for any time without some help."

"I've got a bad feeling about this—"

"You know, my sire always was talking about kismet . . . that there was a certain fate that governed all our lives. You came here today under the impression that you were looking for employment, did you not?" he asked.

"Oh, you aren't saying—"

"Vampires have servants, always have and always will—"

"You don't," Georgia countered.

"Well, my last one died in '72. I never found anyone to replace him. He was one hundred and two. I pretended to be his grandson."

"I don't think I'll need the same job till I'm a hundred and two," Georgia said.

"Miss Sutherland . . . Georgia . . . I am a terrible mess, and you need a job," the vampire said. "Will you take a position as my assistant, so to speak?"

"Define assistant," she said, still sizing up the lumpy bloodsucker.

"Take care of my day-to-day needs, as you did tonight. Bring me food, help me dress, and bring a little life to this wretched place. If I don't do something soon, the disrepair will attract attention. Stefano's assistant did a little outside, but you can only be a recluse for so long before human curiosity takes over," Geoffrey said.

"So you basically want a cook, a butler, and a maid all rolled up in one?" she asked.

"I need to understand this modern era if I am to survive. I need to present myself to society again, or I will forever be Toothless Geoff! Don't you see how amazing this could be? I might not be destined to wallow here until the end of my days with only one Italian undead hoodlum to see me to the great beyond."

"Yes, it all sounds magnificent . . . for you. Not to be rude, but what's in this for me? Do I help you regain your mojo and end up as dessert?" Georgia asked. "I mean, you don't even know me. I've never been any of those things that you need. I can't even clean my own apartment, for Pete's sake!"

"But you have kindness in you," he said quickly. "You could have run, but you got me food."

"I had a moment of weakness. I'm normally a bitch," she replied flatly.

"Good! You need to be forceful to deal with the others of my kind, and I need to present some confidence if I'm ever to escape my dreadful reputation."

"Are you just going to counter every argument I make?" Georgia sighed. She then muttered, "You remind me of my mother."

"You know if I hadn't been turned, I wanted to be a lawyer," Geoffrey said. "You can't deny the strangeness of our meeting, can you?"

"Oh, it's the not the strangeness I'm denying, it's the sanity of it," Georgia said as she hopped to her feet and started rummaging for her purse and shoes.

"What could have brought us together, if not fate?" Geoffrey gushed.

"I rode in on the T, actually," she sighed. "Look, you're a fascinating old dead guy—"

"Undead," he corrected.

"Undead guy, right, but I can't just agree to be your assistant. Like you said, vampires have all these rules and they think I'm lunch, so it's not just something I can do on a whim. Plus if I stick around, I'll need your protection, and no offense, you don't seem like the kind of vampire who can really protect anyone."

As she slipped her purse over her shoulder, she ended up growling out loud. "But I still know all about vampires, don't I?" she grumbled.

"You see the delicacy of this situation, don't you?" he asked.

"You are more devious than I thought," Georgia said. "You told me everything, knowing good and well that you couldn't do the Jedi mind trick to make me forget, so you've been buttering me up to get me to be your little slave. Ugh!"

"As I said, it's fate."

"Don't believe in it," she snapped. "Look, I can swear to you that I will never ever tell another soul what happened today. Vampires aren't the only ones who can keep a promise."

"I'll make a contract with you for one year and a day of service. Please, Georgia, just help me."

"I can't believe this," she muttered.

"And I'll give you one hundred thousand American dollars for your trouble."

Georgia plopped right back down on the rickety little seat. "Excuse me?" she choked out.

"You asked what was in it for you. If you will enter a contract to serve me for one year and one day, I will give you one hundred thousand American dollars," he said. "I will sign the contract without hesitation."

Georgia sat there for a good long while. She rolled the strap of her purse over her fingers until the leather started to curl. "You need a cook, a maid, a butler, and a social planner?" she asked.

"Indeed," he said. "And of course, someone to run about during the day for me. There is so much business that is simply not convenient when you cannot go out in the sun."

"I'm not going to bury a body for you or take part in kinky sex games," she said flatly.

"But you can handle the sight of blood, yes?"

"As long as it's never my own. There is no way I'm going to become a vending machine for you if you start getting peckish."

"Of course," he agreed immediately. "I will draw up a contract that states you are my sacrosanct assistant. I'll have you know that in the eight decades that my last assistant served me, I never once partook in his blood."

"And the contract protects me from your undead friends."

Geoffrey suddenly looked off to the side again.

Georgia raised a brow and let out a long, low, "Geoffrey?"

"There are four laws—"

"Geoffrey!" she snapped.

"It's the law of hospitality that will protect you from the others of my kind."

"Yeah, you gave me a key, didn't you?"

"The key was to protect you when I thought you were leaving. It would have bought you some time, but if it seemed like you were no longer accepting my hospitality—"

"You want me to live here too, don't you?" Georgia sighed.

Geoffrey broke out into a smile so big Georgia could see every gap where a fang should be. She ran a finger along the floor and cringed as it turned gray from a single swipe.

"I really want to say not just no, but hell, no, right now. You know this, don't you, Geoffrey?"

"I'm afraid that is one of my conditions for employment. It's the only way I can protect you and get the care that I need," he said with a little nod. "It's so unnerving to be asleep alone during the day. A few decades ago, I'm sure I could fight off any intruders, but now, I'd only catch a break if they died laughing."

"But if I just randomly move in with a creepy old guy . . ." Georgia said. "I mean, I can't just tell them that I'm assisting a vampire, and somehow with your whole secrecy thing, I can't just claim you're a wealthy software mogul who had a crack-up or something, can I?"

"So, what did you say?" Gail asked, once more leaning in to hear exactly what her interviewer had to confess.

"I kept it simple, really," Georgia sighed. "Gold digger."

It was Gail's turn to raise a brow. "You mean you told everyone that you and the creepy old guy—"

"You do realize that Mr. Lambley might very well end up your employer?" Georgia chastised. She giggled as Gail blushed. "Relax! You know it's funny, but Alice was one of the few people who supported me. She thought that Mr. Lambley must have had an enormous *apartment* for me to just run off."

"But still, you just up and moved in with him?" Gail gasped.

"Well, I waited until the weekend at least," Georgia laughed. "And man, what a weekend. We better get some caffeine in us before I tell you just how awkward those first few days were."

"But what did your parents say?"

"I just told them I was seeing someone new and going to spend a lot of time with him," she said. "They were so used to me saying something disappointing that I don't think they even gave it a second thought. My mom asked if I saw a long-term future with the guy, and I said that I didn't think it'd last more than a year. It's so very nice when you don't have to lie completely, isn't it?"

"And your roommate just let you go?"

"I had the rest of my rent paid up front in the contract. Plus, she got the satisfaction of seeing me run off in a deviant relationship. I guess you could say we were never closer than we were right then." Georgia took a long sip of her drink. "But, man, if you've never seen a vampire contract, it's a work of art. Mr. Lambley really should have been a lawyer. He had everything covered in there."

"And you signed it?"

"In blood, no less," Georgia said with a sly smile. "I was hesitant until I opened the freezer to get some ice for my drink."

"Was there a head in there?" Gail asked, wide-eyed.

"Yeah. We're going to have to give you a soda without the bonus for a few. You're just getting silly. Oh, no, have you ever heard the expression cold, hard cash? Apparently Mr. Lambley took it literally. I opened the door, and a stack of Benjamins fell out."

Gail's eyes widened again. "That must have been . . . wow," she said. By now her cheeks were as bright as the flowers on her sweater.

"Would you excuse me for a second, sweetie?" Georgia asked. "Girls' room."

Gail just saluted her friend and continued to work on virgin soda. As she bounced on her chair, the sultry blonde continued to watch her intently. Unlike the blushing and bubbly brunette, the golden-haired woman lounged with a single wineglass that she sipped periodically. She kept her sunglasses on while her partner in crime seemed perpetually in one of the room's shadows. Gail found herself transfixed by his one visible hand with black-painted nails and pure white skin. He wore a ring made of some sort of swirly mix of metals that he kept slipping off his ring finger and rolling onto his pinkie and back again.

A new waiter, a tall, dark, and handsome drink of water in skinny jeans and a fitted black shirt, drifted by and swept away her glasses. "Can I get you anything?" he asked while flashing a dazzling white smile.

"Your number," Gail blurted out as she stared into his big baby brown eyes.

The waiter just laughed and took up the tray. "If you're still around at closing time, let's talk," he laughed. Gail watched him wander back toward the employee door, taking particular note of just how well he filled out his jeans. Indeed, she was so transfixed she didn't even notice Georgia wander back from the ladies' room in an entirely different ensemble than before.

"Earth to Gail," Georgia said as she waved a hand. "You still with me, or were the drinks too strong?"

"I guess I just zoned out . . . whoa, what happened to the tux?" she asked, blinking at her interviewer's short red dress.

"It was ready for my boss," she said. "Plus, I felt a little more girly after a few drinks. Did I just miss a waiter?"

Gail looked over at the place where the Mexican sampler and her glass had been. She scratched her head. "I really must have been out of it. I missed him too. Did you want something?"

Georgia picked up the remains of her beverage. "Nah, I'm good. I guess we should keep going while the night is young, right?"

"You were telling me how you found cash in your boss's freezer. I mean, is he really that loaded?"

"Well, the advantage of living so long is that over time, your stuff simply becomes valuable. Mr. Lambley was wealthy before he was turned, and with two hundred years of appreciation and interest . . . well, it sort of adds up. He owns a building in Brookline, a whole building. Nothing quite keeps you going like real estate. Don't worry. If you get the job, I'll walk you through everything, like the tax paperwork and the transfers. If I can pick it up, anyone can."

"So that's part of the job too?" Gail asked.

"The job is to take care of Mr. Lambley's needs and his estate," Georgia said flatly. "Some days it's reviewing his portfolio, others it's dry cleaning. All I can say is that it's constantly changing."

"Well, what's the worst thing you had to do?" Gail asked.

"Oh, trust me; the worst is already long over. Mr. Lambley is in great shape now," Georgia said. "You really don't want to hear the gory details . . ." She trailed off as she saw the begging look in the young girl's face— wobbling lip and all. Georgia sighed. "You totally want to hear about the weekend from hell, don't you?"

5

"How does this much dirt end up in the kitchen of a man who never cooks?" Georgia lamented as she tried pushing a mop over a very, very gray floor. Every pass of the twisted white ropes only succeeded in spreading a slightly different shade of black in long sweeping streaks. She wiped a rogue dribble of sweat that had escaped her headband and groaned at the layer of dust that had solidified on each and every hair on her forearm.

"Kitchen, bathroom, bedroom," she chanted. "Just get a kitchen, bedroom, and bathroom."

"Georgia!" the vampire cried from another room. Somehow a two-syllable word managed to take thirty seconds to say. She dropped her mop back in the bucket and darted into the hall. What greeted her made her squeak like a chipmunk.

"Why are you—?" she choked out as she stared at one very big blob of white flesh standing proudly amid a pile of hardware store bags and half-opened boxes. Mercifully, a toilet brush and plunger set blocked most of the Lambley family jewels.

Geoffrey looked down. "Oh, I guess I'm still not used to having a houseguest. My robe wasn't on the landing."

"I told you to leave out any laundry. I put it in the wash."

"The wash?" he asked, wide-eyed. As he moved, Georgia ducked left so that a red and white shopping bag now blocked the view. "What on earth do you mean?"

"I put all my clothes in the washing machine, as well as any of yours I found in the hall, the bathroom, and on the porch. That's generally what laundry means."

"But my robe was silk—handwoven in India. No machine can clean it!"

Georgia laughed nervously. "I'm sure it will be fine. Everything you left out was pretty disgusting. I've never seen so many bloodstains in my life. I've got everything washing in hot water and doused the whites in bleach."

"Stefano put in that machine to take out human stink from the sheets, not for my clothes!" Geoffrey gasped. "It's a terrible, noisy thing that makes a siren at the end that I simply cannot abide. I make his servant come in and do it."

"I'm sure everything will be fine. Look, you want to be ready for the twenty-first century, don't you? It starts with hygiene." She ducked right as her boss turned again. Unfortunately, the bag from this direction was rapidly deflating, so Georgia quickly began studying the missing lightbulb in the entryway fixture.

"Hygiene? I cannot get ill and cannot get anyone ill, so I don't need to concern myself with that."

"You can't go out in bloodstains. They will call the cops, and that would probably end up breaking rule number two, right? Um, do you want to put some clothes on before we continue?"

Mr. Lambley put his hands on his hips. "What is that smell?"

"Probably one of about four hundred cleaning products that I'm trying to use on this kitchen. You might not be able to get sick, but if I cook in here, I might as well walk straight to the ER."

"No, it isn't Christmastime. Why do I smell spruce and cinnamon?"

"It's called air freshener. You didn't give me that much cash, so I got the holiday ones from the dollar store."

"It's vile," he snorted.

"Did you want me to stop what I'm doing and throw them out? Because the smell of pureed rat and mildew is just as disgusting to me."

He was already distracted by something on top of one of her boxes. He pulled out a silky yellow nightgown. "May I?" he asked.

"Go right ahead," Georgia said, throwing up her hands. "Isn't it bedtime for a vampire yet?"

"It's not even noon. How am I to sleep with all this excitement?" he said as he pulled her nightie over his chest. Little tufts of ginger chest hair poked scandalously through the lace edging.

"You have lots of freckles everywhere," Georgia blurted out.

"I'm going back to my room. Oh, and I usually take a snack before bed. I think I heard a trap go off in the back bedroom."

"You want a blended rat?" Georgia asked weakly.

"I want a noontime snack," he said. "I have a servant now, so I want you to make it."

"What if the rat isn't dead from the trap?" she asked.

"The blender will take care of it," he said matter-of-factly.

"Oh my god, you didn't kill a rat in a blender, did you?" Gail squeaked.

"I did preface that this was my worst weekend ever, did I not?" Georgia said with a sigh. She watched Gail grow paler and paler. Finally Georgia tipped her drink and put her companion out of her misery. "No, I didn't kill a rat in a blender," she sighed.

Color returned to Gail's face. Georgia waited until the girl had gulped a full mouth of soda before casually saying, "It was already dead from the trap when I put it in the blender."

Soda sprayed over the little table in front of them. Georgia signaled for napkins. This time the waiter also slipped a note into the interviewer's hand. She excused herself to make a call while Gail recovered her composure.

When Georgia returned, she motioned to a comfy-looking sofa in the back corner of the room. "Let's move over there," she offered. "Oh come on, you didn't think that this job wasn't without some gross-out, did you?

You were a nurse. You can't tell me that blending a dead rat is worse than changing an adult diaper, can you?"

"Did you ever have to kill one?" Gail asked weakly.

"They were always dead when they went in the blender. Did you know that you can get frozen ones online? Mr. Lambley calls them his fuzzy frappes. I should warn you that he needs a new bar blender about every three months."

"And he wore your clothes?"

"Oh, yeah. I learned many valuable lessons that weekend. The vampires may have their four rules, but I learned the first rule of being a good assistant to a vampire is learning how to take out bloodstains. Here's a very big hint—"

"Never use hot water?" Gail offered. "It sets the stain."

"Yeah," Georgia said. "Worst . . . weekend . . . ever . . ."

Georgia picked up the faded and pearled pile of fabric that had once been a silk robe. All around her feet, various shirts and breeches with rust-colored patches littered the floor, while she pulled out a single red thong that had somehow worked its way into a now pinkish load of whites.

She tossed as much as she could into the avocado-colored dryer, turned it to what looked like low, and said a prayer under her breath. She sniffed the air and ran back to the kitchen with barely enough time to pull her ramen noodles off the stove before they boiled dry. As she pivoted to pour her lunch into a new bowl, her feet slipped on the still damp floor. In her desperation to avoid ending up on the tile, the entire pot of noodles ended up splashing on the one clean spot she had managed to create amid the chaos.

"Cursed, I'm cursed," she muttered as she once more reached for a mop. As she looked over to see the pulpy red residue soaking in the blender bowl, her gag reflex took over.

"Well, at least I hadn't eaten," she groaned as she mopped and mopped some more.

Her afternoon consisted of a dust mask and clouds of questionable substances. She closed off one room and actually opened the blackout curtains for a few lovely splashes of sunshine. She shook one little rug and watched puffs of black and gray unknown substances pour out into the alley between Geoffrey's brownstone and his neighbor's. Every bit of furniture in the room was covered with a streaky cloth except for a four-poster bed, where only the lumpy old feather mattress had been covered. She cringed as she saw gnawed holes along an entire side of the mattress and lots of little black presents left along the floorboards.

"I'm so glad I got that air mattress," she muttered. As she pulled another cloth, she was rewarded with a beautiful vanity table in old-world carved rosewood. She groaned at her filthy reflection. Next she revealed a dresser and a full-length mirror and finally some sort of tower with lots of shallow little drawers.

Her final reveal was a wardrobe that filled up most of the wall. She opened it slowly, with a duster handy to swat away any furry guests. Instead of finding more rodents, however, she found hangers with women's frocks from the past century still hanging on delicate wooden hangers. While moths or varmints had attacked many, a few had been wrapped in plastic bags to save them for a twenty-first century viewing.

Georgia pushed them to the side and started sweeping out the bottom. Something small and white caught the afternoon light. Georgia picked it up and immediately cringed as she recognized it as a human-size fang.

"Eww," she cried, but instead of dropping the fang in the dustpan, she set it on the vanity. She started dusting and sweeping with more speed and ferocity and tried not to look at what exactly she was pouring either into a trash bag or the street.

She then started dragging in boxes and bags and smiled as she unrolled a lovely new, clean, plastic bit of bedding. Her smile quickly faded as the air mattress simply refused to fill, no matter how many times she stomped on the foot pump. The more she cursed and fought with the pile of blue plastic, the less and less it wanted to expand.

"What next?" she dared to ask.

She heard the dryer buzz downstairs. She abandoned the pump and quickly discovered that low on an ancient dryer didn't quite behave the same as in a newer model. As she lifted up a T-shirt that looked better suited to fit on a six-year-old, she finally let out a cry of frustration.

"You will not beat me," she warned the appliance. She turned to the washer and a pressing machine that looked like it would be more at home a century ago. "None of you will beat me."

She took a deep breath, walked calmly out to the hall, and managed to find her purse in the chaos. She pulled out headphones, turned up the volume, and then walked right back to snap on some bright pink work gloves. As high-decibel hip-hop pounded her eardrums, she found the strength to scrub, wash, and otherwise make presentable a kitchen, a bathroom, and her bedroom in the back. Undaunted she collected all the bags from her morning's shopping and started stuffing them into the holes in the feather mattress. She then tossed the plastic carcass on top and wrangled a fitted sheet over the mess with sheer grit and determination.

She then took just a moment to marvel at the sun starting to fade through her window. With her headset on, she didn't notice the door opening behind her until it was too late.

"Agh!" Geoffrey cried as streaks of light hit his pale arm. Georgia's nose wrinkled at the scent of burning hair and skin.

"Oh no!" she cried as she yanked the blackout curtains shut. As she tried to adjust to the lack of light, she ended up tripping on the useless hose to the air mattress. She plowed into the moaning vampire and ended up face-first against his hairy chest while she held onto her own nightgown for dear life.

"Oops," she said weakly.

She fumbled for a light and finally managed to see just how badly her boss was injured on her first full day on the job. His entire forearm bubbled and oozed with pink welts.

"Burn cream . . . my room . . ." he whimpered.

Georgia ran past him and darted across the hall. She guessed wrong at first and ended up in another room full of sheets and mouse poop. The second door revealed a pitch-black cavern that smelled like an abattoir. She turned her phone into a flashlight and prepared for the worst. Instead of coffins and body parts, she only found an unmade bed and a crusty glass on the nightstand. She yanked open the nightstand drawer to find all sorts of tubes and creams. She simply scooped them all into her arms, along with a convenient pack of tissues, and ran back in record time.

As she tossed everything on her bed and flipped the light, she discovered not one or two, but five tubes of personal lubricant and another couple of hemorrhoid repair. The only thing not in the pile was anything resembling burn cream.

"Left nightstand," Geoffrey said. "Bandages too."

Georgia ran back and fumbled through the dark until she found the other nightstand. This one contained nothing but burn salves, bandages, and a huge tub of aloe.

She ran back and started treatment, grimacing as a few blisters exploded with the slightest touch. Geoffrey yowled until she finally wrapped a few layers of spongy gauze around the burn.

"Ready to fire me yet?" Georgia asked weakly.

"Well, I still have the other arm," he said with a sad chuckle.

"Should I make you another shake? There was a mouse in the laundry room."

He shook his head. "I'm going to need something a little stronger to heal this, I'm afraid."

"I'm not on the menu, am I?" Georgia asked.

"Of course not, but I need something with fresh and pure blood. Nothing cooked will do." He grabbed his bandage and groaned. "Oh, I'd forgotten how strong the sun was on this side of the house."

"OK, I'm going to find something. You just get back to your room and sit tight until I can fix this. I promise I'll fix this."

She helped him back to the room. As they crossed the entryway, she noticed that the light from the vestibule glass didn't seem to burn him. Once he was settled in the dark, she took a closer peek at the yellow-tinted glass. In one of the corners, she could barely see some sort of film curling away from the frame.

"I'll be right back!" she cried as she grabbed her purse and headed out into the early evening street. A few people sneered at her dirt-streaked T-shirt, but most were too busy studying the screens on their phones to really notice one filthy twenty-something running to Brookline Center on a mission to find raw blood.

She ended up all the way back in her old neighborhood as the sun set. The more student-centered Allston-Brighton area didn't look twice at a girl in a filthy tie-dyed tee and ripped jeans. A bright, jam-packed supermarket advertising all sorts of Far Eastern delicacies lured her in as both her feet and empty stomach started to cramp at once.

She squeezed down the narrow aisle stuffed with bright boxes of cookies and crackers, past a hundred kinds of soy sauce and pickled everything in a jar, until she finally reached a wall of all manner of chopped-up flesh—from pig ears to chicken feet. Everything she could imagine was lined up on dainty Styrofoam trays. It was a couple of bags plopped in the corner of the refrigerated case that caught her eye. She snatched up all of the pig's blood she could carry and hustled to get in line. She could feel the cold, sticky residue dripping all over her left hand, and she tried to juggle the containers. One of the bundles had a dangerously thin rubber band holding it closed on top.

She made it all the way to the register before it finally gave out. All she could do was sigh as cold, thick, red liquid soaked into her shirt. The woman at the counter began to apologize profusely even as a few onlookers began to giggle. Georgia just quietly took out her credit card and proceeded to pay for everything not on her chest and then walk proudly toward the sign marked restrooms.

"Make sure to rinse that in cold water," someone offered as she headed for the door. "If you use warm, it will never come out."

"Now you tell me," Georgia said, laughing as she had to rinse her shirt off in a tiny public sink. Once the biggest blotches were faded and she was soaked to the bone, she grabbed her big bag of blood and shuffled back to Brookline completely on foot. Twenty minutes later the sun had all but set, and she barged into the brownstone to find her vampire boss still whimpering in his room.

The moment she opened her first bag and poured a bunch of blood into a brandy glass, however, the once-mewling undead ran to the kitchen like a cat hungry for tuna. She barely had time to pull away the plastic when he snatched it from the counter and started gulping it down. All Georgia could do was watch as sanguine stains dribbled onto her nightgown.

"I guess you couldn't find anything to change into," she sighed.

He drained his glass and slammed it on the counter. "More," he growled.

She filled his glass again, and again, and again, until all the bags had been drained and only little coagulated messes were left on the counter and floor. He finally collapsed against the fridge with a dopey smile on his face and let the glass shatter on the floor.

"Geoffrey! Geoff! Come on," Georgia cried as she shook his shoulders and tried to rouse him. His eyes rolled back in, and his lashes fluttered furiously. "Is this normal?" she cried as she shook him again. "Geoffrey!"

His head rolled to the side, and pink drool dripped from his lips. Finally he let out a happy little grunt and begged, "More, please."

"That's all I could find—"

"More!" he roared. This time when his eyes snapped back into focus, they were brilliant, almost glowing red. Georgia scrambled back and in the process ended up slipping and slicing her palm on a stray piece of brandy glass.

Geoffrey's eyes widened, and he curled back his lip in a hungry sneer. Georgia scrambled to her feet and dashed for the stairs. Seconds later she managed to wedge the étagère against the trusty bathroom door as she heard roaring and smashing in the apartment outside.

"Mr. Lambley!" Georgia cried through the wood. "Remember rule number three? You invited me to stay here. Remember that!"

The only response was the door shuddering as something heavy slammed into it over and over. "Remember the third rule!" Georgia cried. "You're not a killer, remember, and I'm not lunch. You made a promise."

The door rattled again, this time with even more force. "Remember your promise," Georgia howled again as she hopped in the tub and started rinsing the blood from her hand and arm. As the red faded and steam filled the room, the banging finally stopped.

"I'm sorry, Miss Sutherland," a sad little voice said, just barely audible over the water. "I'm terribly sorry, but it's been a while since I've had so very much to drink."

She kept letting the water pour over her, clothes and all. Only when her shoes were thoroughly drenched did she finally stop the water and peel off the sopping clothes. She stayed, dripping, in the tub until she finally ended up falling asleep, cuddling her own crumpled jeans . . .

"You stayed there all night?" Gail asked, wide-eyed.

"Until I was sure the bleeding stopped, yeah," Georgia confirmed. "You see, blood is more than food to one of their kind. It's a drug and sustenance all in one. Poor Mr. Lambley had been starved for so long that once he had something fresh, he simply lost it. Don't worry, though; he's much better now that we've worked on his diet and exercise program."

"Was it scary?"

"Of course it was. It's important that you know that even a toothless vampire is still brutally strong. You don't need fangs to attack someone, after all."

"Did your weekend get any better?"

Georgia shook her head. "It was the second-worst Saturday of my life, but it taught me so many important lessons."

"Like using cold water on bloodstains?" Gail said with a weak smile.

Georgia tipped her glass. "Yes, like always use cold water on blood-stains. Not to mention putting tinting film on every window in the house, well, every window except the one in my room, but I did put a do not disturb sign out whenever my curtains weren't closed. That put an end to most of the in-house burning incidents."

"A second of direct sun gave him second-degree burns?" Gail asked. "What kind of burn ointment did you have to use?"

"Ah, I almost forgot that we had a professional here," Georgia said. "Well, a vampire can't just go to the doctor and get a prescription. I think your average medical professional might notice the low body temperature and lack of pulse."

"No pulse."

"Not like us. If you listen close, it sounds like they have a dishwasher in their chests, sort of. I get the cream from one of the local sources that are friendly to the families. It's very important that you don't use the regular antibiotic cream, though. The cream has to have silver in it."

Gail furrowed her brow. "That's the opposite of what I would expect—"

"Yeah, something about them being dead and allergic to sunlight might make them react slightly differently to burn cream than we do," Georgia snapped. "Ooh, I'm sounding like I need to switch back to happy drinks, don't I? Yeah, I've got a lot of notes about what to do in the rare occasion one of them gets injured. The number one cure to all ailments, though, is a good drink."

"Did he heal? Do they scar?" Gail pressed on.

Georgia paused to check her phone again. The light on top kept flashing, but she brushed her notifications aside before Gail could pick up what was so important.

"Sorry, I guess I'm just fascinated about some of the medical details," Gail said as Georgia continued to ignore her and tapped her screen.

Finally Miss Sutherland looked up. "Sorry, an assistant's work is never done. Oh, I spent many a night trying to work out just how Mr. Lambley worked, if you know what I mean. I've always been a trial and error sort of girl. I can't just read how to do something. I need to mess it up thoroughly firsthand before I understand it. I can sum it up pretty succinctly, though. Sunlight is bad, antibiotics are bad, garlic in large quantities is bad, and blood is good. Oh, splinters—yeah, they are bad too."

"Like a stake through the heart?" Gail asked.

"Not quite so dramatic. They have an allergic reaction to wood. It's something with cellulose. I probably should have paid more attention when it was being explained, but there were more pressing concerns at the time. Did I mention that Mr. Lambley likes to plan things and then forget to tell you?"

"But there are a lot of details to remember," Gail said. "I mean you could have killed him or been killed—"

"Could is such a pathetic little word, isn't it? I could have done lots of things. I could have studied harder. I could have taken a summer trip to Rome or I could have eaten a chicken salad sandwich today, but I didn't. Could is that word you use to describe things that are either unimportant or uncertain. The important thing is that I didn't kill my boss and he didn't kill me. Otherwise how could we be having this lovely night of drinks and conversation?"

Gail slurped up the last of her virgin cola. Almost by magic another drink appeared, this one garnished with a maraschino cherry and a little umbrella. Georgia was handed the same lime-colored concoction in a martini glass that she had downed earlier.

"I like knowing all the facts, that's all," Gail offered. "I'm used to reading a chart and knowing what to do."

"That's not always a bad thing, sweetie," Georgia said. "Maybe I would have done better those first few days if I had paid attention to details too. The devil's in the details, wouldn't you agree?"

Gail nodded.

"I did actually keep a sleeping bag in that bathroom for about six weeks. It was like my happy place whenever I couldn't handle the day-to-day job, but you know what?"

"What?"

"That first weekend, at my very lowest, when I was about ready to give up and move to some really sunny, tropical island where I was sure no vampire would ever find me, something happened that I never expected."

Gail leaned in again. "What?"

"Here I was, inching out into a hall wearing only a towel and like a dozen Band-Aids, and there was a note and a hundred dollar bill left right outside the door. All it said was, 'Buy some locks, G,' in really pretty cursive handwriting. I don't know, but somehow in that wobbly little note, I could see someone just as scared as me trying to make the best of things. He didn't come out of his room until much later, and he said thank you when I gave him a hamburger smoothie."

"And you got the locks? They could keep him out?"

Georgia tilted her head to the side and showed off her long, clean neck. "You see any bite marks?" she asked.

Gail shook her head.

"Funny thing, though. Something about vampire bites—they heal really quickly. They don't leave scars as long as the victim is still breathing." She waited for Gail to gulp. "Don't worry, Mr. Lambley has never bitten me, and he would never bite anyone under his care. You just seemed so interested in scars, just like the vampires."

Across the room the blonde pushed up her sleeve ever so slightly. Just above her wrist, two neat little slashes cut across her otherwise pristine ivory skin. The man sitting with her, kept his back completely turned to the still-breathing pair.

Georgia patted Gail on the back of her hand. "Don't worry, they're just testing us," she said with a quick sideways glance at the blonde. "Minnie over there likes to add a little color commentary to every social event."

"She can hear us?"

"Yah," the blonde said without skipping a beat. "But you are boring, so I tune you out."

"And she knows Geoff . . . err, Mr. Lambley?" Gail asked, looking quickly between the two women in the room to see who would respond.

"The Jaeger family has known my boss's family for centuries, and I've known Minnie over there for a good year. She's always been one of my most treasured supporters as I was learning the ropes."

"Oh, so she's a friend?" Gail asked.

Minnie and Georgia snorted simultaneously. Gail fidgeted between them, trying to find some way to sink into the velvet cushions while the other two women both sat up a little straighter and sized each other up. Georgia finally broke the spell and plopped down her emptied glass with a flourish.

"I've been such a Debbie Downer!" she declared. "If I keep telling you about my awful first few weeks, you'll never want this job, will you?"

"I never said—"

"Your face said enough, sweetie," Georgia sighed. "Did I tell you that Mr. Lambley's old assistant, the one from the seventies, left a journal in the house?"

"No, you didn't mention it yet."

"Well, it's chock-full of great info for all sorts of things that don't involve technology or people still alive today," Georgia said with a little laugh. "But it did have all the appliance warranties in there. It's helpful when something breaks in the house. The other good thing is that I got cable hooked up. There is simply no problem too great for the combined powers of Home Improvement TV and the Internet. Just be forewarned that you can't let Mr. Lambley too close to the TV. If the show upsets him too much, he tends to accidentally fry the DVR."

Gail actually giggled. "I never thought of a vampire watching TV before."

"Oh, you have no idea. There's one channel that shows like twenty years' worth of soap operas. I actually had to set a timer for a few months because he would stay up until three in the afternoon if I didn't stop him. Mr. Lambley needs at least six hours of rest, or he is a handful."

Gail sat back and took it all in. "So there are normal days too?"

"Most days are quite normal. You'd be surprised how quickly a routine can become your new normal. Mr. Lambley, like all of his kind, likes his routine. I could drone on and on for hours about it, but I bet you'd be far more interested in hearing about a not-so-normal night."

"I guess so," Gail said cautiously.

"I know. I could tell you about the night I first met Minnie and her lovely family. Miss Filipovic, how would you like to hear about a vampire's ball?"

6

"Vampires have balls?" Gail asked.

Across the room both Blondie and her companion burst into a fit of giggles.

"Well, only the male ones," Georgia deadpanned as her companion burst into giggles as well.

"That's not what I meant," Gail laughed. "Oh, man, I think I've had a few too many. I just thought with all the secrecy that they wouldn't be able to have parties and stuff."

"Oh, no, vampires are more social than a boatload of debutantes," Georgia said. "They have a calendar that would make Edwardian nobility jealous. Actually, I'm pretty certain there were some Edwardian nobles at most of the last few shindigs."

"But how? How can they all meet up without someone noticing?"

"You sound just like I did." Georgia sighed . . .

"Hold still," Georgia snapped as she tried once more to yank a comb through a bright orange rat's nest. The vampire squirmed in his chair and yelped and continued to wiggle until she handed him a bright red sippy cup. "That's all you're getting tonight, by the way," she warned.

"I can bloody well have all I want," Geoffrey said with a defiant pout.

"Well, there is only so much pig's blood you can get over the weekend, so you need to make it last—and hold still!" she said as she finally yanked a mat out from behind his ear. "There, that wasn't so bad, was it? No? Good!" she snapped as she tossed the tangle into the trash bucket, which contained a few centuries of gnarled nail shavings, hair knots, and other ancient bodily scrapings. Georgia pulled off her latex glove for a moment to grab her own drink and cool off before returning to her Herculean hairstyling efforts.

Mr. Lambley looked equally uncomfortable as he slouched in his chair with his gut poking out from under the camisole nightgown he still wore from nearly two weeks before. His only concession to modern modesty entailed a pair of silk boxer shorts he finally deemed worthy enough to touch his delicate skin.

As his slumping and pouting became punctuated by intermittent sighs, Georgia finally stomped her foot and bent around to face him. "Look, if you ever want to go out of this brownstone, you need to rise to twenty-first-century levels of hygiene, OK?"

"Who says I even want to go out?" he grumbled.

"You did!"

His lip quivered, accentuating his distinctive lack of a main chin on his doughy face, but he managed to hold still for a few minutes and let the assistant yank a few more sections smooth. His eyes widened as she pulled out a tube of minty freshness and a brand-new toothbrush. His secondary chin wobbled with anxiety.

"Yours is the pink one, mine is the blue," she said. "Don't mix it up."

His eyes widened, and he shook his head vehemently. "There is no way in heaven or this earth—" he started, but his blustering only gave Georgia the prime opportunity to shove the brush in his mouth and start scrubbing. He spit the pinkish foam immediately on the floor. "You! You! You—"

"You have dead puppy breath, deal with it," she said as she shoved it right back in there. "Come on, you don't want to lose any more teeth, do you?"

"Vampires don't get tooth decay!" he protested.

"Well, they do get bad breath, so brush up before I keep brushing for you," she said as she grabbed another bottled water and the waste bucket. "Spit in here this time, if you don't mind."

Reluctantly he swished the toothbrush a few times around his mouth. He then grabbed the bottle and tried his best to rinse out any trace of the minty foam and spewed into the little bucket. Georgia smiled before cleaning up the spray that didn't quite make it.

"This is intolerable," he said before grabbing his kiddie cup. "The smell alone is atrocious. How do you humans stand smelling like cheap strumpets all the time?"

"It's better than what you smelled like, that's for sure. Now, it's almost dawn, and I haven't slept in nearly twenty-four hours. Can I put on your show and send you to bed?" Georgia asked.

"My show isn't on till noon," he said.

"Aha, I've got something from this century that you will actually like. Come with me."

She took his hand and led him out of the upstairs formal bedroom he had once used to entrap her and into his much darker and smaller sleeping chamber. There only a bed, nightstands, and an old-fashioned little television filled the space. She picked up two remote controls, causing her boss to tilt his head in wonder.

"Why are there two of those infernal things now?" he asked.

"Because the cable guy finally showed up this afternoon. That's why I was up all day."

"There was a stranger in my house while I slept!" Geoffrey cried. "Was he in my chamber?"

Georgia rolled her eyes. "I told him you worked nights and were asleep, so he left the last box with me. I hooked it up while you were on your second bath."

"But I already have the cable in my television. Stefano had it hooked up in the eighties—"

"You had crap, so I fixed it. Welcome to the wonderful world of DVR. You can record the show while you should be sleeping and then watch it when you wake up," she said as she started flipping through menus. "I even had the guy set it up so that all the soap operas you like are in the record list already."

"If it's like a video recorder, then it's a waste of time. I always end up destroying the tapes."

"I have it all the way across the room, and there are no magnetic tapes, OK? Just don't fry this cable box. I really don't want to have to pay the replacement fee."

Geoffrey threw his hands up in the air. "This is just too much for me to handle right now. I can't believe there was a stranger in my home. You don't have the right to—"

"I live here too, and I can't live on four hours of sleep indefinitely, so we're going to have to adapt. You need more rest and a better diet too."

"You know nothing—" he started.

"Oh really? I know that you like your blood warmed to exactly ninety-seven-point-five degrees and that you prefer it with a splash of lime. I also know that the extra key is hidden under the second rabbit statue outside and that our mailman's name is Bob. I've learned all this in less than two weeks, and I have the bonus of finding stacks upon stacks of old notes left by a Mr. Higgins, who I can only assume was your last assistant."

"Higgins left notes?" Geoffrey asked weakly.

"You would have found them if you ever cleaned," she snipped. Her face softened slightly as her boss's shoulders slumped and he gave a hang-dog look toward the bed. With a sigh she pulled back the covers and then tucked him in with the remote. "How could someone as helpless as you survive for over thirty years on your own?"

She made sure his almost empty sippy cup was within reach, and she helped him find something sappy and black and white on the very-early-morning cable schedule.

"Trust me, if you could have someone care for you, you'd embrace the opportunity," he said as he snatched the remote and started flipping around the stations again. He stopped as he noticed his short pink nails with nary a trace of dirt hiding under them. "Is the rest of me as well-groomed?" he asked.

"Let's just say, you're a work in progress, but we'll get there," she said as she eased back toward the door. "Hey, if you're ever willing to wear some pants, we might even be able to take a walk one night. Now, can I please get some shut-eye?"

Mr. Lambley was already engrossed with a chef extolling the virtues of a new all-powerful blender with titanium blades. "I'll call if I need anything, Georgia," he said dismissively. "Good day to you."

"Good day to you too," she said as she slipped into the hall. She thought she heard him mumble something about bills and REM sleep or something like that, but she just trudged her way into her own little fortress of solitude. The drop cloths and cobwebs had been swept aside, and plastic crates of jeans and DVDs now mixed in with the classic mahogany furniture.

She pulled her second key out of her pocket and locked the door before flopping unceremoniously on her squishy plastic-topped ancient mattress. None of the lumps seemed to be able to stop her from snoring within seconds of face-planting on top of her fuzzy blue blanket. However, after only two hours of tossing, turning, and sawing logs, her eyes snapped open, as she could distinctly hear someone or something barging through the front door.

"What the—" she said as she then heard loud, heavy footsteps. She rolled out of bed, peeked out the curtain, and had to immediately squint at the glaring midmorning sun. "Burglar, not vampire," she sighed before snapping awake. She immediately grabbed the first heavy object she could muster and unlocked her door.

At the same time, a strange voice said, "Mr. Lambley, it's rather bright, so I wouldn't come down."

Georgia looked at the flatiron she was carrying in her hand. "Am I dreaming?"

"Mr. Lambley, sir, I'll just leave the . . ." The voice trailed off as Georgia appeared on the landing, still wearing the same jeans and cami that she had been rocking during her vampire-scrubbing session overnight. Her bright yellow cheetah-print bra stood out marvelously under the stained-white spaghetti-strap number.

The stranger at the base of the stairs stopped dead in his tracks, and the overflowing pile of mail and grocery bags in his arms nearly ended up on the now-sparkling checkerboard tiles. "Who are you?" he asked.

"Well, who the hell are you—Agent Smith?" Georgia snapped as she rubbed the little crusty bits from her eyes.

The stranger looked down at his neatly pressed black suit, gray tie, and starched white shirt. His jet-black hair was slicked back into a tidy, gel-infused helmet, and his eyes were indeed still covered by black plastic lenses. He even wore one of those black plastic earpieces that characterized both the Secret Service and the executive douche-bag elite and shoes so shiny Georgia could clearly see his reflection in them. Only the mountain of unwieldy plastic in his arms broke the illusion of his being a trained government killer.

"I'll say this again, what are you doing here?" he asked flatly.

"I live here," Georgia said without skipping a beat. "Now are you going to explain exactly who you are, or do I need to wake up Mr. Lambley?"

The stranger just walked right past the stairwell and disappeared into the kitchen. Georgia stumbled down the stairs and followed him. She found him gawking at the new state of the room as he unencumbered himself by setting a veritable mountain of papers alongside a bag labeled "Izzy's Exotic Pets."

"What in the world happened to this place?" he asked as he saw a coffeemaker next to neat little jars marked sugar and salt. "The stain is gone," he said, pointing to a spot near where rat traps has once flourished. He also seemed utterly entranced by clean dishes in a dish rack and a half-devoured loaf of bread sitting in a bag on the counter.

"It's amazing what you can do with elbow grease plus a metric ton of industrial degreaser," Georgia said flatly. "Now could you possibly answer one of my questions, Mr., um—?"

The heretofore plastic-faced stranger finally took the time to pull off his sunglasses and tuck them neatly into his breast pocket. He then extended his right hand. "Ren Matsuoka," he said. He eyed the hair-styling appliance still in Georgia's hand. "Were you planning on straightening an intruder to death?"

Georgia set it down on the counter sheepishly and finally shook his hand. "Georgia Sutherland," she said. "Mr. Lambley forgot to mention that we were expecting company."

"Well, Mr. Lambley is often one to omit certain key details," Ren said, still eyeing Georgia with some degree of suspicion. "And you are Mr. Lambley's—?"

Georgia crossed her arms across her chest. "I work for Mr. Lambley as his personal assistant, and you are Mr. Lambley's—?" she asked in the same bitchy tone.

"I am nothing to Mr. Lambley," Ren said. "I serve Master Stefano DeMarco."

"Master DeMarco? What century did we just enter?" Georgia asked. She found herself fascinated suddenly by just how freakishly light Mr. Matsuoka's eyes were in comparison to his otherwise completely Asian features and coloring. Indeed, his bright gray-green irises simply invited her stare.

"I am Master DeMarco's assistant, and I serve as financier for several related parties, including Mr. Lambley. My master insists that his allies are well-treated, and your master has been an ally for quite a few years."

"First off, Mr. Lambley isn't my master—he's my boss—and how do I know anything you say is true . . . ?" She trailed off as she saw a package of previously frozen whole rats in plastic wrap. "Oh, you're the one who brought the rats before."

"Yes, my master looks after your boss rather well," he said, rolling the word boss off his tongue with particular disdain. His gaze then slipped downward for a moment. Unfortunately, Georgia caught him trying to recover.

"Did you need to do anything else here, or should I let you take a picture?" Georgia asked.

Ren's face remained utterly passive. "Should I tell my master that the food drops are no longer required, and should I arrange for an allowance in Mr. Lambley's operating account?"

"I can take care of getting him rats, if that's what you mean, and he eats much better now, by the way."

"I'm sure he does," Ren sighed.

"Hey, what's that supposed to mean?" Georgia snapped. "Wait, you don't think that he . . . that he and I . . ." She stopped to read his damnably blank face. "What gives you the right to just barge in here and drop off rats anyway?"

Ren placed the bags in the refrigerator. "No offense was intended," he said without even looking at her. "Are you taking any responsibility for his finances as well?"

"I moved the cash out of his freezer and put it in the safe," Georgia deadpanned. "I didn't even know he had a bank account until today."

Ren pulled a business card out of his black leather wallet. "If you need any clarification on his financial matters or status, my cell is on there. I normally work later than average business hours, of course."

"Oh yeah, your master must keep you up all night too," she said. "Look, I haven't had a decent day's or night's sleep in two weeks—"

"I've sorted all of Mr. Lambley's financials for the month, and you can let him know that the property tax is up-to-date. He hasn't specified a stipend for you yet, but if you give me account details, I can confirm all the necessary transactions with your boss."

"Well, thank you for that," she sighed. "Anything else?"

He pulled a red and gold envelope out of the mass of mail. A thick old-fashioned wax seal and embossed lettering caught Georgia's eye.

"You'll want to tell Mr. Lambley that I wouldn't normally bring an invitation over, but this year the Solstice Ball is being hosted by the Pendragon clan for the first time in fifty years, so he might want to consider ending his boycott of society gatherings," Ren said as he handed it to her.

"Vampires have balls?" Georgia asked, wide-eyed.

"Not all of them," Ren deadpanned as he reached for his glasses once more. "If you have any questions, you have my card; otherwise I shall see you at the end of the month with the updated balances."

"What a dick," she muttered as he left without another word. Instead of poking through the pile he left, she ended up stumbling right back to her room and flopping back on her bed with the invitation just lying on her nightstand and her door only halfway shut . . .

"So, every vampire has an assistant?" Gail asked.

Georgia shook her head. "Not everyone, but most of them do. Ren, however, wasn't just one bloodsucker's butler. He worked for several of the area elite as a financial advisor."

"And he's the one who told you about the ball? Were you excited?" she asked.

"Oh, excited wouldn't be the first word I'd use, but I eventually got there . . ."

"So, who is Ren Matsuoka?" Georgia asked as she poured Mr. Lambley's first shake of the night.

"Oh, you met Stefano's boy?" Geoff asked. He shuffled a bit as he tried to adjust to the cotton T-shirt Georgia had finally stuffed him into.

"I wouldn't call him a boy, but I nearly decked him with a styling tool when he showed up unannounced this afternoon."

"Oh, I thought I told you he was coming with the bills. He also brings lunch," Geoffrey said. "Though his cooking is not nearly as good as yours."

"He brought an invitation to something called the Solstice Ball—"

Mr. Lambley didn't even wait for Georgia to finish. He jumped to his feet and shoved away from the table. He actually moved so fast that it took Georgia a few minutes to hunt him down in the dark recesses of his sleeping chamber. She could barely make out him shivering in the little strip of exposed carpet between his bed and the far wall. Little tufts of hair peeked over the comforter, while she could hear his slippers slapping against the ground.

"Oh no, no, no, how could he do this to me?" Geoffrey whimpered. "I gave explicit instructions that no invitations were ever to come to me."

"He said it was because the Pen and Dragon clan or something—"

"The Pendragon clan is hosting?" Geoffrey gulped. "Oh, this is even worse!"

"Calm down, just calm down," she said as she eased down next to him and started rubbing his back. Slowly but surely, the trembling slowed. "Take a deep breath."

"Too much . . . too fast," he choked out. "Too much, too fast."

"Is this gonna be a long night where I end up hiding in the bathroom again?" Georgia asked. "Come on, talk to me. What's so bad about a party invitation? Just don't RSVP if it bothers you so much."

"I wish it was that simple," Geoffrey said. "An invitation from family is considered a formal request. If I see it and refuse to attend, then I might be seen as breaking my word, and that would break one of the four laws."

"Well, you technically haven't seen it, though," Georgia offered.

"But I do know it exists, and it has been accepted in my home by my servant—"

"Assistant," Georgia corrected.

"Assistant," he sighed. "What am I to do? June is not that far away—"

"June is months away—"

"What are months when you live forever? I've blinked, and a month has gone by," Geoffrey gasped. "I cannot even leave my house. How can I possibly go out on the scene? I'll be a laughingstock, an utter laughingstock! Toothless Geoffrey, toast of the ball? No, I'll be the designated fool—the jester."

"How can you panic so much about something so far away?" Georgia said. "What can be so terrifying about a party?"

"They will all be there. The Solstice Ball is the start of the social season. It marks the shortest night of the year and the celebration of ever-increasing hours of darkness in which to revel. It is always hosted in the most exclusive of locales, and all of the local family heads will at least make an appearance. If the Pendragon clan is hosting, then the Pendragons will be expected—" He devolved into wheezing, panicked breathing.

"Geoffrey?" Georgia asked softly as she continued to pat his back. "Geoffrey, you're not making sense."

"The Pendragon family is my family," he said. "That means I'd be expected to attend and even help host. I can't do that, I just can't."

"I'm gonna hunt down that Ren guy and give him a piece of my mind. How could he do that to you?" Georgia snapped. "I thought his master guy was supposed to be your friend. Why would they do that to you?"

"Friendships among my kind are rather complicated," Geoffrey said. "Stefano is a Jaeger, after all. They didn't get the honor of hosting, so it's in the best interests of his family to make the host family look bad."

"Yeah, that doesn't sound complicated at all, that just sounds like he's a jerk. All right, I've had enough of your blubbering for tonight."

"Excuse me?" Mr. Lambley asked.

"That's it. There is only one thing we have to do tonight before it gets too late."

"What?"

"You are going to put on some pants, end of discussion. You are going to put on some pants, and we are going to walk out that door together."

"I can't—" he stammered.

Georgia was already moving toward his dresser. She immediately bypassed his enormous collection of housecoats and frou-frou silk blouses and grabbed the neatly pressed pair of jeans that still brandished a discount store tag. "I used to sell hundreds of these each week, I can guess a size better than a county fair barker," she mused.

"You want me to wear dungarees in public?"

"Oh, you are not going all cranky old vampire on me now," she growled. "Please, don't make me shove you on the couch and slide you into these, Geoff."

He snatched the pants from her and hopped onto the bed. He then waited patiently until she finally dropped to her knees, grabbed the pants back, and started sliding him into them. She shoved his pallid feet through the holes, cursing under her breath.

"I know that language is less formal, but really?" Geoff snorted.

"Just how good is your hearing?" she asked before hunting down socks.

"I look like a workman," the vampire lamented. "How can you stand these?"

"I'm not zipping your fly," she said. "I've got one shirt that should fit you too."

"Everyone will stare at me," he said. "I can't—"

"If you haven't figured it out already, I'm not going to give up. I've got a hundred grand resting on helping you for a year, and I don't want to spend all that time sitting on a sofa watching soap operas."

"But what if I don't want to—" Geoffrey protested.

"I don't care. We're just gonna do this."

"What if people recognize what I am?"

"A shut-in?"

"No, a—"

"Don't say it. Hell, even if you did run down the street yelling, 'Hey, I'm a vampire!' people would just think you were crazy. All we have to do is just avoid a wall of mirrors and a hoard of paparazzi."

"But—"

"We are going out walking on the street on a nice spring evening, that's all. You just have to walk with me to the corner store. We can then turn around or keep going, whatever you want, but it's a Tuesday night, and it won't be that bad. No one goes out on a Tuesday, OK?"

He gathered enough gumption to put on a shirt and a pair of Georgia's old running shoes, but as he approached the landing, his lip began to quiver and he started tugging at his mane of hair. Georgia didn't let him stop, however, and like a desperate mom at a bus stop, she resorted to spit to slick down the worst of his cowlick before she simply dragged him the last few steps to the door.

"Wait—" he tried to protest, but she flung the door open.

"All you have to do is make it to the sidewalk. You have little bunny statues out there. You should totally see them," she said as she grabbed her purse from the newel post.

"Bunny statues?" he asked, wide-eyed.

"Happy little bunny statues," she said as she led him across the threshold.

The door opened, and somehow the world continued to spin on its axis. Geoffrey Lambley took in his first breath of outside air in over thirty years and promptly proceeded to cough as an older truck puttered by. He looked right and left at the few people wandering up and down the street, at the bright lights and the parked cars, until he finally looked back and took in the tiny little stone rabbits that decorated his windowsills.

"Oh, those are rather lovely," he choked out once he caught his breath.

Georgia took his arm and started leading him gently toward the corner. In the mix of streetlamps and shadows, his skin still looked pale, but lost the deathly cast that marked him in the overhead lights. He stumbled a few times in the clunky cross-trainers and baggy jeans until he finally found his footing.

As they reached the main thoroughfare, he watched in awe as a pack of teenagers walked blissfully past him, all of them talking while staring at the glowing screens in their hands. Another, slightly older kid actually brushed right past the vampire, happily bobbing his head to whatever tunes were blaring through his oversize headphones.

It took two more brush-bys for him to finally turn to Georgia and exclaim, "It's like I'm not even here."

"Yeah, a wise man once said, 'You'd care a lot less what other people think about you when you realize just how rarely they actually do' or something like that." Georgia sighed. "It's sad, I remember the quote but not the author, and part of me feels like that's supposed to be ironic. I really hope that wasn't on one of your daytime TV shows."

"I feel like I'm hiding as a ruffian," he said as he once more looked at his pants. Georgia quickly jerked the tag off the back and stuffed it between her cell phone and her wallet.

"Well, you are a ruffian who is outside of his house, so let's just keep walking."

They had made it to the corner when a bubbling whine erupted from Mr. Lambley's bowels. The next round of sputtering could even be heard over the rattle of the next streetcar approaching.

"It happens when I get nervous," he said with an apologetic look. "Or when I'm hungry, or both."

"I'm really glad we aren't in the house right now," she said, fanning the faint but distinctively meaty fumes away.

"Can we just go back?" he whimpered. "I really think I've had enough of the night air."

"Let's just get to the corner store. I want an iced tea."

The vampire took a few more tentative steps but froze as a group of cute young things giggled as they passed. "They are laughing at me," he hissed as he turned tail and shuffled back toward the house.

Georgia rolled her eyes and grabbed his hand. As she gently tugged him back, he passed another round of gurgling gas. Georgia plopped a little box of black plastic into his other palm. He stared in wonder at the screen at the stars shining through where his reflection should be.

"Don't fry it," Georgia warned as she pressed the button and then slid her finger across the screen to unlock it.

"What do I do?" he said as he looked at lots of little candy-colored icons on the screen.

"When in Rome—" Georgia said. "Look, whenever you feel self-conscious, just pull this out and pretend to look at something."

"Look at what?"

"It doesn't matter. Trust me, I have enough stupid apps on this thing to entertain you through eternity. All you have to do is take a breath and look at anything, and voila, you are just like everyone else."

She tensed as her screen flickered, but her boss managed to stop himself before frying her device again. His pudgy thumbs pressed a few random buttons until a little dancing cat took over the screen and started making random silly sounds as he touched it. His eyes lit up as he tapped it and it started to giggle at him.

"No amount of motivational speeches can top an animated cat," Georgia sighed. She let him putz away on the sidewalk until she could gently coerce him to shuffle as he tapped away until before he realized it, he was at the steps of a twenty-four-hour mini-mart. She ended up leaving him to play as she grabbed a bagful of junk food and sugar-laden beverages.

Geoffrey looked up, wide-eyed. A few more folks passed him, and sure enough, as soon as he looked at his screen, no one paid him a lick of attention. He leaned over and whispered in Georgia's ear, "Are you sure these aren't magic?"

"Come on, let's head home . . ."

"So his crippling agoraphobia was cured by an app?" Gail asked in disbelief.

"Not exactly. It took weeks to get him out for more than fifteen minutes," Georgia said. "Mr. Lambley likes his rituals, and you could say his phone is like his totem, his focus. Once he lost the damn thing in the mall, and we nearly had another all-nighter in the bathroom."

She stopped to answer another buzz from her lap and gave an apologetic smile. "He may look slow on the outside, but he can put a teenager to shame with his thumbs," Georgia said. "If you don't have unlimited texting, you'll be broke in a month."

"But didn't you say that he messed up electronics?" Gail asked as another drink was seamlessly slid in front of her.

"He usually only knocks them out for a bit, and we have insurance regardless. Oh, and the emergency phone is in the laundry room since he can't stand the sights and smells in there. If he fries his, you can just transfer the SIM card over until you get a replacement or can make the old one work. I find yelling at them works rather well."

Gail furrowed her brows. "The old vampire . . . texts," she said.

Georgia finally put her phone back down. "Incessantly," she said ever so slowly. "I guess you can figure out by now that Tuesday night is date night. Of course, that is preferable to bath night."

"B-bath?" Gail asked before taking another drink.

"Well, it's not like he can look in the mirror to finish getting ready," Georgia said. "Let's just say it's one of those things you get desensitized to pretty quickly. I thought you were a nurse. I didn't imagine you'd be squeamish."

Gail shook her head quickly. "Sorry, I'm sure it will be fine. It's just not quite what you think of when you talk about being a . . ."—she looked furtively to the left and the right—"vampire's assistant," she finished.

Georgia broke out laughing. "Sweetie, you are a riot! You know, I think I used to do the same thing."

"You did," the other blonde said from her table.

"Minnie, if you are going to keep commenting, I'm going to drag you out of the peanut gallery and make you have a drink with us," Georgia said.

The blonde eased out of her seat, but instead of walking toward them, she straddled the lap of her companion and scooted the chair ever so slightly so that only Georgia could see her bright red lips sliding along his neck. "*Tut mir Leid*, Georgia-dear, it is time for lunch," the blonde purred.

"Is she going to—?" Gail said with a little gulp.

A waiter slipped into the room and quickly set up a screen. Gail blanched as she could hear a moan and watched the shadows move. "He's a consenting adult," Georgia said flatly.

"You mean—"

"Minerva Fenstermacher von Jaeger is not one to let anything but live food touch her Botoxed lips," Georgia said with an eye roll. "Don't worry, she's not going to kill him. That vamp tramp is one of her regulars."

"But wasn't he—" Gail started.

"Wasn't he—?" Georgia asked.

The brunette shook her head. "Never mind, I lost my train of thought—"

Gail sipped a little more and tried to listen to the thumping beats coming over the speakers rather than the mix of slurping and groaning from behind the divider. Georgia took her first big gulp in a while and slid toward the middle of the sofa. After a few more painful seconds, she finally offered, "I was totally going to tell you about the ball, wasn't I?"

Georgia stared in horror at the four digits in front of the decimal point on her phone bill. "Holy Hannah," she muttered. "How did he—?"

She started flipping through page upon page of microtransactions, downloads, and overages. One entire double-sided sheet was devoted to nothing but international talk and text.

"Where the hell is Andorra?" she asked as she got toward the end of the list. "Italy, Monaco, France . . . Japan! Come on!"

"Georgia!" a singsong voice called from above. "Why can I not get any more cows for my farm? These delays are intolerable."

"You have an addiction, Mr. Lambley, and it isn't blood," Georgia muttered. She leafed through all the other stacks of bills on the table and let out a deep, heartfelt sigh as she stared at the column of numbers scribbled on the back of an envelope. Her eyes shifted reluctantly toward a business card shoved under a lobster magnet.

"Georgia!" he called again.

She stomped upstairs to see her boss sitting in front of an unlit fireplace in his sitting room, tapping furiously at little tiny cows, pigs, and chickens in a digital pen. "No one is helping me today," he whined. "I gave SolidSnake583 so much grain yesterday, and today does he even care? No, he gives me some ridiculous excuse about having to go to school. He has to be at least thirteen, he should be in the workhouse by now!"

"Mr. Lambley, you can't keep buying new games and making foreign calls. I mean, who do you know in Japan that you have to call for two hours?"

"Oh, I can get a new straw hat for ninety-nine cents!" he cooed, completely turning back to his screen.

"No, you can't!" Georgia snapped as she yanked the phone out of his hands. "Do you have any idea how much you've spent in two weeks?"

"Give me that back!"

"You have a problem," she said as she started flipping through the menus until she found the parental controls.

"I was talking to Stefano—"

"In Japan?" Georgia asked with a raised brow.

Mr. Lambley nodded. "He has a business there, something with imported food, and I was bored so I called."

"Do you have any idea how much a one-hundred-and-eighteen-minute call to Japan costs?" Georgia asked. "I put you on my phone plan. I have to cough up nearly two grand, or it's my credit that's screwed."

"Oh, just call Stefano's boy. He takes care of all the money," Mr. Lambley dismissed. "No, I need that back. I have to check on the status of the hit against the Bosnian mob, and I have turnips to water."

Georgia held the phone out of his reach. "This is getting charged, and I'm limiting your service," she said.

"You can't do that—" he sputtered.

"It's Tuesday anyway. You are getting dressed, and we are going out."

"If we are going out, I want my phone," he said.

"You'll get it once you're ready," she said, staring right through him.

"Can I just check my Twi—?"

"No!" she barked. The shamed bloodsucker reluctantly shuffled toward his bedroom, yanking off his borrowed nightie along the way. The sight of a sagging pasty butt no longer even made her flinch as she instead focused on sealing off the most expensive options on his latest-generation cell phone technology.

"Vampires should not be on social media," she muttered as she started shutting down apps. She then gathered up empty crusty glasses and wadded tissues to take back to the kitchen before the mess could spread past her designated TV tray containment zone in her newly clean house. As she filled the dishes with hot water and soap, she once more caught sight of Ren Matsuoka's business card.

Reluctantly she dried off her hands and punched in the number on her own phone. She ended up hearing a robotic voice informing her to leave a message at the sound of the beep.

"This is Georgia Sutherland, Mr. Lambley's assistant. He wanted me to call about some bills—"

"Georgia!" The ever-present voice from upstairs cut her message short.

"Just call me back," she finished.

This time she came upstairs to find her boss struggling with the buttons on his new shirt. As she took in just how he had managed to have three extra eyelets on one side and a gap in the middle, she had to laugh. As she started straightening the alignment, her boss conjured up his most adorable toothless smile.

"Are you still cross with me, Georgia?" he asked.

"Yes," she said matter-of-factly. "But I suppose it's my own damn fault. I never should have left a credit card linked to that account."

"I'm sure I have the funds—"

"And I need to teach you about how these apps work," she sighed. "Where are we going tonight?"

"I think I want to walk to the river this time. It won't be too crowded, will it?"

"It's a pretty spring night. You may have to ignore slightly more strangers than normal, but I don't think it will be that bad. We'll just stay away from the Fenway crowds. It's a night game."

They ended up walking for over an hour, sauntering through Brookline and Brighton until they managed to skirt around the never-ending tunnel of a campus that was Boston University and reached the strip of green on the Beantown side of the Charles River. The late spring evening was cool and clear and just windy enough to keep both of them in long sleeves. A few other couples wandered along the waterfront, cooing and making goo-goo eyes and remaining blissfully self-absorbed.

"I'm impressed, Geoff," Georgia said as her boss made it all the way to a bench and actually sat down to watch the twinkling lights of Cambridge on the opposite bank.

"This is not so bad," he said as he took in the smells of fumes and water and something funky wafting from a nearby trash can. Georgia eased down next to him and handed him back his phone, but this time he didn't slide it back on. Instead he looked at the reflection of all the lights in the water.

"They say we don't have reflections because we don't have souls," Geoffrey said, working up his already-bushy brows into an impressive knot.

"And who is this mysterious 'they'?" Georgia asked.

"Oh, it's all a bunch of claptrap," he scoffed weakly. "When I was younger, there were all these stories about how my kind was the devil and we had all these powers. Now we're just shown as pretty boys who smolder and wear too much leather."

"Don't forget the guy-liner and the sparkling," Georgia added as she leaned back to take in the view.

"Can I please forget the sparkling?" he asked with a little laugh.

Georgia smiled. "All you have to do is get through one little party, and then you can come home and I'll let you watch your stories, drink as many pureed sausages as you want, and I'll even make you a vanilla-rodent frappe."

"Actually, I was going to ask you something very important," he said. Georgia took note of how he wrung his hands and how he tapped his feet. She stiffened ever so slightly as she waited for the next few strained words from his cracked lips.

"Yes, Geoffrey?"

"I want you to go to the ball as my escort," he blurted out.

"Um, isn't this a . . ."—she stopped to look to the left and the right to make sure no one was in earshot—"vampire ball? Last time I checked, I had a reflection."

"It's hosted by my family. What can they say?" Geoffrey said. "Anyways, you are my trusted servant, and other retainers will be there."

"But will they be escorts?" she said, choking slightly on the word.

"Well, it has been known to happen. I rather think I'd prefer to have a little scandal than to be dismissed as the poor old fart without a date," he said with a little smile.

"Define a little scandal," Georgia said as she leaned back on the bench. "Are we talking wearing white after Labor Day scandal or wearing a Hitler costume to the Anne Frank Museum level of scandal?"

Geoffrey furrowed his brows again before finally replying, "Well, I suppose that depends on which family you ask. To a Pendragon I would suppose it would be rather like picking one's teeth in polite company—rather rude but sometimes ever so necessary."

"Well, how can I possibly refuse to be your toothpick?" Georgia laughed. "Wait, it *is* the Pendragons hosting, right?"

Geoffrey nodded. "Now, the Jaegers will take rather great exception to a human not being there on tap, so to speak, but since they rather rudely tricked me into going to this dreadful thing, I think I shall take rather great delight in rubbing it in their snooty continental faces."

"Well, that does sound like a moral imperative if I ever heard one," Georgia laughed. "But in all seriousness, what would I even do at a vampire's ball except become the cocktail hour?"

"Oh, you are under my protection as long as you live under my roof. The Jaegers may be snooty blighters, but they do have a healthy respect for the rules. No vampire would dare feed on another kinsman's servant. If a sheriff were so much as to get a whiff of such an infraction, well, it would take more than burn cream to make his or her day livable after that!"

"You really have sheriffs? You mean that's not Hollywood crap?"

"Well, they are technically *vicecomes*, but my family is thoroughly English, so we use the English name. We do still call the high sheriff a *praetor*, though. Otherwise he simply gets unbearable. It took nearly a thousand years to get him to allow the use of languages other than Latin in his court."

"Is he going to be there?"

"I bloody well hope not!" Geoffrey said, eyes widening. "He still thinks that America is full of savages in loincloths and a passing fad for wandering adventurers. He can barely accept the Jiangshi, and our family scholars think that the Chinese clan is actually older than his."

"I'm going to have to take notes," Georgia sighed.

"Oh, most certainly. Each of the great families has slightly different rules of etiquette, but you know the four laws so you should be fine, and you know how to dance, of course . . ."

"Oh, no . . . no . . . no . . . no," she said, hopping to her feet. "I can cook and clean and scrub a toilet all night long, but these feet, they have zero rhythm."

"Oh, don't be a ninny. You'll only have to do a waltz and follow a few rounds, maybe a tango if the Azarola have representatives there."

"You just added more foreign names in there," Georgia protested.

"The Jiangshi are the most powerful clan right now, and they hail from China and are currently not killing us so we are all very happy. The Azarola are the tricksters who pretty much took over South America, and they are also not killing us either right now so we are very happy."

"Well, is there anyone who *is* currently trying to kill you?" she asked.

"The Lung clan from Hong Kong. They pretty much want us all dead, but we have another century treaty so as long as none of us set foot on their land, they won't kill any more of us."

"Um, what about rule number one?" Georgia asked.

"Oh, well, yes, about that. The Lung clan founder may have fallen off a cliff, which normally wouldn't be fatal if she hadn't been stabbed, poisoned, and beheaded before she took the last step. It's something we don't like to talk about, but the Lung decided that since one of us killed their queen, it was fair game for them to retaliate until the guilty party or parties confessed. The Jiangshi blamed the Pendragons since old Uther was fond of axes, and then my clan noticed that the poison came from Cathay—you call it China now—and then someone pointed out that only a Jaeger hunter could have snuck up on their leader, and it just goes on and on. Believe me, if you ever want to get an argument started at a party, just ask who killed Su Min Lung!"

"Good to know," Georgia said, now staring at her feet. "I still don't dance."

"Oh, that's simple enough. I can teach you."

"You?" she said as she sized up his bloated belly and wobbly chin. "You can teach me how to dance?"

"I can teach you a waltz and enough not to embarrass yourself. I make no other promises. After all, you grew up in a generation scarred by disco and working."

"Working?"

"You know, that lusty gyration that makes it seem like you've been stuck on an out-of-control trolley car."

"I think you mean twerking," Georgia offered.

"Whatever. If I wanted to see a diseased marmot in his death throes, I'd watch those nature shows you keep leaving on," the vampire grumbled. "Now, I will teach you to dance and the basics of manners, but you will have to help me get clothes. It specifies modern dress." He punctuated the last remark with a tremendous shudder. "I've seen what passes for fashion nowadays, and I am truly terrified."

"I'm not going to fit in in a room full of your kind," she said as a late-night jogger ran close by.

"I am certain it will be fine. You haven't failed me yet!"

"I ruined most of your laundry."

"Well, other than that, and the burns, oh, and the not feeding my chickens while I was in the bath—"

"I get the picture. Now I'm also getting hungry, and it's about time for us to start wandering back or else Wang's will be shut, and you know I've been planning my Buddha's Delight binge all week."

"Will I get my Shanghai Surprise?" he asked with a giggle.

"Please, try to make that sound a little less dirty," she sighed as she started leading him back through the streets of Boston . . .

"Just how many families did you say there were?" Gail asked as she stared at the little scribbles she had made on the back of a napkin. Georgia pulled out her phone once more and broke out in a knowing smile.

"Oh, I have an app for that," she said with a little giggle. "I took this one that someone made for keeping track of information for like those fantasy role-playing games, and I put in all the families and the powers I'd found in each one. That way if my phone was ever stolen, they'd just assume I was her Royal Highness, Queen of the Geeks, and not some vampire's assistant. See here, I put little icons by each one so I could remember them easily. The sword in the stone is for Pendragon 'cause, well, duh. I have the Chinese character for life force for the Jiangshi, and the little foxes are Azarola. The dragons with the cranky faces equal Lungs—"

"And the arrows stabbed through a heart?" Gail asked.

"Jaegers . . . of course," Georgia said quickly. "The laurels are for the Caesars, and the little winged lions are for Gryffindor."

Gail stopped in her little follow-along exercise and gave Georgia a wild-eyed look. "You can't be serious," she said.

Georgia's face remained impassive. "Oh yes, it's terrible what they did to get immortalized in a series of bestselling children's books!" she said. "And to think they made her portray the Slytherin as the bad guys—"

"No way!" Gail gasped.

Georgia finally cracked a smile. "OK, I was totally messing with you, but yeah, that's the symbol for the Tepes clan."

"Where have I heard that?" Gail mused. She rolled her eyes, and the moans got louder from behind the screen.

"Don't worry, it'll come to you." She too glared at the divider. "Apparently that won't be all that's coming soon," she muttered. "Where was I? Dance lesson montage time?"

Gail nodded, her cheeks getting more flushed. Almost on cue the dee-jay raised the volume to drown out the noisy couple in the room. Georgia flicked away the page full of icons to reveal a wallpaper of what looked like the Eiffel Tower at night.

"Wow, Paris," Gail sighed.

"Tokyo," Georgia corrected. "If it was a daytime shot, you'd see it was red and white. Anyway, you get used to all the families. There are major families who all have big histories and unique traits that tend to rule over what they call the plebs, which are the working middle class of the vampire world. The plebes get to look down on what they call the animals, which are vampires that have been disgraced in some way or who have no powers whatsoever. I never met any of them, but apparently they don't count with the vampire law stuff because I know Steve said he killed a few of them and he's still around. They are apparently less than human, but only just barely, and completely inedible to a vampire."

Gail wrinkled up her nose. "They sound awful."

"They are," Minnie offered from behind the screen. "Oh yah, *mein schatzi* . . . we put them . . . we put them down for their own good."

"Oh come on, you don't multitask while getting laid, Minnie. It's just rude!" Georgia snapped back. "Now excuse me, I'm educating. You know, we could move to that back corner, under the speaker."

Gail nodded furiously, grabbed both their drinks, and shuffled quickly toward an oasis of purple velour and relative quiet. The two girls adjusted their positions so that the screen was all that could be seen. Gail did manage to catch a flicker of movement in the reflection of Georgia's phone, but all she could see was one gray pants leg, even though the shadows clearly showed a feminine form writhing on top of the poor victim.

Gail lifted her own phone again and peeked through the viewfinder. Sure enough, now the gray leg was showing up. Georgia cocked a brow and looked at her interviewee inquisitively. Gail started with an "Um—" and just pointed to the leg.

"The other one left. That's Minnie's takeout," Georgia spat, looking pointedly away.

"He—"

"The other one left, OK?" Georgia snapped.

"So, dancing?" Gail said with a desperate smile. She breathed deep as her interviewer finally eased back against the cushion and started smiling again.

"Well, of all the things I've been surprised by in the past year, the simple fact that Mr. Geoffrey Lambley is actually light on his feet has to be one of the biggest . . ."

Georgia wiped her brow with the edge of her T-shirt before once more staring at the mirror propped against the den wall. As if by magic, her arm stiffened and her shoulders lowered. She watched in fascination as a string of hair moved behind her ear as she kept peering over a freckled shoulder, rather than into the stern gaze of her partner.

"Focus!" Mr. Lambley snapped before swinging back an arm and re-setting the needle on the gramophone that had wandered downstairs for the week. "We will dance all night if we have to."

"It's four thirty, I think we've already accomplished that," Georgia groaned. "Look, I'm tired, and I think I'm getting worse."

The vampire just shook his head and once more adjusted her frame. "Are your shoulders somehow attached to your earlobes? Why do you keep shrugging at me? Now, let's go again!"

He started sashaying her back and forth to the time of the waltz on the record, but instead of maintaining a three count, Georgia managed to step on his toes three times. Once more he stopped, repositioned her, and walked her slowly through the motions.

She howled an expletive as she once more landed on her boss's toes. As she jerked away, Mr. Lambley held his head in shame.

"You do know that children learn this dance, do you not?" he sighed.

"My dancing is limited to the white-girl-don't-spill-your-beer shimmy and the drool-on-your-partner-at-the-end-of-the-night slow dance shuffle. I put my pictures in frames, not my arms!"

"You know, if you spent as much effort on your footwork as you do on making quips, we'd have progress, dear Georgia," the vampire said in a little singsong voice. "Now, again."

They started again, and again, until the sunrise warning alarm on her phone forced her to break away to check the polarized film and the curtains for the morning, as well as fix smoothies for breakfast. Luckily she sniffed her glass of red slush and quickly switched it out with the one in front of Mr. Lambley.

"This one is the strawberry," she muttered in relief as she slurped it down.

"Mmm, is that duck blood?" Mr. Lambley asked.

"Duck, goose, and turkey. The butcher had a blend. Oh, and I added a little marjoram because you said how much you liked it last time, and it was in the window box out back.

He raised his glass for a toast. After they clinked glasses, he promised, "Tomorrow, by tomorrow you'll have this."

One week later he banged his head against the wall as once more Georgia ended up sprawled on the couch with her head buried in her hands. "How can a human have so little rhythm? It's no longer merely comical, it's unnatural!" the vampire asked. He then eyed her shins. "Are they still bruised?"

"The coffee table is a little worse for wear, but I'll be OK," Georgia groaned. "I warned you that I was a klutz."

"Well, let's try a different tactic," he said.

"Oh no, I cannot watch any more *Masterpiece Theater*," she moaned. "I don't care who slighted who or if there are rumors about funny business happening before someone's coming-out, and I really don't care about next week's garden party and if they will ever find proper English roses in time—"

"Oh no, I think that you might need a different partner!" he said, wandering over to his phone.

"Don't call Switzerland anymore," Georgia mumbled as she buried her face in the pillows and tried her best to hide in a sea of plaid.

Not ten minutes later, she could hear the door to the vestibule opening.

"Who the—?" she started.

"You said it was an emergency and to bring athletic wear, Mr. Lambley," a slightly confused yet also ever so slightly robotic-sounding voice said.

"Oh yes, this is definitely an emergency."

Georgia looked over the upholstery to see a tall, lanky form in a neatly pressed dark suit, slicked-back hair, and sunglasses, even though it was most definitely night. "Oh, not Agent Fucking Smith," she groaned as she buried her face again.

"Do I need to get a doctor?" he asked flatly.

"Just get changed," the vampire ordered. "Trust me, Georgia, if I can correct you as you move, I think I can have this fixed! I just need to take a look at those elephant feet you have."

"Fine, but why him?" she asked. "It's not like I'm learning the robot."

"Well, with Stefano off in Japan, I thought his boy was not being put to full use, so I thought he'd have nothing better to do," Geoffrey said. "You keep telling me not to be wasteful, do you not?"

"I say one thing, and yet you always find a way to twist it in some strange way I never intended," Georgia sighed. "So tell me, can this boy of Stefano's even dance?"

"Well, as long as it's the robot," a dry voice said from the doorway. A completely different figure leaned against the jamb in a soccer jersey and sweatpants. His hair was not only slicked back but also captured in a teeny tiny black ponytail that splayed out like an untamed feather duster from the elastic band. His light green eyes that clashed with his classic Asian features stared impassively at the sweaty, red-faced girl on the sofa.

"You totally heard that?" she asked.

"You're rather loud."

"Oh, that is true, Mr. Matsuoka," Mr. Lambley agreed. "Now, would you mind helping me show my dear assistant how to waltz? I'm afraid that all my attempts have been futile so far, but that might be because we are just on such different levels. It's so difficult to slow down enough for a human, you know."

"As you wish, Mr. Lambley," he said with a little bow. He then extended his hand toward the lump on the sofa. Georgia didn't take it, but she did roll to her feet, take a deep breath, and offer her hand to him once Mr. Lambley started to raise a brow.

"Come on, he won't bite," Mr. Lambley chided as Georgia kept her distance.

"He's probably the only one I'll be dancing with that won't," she sighed. As she locked hands with him and he slid an arm around her back, she paused to take in the biceps and the little veins on his arms and just how firmly he held on.

"Is there a problem, Miss Sutherland?" he asked as she continued to stare at the edge of some unidentifiable ink peeking under his sleeve.

She shook her head and let the vampire adjust her posture for the umpteenth time. Mr. Lambley fluttered to and fro, moving an arm and then shifting a foot until he finally got the starting point he desired. Once more the record began to play.

It started just as before, with Georgia's partner falling victim to her amazing left feet crushing innocent toes. Mr. Matsuoka didn't curse or snap or even flinch as he waited for her to adjust. The music started again, and she quickly tripped and planted her face right between his pecs, and still there was no reaction from her partner save a gentle nudge backward. Georgia made a sound rather like a horse as she struggled once more to move in time. This time she made it over twenty seconds before tripping up.

As Mr. Matsuoka gently nudged her back, she gritted her teeth. By the tenth time of no reaction, she shoved away and stomped so hard the record skipped. "Come on! This is totally pointless."

"That time you made it thirty-two seconds, by the way," Mr. Matsuoka said in his infuriating monotone voice.

"You're counting?" she growled.

"I honestly am at a loss," the vampire in the room declared. "If you will excuse me, I'm going to get some air and finish off the rat in the blender."

Georgia slumped back onto her favorite cushion. "I can't do this."

"Only because you keep telling yourself that you can't," Mr. Matsuoka said. "It's rather pathetic."

"What did you say?" she asked.

"I'm sorry, was I unclear?" he asked.

"Oh, you were clear. I was just in awe of just how much of an asshole you are."

"Of course, honesty makes one an asshole in your universe," he fired back. "What a fun world you live in."

"Why you—"

"I'm just a robot, and I can manage this without looking like an idiot," he said as he reached out his hand.

"Oh really?" she sputtered as she grabbed his hand and hopped to her feet.

"Really," he said as he slipped on the record before grabbing her waist and jerking her rather roughly toward him. She responded by stiffening and glaring right into his freakish eyes.

"Just because you think you're so talented and this is easy doesn't mean that it's not hard for normal people," she said as she shifted along with the music. "I mean, you're so arrogant I can actually taste it."

"I think that might just be my cologne," he offered as he kept moving her around the empty patch cleared in the middle of the den.

"All I keep hearing is that Stefano's boy can do this and do that and he can balance the checkbook and pay all the bills and do all the dancing and order the rats and—" she sputtered. Her partner interrupted her by spinning her outward and then yanking her back.

"I do have a name," he said as she stopped right in front of his face.

"Oh, so sorry, Mr. Matsuoka," she growled, taking time to exaggerate each and every syllable.

"My name is Ren," he said with a slight sneer as he twirled her again.

"Ren," she repeated as she suddenly noticed her feet gliding over the floorboards. Immediately she stumbled, but Ren jerked her back to attention.

"Stop thinking so much," he warned. "It will only get you hurt."

She started to speak, but he spun her again and this time when she whirled back, she nearly planted her face into his, but somehow his wiry arms totally managed to stop her. "Stop thinking," he admonished again. "Let your feet just do their job."

"Your voice," she whispered. "Who talks like—?"

"Oh, miracles still happen!" a gleeful British accent chirped as the vampire watched Georgia drift around the room with a rather stunned look on her face. "He's a bit taller, that's it. It was easier for you to get the frame and the steps!"

Georgia kept looking at the chest in front of her. "Yeah, must have been that," she muttered.

"Just let your feet do their job," he whispered before letting Mr. Lambley cut in. A stunned Georgia managed to keep her footing as the shorter, but even more graceful, partner led her back and forth.

"Did you require anything else, Mr. Lambley?" Ren Matsuoka asked in the same damnably calm and even tone as the music finally ended with Miss Sutherland still on her feet.

"Oh, I think Georgia had some bills to be taken care of. You can get them and go," Geoffrey said, still giggling with delight.

"I'll get them," she said, still distracted. Ren followed her dutifully back toward the kitchen. Once they were safely in the oasis of fluorescents and vinyl tiles, she whirled around. "What is up with you?"

"I don't know what you mean," he said. "Mind if I grab some water?"

"You just kowtow and do whatever Mr. Lambley says."

"I'm a servant to vampires," he said flatly. "It's what I do. Mr. DeMarco is not my boss, he's my master. My master has ordered me to take care of your boss, so I do what I am told. That is all there is to it."

"Jesus, do you have any say in all this?"

"Are these all the bills?" he said, picking up the pile on the kitchen table.

"Oh, you do care. You changed that subject pretty damn fast."

"Do you always swear this much?" he asked flatly.

"Only around you," she said back just as flatly.

"It's nice to know that I inspire you," he said before taking the pile to the bathroom and tucking them in his gym bag along with his neatly folded suit.

"Shouldn't you hang that?" was all she could say.

"Yes, I should. Thanks for asking. Have a good night, Miss Sutherland."

"My name is Georgia," she said, imitating his monotone voice with a subtle little sneer at the end of the phrase.

"Good night, Georgia," he said before letting himself out.

7

"Wow, that Ren guy sounds like a total jerk," Gail offered between sips.

"Oh, you have no idea," Georgia said, taking a drink. "But he was totally right. I just had it in my head that I couldn't dance, and he got me over that block. With only a month to prep for a vampire party, I needed to get moving and stop worrying about my feet and start to worry about the rest of me and my nervous Nellie of a partner . . ."

"I am so terribly sorry," Mr. Lambley said as he slouched against the kitchen cabinets.

"Why is it always carrots?" Georgia asked, bewildered as she surveyed the pile of sick in front of the fridge.

"I couldn't help it. When I get nervous . . ." The vampire groaned as he clutched the blender glass to his chest.

His lip quivered, and his face grew more and more pale as his assistant scooped up his vomit and chucked it into the garbage disposal. She picked up a leaf with her pink rubber gloves.

"Did you take my spinach?" she asked.

The vampire burst into sobs. "Who am I kidding? I saw all those tempting, beautiful vegetables, and they called to me," he blubbered.

"You had spinach and carrots! Oh, Geoffrey—"

"The ball is in a week, and I don't think I can do it," he moaned. "I'm just a fangless, worthless—"

"We aren't having this conversation again," Georgia muttered. "Look, if you can't watch what you eat on my biweekly night off, I'm going to have to call that Ren to watch you."

"Mr. Matsuoka would let me do whatever I wish," Geoffrey protested.

"He would *not* put a salad in a blender for you. Oh, god, you've got the shakes," Georgia said. She stopped cleaning, yanked off her gloves, and hopped over the remainder of the goo to help her boss to his feet and lead him to the couch in the den. Once he was tucked in with a blanket and a comforting infomercial on the TV, she hopped back to the kitchen and pulled out a mason jar full of bright red liquid that was marked with "G.L."

Geoffrey wrinkled his nose as she popped open the jar and offered it to him.

"Come on," she coaxed gently as she held up his head and poured a little into his mouth. "I want you to have this so I don't start looking tasty in an hour or so."

He finally choked down a little bit of plain pig's blood. A little flush of color returned to his cheeks, and after a second round, his breath slowly settled down to normal. Georgia pushed the tufts of hair back from his receding hairline.

"You are the strangest vampire I have ever met," she sighed.

"I'm the only vampire you've really met," Geoffrey replied.

"Well, that will all change soon enough. Now, you get some rest while I clean up," she said.

"I can't go. I don't care if—" he muttered.

"Look, if I can waltz, you can mingle for a few hours. Just stop thinking about it."

"There's so much to teach still. You need lessons on etiquette and history and—"

"You need to rest and lay off the human food," she chided. "I'm sure I can find someone with a lot of knowledge who can teach me all this stuff while you get better. Is that friend of yours still out of town?"

Geoffrey nodded weakly.

"All right now, I'm gonna finish cleaning. If you need anything, just yell . . ."

"If there is one terrible fact about the life of an undead assistant, it's that your support options can be limited." Georgia sighed as she settled against the back cushion. Gail leaned in to listen with baited breath. "I only knew one person to call, a person probably not very happy to be called on his night off once more to help another vampire in need."

"Ren Matsuoka, right?" Gail asked.

"The one and only. He gave me the same rundown on the families I just gave you. He also showed up with a gym bag again. I guess he thought I'd had a total relapse after my dance lessons. He was also ever so quick to pass judgment on my early failures in vampire caretaking . . ."

"He did what?" Ren asked with an ever-so-slight break in his normally flat inflection.

"He puked on the kitchen floor. Do I need to do anything special to, you know, dispose of it—"

"You didn't mention that he was vomiting. What the hell have you been letting him eat?" Ren snapped as he ripped open the fridge door.

"He broke into my carrots—"

"Carrots!" Ren snapped. "What is in the bags?"

"Pig's blood."

"Do you have anything stronger?" he said as he rifled through the rather sparse icebox.

"Stronger, like what?"

Ren stared right through her. "You're telling me that you don't keep any human blood in the house?"

"Just my own, but that is staying in me!" she snapped.

"Do you have any idea how much cellulose is in a raw carrot?" he asked, with absolute venom in his now-expressive voice.

"Oh, I'm sure you're about to tell me, Einstein," Georgia snapped back.

"Cellulose is toxic to vampires. A little bit makes them high if they can tolerate it, but too much can kill them. You at least know about stakes through the heart, right?"

"Well, I didn't stab a carrot into his chest. He just mixed my juice into his blood—"

"Vampires are colonial parasitic organisms. It's not stabbing them in the heart that kills them, it's the wood," he snapped.

"Well, of course! Everyone knows that," Georgia laughed.

Ren pulled his phone to his ear. "Not everyone knows that, but you should," he said as he waited for an answer. He suddenly turned from Georgia and launched into a flurry of some melodic Asian language. After a few nods and a quick pace around the room, he jerked his phone away and turned back to the red-faced girl in the kitchen. Georgia took a few deep controlled breaths before finally looking him right back in the freakish eyes.

"Well, did I kill him?" she asked.

"Mr. Lambley is not completely cellulose intolerant. In fact, he has a rather extraordinary tolerance, but if he has gotten to the point of vomit, he is sick and needs to detoxify. Vampires need pure proteins to survive. They are obligate carnivores. Do you know what that means?"

"Do you know what condescending asshole means?" she fired back.

It was his turn to take a deep breath or two. "Gary is going to be by in about twenty minutes with a bag of human plasma. It should be enough for you to thin with a bit of water, salt, and vinegar and feed him for about three days."

"Human . . . blood?" Georgia asked. "How on earth—"

"Gary works for the local Red Cross blood drive. He also has a fetish for being tied up while dressed as a large gopher. His beaver buddy is a friend of mine, and she took many incriminating pictures. Thus we can get small batches of quality human blood with very little cost or effort," Ren said.

"Why is that somehow more disturbing than feeding a vampire?" Georgia asked.

Ren looked back in the fridge. "There are a lot of vegetables in here. The solids aren't tempting, but when you put it in juice form, it's like offering a beer to an alcoholic," he muttered. "Mr. Lambley has always had a problem with watching what he eats. How do you think he lost his fangs?"

"I never—"

"You never asked?"

"You know, I don't think it's very polite to ask your boss, 'Hey, how did you lose your teeth?'"

Ren just shook his head. Georgia stomped off to check on her boss. He gave her a little thumbs-up from the sofa as he watched a woman with very large hair crying over her second husband leaving her for her evil twin.

"Did I hear the door?" he asked.

"Our friend Mr. Matsuoka stopped by to help me get ready so you could rest. I think we're going to get you a little snack too."

The vampire grinned, showing off the gaps in his teeth. "I'm so sorry I made a mess in the kitchen," he apologized again.

"Don't you worry about it, but no more carrots for a while, OK?"

"Oh, I just had a few too many," he snorted. "So what is Stefano's boy teaching you? His family has served our kind for centuries, you know. He's rather an expert."

"Oh, he just seems to know everything," Georgia said with a forced smile. "Need anything else?"

As he shook his head, she wandered back to the kitchen to find Ren spreading a bunch of old papers and Mr. Higgins's journal on the table. He would glance at a page for mere seconds before filing it back in a pile. "You know, you have a wealth of information here if you choose to use it," he said, not even looking up.

"I've read some bits and pieces, but it's not that easy to follow," she said.

"Apparently Mr. Lambley has done this quite a few times," Ren said as he continued to scan. "Oh, and I poured drain cleaner into the disposal.

That plus some hot water should dispose of any infection left over from the vomit."

"Infection?"

"Shall we start at the beginning?" he asked.

"That depends. Are you going to keep going through Mr. Lambley's things and dismissing me?" she asked.

Before he could start again, his phone vibrating on the table interrupted them. "Gary is fast tonight," he muttered before heading to the door. Georgia watched the strange man who showed up in the middle of the night in a suit and tie as he drifted to the door and whispered to the rather unassuming-looking courier in a hoodie and jeans. She managed to get a quick glimpse of puffy cheeks and dark eyes behind coke-bottle glasses before Ren's back blocked her view again. Neither one of them spoke a lick of English as Ren passed a small wad of cash over in exchange for a little red lunch bag with a local insurance company logo on the side.

The courier peeked over the taller man's shoulder and broke into a big grin as he saw Georgia in her slouching camisole top and low-slung yoga pants. "Vamp tramp," she could just hear mixed in with a bunch of foreign vocab. To her surprise, Ren instantly turned from bland and pleasant to frighteningly cold with the slightest shift in expression. The courier blanched and pulled away as bright green eyes bored through him.

"Good night, Gary," Ren said flatly.

"Vamp tramp?" Georgia asked with a raised brow.

"Mr. Chou is aware of whom he's providing services to. He normally only sees women who make a living by assisting vampires . . . in specialized ways," Ren said.

"Vamp tramp, what a colorful little phrase," Georgia mused as they took the bag to the kitchen, where Ren proceeded to show her step-by-step how to decant the plasma into a jar, shake it properly, and thin it with a blend of salt, vinegar, and water.

"You want it just pink to start. We'll mix it stronger tomorrow to give him a bigger dose of hemoglobin. He can take pig's blood too by Thursday, but it's best to keep him on a strict diet until then," Ren said. He then wrote the recipes down for her.

"He doesn't like plain blood," she said.

"He likes the rush from the sugars in vegetables. If he won't take it plain, we can stir it with some lemongrass or a ginger slice. That way we can infuse some flavor without adding solid plant matter into his drink."

"You sound like you've had to do this before," she said, watching him grab a straw and give the blush-colored cocktail a final stir.

"My master is cellulose intolerant," he said. "But he too likes to occasionally have a treat. I can't give him more than a quick swizzle, or he breaks out in hives."

"Well, let's see if I can sell this to Geoffrey," Georgia said. She padded into the den and dragged one of the TV trays over to the recovering patient. He wrinkled his nose as she offered him the plain blood.

"That smells awful," he said, turning his nose away.

"Oh come on, you were salivating the last time I cut my hand," she said. "This is human blood. You should lap it up."

"I can smell the plastic on it. It's bag blood," he said with a little pout, "and it's type A. I don't like type A."

Georgia rolled her eyes. "Well, it's all you are getting until your stomach calms down, so you can either drink it or starve," she said, plopping it down next to him. She then walked away with nary a second glance.

Ren made a point to look over as she came in. "Do you think he will drink it?" he asked.

"He will when he's sure I'm not watching. I've found that the same tricks I used when I worked as a babysitter work pretty well on him. Did you just make coffee?" she asked as she sniffed a distinctive nutty aroma in the air.

"I didn't see any cream in the fridge. You take it black or with sugar?" he asked as he pulled out the mugs.

"Do you have hidden cameras in my kitchen?" she asked.

"I've found that most people adhere to a pretty similar layout, and you didn't change much from when Mr. Lambley was on his own. Remind me to bring cream and better coffee when I'm here next," he said as he poured his cup.

"You do seem like a four-dollar-latte kind of guy."

"We all have our vices," he said, putting a cup in front of her. He then neatly set out the sugar bowl and a spoon before turning to his own cup. "So, do you want to go over the basics, or are we going to banter and bitch for the rest of the night?"

"Oh, I think there will still be some banter and bitching," Georgia said, "But you made good enough coffee that I think I can stay up long enough to learn something."

"Should I get you a notepad?" he asked.

"Only if you want me to doodle."

"Fine," he sighed. "Do you know what vampires are?"

"Besides the obvious?"

Ren nodded.

"You said they are colonial parasitic organisms," Georgia said. "You also mentioned an infection?"

"All vampiric fluids have little bits of the colony in them. All can affect humans, but only vampiric blood can transfer enough infection to control a human. Vampire tears and saliva contain hypnotic sedatives, and vampire semen has been recorded as a hallucinogen—"

"You did not just say the words vampire semen in a sentence," Georgia said as she stared at her guest.

"To be fair, female vampires create a mucus with the same effect . . . Georgia, are you all right?"

"Vampire . . . semen . . . used in a sentence," Georgia said, still shaking her head.

"Georgia?"

"Well, does their shit cure cancer?" she asked.

"Vampires don't produce solid waste," Ren responded without skipping a beat.

"You are way too calm about discussing all this," she said while shaking her head. "Oh, just give me the rest of the gory details."

"You have to be careful to limit your exposure. Vampires can control almost any human if given enough time—"

"And fluid transfer."

"And fluids, yes," Ren continued. "As their sweat evaporates, it creates a cloud of pheromones—"

"The miasma, right?" she offered.

Ren nodded. "So you do know a bit."

"I know that the miasma doesn't work on me."

"That's impossible. Vampire sweat is conditioned to human neurotransmitters. It affects everyone. Your boss is greatly weakened, so you can't compare him to a healthy vampire."

"Is that what makes you so subservient then?" she asked.

"You're the one who asked for help."

"And why did you come here?" she asked back in the same snippy tone.

"I honestly don't know. I serve my master, and my master is allied with your boss. I get one month a year, at most, of peace, but for some reason, I've had to spend it training a complete newbie in the most basic tasks—"

"I am not a complete newbie. I'm just not an expert on vampire semen like you!"

"Do you know what is lethal to vampires?" he asked.

"The sun?" she quipped back.

"Yes, all vampires will die from prolonged exposure to strong ultraviolet light," Ren said. "Some have thicker skins than others."

"Cellulose poisoning, especially a stake to the heart," she said next.

"Including ingesting too much vegetable matter. They are also sensitive to the sulfur compounds of the members of the allium family."

"You mean garlic?"

"Very good. What about crosses and holy water?" he asked.

"Bunch of Hollywood nonsense?"

"Mostly. Vampires are creatures of extremes. Whatever they believe in, they believe completely. Some of the families truly and honestly believe they are cursed by God, and if confronted with holy relics, they will have a psychosomatic reaction as violent as putting them in a tanning booth. This is why they follow the rules so vehemently."

"So they are total drama queens," Georgia sighed. "And Geoff has gone over the four laws and some of the families. The Pendragons are the nice guys, and everyone else are assholes, right?"

"You think you are being funny, but you are going to get yourself a one-way ticket to being on the menu. Mr. Lambley is a kitten. Most of the other vampires you will face are T. rexes."

Georgia waved her hand to stop him. "Not lions?" she asked.

"What?" Ren asked.

"Well, when you said kitten, I thought you'd compare it to another type of cat. Don't you think a T. rex is a little, you know, extreme analogy-wise?"

"You're questioning my analogies?" he asked incredulously between sips of coffee.

"I may still be overwhelmed with the concept of hallucinogenic vampire semen," she said with a little laugh. "But I do get the idea. You think I'm completely unprepared for meeting a bunch of vampires because I got the training-wheels model, right?"

"If you want my advice—"

"You're going to give it anyway," she muttered.

They sat in silence for a while, entertained only by the faint orchestral tones of soap opera credits from the den. Ren tapped his fingers against the side of his mug and tried to lose his gaze into the ripples dancing along the surface of his coffee, while Georgia kicked her feet under the chair.

"Was my analogy that bad?" he asked finally.

"Pretty terrible," Georgia sighed.

"Well, try this one, then. When you go to the ball in two weeks, you want to be like furniture. That's what every good assistant strives to be," he said, once more looking her right in the eye.

"You want me to be as wooden as you?" she asked.

"I'm serious. A good assistant is just *there* in the room. He or she is nice, functional, and utterly forgettable once the vampire has moved on. That is how you stay alive. You don't want to be their friend or their pet or, god forbid, their lover, because that will only make them attached to you. Vampires are not human, no matter what they look like. They don't love—they obsess, and once they target you, it's only a matter of time before they destroy you."

"Vampires aren't the only drama queens," Georgia said under her breath.

Ren pushed away from the table. "I think you've had enough for one night. You're not going to take any of this seriously."

"What did they do to you?" she asked.

"What?"

"I mean, is it just that you've been beaten down by serving vampires your whole life, or was there something more? What has made you so scared of them?" she asked.

Georgia's eyes widened as her guest slowly reached up and loosened his tie. He unbuttoned his stiff white shirt one button at a time until he could pull it apart and yank his undershirt down a few inches. She leaned in to see row upon row of jagged little scars mixed in with the edges of more black, gray, and brown ink. Each puncture mark started a little more than an inch from the next. Before she could gawk too much, he let the collar snap back to his neck and buried the evidence under layers of beautifully laundered and pressed fabric.

He then mechanically took his mug to the sink, washed it without a word, and even took the time to dry it in utter silence. Georgia watched how a few strands of hair had slipped from his normal slick helmet of gel and how more feathery edges of tattoo ink peeked ever so slightly from under his collar as he moved.

"Your master eats you," she finally blurted out.

"When vampires feed, they don't leave scars. They have needlelike appendages that come from their fangs. At worst it looks like a mosquito bite, otherwise it would be pretty damn obvious that vampires were real, don't you think?"

"But—?"

"But when a vampire wants to hurt you, to teach you a lesson, she makes you drink her blood. You can feel it as it slowly takes over your body. First it's numb, then it burns, and then it's simply ecstasy, but then, you see, the vampire wants that piece of itself that it put inside you . . . it wants it back. My mistress likes to rip it out. The reaction of the vampire blood and human in this process causes pain and scarring. As you can see, I needed a fair amount of teaching when I was younger."

"I don't understand. I thought you served some guy named Stefano—"

"My family serves the Jaeger family. If I fail any of them, they can decide to punish me. Lady Claudia Jaeger is not known to be one who forgives any slight, no matter how small."

"She's going to be at the ball, isn't she?" Georgia asked.

Ren nodded. "With the entire Western branch of the family. Just keep that in mind when you're making your jokes. Please, be in the background, don't call any attention to yourself, and you'll be fine."

"Be like furniture?"

"I wouldn't worry too much, Georgia," Ren said as he took her empty cup to the sink.

"Oh?"

"You'll be in a room full of vampires who haven't seen each other in months, some of them as old as the Roman Empire. Do you really think that you'll be interesting to them?"

"Wow, poor guy," Gail said. "You said he had scars all around his neck?"

Georgia stared off in the distance. "Neck, arms, back—you name it. He's right, though. You can never underestimate them. You have to follow the rules at all times. He reminded me to wear my key all the time to show them that I *belong* to Mr. Lambley, mostly so that they don't think I'm an hors d'oeuvre. He's even the one who got me this chain," she said as she lifted it up to let the gold glimmer in the lights.

"So he's a good resource if you have questions?" Gail asked.

"If you can get past the layers of sarcasm and arrogance," Georgia sighed. "At that point, though, he had me terrified. I had only two weeks to prepare myself to face a bunch of vampires, all while trying to nurse Mr. Lambley back to health. I should have walked away. I mean, a sane person would have walked away, but sometimes you have to be just a little bit crazy to do really well at your job, and sometimes you just have to find a really awesome dress on sale when you are walking back from getting your hair done . . ."

"I'd almost forgotten what this feels like," Georgia said as she closed her eyes and let the midday sun pour over her face. "Let's just stay here awhile," she cooed to the man sitting across the wire-frame patio outside a little café on Newbury Street.

He plunged his spoon back into his fruit and chocolate-drenched cup of frozen yogurt, his eyes hidden completely behind a wall of black plastic. He stood out among the waves of New England tourists schlepping along in T-shirts and shorts—with his neatly pressed white shirt, black suit, and perfectly plain black tie. Indeed, one or two of the passersby stopped to see just who this man in black must have been protecting.

Georgia sipped her bright green smoothie, chock-full of kale and carrots and every fruit she managed to have stuffed into a sixteen-ounce plastic cup. "Oh, this would kill our dear Geoffrey, wouldn't it?" she muttered between sips.

"Ah yes, a day of sunshine, cellulose, and garlic bread," he said with a slight smile finally breaking out. "Wouldn't my master and your boss be proud of us?"

"You were right about the pizza though, it was really good," Georgia said. "Breakfast of champions."

"Indeed," her companion said as he pulled out his phone and began scrolling away.

For a few minutes, Georgia slurped away, basking in the rays she had been denied for the past few weeks. However, as her companion continued to stare intently at the little screen, Georgia started to fidget. Soon she was craning her neck to try to read the reflection, but instead of seeing the typical flapping birds or 140 characters, all she could make out were boring blocks of numbers and an occasional graph. Finally, after five solid minutes of staring, Ren set his phone down deliberately, slowly swirled his spoon around a few times, and took a bite before asking, "Is there something I can do for you, Georgia?"

"You know, it's rude to just play with your phone when you have someone with you," she admonished.

"Did you have something pressing you wanted to discuss?" he asked.

"Well, no," she admitted.

"Are we on a date?"

"Um, hell no," she said.

"Then I don't see the problem with me getting a little work done while you enjoy the sun."

"I would say that all work and no play make Ren a dull boy, but you are the one who keeps telling me to be boring to survive," she said before slurping down the last bit of her frosty beverage. "I suppose we should finish today's mission so I can get a nap before the boss man wakes back up. He has been sleeping so much better since we fixed his diet, which means I've gotten more than four hours a day as well."

"I told you it would work," Ren said. He motioned toward the sidewalk. "I'm a master of walking while eating if you want to start looking again."

She furrowed her brows. "You really are enjoying this whole being right thing, aren't you?" she asked.

"One must find pleasure even in the everyday occurrences," he said, even more devilishly monotone than normal. Georgia just snorted and hopped up to toss her cup in the bin. He rose and followed her dutifully, and true to his word, nary a drop of melting FroYo dribbled onto his spotless lapel even as they were forced to dodge and weave through masses of people who had no idea where they were headed.

"That one looks sensible," Ren said as he pointed out a black sheath of a dress in one of the windows.

Georgia shook her head. "I think there's a consignment place a block up. They usually have something funky—"

"You're going to be escorting a member of the host's family. Don't you think you should go for something other than funky?" Ren sighed.

"Am I supposed to dress like I'm going to a funeral?" she asked.

"Black is traditional—"

"So the Goths got something right, that's what you are saying?" she asked.

"Black is traditional and classy. It would also contrast nicely with your complexion, that's all," Ren offered.

"I have never felt more confused by a compliment in my life," Georgia said. "You sound like you're selling a dishwasher or something. Just look at these features—"

"You could have simply taken the money and gone out yourself if you didn't want my opinion," Ren said. "I was only tasked with making sure you had something formal."

"Oh, but I do love having you walking behind me looking like you could totally kick someone's ass," she said with a little laugh. "Tell me, do you always dress like a lost special agent, or do you have so many funerals to rush to that this is just convenient?"

"You only see me at work," he said. "The family expects a certain level of formality in public."

"Oh yes, I am just your job."

"Well, some jobs have to be more difficult than others," he said as he led her toward the next store with a few sparkling numbers behind the glass. "Is this more you?" he said, pointing to a tube of gold sequins.

Georgia shook her head. "Nope."

"This is going to be a long afternoon after all," Ren said in his normal sphinxlike tone. They wandered from storefront to storefront, but the only thing they could agree on was that no sane human being should wear hot pink taffeta or six-inch heels to a vampire soiree.

Finally he managed to drag her into a store or two but kept showing her simple black dress after simple black dress. After the fifteenth refusal, he finally went bold and offered her a number in navy. Georgia shook her head and kept pawing through size eight after size eight, but only sighed at the fluffy masses of sequins and satin with utter disdain.

"See anything you like?" an associate dared to ask after she lingered on a plum number for more than a millisecond.

"Nah," she said.

"Our clearance rack is toward the back," the salesgirl offered as she noticed Georgia's discount sandals, no-name tank top, and clearly off-the-rack jeans. Georgia had to smile as she could literally hear Ren gritting his teeth in anticipation. She promptly snagged the first thing she could find with a four-digit price tag and said, ever so sweetly, that she wanted to try it on.

After slipping in and out of five glittery things and thoroughly perturbing the woman who had to keep letting her in and out of the fitting room, she finally put the poor clerk and Ren out of their misery and grabbed a midrange black number to try on. As she stared at her reflection in formfitting black silk, she couldn't help but notice how it really did set off her pale skin and light eyes.

"My, my, that one does fit well," the fussy clerk noted. "You should let your boyfriend see you in it."

She looked at how it hugged her curves and even made her linebacker shoulders seem less suited for the NFL. "He will never see this," she muttered as she yanked the zipper.

"But it looked amazing," her sales assistant protested as the silk slumped to the floor.

Georgia yanked her clothes back on. "Sorry, just not me," she said quickly as she rushed out the door, leaving a bewildered Ren still waiting for some sort of progress. She made it nearly to the next cross street before she felt a hand on her shoulder.

"What is going on?" Ren asked.

"It's just not me. You're right, none of this is me! No matter what I get, I'm just going to be ridiculous, and I don't really feel like fussing with this anymore. Just pick me out something you think will fit in. I'm a size eight unless I hit the doughnuts, and my feet are size ten."

"Georgia—" he started.

"Look, you know this sort of event way better than me. I'll just mess it up, so why don't we call it a day? Bye!"

She left him standing on the corner shaking his head, but he made no effort to follow her as she wandered farther up the block. Once she was safely out of sight, she ducked onto a side street and flopped against the brick corner of a service alley. She made little fists and pounded her thighs. "What is wrong with you, Sutherland?" she asked. It was at that very moment that she saw the heartbreakingly familiar Mr. Doughnut sign across the street. "Of all the corners," she muttered. She whispered a quick prayer of thanks that the late spring afternoon crowds filled the little shop and prevented any clear view of the staff working behind the counter.

She darted back onto Newbury and kept her eyes on the prize, the side street that led her to a subway station—only a few hundred feet away. She almost made it to safety when a voice behind her called out, "Georgia! Georgie, is that you?"

She turned to see electric blue now mixed into the mass of dreadlocks. She let out a sigh of relief as a girl unseasonably dressed in a black crepe dress and thigh-high bitch boots flagged her down. "Alice!" Georgia exclaimed as she awkwardly wandered back the other way.

"Where have you been, girl?" the chick in three layers of eyeliner exclaimed.

"Oh, you know how it is when you have someone new in your life," Georgia said sheepishly.

"Do I ever!" she cried before tackling her friend with a sloppy hug. "Paul's been getting into the submissive thing, and I never thought I'd find anyone willing to spend two hours in a ball gag while I watch the Sox play."

"Well, I'm glad you finally found a gimp," Georgia laughed.

"A willing slave who isn't a Yankees fan—what more could a girl ask for?" she laughed. "So, how is that bit of aged cheese you've been slathering on your muffin? Is he as filthy in the bedroom as he is filthy rich?"

Georgia took a second to respond. "Oh, well, you know, I never kiss and tell," she said weakly. "What are you doing down here?"

Alice raised her bag of pastries guiltily. "Sorry, I did get hooked when you worked there, and I need a sugar rush to get through the second half of my shift. One of Paul's buddies is a designer, and she opened up a storefront. I said I'd help her out till she could get someone permanent."

"Do I want to know what she designs?" Georgia dared to ask.

"Oh, it's all recycled stuff—art . . . clothes . . . you name it. She does the whole trash-to-treasure thing, and I just lap it up. She made a towel rack for the apartment out of scrap metal and this bag here out of woven strips of billboard ads. It's so fabulously ugly it's gorgeous! Come on, you can come see."

"You know I've not been getting any sleep—"

"Oh, he's that good, eh?" Alice said with a wink. "Come on, you barely text. You haven't stopped by. I mean, if you hadn't sent the check for the rest of the year's rent, I would have thought you never wanted to see me again."

"You got a check?" Georgia asked.

"Heh, you can't play coy when the check is in your name. You're worried that Daddy Warbucks won't be able to satisfy you forever, I can dig it." Alice grabbed Georgia's hand and led her down into a basement studio full of all manner of bizarre and brightly colored creations. A woman with a platinum buzz cut and prominent array of facial piercings waved as they came in.

"You better have something cream-filled for me, Alice," she said.

"Don't you know it? Lisa, this is my good buddy, Georgie. You know, the one that hit the gold-digger jackpot and left me with a two-bedroom all to myself for the next few months."

The artist just waved and went diving for pastries. Georgia, however, was no longer interested in either of the women in the room as a swath of layers of aqua fabric on an old-fashioned dress form caught her eye.

Lisa quickly took notice and plopped a picture of a ridiculously hideous teal mountain of ruffles wrapped around several girls with very big hair and fuchsia lipstick. "My cousin was a sadist at her wedding," she said. "I managed to get a mountain of the ugliest polyester you ever did see. My challenge was to take the worst of the nineties and make something fab."

Georgia smiled at the aqua and rhinestones. "Have you got this in an eight?"

8

Georgia stared at the neat pile of parcels delivered in her foyer as her vampire employer tapped his fingers giddily at the prospect of one of the boxes being marked with next-day labels and a warning that it contained frozen pet supplies. He snatched up the bright white box on top with the glee of a child on Christmas morning. As he took a deep sniff, his companion rolled her eyes.

"What is all this crap?" she asked.

"Frozen rats," Geoffrey giggled. He peered over the box hopefully until Georgia finally yanked it from him, carried it to the kitchen, and started pulling out his blender and favorite milkshake tumbler.

"Just one," she cautioned him before dragging in the rest of the parcels from the vestibule. She furrowed her brows as she saw the name of several boutiques she had visited just this afternoon on a few of the tags.

"What the—?"

She opened the first box to see a pair of size ten black pumps. One by one she uncovered hose, undergarments, a selection of costume jewelry, and the very same sexy black dress she had left crumpled on the fitting-room floor. "You have got to be kidding me," she growled. Just as she was reaching for the phone in her pocket, a little slip of white paper caught her eye.

"Size eight dress, size ten shoes, nothing else for you to worry about, Miss Sutherland – R. M."

"Oh, the nerve of that—" she started.

"Georgia! It's jammed again," Geoffrey whined from the kitchen. After running to stab at a rat carcass with a chopstick, she came back to unwrap a few boxes containing a tux and shiny men's shoes.

"He got you a suit," Georgia said as she stomped back into the fray to clean up. "Ugh, you need to use a little bit of the pig's blood to thin it out, Geoff."

"Mix pig's blood with my rat?" he snorted.

"I do it all the time," she said.

The vampire sneered. "Well, I knew that. Anyway, of course, Stefano's boy bought me a suit. I asked him to get us suitable attire for the ball. He should have spared no expense!"

"Yeah, I know, but, ugh, how does a guy know to get all this? He remembered to get a bra and pantyhose! Seriously, the guy knows how to do everything, and it's annoying. We went out together this afternoon to go shopping, and I had to ditch him after a couple hours. I just told him my size and said to get what he wanted—"

The vampire plopped into one of the kitchen chairs and started slurping up his pinkish gray breakfast. "I don't think I quite follow you, Georgia. Why are you mad when he has done everything you asked him to do?"

"It's just . . ."—she stopped to dump the rest of the rodents in the freezer—"it's just so frustrating! He wasn't supposed to just take care of everything like that."

"But is that not the job of any servant?" Geoffrey asked.

She raised a brow at her boss. "Stop being logical, I'm not in the mood," she said as she yanked a bright red pitcher out of the fridge. She then started a new concoction in the blender with the initials G. S. clearly painted on in blue nail polish. As she peeled a banana and plopped it in, the vampire wrinkled his nose.

"That hibiscus tea is cruel," he bemoaned.

"Oh come on, it doesn't smell even remotely like blood," she chided as she went back to the fridge for yogurt and strawberries.

"Well, sometimes I wake up with a stuffy nose," he said in his defense. "How can you drink that? It's like biting into a lady drowned in perfume."

She poured her own pinkish, thick beverage and settled across the table. The vampire smiled his gap-toothed grin and raised his glass. After a quick clink, she couldn't help but smile as they shared their unique little feast in the early hours of the night.

"You seem less squeamish than when I first met you, Miss Georgia," Geoffrey noted. "You don't even gag when cleaning the blender."

"What can I say? I'm adaptable," she sighed. "What about you, Geoff? You made it all the way to Lansdowne Street with only one little panic attack. You might be tougher than you thought."

Mr. Lambley hopped to his feet and ran toward the foyer. He returned with a quivering lip and a bow tie in his hands. "The suit smells like plastic and paper," he whined. "I think it might have the demon polyester in it."

Georgia rolled her eyes. "You want me to text Ren and have him take it back? I'm pretty sure that every suit nowadays is gonna have something synthetic in it. We can't put you in linen or cotton for a full night. I still have nightmares about the rash you got after sweating in jeans. That leaves silk, wool, and Mr. Polyester."

"Maybe we could do something about the odor," he suggested.

"Well, considering how you hate my candles, the air freshener, pretty much all detergent, and even the smell of toothpaste, what do you suggest? I could fry some bacon next to it."

He gnawed on his lip for a few minutes. Finally he started nodding to himself. "I have it!" he said. "You could wear it for a few days."

Georgia just sat there, cradling her smoothie. "You want me to wear your suit first?"

"You smell much better than plastic," he said.

"I honestly don't know whether to be flattered or creeped-out right now," she said flatly . . .

"Um, so that is part of the job description still?" Gail interjected weakly.

"What, pureeing rats or wearing Mr. Lambley's clothes first?" Georgia clarified.

"The clothes thing. I guess it's finally sinking in."

"Yeah, I had the exact same reaction. Gore is kind of easy to desensitize yourself to, but talking about how you smell . . . ugh, it does take some getting used to. It's kinda like how you can watch a whole horror movie without flinching, but then be terrified when a dog is in jeopardy in a disaster flick. You never know what sort of crazy will freak you out in its ridiculousness, but don't worry, it's just when something is new or back from the dry cleaners. It's not like he rolls it under his nose and leers at you when he sniffs it. You know, some of the Jaegers are far pickier—they only wear leather of men or beasts they killed themselves. Talk about a conversation starter at a party . . ." Georgia trailed off as she saw a slight green hue washing over her companion's skin. "You know, maybe this isn't quite the position for you, sweetie."

"No! I just need a second," she said. "Is the ladies' room back there?"

Gail excused herself and made her way into the relatively calm oasis of black tile and sleek glass sinks. The music was dialed down enough for her to catch her breath as she splashed a bit of cold water on her face. Gail then quickly went to work, blotting wayward eye makeup and reapplying what she could from her limited purse supply. "This is crazy," she whispered. Her heart nearly leaped from her chest as there was a sudden knock on the bathroom door.

"Pardon," a sweet voice said. "Cleaning."

Gail laughed at her shocked expression as a few moments later a round-faced little woman peeked through the door. Gail quickly shoved her lip gloss into her purse and shuffled by to let the small lady in a blue apron slip in with a mop and bucket. The cleaner smiled and gave a little wave as Gail passed her by.

Bolstered by a little fresh air and normalcy, Gail managed to tug her blouse down and once more face the bumping, thumping room inhabited by Georgia and the blonde vampire. As she returned, the blonde was nowhere to be seen, and the good-looking waiter with the perfect wavy hair was cleaning up some sort of spill where she had once been. The man in the gray suit had pulled a Houdini as well, but his jacket laid rumpled next to the now-empty sofa he had shared with the bloodsucker.

Georgia looked up from her phone. "If it's too much—" she started.

"Where did, um, those two go?" Gail asked.

"Oh, Minnie got what she wanted, so she's wandered off to get into her usual sort of trouble. I bet she's dancing out there as we speak."

"And her, um, *friend*?"

"She wore him out, I'm sure. Don't worry, he walked out of here," she said. "A couple painkillers and a steak, and he'll be right as rain in a few days. Actually a regular like him will probably be fine in a few hours."

"Oh," Gail said as she settled back into her seat. "I guess I got overwhelmed for a second. It's a lot to take in."

"Oh, it's just one thing after another. One thing I can guarantee is that if you take this job, you'll never be bored. Well, sometimes it gets a little boring when you find yourself watching soap operas at four a.m.," Georgia said with a little smile.

"So, was it awesome?" Gail asked.

"What?"

"The ball?" she asked as she picked up the fresh drink left for her.

"Oh, it was *so* much work to get Mr. Lambley ready. As for everything else, Mr. Matsuoka took care of most of the details. It was frustratingly easy to find a hotel and a discreet limo service to take us to a manor tucked away in upstate New York. In fact, he had everything so planned out that I simply had to throw a wrench into the works . . ."

"This isn't me," Georgia whispered to the stranger in the mirror. This reflection stared back with familiar bright blue eyes, but they were ringed with smoky dark liner and swaths of iridescent eye shadow. All human imperfection had been brushed away with layers of powders and smears of expensive cream. What little hair she had was swept and frozen in time in a golden caramel arch to frame this new mask that took the place of her normal countenance. A choker of brilliant faux diamonds separated her head from the body tucked into the glorious, curve-hugging, black silk, while her feet snuggled into shiny black heels.

Behind her, a rather squirrely little fellow in a shiny purple shirt and pin-striped pants beamed from behind his thick tortoiseshell glasses. He set down his can of hairspray to start clapping. "I think I've outdone my-self this time!" he cheered. "Now that Beauty is done, I simply must finish the Beast. I think the mask should be just about set."

"Thanks," she choked out. She turned to see poor Mr. Lambley star-ing desperately from behind a half-inch layer of some sort of Peruvian skin mud, while his freshly detangled cropped ginger mop was tucked under one of the hotel's shower caps.

"This had better be worth a pint," the vampire snarled as the other beauty magician kept grinding down his nails with a veterinary buffer wheel. She wore even more makeup than Georgia, enough to mask the stubble and shade a rather prominent Adam's apple.

"Oh, Nikki, you are a wunderkind," Georgia's makeup artist cooed as he surveyed the beautifully buffed left hand. "And how is our Beast this fine evening?"

"Oh yeah, can I offer you an aperitif before you head out?" Nikki asked as she tilted her head to the side and bared her neck.

"Now don't be rude, darling. Our client is going through a rough patch, you know, up there," the aesthetician hissed. He then reached into his bag and pulled out a syringe and cup. "However, if you'd like us to draw a snifter for you, I can assure you that our dear Nicolette is an ex-ceptionally rare type AB negative that is well-seasoned, if you know what I mean."

Georgia stepped toward them. "Sorry, he's on a strict organic diet right now, but thanks for offering," she said.

"Oh, I know what you mean. There are definitely some artificial colors and flavors in here, if you know what I'm saying," Nikki said with a tit-tering little laugh. "Dear boss man, do you want a clear lacquer on these babies, or should I leave him au naturel?"

Her boss began picking at the edges of Mr. Lambley's mask. "I'm going to take him to rinse off and get him dressed. Get the dentures and adhesives ready. I'll decide on the hands once I get him more together."

"Sure thing, Gordo," she chirped as she got out of the way. "I'll just clean up."

Georgia walked in awe as the gangly six-foot-tall woman hopped deftly around in her stripper heels and skintight tube dress and packed up a vast array of toiletries, small appliances, and makeup containers in less than a minute. As the last of the supplies got tucked into her leopard-print case, she swept back one huge black wave out of her eyes and gave a wink to Georgia.

"Oh, it is so nice to be working for your boss, sweetheart. Usually I end up feeling like a toddler's juice box on a long car trip right about now, if you know what I mean," Nikki confessed. "Mr. Lambley is a real gentleman, a real old-world charmer. It's really a shame about the teeth, you know. How long since he shed them again?"

"I, um, don't know," Georgia said weakly, turning back to marvel at her alien reflection.

"Well, it sucks to have 'em pop out right before a ball, but I hear they usually come back in a week or so. Poor guy just got a zit before prom, but we can fix it," Nikki reassured the still-distracted Georgia. "Ugh, I am so low on adhesive. We might need to make an emergency drugstore dive. Oh, I could get us some gummy bears too!"

"All four fangs!" they could hear from the bathroom. "Oh, Mr. Lambley, that will simply be a half pint more . . ."

"You mean they get paid in blood?" Gail asked as Georgia showed her the next page of her contact book.

"Gordon Pembroke, and his lovely assistant Nicolette Tesla—at least that's her stage name. You know, I never have met him out of drag. Well, never mind that," Georgia said. "They are two of the few bondsmen Mr. Lambley will consent to work with."

"Bondsmen? Like bail bondsmen?" Gail asked.

"OK, in the vampire *servant* world, there is also this sort of hierarchy. At the top are the retainer families like the Matsuoka. They've served vampires for so long that they can practically get away with murder, well, as long as they murder humans. Under them are servants or assistants with contracts, that is, me or possibly you if tonight goes well. Still, there comes a point when vampires need a specialist—a doctor, a lawyer, or even a stylist, and since you can only have a contract with one vampire at a time really—"

"Really?" Gail asked.

Georgia raised a brow. "Most vamps don't like each other, and they certainly don't like to share. The issue is, how can you get someone to work for any vamp and still ensure that they obey all the rules while having enough business and connections with the outside world to be good at their jobs?"

Gail started gnawing on her lip. "You have some sort of leverage over them?" she asked.

Georgia broke into a huge smile. "Bingo! If you haven't guessed by now, or by watching most vampire fiction, vampire blood can have a controlling effect in the short term. It gets in your brain and leaves you with an infection until it is sucked back out by a vampire or your immune system kills it all off."

She paused as Gail turned a bit green again. "I'm still getting used to vampires being an infection," Gail said. "So they infect your brain and take control, like those fungi that control ants? And these bondsmen are like zombies?"

"Whoa, there are zombie ants?" Georgia asked. "I'm so gonna have to look that up after we are done, but no, it's nothing so dramatic as all that. Vampires are like any other infection, you start getting better and better at fighting them off after a while, but vampiric infection has a great side effect. Vamp blood is a bit of a bully in the infectious disease world. I mean, it is like the probiotic of all probiotics. If you take enough of it, it will slow down and even cure a lot of conditions. It can add years to your life and protect someone whose immune system is all but gone."

She trailed off and took a sip. "So, I guess ages and ages ago, some enterprising and desperate folk figured out that they could sell themselves out to vampires in exchange for a reprieve from a death sentence."

"So they drink vampire blood and are like supermen?" Gail asked.

"They drink a bunch of vampire blood and become addicted to it. If they run out of business, they die. They have their own code, but I try to stay out of it. They run their little groups and make deals with the families. The only condition is that they have to be truly dependent on the blood and they can only charge blood for their vampire clients. Oh, and of course, if they say anything, it's a pretty gruesome end from what I can tell."

"So they need vampire blood to survive."

"And they are pretty much the lowest men and women on the totem pole. Gordon and Nikki are far nicer than most."

"So why do they need the blood? Is it . . . you know . . .?"

"It's kinda rude to ask your hairdresser, 'Hey, how did you end up a vampire blood addict? Did you like get AIDS or something?' Don't you agree?"

"Yeah, I guess so," Gail said sheepishly. "So did they actually get you guys all ready for the ball? Is that why Mr. Lambley likes them so much?"

"Of course, but it wasn't so easy . . ."

"You both look so—so—" Gordon said as he surveyed Georgia and Geoffrey standing stiffly in the middle of their affordably priced chain hotel room. Georgia tugged at the deep neckline, while Mr. Lambley incessantly picked between his lips until a piece of off-white pointy plastic popped into his hands.

Nikki was the first to hop to her feet. "They look like Barbie and Ken gone to hell, Gordo," she said. "I've seen corpses with more life."

"Why all the doom and gloom, you two? You are the picture of formal perfection. You'd be the toast of any of the past five balls. You have A-1 couture on both of you!" Gordon paused. "Oh dear, that is totally the problem, isn't it?"

"You can put a cheeseburger on china, but that doesn't make it fine dining, sweetie," Nikki said, shaking her head. "Boss man, we've missed the mark."

Gordon began to pace, sizing his clients from slicked-down head to polished toe. He then strode confidently over to the vampire, lifted a few of the plastered locks of ginger, and sighed. Although the red mane had been tamed, its smooth look against his puffy, pasty face only exaggerated the image of a well-oiled swine in the moonlight. Next to him the well-painted starlet continued to frown and sweat, forming unattractive lines from eyelash to neck crease.

Gordon reached into his breast pocket and whipped out a comb. "We have, what, thirty minutes, Nikki?"

His assistant yanked out a spray bottle and some tissues. "We have an eternity. Say, Georgia-dear, I saw that you packed one other little number in your bags. What do you say we give it a try?"

"Won't the others be offended if we aren't traditional?" Mr. Lambley asked as he saw Gordon pull out an iridescent purple bow tie from one of his bags. "And Stefano did pay for our—"

Georgia, on the other hand, broke out in a huge grin. "Come on, Geoffrey. This is your family's party, right? Don't you think we should go as ourselves?" She reached over and took his hand. As she felt shockingly soft skin and nicely rounded nails, she muttered, "But I do need to find out Nikki's secret for that."

Mr. Lambley smiled weakly. "Well, I suppose if I'm going to be a laughingstock anyway, then I might as well be comfortable."

"Trust me, if you're comfortable, they won't be able to laugh at you," Georgia reassured him.

"Really?"

"Really. You can't mock someone if they are confident in who they are. Just trust me, OK?"

"But—" he stammered.

"Oh, she's right, Mr. Lambley. If you can't be yourself, you have to pay a hell of a lot more than you are willing to pay us to fit in," Nikki said as she rummaged through Georgia's bag. "Get some steam on, boss man, we have wrinkles to deal with."

Georgia squeezed her boss's hand again. "Come on, Geoffrey," she said. "You're a Pendragon, remember? This is your night."

"Half an hour till sunset, chop chop!" Gordon cried.

Geoffrey nodded. "I'm a Pendragon, and this is my bloody night!"

"Damn right," Georgia cheered him on, but before she could say another word, the force of nature that was Nicolette Tesla grabbed her by the hand and dragged her into the bathroom—already unzipping her current frock before the door could even be shut. Georgia looked into the mirror as her shoulders slipped fully into view, and while she couldn't see her date turning red from his vantage point on the bed, she could certainly hear his gasp.

Exactly twenty-nine minutes later, Nikki shoved a completely different woman into the back of the chartered limo. The last few traces of sunlight kept Mr. Lambley inside for a few minutes more. Georgia wiggled her toes, which were now tucked into a much more dancing-friendly pair of sandals, smiling at the bright blue polish her new companion had managed to get on and dry on twenty nails with little more than pinpoint accuracy and an industrial-strength hair dryer. The only item that had stayed put was the sparkling diamond choker because, as Nikki had said so eloquently, "Bling is definitely the thing."

"These are awesome fakes," Georgia mused as she tilted her head back to get a better look at her reflection in the wall of glass that separated her from the driver. She tousled her hair once more, enjoying just how delightfully, purposefully, messy Nikki had managed to make her pixie cut, and marveled at what a few dozen less layers of makeup did for her skin. She squiggled under her lacy, gauzy wrap that Nikki had improvised from one of her Cher costumes that she happened to have stashed in her trunk. Finally, as the last traces of the sun dipped below the horizon, the limo door opened once more, and a wild-haired, purple silk shirt-wearing, velvet jacket-clad creature of the night slipped into the seat next to her. He smiled, showing off his comforting gap-toothed grin.

"Oh my," he said as he surveyed her ever so closely.

"Is that a good oh my, or a dear god sort of oh my?" she replied.

"Why you look like—" His pale eyes darted off to the side as he chewed a bit on his lip. "Holly Berry! Yes, just like her."

"Did you just call me a Christmas decoration?"

Geoffrey's eyebrows furrowed as the limo started to move. Georgia rolled down the window to wave at the beaming pair of bondsmen who were grinning proudly and holding hands as they watched their creations leave.

"You know, the woman in the movies with the same hair," he said, still too lost in thought to wave as well.

"Oh, Halle Berry." Georgia sighed as she nudged him until he too gave a little wave to the people who had spent the greater part of an afternoon slaving away in a cramped motel room.

"Yes, Holly Berry, of course," he said quickly as they waved their final farewells. Gordon nodded as he raised his cooler full of payment in respect. "I certainly got a pint and a half's worth, it seems," the vampire said as the window rolled up.

He rubbed his wrist a few times until Georgia pulled his hand away. "Leave the bandage on for the trip," she snipped. "Remember, you don't heal instantly when you're a pint down." She then pulled a sippy cup out of her purse and handed it over.

"I don't like type A," he grumbled as he took a tiny taste. "And I think this person was Irish."

"Wow, racism in a cup," Georgia sighed. "Look, it was all Gary had this week, so you can have this, or you are going to be stuck with whatever party food your family has on tap tonight. Do you want to risk it?"

The vampire sank back in his seat, pouting as he took the first few sips. Eventually hunger took over, and he began contentedly sucking away as their limo eased out of the parking lot. Georgia took a moment to play with the seat warmer and individual AC controls until the minibar fridge caught her attention. Once she had thoroughly exhausted each and every button, gadget, and gizmo, she turned back to verify that her charge had indeed finished his much-needed breakfast.

"I don't know if I can do this, Georgia," he said before gnawing on his lip. "I've skipped so many recently. I don't want them to see me like this—"

She gently squeezed his hand. "At least you won't be confused for the catering," she comforted with a weak little laugh. "All we have to do is make it through one night, right?"

He nodded a little too quickly. "Yes, just one night. Oh, before I forget, there is one ever-so-important thing you must remember."

"Now might be a good time to tell me," she said as she noticed the time they had already spent in the car. Her phone listed the venue as only being twenty minutes from the motel in light traffic.

"Whatever you do, don't mention Mordred," Geoffrey warned earnestly.

"Mordred? Like, um, that guy from the story of King Arthur?" she asked.

The vampire nodded vehemently.

"Um, it's not exactly something that comes up in everyday conversation," she sighed. "Wait a second, am I missing something?"

"It's a Pendragon-hosted gala tonight. Since my parents are presenting and they are direct descendants of our founder, it would be in exceptionally bad taste to mention the name of the traitor that almost had our entire bloodline eliminated as kin killers."

"And what exactly does that have to do with King Arthur again?" She clicked her tongue a few times as she furrowed her brows. "Oh, hold the phone—"

The vampire responded by grabbing for his cell. "Do I need to call someone?" he asked in a hushed whisper.

"Pendragon?" Georgia repeated. "You mean that you literally have the name Pendragon, and it's not just some hey, rah, British legendary callback sort of name?"

"I don't quite follow your idiom," Geoffrey said. "One of my sires, Lorcan, was bitten by Arthur, son of Uther, founder of the Pendragon family."

"Arthur—King Arthur was your grandpa?" Georgia asked, once more bursting into giggles. "You're putting me on, aren't you?" She trailed off as she saw a frightfully serious look on her boss's face all of a sudden. "You're not kidding, are you?"

"Quite some time ago, long before I was born, our founder was murdered—stabbed in the back by one of the vilest traitors in vampire history. Mordred committed the ultimate sin and not only killed one of our kind, but his own father, at the Battle of Camlann. He was eventually slain by his younger blood brother Lorcan, but it's all very sordid business, and discussing it is an easy way to turn a night ugly. Even mentioning his name is considered a vulgarity among the Western families."

"I'm still a little hung up on King Arthur not only being real, but a vampire—"

"What, you thought it was water in the Grail?" Geoffrey scoffed. "Now who's being silly? Anyway, I forgot to warn you."

"Just how old is your father?"

"He celebrated his eighteenth back in the eighties. It was an amazing spectacle," Geoffrey said. "They actually found an entire choir . . . Why do you look so confused?"

"You said you're over two hundred years old, but your father is eighteen. I was never that good in math, but something doesn't add up."

"Well, it's rather like you do with your own young, isn't it? You count months until they are a year old, and then you switch into something more suited to the scale of your life span."

"Oh, he's eighteen centuries, isn't he?"

"Indeed!" Geoffrey said. "Mother turns fifteen in just a few years, but if you say anything about her age, she is liable to kill you with a glare . . ."

"King Arthur, really?" Gail asked incredulously.

Georgia raised her hands into a semblance of a scout's salute. "I swear," she said with a laugh before taking another drink. "Believe me, I thought it was crazy too, but after some of the other crazy shit I've seen, it kinda becomes normal after a while. I mean, the legendary King Arthur is totally different, but the founder of the Pendragon clan was named Arthur and had an offspring named Mordred who killed him, and it's the vampire legend that one day Arthur will return and lead them."

Gail burst out laughing and took another drink herself. "Was Lancelot at the party?" she asked.

"Oh no, as far as I've heard, and this is just rumors, mind you, he was a human and died centuries ago after totally having an affair with Arthur's also human sweetie, and that might have something to do with our whole legend."

"So, you're killing me with suspense! What happened at the ball?" Gail asked again.

Georgia kicked up her feet and took a deep satisfying breath. "Well, I got to meet Mr. Lambley's friends and family at last, and believe me, nothing can quite prepare you for that . . ."

9

The limo rolled through a set of gates straight out of a Hollywood horror movie, complete with pointy finials and marble statues lining the pebble drive. The eerie atmosphere faded slightly when Georgia could see cheerful beds of mounded flowers and a gazebo of twinkling lights as they rounded the bend. Indeed, the Georgian mansion hiding behind a wall of trees, with its bright white columns and dainty hedgerows, seemed more like an escapee from *Pride and Prejudice* rather than the *Amityville Horror.*

Their car joined a procession of idling black vehicles as a rather gaunt older man in a tuxedo and spectacles continued to motion all the other servants to hold as he kept moving some sort of device all around the front lawn.

"What on earth is he doing?" Georgia asked as they rolled to a halt.

"In the old days, they would just walk out an animal to make certain that the sun was fully set, but now the head man has one of those fancy little devices that can tell if it's safe to be outside," Geoffrey said. "Oh, and the dogs are out too."

Georgia peered over her boss to see a trio of all-white German shepherds sniffing around each vehicle in front of the house. One began to bark furiously at a silver Rolls Royce until the driver was forced to open the trunk and let out a woman that was still dribbling red from her neck.

"Seriously, will they ever learn?" Geoffrey scoffed. "This is a strictly catered affair."

A pair of young men in plain black suits came to escort the rather pale young lady toward a smaller house on the edge of the property. The sign, marked "Deliveries and Catering," made Georgia shudder. Her unease continued as a very large canine slammed against her window and began yowling.

As she squealed and hopped away, she found herself actually sitting on her master's lap, which made for quite the image as his window rolled down and one of the servants began peering intently at the flushed girl sliding back onto her own seat.

"This is a catered event," the man at the window said flatly.

"Oh, she's my servant and my date," Mr. Lambley said with glee. "She's under my protection. Georgia dear, let them sniff you."

"Excuse me?"

"Just let them sniff you. That way they will know that I haven't been feeding off you," he said.

She gingerly stuck her hand out the window. The white fluffball sniffed her a few times and sat down, satisfied that Miss Sutherland was not on the menu tonight. She also lifted the key that had been tucked into the bodice of her dress. "See, I serve Mr. Lambley," she said. "He gave me the key to his place and everything."

The tuxedoed guard looked back to the man in pince-nez frames, and after a quick dismissive nod, the dog was led away and their limo was waved toward the grand red carpet procession. Georgia strained to catch a glimpse of the few groups who were being escorted toward the door now that it was deemed safe to let the creatures of the night into the open air.

Despite the warm June evening, most of the procession chose to wear long coats, often with fur trim, and very large hats to obscure most of their faces. Only an occasional flash of skin could be seen—all of it dreadfully pale.

"I guess you don't have to worry about the heat," she noted as they rolled one place closer.

"We aren't very sensitive to temperature at all. I'm always ever so afraid that I've got it wrong," he fussed. Georgia kept an eye on just how tightly he was squeezing his knuckles with each inch they crept forward.

"You'll be OK," she said, doing her best to sound convincing for both of them, but even she had to gulp as the door opened and she took in the bright lights and stark carpet that cut from the drive toward the very large and stately manor that housed the majority of the vampire population of the United States that night.

"Just breathe, Georgia," she told herself. Somehow gravity had managed to change in the small bubble of space surrounding their limo, rendering once-normal limbs into lead weights. She choked in a taste of the air within the singularity and immediately wrinkled her nose at the mix of diesel and freshly watered mulch. However, her own stone-cold panic paled in comparison to the fugue state that had overtaken her undead companion. He stopped breathing as he took in the scene.

"You have to move, Geoffrey," she hissed. "Move!"

She could feel the crushing weight of every stare as they remained frozen against the leather seats. "Move," she growled again while shoving her leg against her boss's.

"Welcome to Sunny Acres," a strained yet still polite voice said as a hand was extended to help the frozen guest of honor . . .

"Sunny Acres?" Gail asked incredulously.

"Vampires are experts at two things—blood and irony," Georgia quipped. She peered down at her phone once more and smiled apologetically. "So sorry, I have to take this."

Gail leaned back and took the time to check the messages on her own phone, but was rewarded only with a boring system update notice and an obnoxious lack of reception bars. "I wonder what carrier she is using," the brunette muttered as she watched Georgia chatting away by the back door. Her ears perked up a bit as she heard something along the lines of, "I think she just might be the one." As soon as her interviewer noticed the interviewee's gaze, she turned around and put her hand up to block her lips.

Gail smiled a little more as the hot waiter swept by and put down another tray of chips and a big glass of water. "On the house," he said sweetly, with teeth so white it seemed like there had to be a black light in the room. "Can I get you anything else?" he asked.

"Your phone number," Gail joked weakly.

"Well, if you're still around at closing time, we'll talk," he said with a little wink. Gail lost herself in watching the hot young guy saunter back toward the kitchen door. Her face fell a little as he leaned over to check out the sizzling blonde vampire who had drifted back in to take a seat on a stool.

"He is easy on the eyes, right?" Georgia said as she plopped back down, somehow now in a scoop-back red tank top and plaid schoolgirl skirt.

"Did you—?" Gail started. She shook her head. "Never mind. Did you ever get to the ball?"

"After what seemed like an eternity, I finally shoved Mr. Lambley out onto the carpet. He stumbled, but I managed to pass it off as us both being drunk from the ride. I think he might even forgive me for that someday . . ."

Mr. Lambley pushed up from the carpet and gulped as he found himself staring at a very long, very bare leg extending from a slit in a tailored black evening gown. Next to him Georgia giggled and jerked him to his feet. "Don't mind us," she said quickly with a little hiccup as she rushed him along, focusing only on the door and the pair of tuxedo-clad ushers waiting to open the door for them. "Just keep moving," she hissed in his ear between fake tipsy giggles.

Somehow one hurried step became two and two became a dozen as they stumbled past a few more-dignified entrants to make it at last to the entrance. Georgia yanked the invitation out of her boss's pocket and handed it to a white-gloved hand.

"Lord Geoffrey Lambley of the Pendragon family," an extremely British voice read aloud. "And . . .?"

"Miss Georgia Sutherland," Mr. Lambley managed to choke out as he straightened his lapel and flipped the ginger mess from his eyes.

"No family?" the gentleman asked. He then took in the decidedly rosy blush on Georgia's cheeks and the heat radiating from her decidedly living, breathing chest. "Oh, oh my," he said, clicking his tongue.

"My family couldn't make it tonight," she said with an imperturbable smile. "You'll have to just deal with me."

"Human and American," the doorman said with a little sneer.

"Is there going to be a problem?" Georgia asked as she finished straightening her boss's tie. "I'm pretty sure the Pendragon family is hosting this little shindig."

"Human and extremely American," he sighed before waving the pair through the door.

"The whole evening is going to be like this, isn't it?" Georgia whispered as they were ushered toward a small army of obsequious penguin men who whisked away Mr. Lambley's overcoat and Georgia's shawl in record time and shepherded them past a heady array of flowers and glittering metallic balloons and then dropped them smack-dab into the middle of a gloriously retro marble and gilded ballroom.

"This looks just like a bar mitzvah I went to," Georgia said, wide-eyed.

A huge banner hung from between the columns with the words "*Felicem Natalem Meenakshi*" written in bold script. Georgia's eyes widened farther as she saw a rainbow of silk streamers and piles of cheap metallic confetti strewn over the plastic tablecloths. This dazzling array of party-store chic contrasted with the designer gowns and thousand-dollar shoes covering the pallid party guests. Georgia tried to contain her gawking as a pair tittered over plastic champagne flutes filled with a rusty red liquid.

"Um, are we in the right place?" Georgia leaned in to whisper.

"It seems that they have decorated the venue in Mother's style," Geoffrey said as a three-tiered fondue fountain was wheeled to the center of the refreshment tables.

"That's not chocolate," Georgia moaned as she took in a slightly beefy odor in the air.

"Warm marrow-fat fondue!" an onlooker gushed with glee.

"I'm so glad I didn't eat before we came," Georgia muttered as the punch bowl rolled by. "The chianti is coagulating."

Still, she put on her best brave face as she stood among all the pale countenances in dark-colored dresses and starched classic tuxedos. Mr. Lambley took a step back to marvel how his escort's light aqua and rhinestone number perfectly matched the glittering décor.

"I've never seen quite such a gown," he said appreciatively at how the bleached blue matched her pale eyes. "I don't care what they say. I'm the luckiest man here."

Georgia smiled her first genuine smile of the night and gave her partner a little curtsy. He extended a hand and led her away from the catered supper, well aware that his date was being sniffed out as a possible canapé.

"This is insane," she whispered as they slipped past yet another generic pair of slicked-back dark hair in a tuxedo and mysterious brunette in a little black dress. "It's like being stuck in a pile of photocopies," she muttered as she counted how many dresses looked almost the same.

"I cannot hardly tell them apart either," Mr. Lambley said as he kept scanning the crowd. "I must say the commoners do tend to blur together."

"The commoners?" Georgia said in an exaggerated imitation of his poncy British accent. "Oh dear, there goes the neighborhood. Next thing you know, they'll let a human in here."

Mr. Lambley burst into a little giggle. They continued to titter and mock the crowd of anemic faces that pointedly tried to ignore them until finally a very different face in the crowd made Georgia's boss turn even more deathly pale than usual.

"Geoff—?" Georgia started, but she too trailed off as a radically different pair caused the entire crowd to part.

The taller of the two new arrivals wore a shockingly bright red dress to match her brilliant, mirrorlike lipstick. She stared witheringly from under a fringe of golden blonde hair and tapped a mighty red stiletto as she took in the human who dared to stand before her. She muttered something foreign and guttural to the tiny woman beside her—a dazzling redhead wearing little more than what looked like dental floss connecting the leather scraps that covered her petite ice-white assets.

The redhead wore no makeup to conceal her mask of freckles, choosing to flaunt the stark contrast between the spots and her smooth, pale flesh. Instead of wearing diamonds, she adorned her neck with a string of gold-studded teeth, and the bangles on her wrists looked decidedly like carved bone.

Mr. Lambley gulped as the smaller one approached and took a deep whiff of the aroma of his human companion. "I see," she said in a thick German accent. "The best you could do?"

"Good evening, Madam Jaeger," Geoffrey said, giving a stuttered little bow. "It is so *nice* to see you back in the Colonies for a spell."

She snorted a little. "We all have sacrifices to make, *Herr* Pendragon." She then waved dismissively at the blonde in red. "You know my offspring, yes? Minerva will be staying in Manhattan for a while to take care of business. You had best be aware of her claims. Who is this cattle with you, Pendragon? It's slumming even by your standards."

"I'm right here," Georgia snapped before any sort of rational thought stopped her tongue.

Madam Jaeger simply rolled her eyes. "I know this."

Geoffrey gulped and took a slight step forward. "Lady Claudia Schwartz von Jaeger, please meet my assistant, Miss Georgia Sutherland. Georgia, this is Madam Jaeger, consort to the esteemed Brynjulf Jagäre and mistress of all his affairs in the outer territories, and this is her lovely daughter, Minerva."

"Minerva Fenstermacher von Jaeger," the blonde added.

"Hi, I'm Georgia," she replied before combining wave and a bow into a single awkward motion. The vampire women rolled their eyes as they turned away to converse in German without so much as an acknowledgment to the human flushing brighter and brighter by the moment. As she began to choke out a guttural "h" sound to summon them back, Georgia became painfully aware of another set of eyes boring into her skull. Someone moved quickly as she whipped her head toward the source, and all she was left with was an unsettled feeling and a tipped-over glass at one of the tables near the little stage in the back.

Before she could catch her breath, a wave of dizziness came over her. She stumbled toward her boss and ended up falling in his arms just as the greeter at the door requested all parties to be silent.

"I cannot believe this," Mr. Lambley gasped as quiet descended upon the room. Even the haughty Germans hushed instantly and bowed their heads in deference. Georgia straightened herself up and peered over Geoffrey's shoulder as a bona fide amazon strutted through the door. Georgia grabbed her head again as the beast of a woman took another step inside. The stranger merely waved her hand, and a path cleared instantly. Only the dizzy human remained frozen for a second too long, giving Georgia a perfect view of all seven feet of golden-haired muscle somehow shoved into a gold mesh cocktail dress. The stranger cocked her head and gave a withering glance through her false eyelashes and multiple layers of eyeliner, causing Georgia to shuffle backward. The stranger raised a bleached brow, showing off more of her staggeringly bright eye makeup, straight out of an eighties' Kabuki carnival act. Now every other pair of eyes in the room was firmly trained on Georgia until the greeter at the door finally broke the spell by announcing, "Lady Asrun von Jaeger would like to call you all to attention!"

The giant nodded and swept her arm ever so gracefully to her left. "The Jaeger comes," she said simply, but the news tore through the room as if she had announced the second coming of Christ. The contents of the room immediately dropped—either literally to the floor or into a deep bow or curtsy. Once more Georgia's human reflex speed failed her. Before she could bend her knees, the giant was somehow right next to her. Asrun shook her head and flipped a finger upward.

"You, human, stay," she whispered.

Georgia gulped as she looked at everyone groveling except for her and the colossus in gold. The sudden close proximity to the giantess revealed that at least part of the amazon's height came from platform heels. Georgia shifted uncomfortably as the black hole had moved from the red carpet to the ballroom and time dragged painfully close to a halt. Next to her, Asrun looked down and surveyed every inch of Georgia, paying especially close attention to the pair of necklaces resting against her wobbling throat.

Georgia became aware of just how loud her breathing was compared to the utter silence in the room. Each breath echoed against the cold un-feeling stone at her feet and seemed to make her teeter-totter more and more as her head continued to pound. Meanwhile Asrun continued to stare ruthlessly until Georgia shifted her feet and crossed her arms over her chest. That simple movement caused an audible gasp throughout the entire room.

Asrun finally took a step back, giving Georgia a few blessed inches of personal space. However, her moment of relief faded quickly as the doors to the ballroom opened once more. Georgia grabbed both her temples and winced uncontrollably as a new figure stepped into view. As she focused on the gentleman easing his way toward her, it took a few blinks to make out his long pale face, even though he was only across the room. He had a stereotypically European set of features poking out under skin that must have been quite tan in centuries past. He too wore a slick coif of jet-black hair, but it was close-cropped and expertly manicured along the sides to show off absolutely perfect shades of silver to complete a dapper old-style Hollywood look. He wore a deep red silk shirt under a leather jacket and showed off a similar toothed necklace to the one the redhead sported for the evening. A single scar nearly bifurcated his otherwise flawless face, drawing a graceful line through his icy blue eyes.

He seemed to float his way to the middle of the room, where his giantess towered over everyone—including the still-standing Georgia. He cocked his head in the same amused fashion as he looked over the girl in aqua. At this distance, Georgia noticed that his pants and shoes were the same unusual leather, but the arms seemed to have a pattern etched into the ebony sleeves. The Jaeger began to pace around the object of his curiosity until he finally noticed the ginger cowering next to her.

"*Intressant*," the Jaeger said in a low voice. He then leaned up to his taller consort and hissed something in her ear so soft a dog might have trouble making it out. Asrun nodded and waved to the room.

"I think we've had quite enough theater, good friends from the north," a new and lilting voice said, breaking the spell. Everyone looked up to see a vampire gesturing warmly from the stage, showing off to all just how beautiful a dark-haired woman could be in a shimmering silver dress. "Everyone please welcome Lade Asrun von Jaeger and our most esteemed of all guests tonight, Brynjulf Jagäre, the Jaeger," she said with a grand flourish. "It is such a grand compliment to have you attend this night, where we all celebrate the end of waxing days and give thanks to many long nights to come."

The Jaeger nodded toward her, his apparent version of a bow. "Lady Pendragon, the honor is mine," he said, his voice simultaneously gentle and commanding. "Since your founder could not be here to celebrate with you on this, the sesqui-millennial anniversary of your death, I thought it fitting that the Jaeger clan join you in these wildlands. Please, all, let the festivities begin."

With those words everyone returned to their feet, and the din of excited conversation filled the room. Geoffrey, however, remained shaking near the floor until Georgia finally yanked him to his feet. "What is going on?" she hissed.

Before he could answer, the woman from the stage popped in front of Georgia, creating an instant social barrier between the misfits and the two terrifying Jaegers. Georgia had to marvel at the stranger's waterfall of supremely shiny dark hair, which drifted in luxurious waves all the way down to her waist. Her skin, like the Jaeger's, seemed closer to human tone—a rich ivory as opposed to ghastly white. She smiled sweetly through wine-colored lips and batted the lashes around her dark brown eyes with the grace of a master coquette.

"Why didn't you tell me that you were coming, Brynjulf?" she asked.

He looked over her shoulder, right at Georgia. "I did not want to cause you to make a fuss over me. Still, I did not think you brought live food to your parties, Lady Pendragon. Is it for your deathday?"

"Excuse me—" Georgia started. The very fact that she spoke made the blonde giant do her terrifying eyebrow motion again. The previously unflappable Jaeger even twitched slightly.

Lady Pendragon, however, didn't miss a beat. She smiled broadly once more. "Oh no, you and I still agree to disagree on the role of humans in our society, Brynjulf," she said sweetly. "The lovely young lady is here with my son, and as you can see, my son has an excellent eye for the unique. Wouldn't you both agree? Now, I see your other consort just over there, old friend. I would hate for her to not get a chance to greet you after all this time."

The Jaeger merely nodded. "Oh, and where is your mate, lovely Lady Pendragon?" he asked. "You have not been fighting again, have you?"

Georgia put her hand over her mouth as a wave of nausea came over her. She closed her eyes for a millisecond, and as she opened them, a new vampire stood next to the Lady Pendragon, but unlike the relentlessly genial lady beside him, this extremely pale-faced stranger made no effort to hide the contempt on his face.

"That's none of your business, Jaeger. Now, why don't you go and have a grand old time threatening the rabble?" the stranger snapped.

Asrun immediately glowered and took a threatening step toward the relatively small and scrappy man in a pin-striped suit, however, the Jaeger held her back with a gentle wave of his hand. "It is good to see you again, Lord Pendragon. Come, my love, Claudia is here."

With that Georgia and Geoffrey were left with two of the most beautiful creatures ever dropped into a dinner party. While Lady Pendragon could easily be labeled as classically beautiful, with her smooth skin, delicate bone structure, and graceful feminine curves, Lord Pendragon had a more quirky, unusual set of features, which still made many sets of eyes cast come-hither looks his way. The only thing that marred his fantastically pale face, razor-sharp cheekbones, and crystalline emerald-colored eyes was an expression firmly planted on his face that made him look like all he could smell was a flattened skunk while he was simultaneously watching his girlfriend make out with another man. He flipped a wayward wave of rich brown hair behind his ear, revealing a strange earring of what looked like an old cross made out of bone, but before Georgia could examine it further, Lord Poo-Face turned his glare toward her and Geoffrey.

"Is this some pathetic stab at attention, boy?" he growled.

"I didn't—I couldn't—" Geoffrey stammered.

"Hey, he didn't know the Jaeger of all Jaegers would be here," Georgia said, quickly moving in front of him. Lady Pendragon's eyes actually lit up as she saw apocalyptic levels of ire brewing along her companion's jaw.

"You," Lord Pendragon grumbled as he eyed her again. "You can't be here."

"I came as Mr. Lambley's plus one, and there is nothing to say you can't have a human as a guest. I had an expert look it up."

Lord Pendragon narrowed his eyes and stared at her again. Something deep within that stare kept a tally of Georgia's distinctive light eyes, perky pointed nose and chin, and the little way she seemed to pout as she faced off with a centuries-old bloodsucker. "*You* . . . you can't be here," he said again.

Lady Pendragon wrapped an arm around his waist and eased him back. "Now, sweet Lorcan, this young lady is here with our son. We should introduce ourselves properly," she cooed.

Lorcan snorted and waved dismissively. "I have things to attend to. We will talk later, boy," he snarled at Geoffrey before storming off and leaving Lady Pendragon with an arm free to wrap around each of them without warning.

"It is so lovely to see you, Geoffrey!" she said as she drew them both in. "It's been decades."

Geoffrey nodded and politely tried to break away. "Decorum, Mother," he said sheepishly at her public display of affection. She rolled her eyes and turned her full attention to the utterly confused girl in aqua.

"And who is this lovely creature you've decided to bring to our little party?" she asked.

"Mother, this is Miss Georgia Sutherland. Georgia, I'm pleased to introduce you to Lady Meenakshi Thakkar Pendragon, my mother."

"Oh, pishposh! Call me Mina, child," Lady Pendragon said as she swooped in and gave Georgia a hug. Although the intentions seemed warm, Georgia shivered at the embrace of the room-temperature woman. She winked as she stepped back. "Geoffrey hates how I've embraced twentieth-century manners in my old age, but I simply can't abide being all stodgy."

Georgia began to compare the beautiful, slightly exotic features of Mina to the puffy awkward ones of Geoffrey. Other than the distinctly British tones in their voices, nothing seemed similar between Mr. Lambley and his mother.

Mina broke out laughing. "Oh, our kind isn't like yours. Each shell is different, and my dear son and I wouldn't have anything in common on the outside," she said.

"Can you read minds?" Georgia gasped.

Mina leaned in and whispered, "Just faces, love." She then popped back and stretched her arms longingly toward her son. "Now please come with me, sweetie, and let's go sit and chat. I simply must hear all about you both . . ."

"So you can only imagine what it's like to have family members catch up after decades of being apart, right, sweetie?" Georgia asked as Gail gawked across the sofa.

"Was she the first vampire to be nice to you? Everyone you've described so far—" Gail started.

"Was an asshole?" Georgia laughed. "I didn't even tell you about the foodies! Oh my god, if you ever want to feel like a hunk of meat, then try mingling with a group of undead who start describing your bouquet and the quality of your flavor."

Gail blanched. "You mean?"

"Lady Pendragon and Mr. Lambley spent the majority of the night talking, so I wandered a bit and quickly figured out exactly why Mr. Matsuoka thought it was such a terrible idea for humans to be at vampire functions. Apparently my diet and lifestyle make me smell rather like kale according to one of the foodies." She stopped to take a sip and watch her companion's quivering lip. "Oh, the best part was a certain bloodsucker from Virginia that worked as a phlebotomist for a bariatric clinic. She used her job to create a tasting bar for those who prefer richer blood."

"You mean there are certain vampires who like blood with more fat and cholesterol?" Gail asked incredulously.

"Oh, some only drink from the elderly, some only from certain ethnicities, and many love America because our blood on average is like *foie gras*—rich and fatty and not too heavy on the vegetable flavors. To them we are just different breeds of livestock, if you think about it."

"I'm just imagining a vampire infiltrating the medical profession," Gail said with a furrowed brow.

"You mean a twenty-four-hour profession where you can work nights and have access to blood?" Georgia said, laughing again. "Yeah, that doesn't sound like anything a vampire would like. In all seriousness, most of the families have connections to hospitals and blood banks. It's simply the easiest way to feed in an industrialized nation."

"I just can't imagine. Then again, before tonight I couldn't imagine a vampire ever being anything more than a story," Gail said in wonder. "I mean, I've seen some pale night owls around the hospital at night, but I'd never think—"

"Well, that's the thing, you wouldn't ever think about them, or even notice them if they didn't want to be seen. Vampires secrete so many pheromones that it clouds your mind. Most people just look away and think nothing of them. I, on the other hand, seem to have a rare genetic trait that makes me react differently."

"You mean that you can see them, right?" Gail asked.

"See? No. To me, vampires kind of stink. If I'm around too many of them, I can get a headache and nausea. In fact, after a few minutes of talking to Mr. Lambley and his mother, I started feeling so bad that I had to excuse myself to the gardens for a little fresh air . . ."

Georgia grabbed onto the railing along the deck and seriously contemplated if the wall of azaleas could conceal vomit as she tried to make the world stop spinning. One of the penguins patrolling the perimeter eyed her menacingly as she shuddered against the shrubbery.

"Evening," she said weakly.

"Try this," a comforting monotone voice said as a plastic flute full of tan bubbly liquid was shoved in front of her slightly green countenance. She turned to see a familiar face among the starched white shirts and sleek black suits she had seen on all the servants at the gala.

"Ren?" she said softly as she sipped on the miraculous ginger ale. "Where have you been all night?"

He pointed toward the sign marked catering before handing her a little ziplock baggie full of saltine crackers. "I had to arrange for my master's dinner and then tend to the Jaeger delegation's affairs. It's a special night if the Jaeger decides to make an appearance."

"The Jaeger? What, does he have brothers named 'And' and 'Or'?" Georgia snorted as she started to return to a normal color.

"Lord Brynjulf Jagäre is the original hunter, Georgia. He founded the clan and was given the right to pass on his name."

"You mean that he—he's—oh," she said as the realization slowly dawned on her. "So, how many centuries old is he?" she dared to ask.

Ren looked over her shoulder and then checked behind him before daring to speak. "He was considered old at the sacking of Rome, if that says anything. No one knows for certain, but he is feared even by the Caesars to the point where he is granted dispensations not allowed to other clan founders."

Georgia munched on a cracker before daring to speak. "You act like I should know what that means," she said, rolling her eyes.

Ren's face remained calm, but he did pause to take a deep breath before replying, "The Jaeger is the one granted the right to mete justice by the Caesar and the sheriffs. If a vampire or servant breaks the four laws to the point where the transgressions are considered unforgivable . . ."

Georgia gulped. "No wonder everyone is so afraid of him. He's the executioner, isn't he?"

"He rarely comes to these sorts of public events, so everyone is on edge."

"So why tonight? Mr. Lambley's mom seemed unfazed by him. Do they have history or something?" Georgia asked. "By the way, thanks. I think the urge to hurl has passed."

Ren nodded and dutifully took back the now-empty glass. Georgia shivered slightly as his fingers lingered just a bit longer than expected. "You're cold," she said as she pulled away.

Ren whisked her garbage away to a serving tray without another word. She watched him rub his hands a few times before returning. "I apologize. I've been handling cold packs for a while now. No one else here would notice."

"You mean not everyone is bringing in live food?" Georgia snorted as she once more eyed the catering sign.

"How are you doing now? Should I get you another drink?"

"You're totally changing the subject again, Ren. What are you not telling me?"

"I don't want you passing out here," he said without skipping a beat. "There isn't much, but some of the other servants have a little picnic in the back for when we aren't required. I can bring you something if you like."

"I think somehow that all the vampires are making me woozy, especially 'The' and his womenfolk. I thought I was seriously going to puke on those hideous gold wedges that Xena Warrior Vampire was wearing."

"Did you just call Lady Asrun . . . Xena?" Ren asked, barely containing a grin.

"She's an amazon, isn't she?"

Ren shook his head and handed her a napkin without her even having to ask. "If you need any lipstick, there is a powder room just inside the south door. And to answer your question, Lady Asrun is from much farther north than the amazons. Both Lord and Lady Jaeger are from what is modern-day Sweden."

"But the name is German," Georgia said. "Oh, don't look so surprised. I have a smartphone and more than a little bit of curiosity."

"Lady Claudia is German," Ren said.

"Oh, yeah, that's his other woman, right—the one who scares you and tells you what to do?"

Once more Ren looked all around. He leaned in and hissed, "Be careful what you say. Their hearing is far better than ours."

"As with our speed, sight, and strength," a new voice said from be-hind. "So tell me, Ren, is this the distraction that has been keeping you from refilling my glass?"

Georgia watched as Ren moved faster than she had ever seen before—darting back toward the bar and returning with a carafe full of viscous red fluid. She turned to see a vaguely familiar figure in a well-tailored black suit with a similar bloodred shirt to the Jaeger but without the instant nausea aura surrounding him. The stranger smiled warmly to show off brilliant white teeth so straight and clean that they simply had to be the product of modern dentistry.

He didn't even look at Ren—merely waved his arm dismissively to reveal an empty brandy snifter. Instead, his dark eyes starred unabashedly at the low swooping neckline on Georgia's gown, but instead of taking note of the cleavage, they studied the long pulsing artery running along the side of her bare throat. Ren dutifully filled the glass, his head lowered. The stranger took a sip and waved him away without so much as a thank you. Instead, he gave a little bow and twirled his free hand toward Georgia with a gentle flourish. "Stefano DeMarco, at your service," he said.

"Oh, so you're the master Ren keeps talking about," Georgia said as she smoothed her dress. "You're a Jaeger, right?"

"I have the honor of being a direct descendant of the Jaeger, yes," he said, still sporting his dayglow smile. "And you now serve my dear friend Geoffrey, right?"

"Yeah, he's my boss." She stuck out her hand. "I'm Georgia, Georgia Sutherland."

He took her hand and kissed it rather than giving it a hearty shake. "What a lovely name, Georgia."

"That's, um, quite an accent," she said, cocking her head. "I've never heard anything quite like it."

"It's from the old country," he said quickly. "I've traveled to many countries in my time as well."

Georgia giggled. "I'm getting a bit Chef Boyardee meets Dracula. It's unique."

Stefano blinked a few times. "Never heard that before."

"I'm sorry. When I don't feel well, I tend to lose the filter between my brain and my mouth. Don't mind me," she said quickly.

The two stood in awkward silence for a while watching the various lights twinkling in the gardens. Georgia looked over to see Ren doing his best statue impression.

"I am surprised to see you again," Stefano started.

Georgia furrowed her brow. "Again? Did I meet you before somewhere?"

"Only in passing," he said with an accent that softened slightly.

"Oh yeah," she said, her eyes lighting up. "You helped Mr. Lambley pick up desperate women off the Internet. I vaguely remember meeting you in the hall, right?"

"So, you are saying you're a desperate woman then?" he fired right back.

"No, that would be my roommate, and she's not really desperate, just adventurous. I was caught in the crossfire and ended up with the job. All's well that ends well, I suppose."

"And now you are here with old Geoffrey as his date? You must serve him well."

She rolled her eyes. "It's not like that. It's my job to make sure he gets better, that's all. You're friends with Mr. Lambley, right? Why don't you ask him why he needed an assistant so badly?"

"Geoffrey isn't one to ask for help anymore. You have to force it upon him," Stefano said with a sad shake of his head. "I suppose that it is for the best that he has you now."

She motioned to the statue to his left. "Well, I wouldn't be any use at all if it wasn't for Ren. He's been a lifesaver," she said.

"He's a Matsuoka. It's his duty to serve. I would expect nothing less. Ren, I hope you haven't been boring this beautiful young lady to death with all your facts and figures." He leaned over to Georgia a little too closely. "I tune him out most of the time. He sounds like a robot, does he not?"

Georgia finally burst into a fit of giggles. "I'll give you that," she said. "Not to mention the normal state of being a rude know-it-all."

It was Stefano's turn to laugh. "Oh, good! For a moment I thought something had happened to my faithful servant."

Ren remained impassive, watching the level in his master's glass like a hawk. Stefano sipped a few more times before motioning again. "Get me something a little more refined, now, and do get something for the lady as well," he said.

"Very well, master," Ren said with yet another infuriatingly polite bow.

"So, you're an Italian vampire in a German family with a Japanese assistant?" Georgia said as she watched Ren retreat. "That's like the winning card in Axis powers bingo."

Stefano cocked his head in the same infuriating manner as his ancient relatives. "I never quite thought of it that way," he said, suddenly lost in thought. "You think I'm the enemy then?"

"I don't know about for you, but for me, World War II was more my grandparents' thing. Were you, you know, around for it?"

He waved his hand dismissively again. "The years all blur together. I remember it, but I try not to get in human politics. It's like worrying about the weather—if you don't like it, just wait a little while and it will blow over. Do you study history, then?"

Georgia shook her head. "I've never been too into it actually, but I suppose working with, well, you guys has given me a new interest in the past."

"Oh, is there anything you want to know?"

"I don't know. I never thought I'd get a chance to ask someone for a firsthand account of ancient Rome or what Abraham Lincoln sounded like. I don't even know where to begin. Is it rude to ask a vampire their age?"

Stefano burst into a hearty laughter. Despite his genteel Eurotrash exterior, he managed to let out a ruckus of guffaws that was rather like the sound of a donkey and a hyena mating violently. He finally shook his head. "I wouldn't worry too much about it, but I wouldn't expect half of them to even remember how long they've existed. The years blur after a while. Some of them wallow in the past when you could get away with munching on a few peasants without a care in the world, while others are obsessed with the latest and greatest fashion and fad. It really depends on the vampire, I suppose."

"So do you still count your age in years or have you moved onto centuries?" Georgia asked.

Stefano smiled. "I like the way you think, Miss Georgia Sutherland. I try not to worry too much about my age. Let's just say I've seen a fair amount of Europe merge together, then break apart again."

"Well, that's vague," she snorted. She was distracted by the sight of a tall brunette in a silver dress standing in the window and getting her hand kissed ever so slowly by a tall, dark, and mysterious man in a delightfully anachronistic red military coat.

"Oh, the Tepes are here. Lady Pendragon must be making the rounds."

"I don't see Geoffrey with her. I better go find him—"

"He's probably with Lorcan now, and I wouldn't interrupt that conversation if I were you," Stefano warned.

Mina Pendragon continued to flirt and smile with the exotic stranger. Georgia quickly looked away as the vampire lady moved even closer.

"Old Vlad and Mina have a fair bit of history," Stefano said. "I think the affair has lasted a good four hundred years now."

"So I'm guessing vampires aren't into the whole monogamy thing. I mean, she's with Lord Pendragon, right?"

Stefano laughed again. "Oh, the American puritanical tradition lives on," he dismissed.

"It's not like that. I just don't know how it all works. I mean the Jaeger has two women, right? Does it work both ways, or is it like humans, where if a man has two women he's a player, but if a woman dates two guys then she's a slut?"

Ren interrupted briefly to hand a new glass to both Stefano and Georgia. She briefly inspected the red liquid in the glass and took a quick sniff before daring to take a sip of something that tasted very expensive and alcoholic.

"Ren, can you ask if Geoffrey is indeed meeting with his sire? I wouldn't want his date to worry."

"Very good, sir," Ren said with another bow.

"You look a bit surprised. I take it that your relationship with Geoffrey is more *modern?*" Stefano asked.

Georgia resisted the bait and instead snuck another peek at the window, but both Lady Pendragon and Vlad had disappeared. "You didn't answer my question," she said.

"Come, let's have a stroll in the gardens and talk, and don't worry, I won't bite . . . unless you ask me to."

"That must be such a classic vampire pickup line," she said, shaking her head. Still she started following him as they meandered through the hedges and fairy lights.

"You really aren't fazed by us at all, are you, Miss Sutherland?" Stefano asked. She shook her head again and took a sip of the wine. "Well, I suppose there have to be some humans like you just to keep it interesting. In answer to your question, there is no difference to us whether the shell looks male or female, and we don't have the same conceit that only one soul is meant for another. Existence is too long to be tied down by that, don't you think?"

"I wouldn't know. I've only got sixty or seventy odd years more to ponder that idea," she snorted. "So the whole mate thing is temporary for all of you?"

Stefano shrugged. "There are those that choose to have long-term relationships, to be sure. We are all part of families, same as you, but our families come from ideals as much as blood. Meenakshi Pendragon is what you'd call a free spirit. She might have been made to be the mate of Lorcan, but come on, no one could endure that much brooding for more than a century. Quite frankly, the council was shocked that they even produced one successful offspring, let alone two."

"Two?" Georgia said, suddenly interested.

"Oh yes, Geoffrey's brother, Edwin, is around here somewhere, but I'll warn you that he totally takes after his father. Between the two of them, they make listening to Emily Dickinson seem cheery."

"It's so weird to think of vampires having two parents," she said.

"Why? Don't you have two parents?" Stefano asked. "You've seen too many Hollywood movies. I mean, if you believed them, then anyone we feed on would sprout fangs. It would be as if every Big Mac consumed could turn into a human."

"And your parents are in there?" she asked, motioning back to the house.

"One of them is. My other sire, Klaus, doesn't like to travel. I only see him when I'm in Austria for the summer."

"Austria, Japan, you seem to travel a lot."

"My servant likes to tell you my plans?" Stefano asked.

"I just remembered that's why you were away. Ren doesn't talk about you very much. Mostly he's been helping me learn how to take care of your friend." Georgia watched as the vampire's face sank a wee bit. She quickly piped up with, "I would like to know more about you though."

"Oh really," he said, his smile returning. "What would you like to know?"

"How you and my boss became friends. You two don't seem like you have a lot in common except how you love ordering Ren around."

Stefano tilted his head side to side and stared off over a rose garden. Georgia watched him pace a bit with a bemused little smirk on his face, as if he wasn't quite certain where to begin. A fresh scent of jasmine and cut grass replaced the deadly vampire funk in the air and let Georgia catch her breath and take a few more peaceful sips of wine. As she looked over her glass and took in the sharp jawline and big baby brown eyes of her new companion, a little bit more of a blush crept across her cheeks.

She quickly looked away again. Stefano took notice, and she cursed her lack of vampiric reflexes under her breath as the creature definitely noticed her reaction. He motioned to a bench between the trellises.

"We actually met during the war, that one you mentioned before," Stefano said. "At that time my family and the Pendragons were at odds, so I was asked to visit Geoffrey's estate and try to open up a dialogue between the families again. Claudia and Lorcan, in particular, can't stand each other, so the sheriffs thought if their children could play nice, it might help ease the tensions."

Georgia eased onto the stone and kept nursing the wine. In the meantime Stefano paced around her, slowly circling in with each anecdote.

"London wasn't the most glamorous of places back then, so our good friend Mr. Lambley had stowed away to Boston to take over one of his mother's many random houses throughout the world."

"The one I now live in?" she asked.

He nodded, "That very same one. Oh, if you could have seen it then—always full of life, full of music, and never wanting for a fresh supply of immigrant women looking to make it big in America . . ." He trailed off and coughed slightly as he noticed the furrow starting in her brow. "But it turned out that Mr. Lambley and I liked many of the same things—jazz, opium . . . jazz singers on opium. The adventures we liked to have! The local police chief was a bondsman then, and while the humans had a lovely calm town to live in, the two of us had virtual free rein to cause mischief and eat very well."

"That doesn't sound like Mr. Lambley, plus aren't his family against eating people?" Georgia challenged him.

"The Pendragons object to *killing* humans, a sentiment I both admire and respect, but that certainly doesn't stop them from feeding, my dear. Geoffrey was a master with the British accent and the puppy eyes and his copious amounts of cash. He was truly a vampire's vampire back then. If he ever grows his fangs back, you'll see what a charmer he can be. There was this one night where we snuck into Fenway Park and dined on three stewardesses, most of the grounds staff, and the first baseman until almost sunrise. It was magic. The popcorn vendor, he actually tasted like popcorn! Did Geoffrey never tell you about that night?"

"Did you ever meet Ted Williams?" she asked without skipping a beat.

Stefano broke into a huge smile, showing off all his fangs to full effect. "I saw him play and even caught one of the men who caught one of his home runs. I still have the ball on my mantel! It's right next to my autograph from Babe Ruth."

"I never knew that European men were so into baseball," she mused. "You're not a football fan?"

"Geoffrey has tried to get me into it, but I'm probably the only Jaeger who doesn't cheer Germany on in the World Cup. I've always preferred the more laid-back pace of a good baseball team. I like the stats, the atmosphere, the strategy of it all, but there is something I must confess to you, Miss Sutherland," he said, easing beside her with a deeply apologetic look in his eyes.

"Oh?" she said, trying not to laugh at his exaggerated hangdog face.

"I . . . am . . . a Yankees fan and have been for nearly a century," he said. "As a lady from the Boston area, can you ever look past this?"

Georgia raised her hand to her forehead and looked away in disdain. "Oh Stefano, you may be an infectious colony of microorganisms inhabiting a dead body and you may very well think of me as a light snack, but I could overlook that. However, your love of the evil empire simply cannot be forgiven," she gushed.

Both of them burst out laughing again. "You're a better actress than most of those dames on Geoffrey's soaps," Stefano said. "Did you know that once we spent a weekend in Hollywood doing a mock casting call?"

"You and Geoffrey?"

"Oh yes, he had me write out all of this terrible dialogue, and we'd watch them perform for us. The best-looking ones were invited back to our suite, of course."

"Oh, of course!" Georgia said. "So, your epic bromance is based on soaps, drugs, and baseball?"

Stefano nodded. "That wouldn't be entirely incorrect," he said, inching closer to her. "But what I want to know is how you ended up responding to that advertisement, and then here, tonight, in this *stunning* dress . . ."

"I ended up telling him the whole story, which you know by now," Georgia said to an eagerly listening Gail. "And he regaled me with all manner of oversharing stories about him and Mr. Lambley. Let's just say that if you do get the job, you won't want to sit on the gold velvet sofa in the formal living room. Just trust me on that one."

"So this Stefano sounds pretty, um, pretty," Gail said, giggling slightly before taking another drink.

"Oh, everyone knows just how good-looking and charming Stefano DeMarco can be, especially Stefano," Georgia snorted. "I can sum up ninety percent of my conversations with him by simply dropping a random famous person's name, inserting a fabulous locale, and then finishing with a line about how delicious someone tasted."

"Oh?" Gail said.

"You know that really good-looking guy at the party, the perfect one that you don't dare approach?"

Gail nodded.

"Well, Stefano is his not-quite-as-attractive but really chatty friend who talks your ear off all night, buys you drinks, and makes you forget pretty much everyone else for a while. Between him and Mina, I have never seen two individuals who can talk quite so long to anyone and say so little, and then—like social ninjas—they can just go poof and reappear in another group and start the cycle anew. I'm pretty sure that they take pride in mingling. It may be an Olympic sport in the making, at least at their level."

Georgia eyed the level in Gail's beverage and then signaled to the hot waiter at the bar. "Still, if it wasn't for them, I wouldn't have met and promptly forgotten so many bland bloodsuckers that night. At one point I got the rare privilege of seeing them both in action. You see, these affairs start with so much talking. You hear who's sleeping with whom, who's feeding on whom, and just where the vampire hot spots are for this decade. Apparently Norway is the perennial favorite to go for winters, while Sydney is where you should spend your summers."

"Our summer or theirs?" Gail asked.

"Well, it's winter in the southern hemisphere technically then too," Georgia conceded. "South America is also a hot spot, since there aren't as many legal issues to deal with if random people show up missing. The Azarola, in particular, have connections there that make it easy. Although the family started in Europe, most of them now live below the equator and have taken up the pharmaceutical or agricultural professions, if you get my drift."

"So there are vampire crime lords too?"

"Oh, that can't possibly surprise you at this point," Georgia laughed. "I was honestly more shocked to meet a vampire accountant. I mean, he's had an eternity to perfect math. How sad is that? He seriously tried to talk my ear off for an hour on just how modern general ledger codes evolved from something in ancient Sumeria or Egypt or something like that. To this day I'm not entirely sure what a general ledger has that makes it so much more fascinating than a specialized ledger, but I will forever associate it in my head with ancient kings and goats."

"Well, are there vampire doctors and lawyers too? I know you said there was a phlebotomist," Gail asked as she ogled the waiter. He set down an electric blue concoction in front of Georgia, prompting her to raise a brow.

"Lawyers—" she said, still checking out the frosty drink in a high-ball glass that looked rather like nuclear waste created by Smurfs. "Oh, there are plenty of lawyers in the group. Doctors are a different story. I found most of them to be mad-scientist types, and what we would call a doctor, a vampire calls a veterinarian. Excuse me, what is this?" she turned to ask.

"It's from an admirer," the waiter said. "It's a Tsunami—one of the house specialties."

Georgia paused to take a deep breath. "You can take it back. I don't accept drinks from strangers, even ones that admire me."

"Are you sure?" the waiter asked, still hovering over the drink.

Georgia nodded. "Tell him that I get the message, but I'm not looking to play tonight. Oh, and can I have a real drink as well? Vodka martini, extra dirty."

"You have an admirer," Gail teased. "I wouldn't turn down a free drink."

"That wasn't a drink, it was sugar, food coloring, and way too much Malibu for any human to consume," she scoffed. "Don't tell me you like little umbrella drinks."

Gail raised her fingers in front of her face and made a little pincer. "Maybe a little." She then did the pincer again to frame the waiter's shapely butt, which was brilliantly in view as he leaned over the bar to whisper something to the bartender. She quickly snapped back to attention as Georgia cleared her throat. "So, the party was a bust? Vampires don't throw the best soirees?"

"They are apparently great fun if you are a vampire," Georgia sighed. "But they are similar in that they start with a whole bunch of boring and awkwardness, and then there comes this magic moment when enough alcohol enters everyone's bloodstream and the band starts getting louder, the conversations start getting louder, and then people start to forget just enough of their manners that the whole affair begins to get fun . . ."

"So, you can get drunk," Georgia giggled as she watched a pair stagger past the coatroom as she and Stefano dared to reenter the fray of the main ballroom.

The young vampire nodded. "Once the alcohol is suspended in the blood, we can enjoy it just as much as you, but, sadly, only for a brief while. No matter how hard we try, it always fades far too quickly. It's the same for other intoxicants," he lamented. "Did I tell you already about the night in Bangkok where I managed to sober up just in time to realize that—"

"Oh, there you are!" a lilting British voice cried just as she rounded the corner. Somehow Mina could project her voice over not only the din of the crowd but over blaring strains of eighties' guitar solos.

"Is that . . . Billy Idol?" Georgia asked as a guttural voice began to shout, "It's a nice day for a white wedding," over the music.

In the blink of an eye, Lady Pendragon had swooped to Georgia's side, dragging a wild-eyed Geoffrey in tow. "Isn't he magnificent?" she gushed as she swooped around the confused human. "I was so tempted to break the rules just once to keep him forever."

"Oh yes, you did have quite the time in Thailand as well, didn't you, Mina?" Stefano laughed. "I remember you and those birds. Wow."

"Come on, Stefano, not in front of Geoffrey. That's his mom!" Georgia snapped.

Mina burst into uproarious laughter. "Oh, sweetie, how charmingly American of you," she said. "Geoffrey was far too busy with those fourteen hookers and the donkey to play with me. Oh, that was a fun Christmas, wasn't it, Stefano, darling? Anyway, I was so close to just ruining his career so I could keep him to myself, but I knew that I couldn't keep such wonders from the world so I let him go. He has no idea, but he had a dop-pelganger in the seventeenth century—a Welsh mercenary who liked to drink and get in fights too. I should have kept that one, but alas, the plague is so unpredictable, isn't it?"

"I never really thought about it . . ." She trailed off as "White Wedding" faded into sitar music. "Who is the deejay?"

"Oh, I picked the playlist with my favorites from the past few centu-ries," Mina said, breaking into a huge smile. "Yes, and I think there is a little jazz in there too, for my boys. Stefano, dear, I hope you haven't talked this poor girl's ear off. I have so many more wonderful people to introduce her too."

"You know, I really haven't gotten to spend any time with your son," Georgia said quickly. She eyed the packed dance floor. "And I promised him I'd dance."

"You did?" Geoffrey said, wide-eyed. He then watched as Stefano and Lady Pendragon both were motioning over more people to mingle with. "Oh, yes, of course. I know how you love to dance, Miss Sutherland."

Before Mina and Stefano could so much as turn around, Georgia and Geoffrey had slipped into a mass of widely different dance styles. The vampire settled on a pseudo-waltz step that almost fell in line with the twangy Indian-inspired music. Georgia stumbled a few times at first but finally managed to find her rhythm in the corner of the floor.

"I thought I'd never get away," Georgia said. "And you looked like you were one conversation away from a coronary. Can vampires have heart attacks?"

"I'm starting to think that they can," the vampire sighed.

"What?" Georgia asked as they swayed too close to the speaker.

"Never mind," he said, sweeping her along the floor. As they got to-ward the edge of the dance floor, however, the vampire's eyes widened again as none other than the trio of hunters themselves lay in waiting by a table full of empty wineglasses. Next to them a heated argument in some foreign language raged even louder than the music. Geoffrey tried to swing his dance partner away from the scene, but before either of them could blink, a short and scandalously dressed redhead had yanked away

Mr. Lambley and led him out toward the center of the dance floor, calling something back in German that didn't sound particularly kind.

Georgia smiled weakly at the enormous blonde woman who was snapping at two other, much smaller, vampires. Finally, one of them pointed to Georgia and said in English, "How can you deny that a creature such as that has an eternal spirit?" he said.

"Wow, this is a little heavier than the last party conversation I was in," Georgia said, looking furtively around for a familiar face. "Sorry to intrude."

The amazon snorted. "Parrots imitate speech too," she growled.

"I really don't have anything either polite or relevant to say to that," Georgia said. "But I'll leave you to it."

The blonde moved closer. She leaned down and peered into Georgia's eyes—so close that the potent mix of alcohol and iron in Asrun's breath got right into the human's nose. The vampire muttered something in what was presumably Swedish, causing the Jaeger to snicker before sipping on the tail end of his glass of spiked blood.

"Just because you want to dismiss the importance of the human soul in our existence doesn't make our point any less valid. You've seen with your own eyes tonight that a human can resist—" one of the little strangers said.

"Exceptions prove rules, professor, and you won't get any money from us to continue this pointless research. Go beg the Pendragon fools if you want," the blonde snapped.

"You know, I should be going," Georgia said as she tried to slip out from under the stare of Asrun. As she tried to wheel around, she nearly plowed right into the chest of probably the single largest man she had managed not to notice in a party full of vampires. Behind her she could hear the Jaeger say in his thickest Scandinavian accent, "My good sheriff, I see you have joined the party. It is wonderful when the *vicecomes* decide to maintain a little order in these crazy times."

"Wow," slipped out of Georgia's mouth as she stepped back. The barrel chest was connected to two massive arms and tree trunklike legs, all topped with a brilliantly smooth and shiny head. The stranger smiled

warmly, flashing a mix of golden and pearly white fangs that were perfectly offset against his rich brown lips.

"You must be careful there, missy," he said. Georgia continued to
study the stark contrast between the stranger's bulk and fearsome facial
tattoos and his sparkling brown eyes and warm grin. He then gently took
Georgia's hand in his and raised it to his lips. "Pleasure to meet the only
guest here raising more eyebrows than I am."

"You're warm," was all she could spit out.

The stranger burst out laughing, while both Asrun and the Jaeger
continued to watch the new person with a mix of caution and disgust. The smallest vampire tried to resume his argument. "As you
can see, there are clear examples of humanity transcending into our
existence—"

"Oh dear, I've walked into that argument again," the huge stranger
said, shaking his head. "If you would please pardon me for a moment."
The giant then turned to face Lady Asrun, and Georgia had to smile as the
amazon finally faced a man taller and broader than herself. Even in her
monstrous footwear, she still had to tilt her chin slightly upward to glare
at him right in the eye.

She spat out something in Swedish that didn't need any translating.
Georgia blinked a few times at the raw, unabashed name-calling of the
only truly dark-skinned individual in the room. Brynjulf finally rose to
stand beside his woman and gave a slightly apologetic bow. "While we
respect the right of the sheriff to be here—" he started to say.

"You better not finish that sentence, my dear Jaeger friend," a British
voice cut in.

"She must have superpowers," Georgia muttered as somehow Lady
Pendragon had managed to slip into the conversation moments before
one of the Jaegers managed to completely start a riot on the dance floor.
This time both the sullen Lorcan and another rather handsome vampire
with dirty blonde hair and perfect amber-colored eyes were flanking her
as escort.

"Mr. Sugar! I knew you'd come to see us," she said, fluttering over between the two bristling giants. "Have you met my son's date tonight? Mr.

Sugar, this is Miss Georgia Sutherland, and you simply must spend some time with her, she's causing quite a tizzy."

Mr. Sugar took a careful step back from Asrun. "We are in the house of Pendragon tonight," he said. "And I'm here to visit one of my dearest friends, not to talk philosophy with my less-enlightened cousins," he said with a slight sideways nod toward Asrun.

The blonde started to take a breath, but her mate took her arm and gave her a look that quieted her instantly. "I still have not had a dance, my love," he said. He nodded toward Mr. Sugar. "Sheriff," he said before leading the blonde away.

The weasel of a vampire who had started the argument tried to take a step toward Mina. "Oh Lady Pendragon, I was hoping—"

"Humans have souls. You don't have to convince me. Go talk to Neeha, and she will write you a check just to shut up and leave my other guests alone," Mina said with an exaggerated roll of her eyes. "Now, has that Jaeger bitch finished with my son, yet? I think they are all quite a bit drunk by this point."

"I'll handle it, Mina," Lorcan said, still managing to scowl while saying the simplest of phrases. The other brooding sentinel tried to make his escape as well, but Mina swept her hand back and grabbed his without even having to turn. "Edwin, you have to mingle too. It's not every decade that your brother brings a date to one of our parties."

"Oh, you really did come with young Geoffrey," Mr. Sugar said, all smiles again. "I thought that was just silly rumor."

Georgia half curtsied, half bowed to the giant. "I am here with Mr. Lambley, yes . . ." She trailed off as she noticed a dark shape obscuring her reflection in one of the many Mylar balloons. "OK, I'm a little confused."

Behind her she could hear furtive whispers, including such words as freaks and abomination. For the first time all evening, Georgia had some doubts as to whether the words were being used to describe her. Some even dared to point at Mr. Sugar openly. She blinked and looked into the reflection again, but this time she could only see herself.

Mina remained her usual unflappable, chipper self. "I must apologize to you both. I knew that Harvey would be stirring up trouble to get donations tonight, but I underestimated just how fast the champagne would get to Asrun. She can fell an entire army with an arm chained behind her back, but she certainly cannot hold her liquor like a born and bred citizen of the great British Empire." Both she and Mr. Sugar stopped to laugh, while Edwin tried his best to melt into the crowd. "When Asrun and Brynjulf are both into cups, it can get a bit *testy* in the room," she continued. "If the sheriff hadn't been here, I'm certain it would be quite a scene."

"Well, I mean, the sheriff is huge and terrifying. Why would they even think—?" Georgia stopped as Mina, Mr. Sugar, and even sullen Edwin all burst into laughter.

"You thought that Mr. Sugar was the sheriff?" Edwin snorted, revealing his decidedly flat North American accent in comparison to the lilting British of Mina and the dulcet island tones in Mr. Sugar's deep voice.

"I am so confused," Georgia said as she took in the swarm of undead around her. She bit her tongue as the nausea swept over her once more.

"Don't worry, you don't have all that long to be so befuddled," yet another voice chimed in as Georgia's head swirled even more.

This voice belonged to a tiny form that had been completely eclipsed by the sheer mass of Mr. Sugar. A teeny, trembling bird of a lady took a few tottering steps toward Georgia, leaning against an ivory cane with one hand while carefully patting her silver curls into shape to frame her delicate wrinkle-hatched features. She watched Georgia from behind her dainty silver spectacles, clucking her tongue a few times in disdain. "The necklines are so low nowadays," she sighed. "While convenient, it leaves ever so little to the imagination."

"Sheriff, have you had refreshments already—?" Mina started.

"Oh, don't you worry about me, Lady Pendragon. I ate before I came," she said, still tottering ever so closer to the human. The closer the crone inched, the more the human's stomach turned.

"Oh, you must be the sheriff," Georgia said. "Nice to meet you, ma'am," she choked out before having to quickly cover her mouth.

"You're one of those people," the sheriff said dismissively.

"I get that a lot," Georgia muttered.

"So, did you want to catch up?" Mina offered.

The sheriff continued to pace her agonizingly slow circle around the confused human. In her sensible violet velvet gown, understated jewelry, gloves, and hairpins, she looked just like a grand dame straight out of the latest episode of *Masterpiece Theater.* By the time she finally finished her three-sixty, Meenakshi Pendragon's immediate family had returned in full, with a red-faced Geoffrey trying to conceal his abject terror at the sight of the little old lady just within arm's reach of his delicate human plus one.

Without warning the sheriff snapped a hand out and plopped it unceremoniously on Georgia's. Unlike Mr. Sugar's, this hand was deathly, freakishly cold, and surprisingly strong. "You annoy the Jaeger," she said. "Which means I rather like you personally."

Georgia almost managed to form a smile before the sheriff continued, "However, it is my job to keep order and enforce our laws. Your nature makes you a liability to our kind. You need to be careful, young lady. I would hate for you to cause any incidents that would reflect badly upon the Pendragon family. After all, it's not just like we can wave a hand and make you forget."

"I'm sure that she will be fine," Mina interjected.

"Oh, I'm sure she will, as long as you keep a close eye on her," the sheriff said. She then turned right to Lorcan. "I mean, your family wouldn't want any more . . . incidents."

"Of course not, my sheriff," Lord Pendragon said a little too quickly.

The sheriff turned right back to Georgia. "You're curious, aren't you, little thing?" she asked.

Georgia's eyes turned involuntarily to Mr. Sugar. The sheriff simply petted her hand. "You've been given some sort of education by the Pendragon, yes?" the sheriff asked.

Georgia nodded.

"That fool Professor Harvey keeps stoking the fires between the progressives and the classicists here by trying to argue whether we vampires simply live in our human shells or if we somehow are born from the humans that gave their lives for us in addition to our true blooded parents. It's rather contentious talk and never suited for a party, in my opinion.

Usually Lady Pendragon and her kin end up arguing that humanity influences us, while the Jaegers stomp their feet and call it ridiculous. I, for one, never deign to take part in such things. It's bad for the digestion, you know."

"Anyway," the sheriff continued, "vampires are born when humans die, and our kind likes to debate what happens to that human just as much as you humans like to debate what happens to yourselves when you expire. However, every once in the rarest while, something happens that completely upsets the argument."

She motioned to Mr. Sugar with her cane. He gave a little bow.

"He has a reflection, and he's warm," she said. "Is he——?"

Mr. Sugar bared his fangs proudly. "Not human, no," he finished. "But not entirely vampire either. They call me so many names—abomination, stillborn, half-dead, but the Tepes have a good word for my kind. They call me a *dhampir*, which at least only translates to half-breed, or so they tell me."

"A half . . . vampire?" Georgia asked.

"My dear Mr. Sugar is one of the rare humans that did not die when the vampire came to be within him. I'd rather not get into the details, as it's not polite conversation for a party," the sheriff said, switching her hand from Georgia's to his.

"So you're still alive?" Georgia asked.

"Are we not all alive in some way?" Mr. Sugar said with a sad little laugh. "What they mean is that my human half is still alive. My vampire self simply could not kill this old pirate dead."

"And since the Caesars do not formally recognize a vampire until their date of death, poor *dhampirs* like Mr. Sugar are treated terribly," Mina chimed in. "If they aren't taken in by a major family, well, let's just say——"

"You don't last very long," the sheriff finished. "Lucky for Mr. Sugar, he has been a fine servant of my office here in North America. His unique abilities help keep all of these gentle people on their best behavior. Now, I do believe that I see a few gentlemen that I need to discuss terms with. Mr. Sugar, I'm sure you want to spend some time with your friends before I steal you for the rest of the night."

The moment the sheriff tottered away, Georgia could breathe easier. Mina, Geoffrey, and even Lorcan immediately swept around her and formed a barrier between her and the curious onlookers.

"Are you all right?" Mina asked.

"She is a little intimidating, but I think I'm OK," Georgia said. "Did I miss something?"

"Do not worry, child. I'm sure if my mistress was more than curious, she wouldn't approach in the open." Mr. Sugar turned to Mina. "She simply wanted to take a look at this guest of your son."

"I'm still kinda stuck on the half-vampire thing. Geoffrey, why didn't you tell me about them? Also, you OK?" Georgia asked.

Her boss nodded vehemently. "My feet did survive the Teutonic tramp for another evening. I swear, Georgia, she makes you seem graceful on the dance floor."

"The half-dead are so rare that you wouldn't think to mention them," Lorcan interjected flatly.

"Indeed, I am the only living *dhampir* in the United States, and one of only three known in the entire world," Mr. Sugar added. "You have a better chance of getting struck by lightning a few times than ever meeting another creature such as me . . ."

"So, there are half-vampires too?" Gail asked.

Georgia tilted her head from side to side. "Not really half-vampires per se, rather like a vampire living inside a still-living human. It's as awkward as that sounds. It's not really a subject that vampires like to talk about. Well, that's not true either. It's kind of something that they don't talk about openly," she said as she stared off into space. Finally she managed to hunt down her next sentence. "I think it's rather tragic, honestly, and talking about it is a fast way to get a vampire either irritated or ready to overshare with you. Anyway, the way it's supposed to work is that you have a mommy vampire and a daddy vampire, and they both bite some poor human and transmit a special infection into the lucky person. Those happy little bloodsucking germs hook up and recombine and then go forth and multiply, all the while attacking and systematically killing the human host.

Once the host is deceased, the little cells go crazy, and in a few hours—poof, a new little monster wakes up. And that, Miss Filipovic, is where baby vampires come from."

Gail tried to stifle a little giggle. Georgia tipped her drink toward her in a pseudo-salute. "You never thought about it that way, huh?" Georgia asked. "Anyway, sometimes the baby vampire isn't strong enough, and the human body stays inanimate. Apparently this is more and more common nowadays, and most of the commoner vampires can't even reproduce at all."

"But sometimes the human doesn't die at all?" Gail asked.

Georgia shook her head. "Very, very rarely something totally wacko happens, and the vampire wakes up with a living body. Mr. Sugar doesn't like to talk about it, but it's . . . it must be . . . it must have been very painful." She stopped to take a large drink. "Mina told me that usually whatever wakes up goes mad within a day and has to be, um, put down, but in a few cases, the half human–half vampire can find a way to cope."

"Like Mr. Sugar?"

Georgia nodded. "Exactly. He somehow managed to make peace with himself, and he's worked under the sheriff of the United States for over a century. It's not easy, from what I've managed to find out from Mina and others, but he has a very strange inner calm around him. I hear he does a lot of yoga."

"But don't vampires—I mean, aren't they undead humans?" Gail asked.

"Well, if you watch fiction written by humans, sure they are, but if you ask a vampire . . ."

"So, are you one of those humans who think that we're just like you, but dead?" Stefano asked. The cluster of vampires around Mr. Sugar had left Georgia once more seeking fresh air, and her new Jaeger shadow had been more than happy to escort her and his dear friend Mr. Lambley back out to the garden. While the dapper young Jaeger sipped from a brandy snifter, Geoffrey had taken refuge with a plastic coconut cup, complete with a fancy bendy straw and bright yellow umbrella.

"That depends. Are you one of those arrogant vampires who assumes that every human is an ignorant walking lunch?" she fired right back.

The ginger-haired vampire looked back and forth as he slurped his beverage, doing his best impression of a young child watching Mommy and Daddy fight.

"Well," Stefano said, sizing up Georgia's leg as it peeked out of the slit in her gown, "I think you'd be a far more substantial meal than lunch."

She raised a brow. "You did get the memo that sexy and creepy aren't the same thing, right?" she asked.

"Normally women are not as difficult as you, Miss Sutherland."

"What can I say? I'm an overachiever," she said with a wicked little smile.

Stefano finally leaned back to his ginger-haired friend and whispered just a touch too loudly, "You lucky limey bastard."

Georgia rolled her eyes as a response.

"I am fortunate to have a new assistant," Geoffrey answered diplomatically. "Miss Sutherland, are you feeling better?"

"I'm fine as long as I get a little fresh air." She looked back at Stefano. "You know, we really don't need an escort. I'm sure you have plenty of vampire ladies to charm, Mr. DeMarco."

"I'm not interested in any vampire ladies right now," he replied.

"Well, then, I saw plenty of vampire men in there."

Stefano let out a chuckle and took a step toward her. He gave a little bow and held out his hand. "Since you seem a bit feisty again, my dear, how about a dance?"

"Thanks, but no thanks. I'm not much of a dancer," she said flatly.

"You've never had a partner as good as me," he fired right back.

"Then I don't want to make you look bad."

"No one could look bad in my arms."

Georgia still shook her head. "I'm kinda here with someone else, Steve, you know, your friend, Mr. Lambley—"

"Oh, Gingersnaps here wouldn't mind if I take you out for a spin, would you, old boy?"

"Gingersnaps?" Georgia mouthed while eyeing the now red-faced vampire.

"Miss Sutherland is free to dance or not dance as she chooses," Geoffrey stammered out.

"Then choose to dance with me, sweetheart," Stefano said, holding out his hand once more.

"No, really, I am terrible and don't want you to look bad," she protested again.

The vampire didn't back down. "The dance floor is packed. Who is even going to notice you in the crowd, hmm? Come on, one dance to one song, and then you'll be rid of me if you so choose."

"One dance, and then you will leave me alone?" she sighed.

"If that is what you desire."

"Fine, but only if there is something from this century playing," she muttered as she took his hand. Stefano nodded to Mr. Lambley and gave a little wink. "Well, then, we shall simply have to request a little twenty-first century ditty, won't we? Wait, you're not into country music, are you? That would pretty much be a deal breaker right there."

"Wow, I've never wanted to be a Kenny Chesney fan so much in my entire life," Georgia said. "But no, I prefer something more urban."

"Interesting," Stefan said. "Well, I'm sure we can find something that you can dance to."

She let him lead her back into the crowded hall. A few rolled their eyes or gave a brief hushed titter as they saw the girl with a rosy tint and an aqua dress once more step into the room, but that was pretty much it. Far too many were focused on Mina doing a barely legal tango with that Tepes guy, or on the Aryan threesome holding court in the back. She tried to turn back to Mr. Lambley, but the surprisingly nimble little toad had slipped off into the crowd.

"I'll wait for one or two more songs, but that's it," she sighed as the tango faded into some sort of medieval folk tune.

"Geoffrey is just taking care of the deejay, sweetheart. Never you fear," Stefano said.

"Oh, I'm just in a strange place surrounded by humanity's chief predator. What do I possibly have to be afraid of?"

Stefano raised her hand to his lips and purred, "Certainly not me, darling."

"Ugh," she sighed as she kept looking for familiar red hair. Stefano continued to chatter away, while Georgia did a bit of vampire watching from the sidelines. She noticed the smaller blonde Jaeger slip out a side door with a suspicious glint in her eye—licking her painted lips like a starving cat. On the other side of the room, the perpetually perturbed Pendragon, Lorcan, looked absolutely miserable as the professor talked one ear off while the sheriff and Mr. Sugar gabbed into his other. In the middle of the room, a writhing swarm of pale faces continued to dance in all manner of styles—from a Dark Ages ronde to a decidedly more modern group doing the frat-boy shuffle.

Georgia let out a deep sigh. "No one is going to see this or remember it, so let's just get it over with," she said.

"You don't want to wait for one of your songs?" he asked.

"Whatever," she said, grabbing his hand. She hadn't made it ten feet into the throng when the genre changed again, from lilting harpsichord strains to clanging synthesizers. Georgia began to giggle as a group of vampires began to flail around to an eighties' one-hit wonder.

Stefano pounced on her good mood and broke into a dazzling white smile. "Who doesn't like "The Final Countdown"?" he asked as he jerked her into hold and led her to an open spot smack-dab in the center of the dance floor. Georgia stumbled a few times before she relaxed into a sort of fast waltz, ducking in and out of frenetic undead couples.

"I remember this from when I was a kid. It's the kinda song you hear in commercials or movie trailers," she laughed as Stefano swung her out and then snapped her back into hold. True to his word, he was exceptionally nimble on his feet and able to flick and kick around her large and ungraceful feet. Every time she so much as swerved, he was able to adjust and guide her into a position where she managed to look graceful among the discordant mix of dance styles filling the room. As the music swelled into the first chorus, she even allowed him to lift her and swing her around into the heart of the dance floor. Finally she looked up and gasped as she realized just what sort of mischief Mr. Lambley had gotten into while Stefano had lured her away.

"Oh . . . my . . ." she breathed as she looked up at the wall of metallic balloons, which had been expertly turned and shifted to form a wall of a hundred mirrors, a wall where Georgia was the only reflection, suspended in thin air as her partner lifted her higher.

All of the chaos melted away as he continued to guide her around, always keeping her floating in the magical image. He burst into a huge smile as he dropped her into a dip. "Now you see the world just as I do," he whispered in her ear as she snapped back against his chest. "In this room there *is* only you."

Georgia relaxed and let him swing her about for the rest of the song. As the final chorus swelled, she let him lift her completely to his shoulders and spin frenetically, forming a swirl of aqua as she giggled with delight. As he eased her down, she slid against his long, lean frame and could feel just how well-built this hunter really was under his fancy suit and tie.

She looked right through him into her own reflection, blushing more than she probably should have. She watched a stray hair slip behind her ear as she felt cool breath against her neck.

"Can we go outside?" she managed to choke out.

"But of course," he said, leading her out as the music blended into yet another Billy Idol tune, this one more soft and slow.

"I danced with a vampire," Georgia gushed as they swept back out into the gardens. "I really danced with one."

Stefano shook his head in amazement. "You just realized this? You do know we've been there all night, right?" he said with a little laugh.

"You know what I mean," she said, punching his arm. Her smile only widened. "It was like I was flying."

"There is magic in the air tonight, sweetheart," he said, kissing her hand again.

"You were right. That was amazing," she said. "I guess I was so busy being annoyed with all of you that I never thought to just relax and . . ." She trailed off as she noticed a strange bit of movement behind one of the trellises.

Both she and Stefano looked at each other with a conspiratorial wink in their eyes as they heard a soft moan coming from the bushes.

"Sounds like someone is having a better time than us," Stefano chuckled as he nudged Georgia.

"You mean you—well, yeah, I guess your kind—wow, I think I can hear slurping. You want to move farther down the path?" Georgia said over the rustling.

"It's not the kind of thing that gets you excited?" Stefano teased.

"If you are about to say something to the effect of 'how American of you,' then I will seriously knee you in the crown jewels, Mr. DeMarco," Georgia snapped. The rustling stopped suddenly, and Georgia ducked in close to her vampire companion, as she could hear heels clicking on the garden stones. Still, she couldn't resist peeking over his arm to see a leggy blonde stopping under one of the trees to tug the hem of her little red dress and to double-check that her twins were safely tucked back into their holsters. She then ran her finger slowly around her lips and flung something off into the vegetation. Finally, she applied fresh lipstick and tossed her tousled hair back over her shoulders.

Stefano burst out with something that sounded both snide and guttural at the same time. The blonde snapped back in German so quickly that Georgia didn't have a chance to even try to figure out what was being said. After a few more rapid-fire exchanges, Stefano gave her an obnoxious thumbs-up.

"Sorry, sweetheart," he said while turning back to Georgia. "She just wanted to know if her lipstick was back on. She decided that she didn't like the catering and needed a light snack."

The blonde made a rude gesture at Stefano. He smiled as she stormed off. "My sister is such a bitch," he sighed.

"Minerva, right?" Georgia asked. "You mean she screws a guy while she drinks his blood?"

Stefano laughed again. "Blood is one type of sustenance, yes, but my dear older sister has a taste for something a little easier to get at a party, if you know what I mean."

Georgia rolled her eyes. "Oh, she fancied a little protein shake from a lucky fellow? How nice."

"She does have a mouth that is the basis of legends," Stefano said with a slow and respectful nod.

"Eww. Isn't she your sister, Stevie-boy?"

"Not human," he fired back. "Still, she's not my type at all. I prefer . . ." He trailed off to start a sarcastic round of applause as the second party made his walk of shame from the shadows of the bushes. Georgia joined him for a second, but stopped cold as she saw the unique combo of pale green eyes and Asian features in the moonlight.

"I see that she ordered the usual tonight," Stefano cracked as Ren immediately stiffened and lowered his eyes.

"Do you require anything, sir?" Ren asked softly while pointedly not looking at Georgia.

"Oh, it looks like you've already been of plenty of service tonight," Georgia snapped.

"Yes, why don't you go freshen up and see if Mother needs anything? That is, if you have anything left to give," Stefano said.

"As you wish, sir," Ren said with a quick bow before hustling toward the main ballroom.

"You know, I think I'm going to find Mr. Lambley now," Georgia said flatly. "It's probably about time for us to go."

Stefano grabbed her arm and pulled her back. "Go? Why would you want to go now?"

"I want to go because I remember now exactly why I'm here for creatures like you," she snapped.

"I don't see you like the others do," Stefano said, pulling her closer again.

Georgia shoved back again. "Yes, you do. To you I'm just an after-dinner drink. Wait, I am the dinner and the drink!"

"Sweetheart, please—"

"My name is Georgia, Steve," she snapped. "Not honey, not dame, and certainly not sweetheart. So if you would excuse me, I'd rather just forget about tonight."

"Fine, if that is what you want," Stefano said before yanking her against his chest. "Your wish is my command," he purred before sweeping her into his arms and kissing her passionately.

She froze for a moment, taking in the heady mix of night air, alcohol in the blood, and his firm grip until the chill from his lips passed to her own and her eyes snapped open again. She pushed away and stood there, stunned for several seconds.

Stefano sighed and shook his head. "Such a pity."

Georgia continued to stand there, staring off at the distant fairy lights until her vampire companion's face melted back into his familiar cheeky grin.

"Oh, hello there, are you all right, *signorina?*" he said. "I just noticed you alone out here, and I thought I'd introduce myself. I'm Stefano DeMarco von Jaeger, and you are?"

Georgia blinked a few times. "Georgia Sutherland."

"Ah, such a beautiful name. A pleasure to meet you, Georgia."

Georgia raised a brow. "I wish I could forget tonight, but no matter how hard you try, Steve, I'm not giving you a do-over. Ugh, kissing you was like kissing a raw piece of meat. Yuck!"

"What?" Stefano gasped. "You mean you can remember me? Remember tonight?"

"Like I said, I want to forget, but, ugh, no," she said as she wiped her mouth with the hem of her dress. "Good night, Steve. Let's hope we don't meet again."

10

"You kissed a vampire," Gail gushed. "You really kissed one?"

Georgia waved her hand contemptuously. "It's not quite what you think. Imagine kissing a hunk of raw meat."

"Oh, I bet he was a hunk," Gail said between sips of her drink. "Come on, you have to tell me more."

"It was nothing, really. Really, Stefano is just that type. He moves fast and normally hops from girl to girl without a thought, quite literally. I learned that night that Stefano is a little different than your average blood-sucker . . ."

"You actually remember him kissing you?" Mr. Lambley asked as they settled into their limousine for the return trip. Georgia stared at the clock on the dash with a furrowed brow.

"Will we make it back to the hotel well before sunrise?" she asked the driver, not acknowledging Mr. Lambley for a second. "My companion is not the best during the day."

"No worries," the driver said before closing the polarized screen between them.

"But, but I've never heard of anyone . . . even vampires are affected by Stefano's charms," Mr. Lambley stammered. "Are you certain that he kissed you?"

"I'm certain that vampires have pretty bad breath," Georgia muttered. "Yes, Geoffrey, I remember him kissing me. What is the big deal? It wasn't that great an experience for me."

Mr. Lambley started wringing his hands. "All of our kind have the same basic abilities—the immortality, the lack of reflection, the resistance to heat and cold and all of that, but a very few of us have extraordinary gifts," he said.

"You mean like how you can scramble electronics when you get stressed?" she said, pointedly eyeing his phone going haywire on the seat next to them. "Calm down, Geoffrey, or I'm going to have to spend another two hours stuck at the phone store."

"Stefano is special even among special vampires. He's known as the Great Shadow throughout much of the vampire community because he has what is known as a universal ability, one that affects all kinds—"

"Geoffrey, what are you babbling on about?" she said as she snatched up his now completely black phone and tucked it as far away from him as possible.

"You know how we all have miasma? He has a most concentrated form in his saliva, one that can make you forget almost anything if exposed to it. The Caesars called it *osculum oblivio*—the kiss of nothingness. I've watched him make a woman forget an entire week once, but the longer the kiss and the more passionate he becomes, the greater the effect. All he has to do after causing the amnesia spell is use a few suggestions to replace whatever the victim missed. He's used by the sheriff as a means of last resort to help clean up messes our kind makes all over North America."

"Well, I wish I was like everyone else, because he's a rather terrible kisser," Georgia said.

"Does anyone else know?" Geoffrey asked.

"Know what?"

"Does anyone else know that he kissed you and you can remember it?" he asked, this time grabbing both her hands.

Georgia shook her head ferociously. "Just you."

The vampire let out a sigh of relief. The flush of color left him, and he returned to his normal pallor as his phone flickered back to life on the edge of the seat. "Please, Miss Sutherland, promise me that we will keep this between ourselves. I'll call Stefano and make certain that this is kept quiet."

"Really, what is the big deal? They already know that vampire voodoo doesn't work on me."

"They know that you are one of *those* people, the rare few unaffected by the miasma, but in my decades of knowing Stefano, I have never met anyone immune to his kiss, and neither has the sheriff. If she were to find out that even he could not control you, well, let's just say it wouldn't be pleasant for either of us."

"Wait, was he some sort of backup plan for you? Did you think that if things didn't work out that he could just pull a reverse Sleeping Beauty on me and I'd be out of your hair or something? Tell me the truth, Mr. Lambley."

"Well, no, not really," the vampire said as he looked away. "Stefano was supposed to be my backup in the beginning if my miasma was too weak to control a girl—you know, when I was looking for something else and not an assistant—but even his kiss couldn't take away our time together. The sheriff is just more comfortable having someone like you around our kind if Stefano is tasked with erasing any mistakes."

"So, if I see something I shouldn't, he's the cleanup crew? You know, like seeing Ren being used as a toy by that blonde bitch? I really wish he could have erased that."

"Oh, I see Minerva got hungry. She's always been the pickiest of that lot. Stefano's boy is her personal favorite as of late. She'll even come up from Washington for days to feast on him. I thought you knew."

"Well, no, I didn't, and it just reminded me what I am to . . . to all of you."

"No! Please do not confuse the Jaegers with my family. I see you as a valued assistant, Miss Sutherland."

"Except when you have too much blood in your system and I end up sleeping in the bathroom," she snapped.

The vampire continued to hold her hands, draining the warmth from her fingers. He finally craned his head around to look her right in the eyes.

His normal placid expression tucked away among doughy pillows of flesh was replaced by something far more intense and focused. The sheer power of his glare actually gave the furious human girl pause.

"I made a promise to you, Miss Sutherland, and a vampire's word is his bond. I do swear to you that I will never hurt you, never betray you, and never so much as think of you as food. So help me god, Miss Sutherland, I am devoted to you and your service and would be lost without you. Are we clear?"

"We're clear," she said, squeezing his hands.

"As I said, I'll call Stefano and ask him to keep this quiet. The sheriff of these lands may look unimposing, but she is a force to be reckoned with. I must say, though, it's rather charming to see Stefano all flustered for a change. Usually it's me at the end of the night looking as he did. Now I know why."

"How *are* you friends with him? I still don't get it, but come on, let's just relax and enjoy one more day in our hotel before we take the trip back to Boston. Who knows, if you're good I might even get you some pay-per-view . . ."

"So you're like superwoman?" Gail asked. "You're immune to all the vampires? Wow!"

"A little less loud," Georgia said as she motioned her head toward the blonde sitting at the bar. "We don't like to bring that up too much. Of course, I might *not* be immune, and I just can't remember it. Stefano DeMarco is a trained hunter, after all, and if he wants something, he can stalk it for a very, very long time."

"So, you never saw him again?"

"Oh, I've seen him plenty of times, but you don't really want to hear about that, do you? Wouldn't you rather learn about the day-to-day job?" Georgia teased.

"I just get this feeling that you're not telling me everything," Gail said with a sly little smile. "Like why you would give up an apparently easy job that pays one hundred thousand dollars a year, hmm?"

"Maybe I just want to give someone else the same amazing opportunity," Georgia said flippantly.

"Come on, what you've described is way easier than cleaning up old men in diapers. You're still holding out on me, aren't you?"

Georgia smiled slyly and took a sip of her drink. Gail's eyes widened as she noticed the sparkling diamond on the third finger of her left hand. "Oh, come on! Are you going to tell me everything?" Gail gushed.

"Well, I don't know—" Georgia said coyly.

"I mean, if you don't have some story to tell, then the job must be horrible, but the way you keep smiling and talking about the ball and everything. I mean, I think I know what really happened!" she said rapidly, flushed from a mix of alcohol and excitement.

"Oh, you think you know the truth? I must say the last six months of my employment are quite the story, but does it really have to do with the job?" Georgia said.

"You danced with a vampire, a vampire who has a kiss that makes everyone forget him, but you are immune. You get this look in your eyes whenever you say his name. Come on! Tell me what happened between you and Stefano. Tell me that he's the reason you're quitting your job!"

Georgia let out a deep sigh and flagged over the waiter. "We're going to need more drinks. It's gonna be a long night," she cooed. As soon as he was gone, she leaned over to Gail and said, "You're right, Stefano DeMarco is the reason why I'm here tonight, and I suppose I owe it to you to tell you everything, don't I? After all, who else can I tell about what happened?"

Gail broke into a huge smile. "You mean—?" she prodded.

"A week after the party, a dozen roses were delivered to Mr. Lambley's brownstone, along with an invitation for dinner downtown. My boss advised me not to refuse, so I asked for Nicolette to drop by and keep him company. Did I mention that she can play board games for hours and is a champion at Scrabble? If you ever need a night off, she will come by for only a shot of blood. Mr. Lambley loves it."

"He invited you to dinner?" Gail gasped.

"Yes, he invited me to have dinner with him—unlike most vampires, who invite you over to *be* the dinner. He managed to get reservations on the waterfront at someplace ridiculously gourmet, expensive, and fancy— the kind of place that sneers at you if your tie isn't expensive enough, but I somehow managed to dig up an old cocktail dress and join him on a warm summer night just before the holiday . . ."

"Oh, nice to see you again," Georgia said dismissively as Ren Matsuoka arrived at her door promptly after sundown. He was once again in his stark uniform and slicked-back hair, only lacking his plain black sunglasses to complete the Secret Service agent attire. "Well, nice to see you with your fly zipped this time."

"I've been told traffic is terrible tonight. We should be going, Miss Sutherland," he said in his damnably calm voice.

"I thought my name was Georgia," she snapped back.

"As you wish, Georgia," he said as he motioned toward the car double-parked on the street. From the doorway the drag queen babysitter waved joyously with one hand while she played with Mr. Lambley's slightly more bushy and growing-in ginger hair with the other.

"Have a blast, darling, and don't you worry. Dinner is already taken care of! Night, dearie," Nicolette called sweetly.

"Please, have a good time, and you don't have to hurry back. Nicolette brought my favorites—dry gin and Pictionary!" Mr. Lambley said.

"You just like her because she spikes the drinks. Now you two behave, I'll be back by midnight," Georgia said as she waved back. Her smile faded the moment she was tucked behind tinted windows. Her frown deepened as Ren slipped into the backseat with her once he'd given instructions to the driver.

"Would you prefer I took the front?" he asked.

"I'd prefer if you'd told me about the services that you provide to the Jaeger family," she snapped bluntly.

"Excuse me?"

"I'm sorry, but it was just a bit annoying to see you, you know, ugh, I don't even want to say it."

"I am a Matsuoka, and it is my duty to serve the Jaeger family. If that service includes feeding them, then I am obligated to offer myself," he said, even more flatly than normal.

"So, you just let them feed off you whenever they want? I can't believe it." Her voice softened a little. "I'm sorry you have to do that."

"I don't want your pity," he said.

"Well, you didn't look pitiful at the ball. In fact, you looked rather pleased with your situation," Georgia snapped.

"You're right. I was not suffering at the ball, and believe me, if given the choice between Lady Asrun or Lady Claudia chomping at my throat or getting a blow job from Minerva, I will choose the latter option each and every time."

"So are you and Minerva . . . like a thing?"

"Like . . . a thing?" he said, mimicking her drawn-out inflection.

"Stefano and Mr. Lambley both seemed to think that she comes to you a lot for feeding time."

"And this is your business . . . why?" Ren asked.

"Forget about it."

They rode in silence for a while until they got stuck in a particularly long backup around the Boston Common. After staring at the same set of blinking lights for a solid five minutes, Georgia couldn't contain herself anymore. She turned back to look at Ren, but before she could even open her mouth, he said softly, "No, Lady Jaeger and I are not . . . a thing."

"You were right, it really wasn't my business."

"Minerva Fenstermacher is considered my family sponsor. I'm required to do *special* services for her whenever she is in town. She has a fondness for AB negative blood, which is rather hard to come by unless you happen to be me. She also prefers to feed on—"

"Yeah, I get it: she never spits, she swallows, and you have her favorite drinking straw. Should we leave it at that?"

Ren nodded.

"She just uses you?"

"I am what she considers delicious, nothing more, nothing less, and quite honestly I prefer it that way." Ren sighed while looking out the window. "Anyway, it doesn't matter what I think, I live to serve."

"How can you be so passive about this? Aren't you angry at all?" Georgia asked.

"Of course, I'm angry. I've been angry for a very long time, but there is nothing I can do about it, so I've stopped fighting. The question is, why do you even care, Georgia? You're not the one who has to live like this," he said, still looking outside rather than at her.

Georgia sat back. "I don't know. Maybe I just don't like the thought of us being meat to them."

"Then you shouldn't have chosen to serve a vampire," Ren replied.

She watched him pull out his phone and start flicking away at stocks and bonds, spreadsheets and calculations. In the light, though, she could see the tension in his jaw and the furrow above his brow.

"Checking the Internet?" she asked innocently.

"I was just following up on a trade. We are up one fifty on our portfolio this month," he said. "Dropping oil prices are good for what I hedged on."

"Wow, one hundred and fifty thousand, not bad for a month's work," she said.

"It's million," he muttered.

"Excuse me."

"We're up one hundred and fifty million. I just sold some Indian antiquities for the Pendragons and divested a failing small shell company to a sucker in Dubai. It's not typical, but I've done even better in the past. Vampires are big business if you know how to manage it."

Georgia just sat there, blinking. "I never thought of it that way."

"Think about how many assets you can accumulate in one lifetime, now multiply that times a hundred. Plus vampires have an issue with having to disappear and reinvent themselves every few decades—new identities, new documents, new everything. There is a brisk trade in identification management for the undead in the twenty-first century, and my family is the pioneer of life fabrication."

"I guess I never thought about that either."

"I went to school for business and investment management by day, and had a very different education by night. Let's leave it at that."

"But we never leave it at that, do we?" Georgia said as the car finally started to move again thanks to a patented Masshole cutoff maneuver by the driver. "Ren, are you like a gangster or something?"

"Oh yes, all these tattoos are totally Yakuza," he said drily. "I'm far more white collar than bust a cap in yo' ass, if that's what you need to know."

Georgia burst into a fit of giggles. "Did you really just utter the words bust a cap in yo' ass?"

Ren cracked a little smile. "Something wrong with your hearing?" he asked.

"So, you are the fake ID king of vampire land? Can you fix my credit score or anything fun like that, maybe erase the fines on my library card?" she asked.

"If I had the time, I could give you a whole new life if you wanted, Georgia, but I'm not cheap."

"Even for a blonde?" she asked with a little wink.

"You really hit below the belt at times."

"No, I'm pretty sure that was Minerva."

"You're giving me that look again," he said as Georgia continued to stare at him. "You want to ask me something inappropriate and obnoxious, so just go ahead and ask it."

"Who, me?" Georgia asked innocently.

"Yes, you, but I will warn you, I can be just as obnoxious."

"Oh, that is without a doubt."

"We're getting close to the restaurant. You had better hurry up."

"So, have you and Minerva—"

Ren responded by burying his face in his hands. Georgia could barely make out a muffled sound like "Hi" from behind his mask.

"Hello to you too," she quipped.

"Not 'hi'—*hai*," he said, finally dropping his hand. "It's Japanese for yes."

"Wasn't it cold?" she blurted out without thinking. Ren slumped back against the seat.

"Sometimes. A vampire's body temperature is much closer to the ambient room temperature at all times, but in the summer, it isn't so bad. They warm up quickly when they feed, if you must know."

"So, other than the cold, it's the same, um, you know—"

"Yes, it's a lot like having sex with a human, only with the added benefit of hallucinogenic bodily fluids. After a few minutes, you're too high to care what they do with you. I thought we already had this talk."

"Well, I didn't know that you got your information firsthand. Sorry if I was surprised."

"Well, now you know, and knowing is half the battle."

"I've heard that before."

"It's an eighties' cartoon reference, probably from before you were old enough to remember. Look, if you want hours of details sometime, we can have breakfast, but for now can we drop the subject? Please?"

"Then let's have breakfast. I'm off on every other Monday right now. How about you?"

"I have a few hours each Monday as well. Would you prefer sushi or burritos?"

"Never been a big fan of Mexican, but I love a good cucumber roll."

"I'll pick you up at six then. That should give us both a good two hours before my master and your boss start roaming about."

"It's a date," she said before any sort of filter activated between her brain and her mouth. "I mean, you're on . . ."

"It actually became a tradition, you know. Monday night is breakfast lessons with Ren, Tuesday became Date Night for me to get Mr. Lambley out of the house, Wednesday is movie time, and the weekend, well, the weekend became a mix of whatever the local vampires wanted to do. Oh, Nicolette works on Thursdays and Sundays normally, so it's tough to get her to vampire-sit on those nights," Georgia noted to the wide-eyed and eager Miss Filipovic.

"But you went to dinner with Stefano?" Gail asked, circling the subject back around. "What happened?"

"Oh, it was ridiculously fancy and expensive, with foams and gastriques and all manner of fancy pseudo-sauces on our plates. I think he even had something with bacon air as a component. I guess you can charge extra if you just rename the same smell you get from opening a bag of doggy treats."

"And?" Gail prodded.

"And the night went a little something like this . . ."

Georgia stepped out into the warm summer night as Ren darted ahead to whisper something in the doorman's ear. She stared right past them to see the last rays of light sinking behind the skyscrapers and slowly transforming the Boston Harbor into an inky mass dotted with the lights from the city. She breathed in the mix of salt and fish funk that permeated the waterfront when it was warm and took delight in how her wedges clattered against the walk. The breeze picked up a little, giving her the perfect wind-blown look before being led in the door.

The front desk gave her a round of pleasantries and let her know her table was ready on the terrace. Ren had managed to melt into the shadows somehow, leaving Georgia to be led to a lovely table for two with a perfect view of the bay and a bottle of something that looked dreadfully expensive chilling in a silver bucket. The only thing missing was her dinner date.

Georgia let herself be eased into a chair. A few minutes later, a familiar vaguely European accent chimed in with, "Ah, it's so good to see that you made it, sweetheart."

Georgia bit her tongue. Instead she watched in fascination as her vampire companion eased into the chair beside her, seemingly unfazed by the traces of sunlight surrounding them. He motioned for the waiter to break into the bubbly. And once the cork was popped and the menus passed out, Georgia's fascination turned to shock as she saw just how much each bite of food was worth at this fine establishment.

"*Prix fixe, s'il vous plait,*" Stefano said. Georgia was still gawking at ten-dollar glasses of water, too busy to notice the flurry of French darting back and forth between Stefano and the waiter. The only words that she managed to pick out toward the end were, "No, vegetarian," as he pointed right at her.

"I thought this was just fancy. I didn't know it was French."

"The waiter is from Marseilles. It's just easier to get what you want if you can speak in someone's native tongue," Stefano said. "Mmm, have you ever had Cristal before?"

"Can't say that I have," she said before taking a sip. "But it's not bad."

Stefano left his glass untouched, opting instead to stare at the bubbles until Ren magically appeared with a second glass and carafe of a slightly more viscous-looking golden liquid. In a matter of moments, the glasses were switched, and Ren disappeared back into whatever dark corner he came from.

"There is nothing like fresh plasma with a shot of champagne in it," he cooed.

"That one I'll just take your word on," Georgia said. "So, you asked me to dinner—any reason why?"

"I think we've gotten off on the wrong foot, sweetheart."

"Partially because you refuse to use my name, Steve," she snapped. She had to pause to receive a description of watermelon salad with cucumber spheres and chili-lime vinaigrette. Across the table Stefano was greeted with beef carpaccio.

"Touché," he said. "Fine, Georgia, I think we needed a fresh start, a proper introduction. I'm Stefano DeMarco from the Jaeger family. It's a pleasure to meet you."

"And I'm Georgia Sutherland, assistant to your friend," she said, raising her glass. "You should know that he's the reason I'm even here tonight."

"I must say it is truly one of the great mysteries of this world how a vampire such as he secured an assistant as beautiful as you."

"What do you mean, 'such as he'? He's a nice guy who needed help. He's also the person who pays me, and he doesn't look at me as if I'm a walking, talking T-bone."

"Touché again," he said between bites of raw meat. "Still, Gingersnaps is not in the prime of his life right now. I didn't think he'd manage to lure anyone into our little trap."

"We've been here, done this conversation already," Georgia sighed.

"You really are not affected by me at all?" Stefano asked. "Extraordinary."

"So I'm guessing you've had to repeat a lot of conversations to girls on dates," Georgia offered. "I mean, if you kiss them, they forget you, right?"

"Sad but true. One kiss is usually enough to have them reeling. I've tried a few second dates, but they always end up just like the first ones."

"That is kind of sad," Georgia said. "So all you've ever had to do is focus on a good set of pickup lines. You never really get to know anyone, do you?"

"Oh, I get to know them, but they never really get to know me."

Georgia munched the rest of her first course in silence. She watched Stefano slurp down his drink with morbid curiosity. Through the glass she could just see the flickering motion of two tiny red tendrils slipping and sliding from the tips of his fangs to the bottom of the plasma.

"I know, they are particularly long," he said with a little wink. "But it's not the size of a man's fangs, it's how he uses them that matters."

"I just hadn't ever seen them. Does Geoffrey—"

Stefano shook his head. "Without the protection of enamel, fangs tend to retract or get torn. I think Gingersnaps lost his last one somewhere around 1988. Now he's stuck with syringes and sipping cups."

"So that's when he lost them," Georgia said softly. "And you're basically a bunch of bacteria making a man into a mosquito."

"You have quite the perspective on our kind, Miss Sutherland," Stefano said as he tipped his glass to her. "I must say it's refreshing."

"Let me guess—you usually get someone fawning and hoping that you'll drink her blood and she'll become immortal. They fantasize about you sinking your fangs in their neck and running your cold hands down their spine until they shudder. After all, you can pull the vampire card, can't you? Unlike most of them, you have the industrial-strength amnesia spit, right?"

"As of late I have them ask if I sparkle in the sun and only drink animal blood," he sighed. "Or they want me to wear nothing but bondage gear. I must say that Goths are easy prey."

"I bet they are. That's what you were looking for to help Mr. Lambley, an easy victim that you could just slip your Mickey to, but, surprise, you ended up with my crisscrossed cell action and me."

"You look disgusted."

"Maybe I'm just disappointed. I mean, aren't you Jaegers supposed to be the great hunters? You're picking off the wounded gazelles."

"That was just for my friend. He needs the help."

"Yes, he needs help. He needs someone not to coddle him, to make him go out and face the world, not shelter him from it. I can see the way you look at him. You pity him."

"And you don't?"

Georgia paused slightly too long. Long enough to be interrupted by a salad of goat's cheese, pistachio, and beets. Stefano smiled triumphantly from across the table. Instead of firing right back, she took the time to slowly slice and savor each and every morsel of the bright red salad. Once she had scooped up and devoured the last drops of the blood-orange dressing, she dabbed the napkin to her mouth and smiled. "I see a theme in our dinner," she said. "And you're right, I did pity Mr. Lambley at first, but he's trying—"

"Very trying," Stefano interjected.

"He's trying to be better."

"And you think I am coddling him? You do realize that I'm the one that sent him that invitation? I was afraid if he didn't join any society event soon that he might fully descend into the withering, and despite what you might think about me, sweetheart, he is my friend, and I don't want that to happen."

For the first time since Georgia had ever spoken to Stefano, a sincere burn replaced the sparkle in his puppyish eyes. He gripped his fork so hard that the handle actually curved.

"You really are his friend," Georgia acquiesced.

"And you really look out for him," he said.

"So, what is the withering?"

He waited for the waiter to change out the plates once more. As Ren slipped back to refill Stefano's glass, the vampire grabbed his servant's wrist. "*Jioruja-chan ni nan to itta?*" he snapped.

"*Nandesuka?*" Ren said.

"*Osoi-Shi o setsumei shimashita ka?*"

"*Iie, kyūketsuki-sama,*" Ren said. "*Naze desuka?*"

"I'm still here, by the way. Don't make me break out the translator on my phone," Georgia threatened from behind her plate of deconstructed ratatouille. Stefano raised his hand and then whispered in his servant's ear. Ren bowed quickly and muttered something that could only be an apology in Japanese.

Once he had disappeared back to wherever he seemed to like to hide during dinner service, Stefano said apologetically, "I thought my servant was teaching you. I guess he's been omitting a few things."

"Usually when it's something called 'the withering,' there isn't really a good point in the conversation to bring it up," she said. "Is it some kind of slow death?"

"In Japanese it's known as *Osoi-Shi,* literally 'slow death.' It's what happens when you stop being able to heal and maintain your human shell. Year after year you fall apart, aging and withering just as any mortal man would. At some point your fangs fall out and you can't feed. If you don't fight back, then it is a one-way ticket to oblivion. All the billions of other tiny creatures that want to feast on the suit of meat you wear start to win, and eventually you just disintegrate. I'm told it's exceptionally painful in the end."

Georgia dropped her fork. "So Mr. Lambley is . . . ?"

Stefano stared off into the bay. "Usually once a vampire loses his fangs, he only has a few decades left. The modern obsession with cleanliness and vaccines has made it easier to survive longer. There is less competition, so to speak, but I must confess, until recently, I thought I was going to have to say good-bye to my best friend sooner rather than later. My only hope is that he's a Pendragon and not like most of our kind."

"All the families are different. I do know that."

"The only vampire ever known to recover from the withering was Arthur Pendragon. Yeah, all that Grail and King Arthur mythology has a little bit of truth to it—who knew? The Pendragons might not be as strong as the other clans, but they are a scrappy lot. It was a terrible shame that their founder managed to cheat the worst death our kind can have and beat the unbeatable, only to be killed by his own offspring. Talk about irony," Stefano sighed. "I just hoped it ran in the family."

"How do we help him? How do you beat this?" Georgia asked.

"Well, the only one who ever has beaten it is, unfortunately, quite dead, so I have to work on the same rumors that everyone else has, but the general consensus is that the withering is tied to one's will to live. If you can restore that, the body regenerates. I've already seen the signs."

"What signs?"

"Have you had to trim his nails? Cut his hair?"

"Yeah, and it's not the most pleasant thing in the world. He hates to sit still."

"He hadn't needed his nails clipped for at least a year before you came along," Stefano said with delight. "I think he might be fighting back. I don't know what you are doing, but it's working."

"Well, I can only imagine that staying in one dark dirty little house with only soap operas to keep you company wouldn't give you much reason to live. His old servant died after serving him for decades, and he was losing his teeth, right? I bet he was just shutting himself away."

"Of course he was, but he would never tell us why—not me, not Mina, not even Minerva, and they used to be as thick as thieves."

"You mean your lovely sister was *friends* with Mr. Lambley too?" Georgia asked with a bit of venom in her voice.

"Oh, not the kind of friends with benefits. Minerva can be abrasive, but she was always fascinated by the Pendragons, as I was. The two of them would hunt together, not for the normal prey, but for rare books and pieces of art. I don't think they even liked each other, but they could go on and on for years about something Baroque or a limited-edition Bible print. I once had to hide for six months in a monastery outside Florence where they forbade talking, just so the two of them couldn't babble any more around me. Then when he lost his first fang, it was suddenly silent, and I must admit I even missed it, but Minerva says she doesn't know what happened either."

"And you believe her?"

"Oh, my sister is the biggest bitch in Western Europe. She's ruthless, heartless, and prone to violence—also she has a shocking obsession with oral sex—but she's no liar," Stefano said. "Whatever broke him is his little secret."

"It must have been terrible. He's never said anything to me either, if that's what you're looking for," Georgia said softly.

The two of them picked away at their respective food in silence for a few long drawn-out minutes. The vampire watched her closely as the night breeze toyed with her hair and her bright eyes stared off into the far horizon.

"I just want to get to know you, and I'd very much like for you to get to know me, sweetheart. Is that too much to ask?" Stefano finally said.

Georgia turned her attention back to the man across the table. "You've never really had a girl to talk to, have you?" she asked.

"I'm desperate for an education beyond banter. Will you help me, as you've helped my dear friend? Will you consider going on a second date with me?"

"Maybe, but don't you think we should focus on fixing Mr. Lambley first?"

"Well, I don't think pitying him and acting like he is dying has worked in the past," Stefano said. "So I wouldn't do anything different than what you are doing. After all, it takes decades to die as one of our kind, it might take just as long to heal."

"Well, I suppose I might be convinced to see you one more time—especially if this meal ends in something chocolaty . . ."

"So you said you'd see him again?" Gail gushed.

"Well, the last course was a seven-layer chocolate and chili cake with cinnamon ice cream, so I felt honor-bound to see him at least one more time."

"And Mr. Lambley, I assume—"

"Well, you know what assuming does," Georgia said with a little wink. "But I can assure you that Mr. Lambley is recovering slowly. But now you see why it's so important that he has an assistant, don't you? I know you are a nurse, but do you believe in the whole mind-body-spirit thing?"

"Well, I don't know enough about vampires to really comment," Gail said.

"If you let yourself just be alone and miserable, you don't get any better. I want to make sure that Mr. Lambley has fresh life and energy in the house. He eats well now, gets out and about, and has someone to talk to. Vampires are so obsessive over things that I really think it's a case of mind over matter. I want to make certain that whoever follows me will keep him on the same path."

"Oh, of course," Gail said, suddenly back into interview mode. "I always do my best to take care of people. Chronic care and hospice was my thing. Stefano said it would take him years to recover, right, so we are talking about long-term care?"

"I see that we understand each other."

"So, did you ever find out what made him sick?"

"Mr. Lambley has his secrets, and I respect them. If he ever wants to tell you or anyone else what happened, then that is his choice. I did, though, learn a lot from Ren at our Monday night breakfasts. Things like how pig or human blood is best, or that you need to give a vampire a balanced diet of types for optimum nutrition, no matter how much they fuss and complain."

"Night breakfasts?"

"Well, when work starts at sunset, everything gets flipped around. Ren and I would always meet up at Little Jiro's Sushi Hut a few hours before dark. It's a hole-in-the-wall with amazing miso soup, and the chef there always gave me extra cucumber in my rolls, but that's not really important, is it?"

"Is it?" Gail asked.

"Breakfast was when Ren helped me set up the app and my calendar. This phone might not look like much, but it's my lifeline. I have one program just to track Mr. Lambley's steps each day. If he doesn't get close to ten thousand, it will warn you, and you can take him for a walk. He likes the Common in the warm months and the CambridgeSide Mall when it snows. Even though vampires aren't bothered by the cold, he absolutely hates getting his feet damp. I once had him throw a hissy and lock himself in his room because I let him land in a particularly nasty puddle."

Gail leaned forward again, her cheeks obviously flushed. "But you have to tell me," she insisted.

"Tell you what?"

"What was your second date?"

"Well, the second date was expensive dinner again, and then he took me on a helicopter ride over the city. We had box seats for the opera and for any show we wanted, and I even got to slip into a fancy charity thing with an extravagant open bar and waiters who passed around lollipops frozen with liquid nitrogen. The best time, though, was when we went to a Boston classic film series. Hearing him talk about when *Casablanca* was in theaters was an amazing experience."

"Oh wow, those sound great."

"Oh, those were just the appetizers. Soon he decided to up the ante . . ."

"Georgia, am I getting time with Nicki?" Mr. Lambley asked anxiously as he saw his assistant primping in the mirror in a brand-new minidress.

"Nicolette is on tour in Denver and San Francisco this week. You are going to have to get dressed and join me for a change."

The vampire pouted as he looked down at his new emerald green smoking jacket sent right from India with his name embroidered on the lapel. Mina had spared no expense and mercifully provided several pairs of silk drawstring lounge pants as well, so Georgia had been spared surprises on the landing for nearly a month—save the one time he simply had to run out and tell her that someone named Blake had hooked back up with his ex-wife Marissa after she recovered from a coma.

"Not a shower again. I've had one this week," he whined.

"Nothing that drastic. You just need to put on a shirt and pants to get to the car coming for us. Ren says that Stefano has a surprise for us both, and he's going to keep you while I go out with Captain Eurotrash."

"Stefano's boy isn't nearly as fun," Geoffrey pouted. "Last time he made me drink Irish."

"There aren't that many sources of cheap, clean human blood available, and after that hissy you made last time, well, let's just say I had to learn enough Cambodian to write a formal apology to Mrs. Q, as well as get her a live duck."

"How was I supposed to know that she'd be offended?" the vampire sniffed.

"Mr. Lambley, you called her a tasteless slut," Georgia sighed.

"Oh, was that what that meant? I meant to say that the blood she got me was tasteless."

"And this is why I had to clean your phone again. You can't just trust any random translation programs—" She was cut off by the doorbell. "You. Shirt. Now! I don't care if you keep on the comfy pants if it will keep you quiet."

She fussed one last time in the mirror and applied a fresh coat of flavored lip gloss on her already-shining lips. Once she was sure her hair was perfectly imperfect and her mascara wasn't clumped, she bounded down the stars to see a familiar face in a familiar black suit.

"Why do you ring the bell when you have a key?" she asked as she yanked open the door.

Ren responded with his usual little bow. "I wouldn't want to just barge in when I know you are home and getting ready," he said.

"You were afraid that Mr. Lambley wouldn't be in shorts again, weren't you?" she teased. "Mina sent a care package from her latest trip. It's safe. I swear."

Ren's eyes darted all over her low neckline and short hemline, pausing at the twin highlights on the tour for slightly too long. "Mostly I wanted to be respectful of you. I would hate to barge in while you were still getting dressed."

"Oh, I bet you would," she said with a little wink. "Sorry, I don't have any animal print for you today."

"The purple does look quite pretty against your pale skin though," he said. "I don't know why you don't wear dark colors more often."

She twirled around for him. "So, you like it?"

Ren cleared his throat. "I only meant that my master will be quite pleased, I'm sure," he said softly. "I hope you enjoy your evening."

"So, what's this big surprise?" she asked.

"By very definition, a surprise is not revealed early," Ren said. "And it seems that your boss is as ready as he'll ever be."

Georgia had to shake her head as Mr. Lambley padded downstairs with his belly poking out where his buttons didn't quite meet the right button-holes. She could clearly make out one blue sock and one black peeking over his loafers, and his pants were half-tucked into each shoe. In his left hand, he carried a beach bag stuffed with his smoking jacket, some cards, and a pair of knitting needles, while in his right he had a crusty plastic mug.

Georgia hopped over and made quick work of the chaos, handing the mug gingerly to Ren while fixing the shirt. "Oh, you're making a new scarf?" she asked sweetly. "I hope you picked up acrylic yarn this time instead of the cotton stuff."

Geoffrey sighed as he endured having his hair finger combed. "I know I might see Stefano, my dear. I'm not that addled yet," he sniffed.

Ren returned with a travel mug. "It's pig, don't worry," he assured his vampiric companion. "I even added a twist of lemon since I hear you've been doing so well this week. Now, if you will both follow me, my master is waiting."

Georgia and Mr. Lambley followed Ren out into the warm summer night. An honest-to-goodness limousine awaited them, complete with tinted windows and a driver in a jaunty hat. As Georgia slipped onto the devilishly soft leather seats, a card with her name in gold letters was waiting for her.

As the vampire plopped beside her, he immediately started poking in the mini-fridge in the back. He squealed as he saw both bottles of wine and dark bottles marked with type B and type O. Ren eased into

194 R E C A R R

the seat across from them, tapping furiously on his phone. He nodded deferentially to Mr. Lambley. "My apologies, sir. I was just finalizing the arrangements."

"Ren, you are being more Renlike than usual," Georgia said. "What are you up to?"

His face changed to one of pure innocence. "I am not up to anything. I am merely the facilitator tonight."

"Nice ride," Georgia said as she relaxed into her own private wave of air-conditioning. "And it caters to all kinds, I see."

Ren nodded. "Always use Sunset Limousine. It's the only reliable bonded-driver service on the East Coast. Don't worry about the cost, my master has already paid."

The limo soon filled with the local hip-hop station, causing both Georgia and Geoffrey to start tapping their feet and swaying to the beat. Even Ren could be caught from time to time nodding his head as they drove around town. Georgia finally took the time to slip open the vellum envelope and open a very formal invitation.

"I hereby invite you into my new residence – S. D.," was scrawled in rather rough script in comparison to the elegant stationary.

"New residence?" Georgia asked.

"An invitation," Geoffrey gasped.

The limo rolled to a stop in front of a rather imposing-looking brick building not far from the location of Georgia and Stefano's first date. Ren exited first and walked around to let out both Georgia and Mr. Lambley to the doorstep. In lieu of a doorman, an impressive key-card lock and a number pad awaited them. Ren swiped his phone in front of the sensor and then held open the door.

"Don't forget your invitation please, Georgia," Ren warned.

"You managed to find a place in Boston? I wonder what the rent is like here," Georgia said as she stepped into a lobby straight out of an old movie. Her shoes clicked delightfully on a checkerboard of black and white marble and echoed up through the spiral staircase.

"Did this used to be a hotel?" she asked as she saw a massive desk running along one wall.

"This was the Intercontinental, wasn't it?" Geoffrey asked in awe. "Miranda used to sit right over there," he said, pointing to an empty chair. "But I thought—"

Georgia eyed the long, narrow windows, all of them fitted with either dark stained glass or blackout curtains. Every surface was glass, metal, or stone, with the rare exception of some massive flowers in vases along the floor. Georgia couldn't resist running a finger along them to feel the silken leaves.

"Was this a hotel for vampires?" she asked.

"Very perceptive, sweetheart," a new voice said from the stairs. "It was a home away from home for visiting vampires from the 1820s all the way through the 1960s. The vampires that owned it suffered a rather terrible fate when one decided to test a Lung's patience over the Newark Armistice Zone, so it was left abandoned. A developer decided to turn it into lofts recently, but when the real estate market crashed, the project was abandoned."

"You bought the Intercontinental?" Mr. Lambley said as he padded around the room, still wide-eyed. "You really did it?"

"Parts of it were parceled off, but I was able over time to purchase the bits back. I can be very *persuasive* when required." Stefano laughed as he skipped down the stairs. "I think at one point they were even thinking of tearing this place down."

Georgia followed her boss to an out-of-place modern sectional and television tucked in one corner. "The remodeling and restoration is obviously still a work in progress," Ren said. "My master chose to focus on the penthouse first. However, he did remodel two additional rooms on the fourth floor just for you, Mr. Lambley."

"You mean . . . ?" Geoffrey said hopefully.

"Yes, the blue rooms are restored as best I could," Stefano said. "I even managed to get the fountain on eBay."

Geoffrey giggled and took off up the stairs with speed that Georgia had never seen before. She tore after him, not caring as the hem in her skirt kicked up. Stefano and Ren caught up around floor three. All of them ran past painters' cloths and scaffolding until the dusty stairs gave way to temporarily tacked-down carpet. Geoffrey bounced up and down as he reached the freshly painted white door until Ren finally put him out of his misery and swiped his phone over the lock.

"Wow," was all Georgia could say as she took in bright blue walls and stark white trim. A massive Moroccan-style canopy bed filled one half of the room, while a mosaic fountain and full bar made up the other. "What is their obsession with mirrors?" she asked as she stared at Ren's reflection through the silk curtains.

Geoffrey walked slowly around the bed, poking at the fluffy rainbow of cushions and throws. He picked up a rather faded blue and white number and brought it slowly toward his face, breathing in the heady aroma of the antique cloth. "How did you get this?" he asked, also looking at Ren in the mirror.

The servant gave a curt bow. "Most of the soft furnishings and linens from this place were sold in a lot at Christie's a few years back. With the assistance of Lady Minerva, I was able to retrace several of the original items. Those from the finished rooms are already in place, but I have several boxes in the basement if you want to help me unpack them, Mr. Lambley," he said.

The vampire dropped the pillow and snatched up a surprised Georgia's hand. "Oh, the stories I will have to tell you," he started. "Miss Sutherland, you would not believe the individuals who have stayed in these walls."

"Is it any crazier than having King Arthur for a grandfather?" she asked with a little wink.

"I never understood the obsession with him," Stefano piped in as he plopped unceremoniously on the bed.

"Seriously? You can't understand why King Arthur is a legend?" Georgia asked incredulously.

The younger-looking vampire started playing with the cushions, toying in particular with a gaudy golden tassel. His big brown eyes opened wide with mock innocence. "Not that I would ever mock the founder of the great Pendragon line, Gingersnaps, but you have to admit the only reason why your grandfather could get away with so much was that he had a big sword and a shining crown," Stefano explained.

"Not this again," Geoffrey protested.

"He united the British people," Georgia chimed in.

"But he's most famous for his wife running off with his best friend," Stefano fired back.

"Round Table," Georgia offered.

"Got a whole mess of knights killed chasing a magic cup," was Stefano's response.

"Was the sword and the stone part real?" she asked Geoffrey. Her face fell as he shook his head. "He still founded a vampire clan, right?"

"And got killed by his jealous son—a kid that I might add was begot by his sister—in a battle that killed a fair lot of humans from what I've heard. If he was around nowadays, he'd be paraded out on daytime TV before being a victim in some crime show that same night."

"And you can judge Geoffrey's family . . . why?" Georgia asked. "From what I could see, your grandma's a racist and grandpa's a bully that I've never heard of in all my history classes."

Stefano burst out laughing. "You have quite a set of balls, sweetheart," he said. "I can't really argue about the fame. Unlike some families, the Jaegers take the whole rules about vampires staying out of humans' perception a bit more seriously than others. I mean, don't get me wrong, your family at least has the decency to hide being vampires in all their family stories, Geoffrey, but you have to admit they love to flaunt the drama."

"Don't you dare put us in the same class as the Tepes," Geoffrey warned. "Now, all this talk is getting far too prickly for an evening out, don't you think?"

"You are still so terribly limey, Gingersnaps," Stefano sighed before turning his attention right back to Georgia. "But he is right about one thing. Tonight is supposed to be a night for romance and celebration. I still have so much more to show you, sweetheart."

Georgia sighed deeply and gave an exaggerated roll of the eyes but still extended her hand. "Well, why don't we finish the tour before you crazy kids start calling each other names again?" she said.

Ren turned to Mr. Lambley and gave another little bow. "If you would like, the bar is stocked with your favorite," he said before pulling out an industrial-looking blender.

Once more the ginger-haired vampire was all smiles. He bounded to one of the stools and looked on hungrily as Stefano's servant pulled out an ice bucket and a plastic bag of what could only be described as rat-sicles. Georgia allowed herself to be swept away in the arm of the Jaeger and slipped out of the door just as the first crunching sounds were audible.

As they climbed the stairs slowly, she finally slipped out from under his arm and formed a mini-blockade at the first landing. He smiled be-musedly as she crossed her arms over her chest and pointedly asked, "So, what is really up between you and Mr. Lambley? Sometimes I'm positive you hate each other, and other times you do . . . well, you do this," she said as she motioned to the work in progress.

"Like all relationships, ours is complicated," he said with an exagger-ated European accent.

"That isn't an answer."

"Well, it is an answer, just not one that you like," he corrected. "You went to the Solstice Ball. I know you weren't listening to every conversa-tion, but I'm sure you could feel the underlying tensions."

"Oh, I got the general idea all too well. Jaegers and Pendragons equal Montagues and Capulets. It's all rather Shakespearean."

"You're far closer than you even realize there," Stefano laughed. "There are some stories I'll have to tell you at another time."

"If you try to tell me that William Shakespeare was a vampire, I will personally go find a wooden stake with your name on it."

"Shakespeare? No," he reassured. "Now if you want me to introduce you to Christopher Marlowe sometime, he's undead and well and living in Uruguay."

"You're kidding, right?" she asked.

"Ask Mina Pendragon about the real reason why that old playwright was suddenly incarcerated and then stabbed before any sort of trial. Seriously, ask her and see what she says," he said. "I can see the way you look at the Pendragons and then how you look at my family, but I swear to you, there are no angels in the world of vampires."

"Well, to be fair, it was your family that looked at me like I was a thing and questioned if we had souls," Georgia said. "Geoffrey said that most Jaegers think humans are cattle."

"Did you ever wonder if your hamburger had a soul? Do you think you could justify eating bacon if you found out that pigs were the same as you?" Stefano asked.

"You're asking the wrong gal about that, Steve," she snapped. "Still, last time I checked, cows don't talk."

"Maybe they do when you are not around," he said.

"So you think we are animals to justify eating us? I get it, but I think that's why it's a little easier to hang out with Mr. Lambley's family."

"So you think it's better to feed on sentient, thinking, feeling creatures? Just to take that argument all the way to its end. Would it be right for you to feed on another human too?"

Georgia rolled her eyes. "This is like one of those stupid arguments I got into at college. You can go on and on about terrible what-if scenarios until you are blue in the face, but ultimately they are ridiculous. The Pendragons I've met all say that they feed but don't take human lives. I'm sure it's bullshit for some of them, but Mr. Lambley never treats me like walking steak. You're just trying to change the subject."

"I am?"

"What is all this crap between you and Mr. Lambley? I think you're friends but your families are in the way. Is that really all it is?"

"Of course," Stefano said quickly, but he shook his head involuntarily at the same time. Georgia continued to stare right through him until he finally raised his hands in defeat and splatted right down on the stairs. "You have to be the single most frustrating woman I have ever had the pleasure of meeting, Miss Georgia Sutherland!"

"Still not actually answering me," she said flatly as she plopped down beside him.

"Just like you say, the Pendragons have their bullshit, and my family has it in equal share," Stefano muttered.

"Go on," she prodded.

"Even Asrun knows deep down that humans have something more to them, but to the Jaeger, a human dies when a vampire is born. There is nothing in common between what was before and what you are now. You think the Pendragons are so noble? Look at what they do. The Pendragon family only picks the very best of humanity, well, the best in their opinion, and turns them. They think that who they were before they died actually matters."

"They think the human becomes a part of them," Georgia said.

"But only the best of the best of humanity is worthy of such an honor."

"Well, I've heard of King Arthur, but—"

"Each and every one of them was selected not because they were some amazing soul, but because of what they could offer the clan. Other than Lorcan, the accident, all of them brought riches, influence, or titles into their happy little family. Your boss was no exception. He was picked because he got them access to lucrative lands and a great deal of creatively acquired pounds sterling. His brother, Edwin, had to disappear so that they could eliminate a rival Canadian shipping company that dissolved without a clear heir. Did Geoffrey ever mention that he and his darling mother were the major shareholders that profited?"

"Well, no," she admitted.

"You won't find any poor Pendragons, nor will you find any without a thoroughly vetted pedigree," Stefano sniffed. "You think they care about humans? They care about how humans can serve their interests. You are more than food, you're toys to them."

"Wow," she said, shaking her head. "So is this about money?"

"This is about the simple truth that no matter what is said or done, the Jaegers are the killers, and the Pendragons are the heroes. I'll tell you something, sweetheart; those heroes are the ones that spin the tales. They're the only family with a millennia-old public relations team, that's for damn sure."

"I assume you mean Mina."

Stefano nodded. "She was personally selected by Lorcan for her unique abilities. She likes to influence storytellers, writers, religious and political leaders, but above all, she weaves her way into the media of every age—making certain that every generation knows exactly how great and wonderful certain vampires can be."

"You want me to believe that, um, King Arthur and the Round Table is a PR stunt?" Georgia asked.

"King Arthur is a human legend that comes back over and over—"

"Because it's a universal theme!"

"Because they want you to associate them with absolute good."

"So it's all a plot," Georgia laughed. "All those stories were really made up by vampires?"

"Not all of them, no, but Mina is a master manipulator. She knows how to plant a seed of inspiration in just the right place, and like a weed it grows and grows. There are no limits to a prodded human imagination, and all she has to do from time to time is light the spark," he grumbled.

"Now I see where Ren gets his amazing ability to mix metaphors," Georgia muttered. "So this is what bothers you? Geoff's mom?"

"It's not just that. I can see the way you look at my family, and I can see the culmination of thousands of years of manipulation. Maybe we're just too honest. We never try to claim that we're human."

"So you don't remember being alive at all?" Georgia asked.

"That's a ridiculous concept. I'm Stefano DeMarco of the Jaeger clan. That is all that matters."

"So tell me this, when a vampire is born, is it like some helpless thing? Is it like an infant?"

"No."

"How do you know how to speak and walk around and hunt humans?"

"There are certain echoes," he said. He buried his head in his palm. "But it's not like we are that same human *at all*."

Georgia sat back and watched the vampire as his face grew more and more red. She gave him a minute to recover before setting a hand gingerly on his shoulder. "You kinda agree with the Pendragons, don't you?" she asked softly.

"I asked the same questions you did when I was younger," he confessed. "I defended the Pendragon clan to my family time and time again. I mean, I was supposed to be an ambassador to the progressive families, right? I thought, as I suspect you still do, that they were somehow better than us and Geoffrey was my friend."

"I'm sensing a 'but' coming," Georgia said.

"When I needed my friend, he just abandoned me without saying a word. He shut down and stopped talking to me, and to Minerva. We suddenly weren't good enough for him to come to us, and let's just say, I could see Mina's influence in a few too many places."

"So you're mad because he left you at a bad time. Did you ever try to talk to him?"

"He was sick, I know that, but for decades he refused to see me. It was only last year when he decided to talk to me again, and he just acts as if nothing happened."

"Well, maybe you should talk to him," she said, starting to rub his shoulder. "Just try it?"

"There is a lot of history between us, Georgia," Stefano sighed.

"Well, you're vampires. I think that goes with the territory."

Stefano eased farther back, forming an awkward bridge over the marble stairs. He stared at the skylight above and blew a wayward curl out of his eyes. Georgia watched how the softer lights played with his face; the mix of darker skin and awkwardly European features didn't conjure up the stereotypical image of the angular, ghastly, exotic vampire. As he shimmied and adjusted into place, she couldn't help but smile.

"Isn't that dangerous?" she asked, pointing to the huge window over the stairs.

"These are the servants' stairs. The original owner was very close to her humans and wanted to give them one area of refuge," he said. "There was one older lady, Miss Darla, whose room was just off these stairs on the top floor. The entire ceiling in there was glass, with a little ladder that could get you to the roof. Eh, it was never really my problem. She always hated it when I came by."

"You really don't burn in the sun?" she asked.

"Burn? No. Some of the older vampires practically combust with a second of sunlight, but most of us just break out terribly. I, on the other hand, can wear a little sunscreen and a hat and last for hours. It does get itchy after a while, though."

"So what makes you different?"

"I've always been different, sweetheart, but it's part of the Jaeger test, the test to make sure you're really a pureblood and not some upstart. Every one of us when we die is put through a trial. We get dumped in the middle of nowhere at dawn and have to survive until sundown. Claudia kicked me out of a tower into the middle of a burned-out battlefield. There was no real cover for a kilometer in any direction, and all the remaining trees had lost their leaves. Back then we didn't have all these wonderful creams and spray sunscreens. I had to claw my way out of there and get to shelter by midday. She had also dressed me up as an enemy soldier, so not only was I trying not to die from the sun, but there were bullets involved."

"Well, you seemed to get through it."

"That I did. Claudia is not fond of many humans, but she always had a soft spot for Friedrich Wilhelm Nietzsche and his beliefs. I think he's the one who said, 'what doesn't kill us makes us stronger,' or was that Conan the Barbarian?"

Georgia started to giggle. "So, are you going to talk to Mr. Lambley?" she asked.

"I really can't get away from you, can I? You just always cycle back around—"

"It's part of my infuriating charm," she teased.

Stefano curled up to his feet and yanked Georgia up as well. "Come on and see what I've done with the place," he said as he started up the stairs. "After all, that is why I brought you here."

He led her up to a freshly painted door at the very top of the stairs. Across the way, Georgia couldn't help but notice a very different door— one still marked with claw marks from corner to corner and a jamb that had obviously been repaired.

"Welcome to my humble home away from home," he said as the door swung open to reveal a cavernous space with exposed brick and sleek leather furniture.

"This looks like something out of the movies," she said as she took a few tentative steps inside. "Normally I'd ask how you could afford something like this in Boston, but I've talked to Ren too much."

"The Matsuoka family has done rather well for us," Stefano said. "Can I get you a drink?" he said as he pointed to the delightfully old-fashioned wooden bar in the corner. "Or if you prefer, there is a hot tub and a pool on the terrace."

"I didn't bring a swimsuit, sorry."

"Well, that's certainly not a problem in my book," he said with a little snicker.

Georgia just rolled her eyes and continued to survey the loft. One entire wall was filled with old posters with everything from *Gone with the Wind* to *Star Wars*. "You actually have a *Revenge of the Jedi* poster?" she asked as she made it to the end of the display.

"Ren said it was super-rare. It was something he picked up last time he went home," Stefano said as he walked over, drinks in hand. He then pointed to a rather tattered and faded black and white image of Humphrey Bogart mounted in a frame. "It's a still from the *Maltese Falcon*," he said. "I got him to sign it. That was one of the greatest nights of my unlife, but he will never remember it."

"Do I want to know what you did to Humphrey Bogart?" she asked warily.

Stefano smiled slyly and handed her a lovely tea-colored beverage. "Oh, it was magic," he purred. "We went back to his mansion, played some chess, and I won't get into any of the particulars about what darling Lauren may have said or done to me . . ." He trailed off as Georgia crossed her arms in front of her chest and raised a brow. Finally he tipped his glass and gave a little wink. "I got the signature, spat in his whiskey sour, and he never so much as thought of me again," the vampire confessed.

Georgia eyed her drink suspiciously.

"No! I wouldn't do that to you, not that it would work anyway," he reassured her.

She started pacing back and forth among the memorabilia.

"Wow, Steve McQueen, Cary Grant, Harrison Ford—" she said as she saw scribbled line after scribbled line.

"It's easy to be a vampire in Hollywood," Stefano said. "They see so many people and keep such weird hours that it's simple enough to slip in, get a signature, and never be given a second thought, even if you don't have superpowers. I like to go there from time to time just for a few nights."

"I'm sure you've got a million stories," she said, still taking in the scene. She finally settled on one of the sofas in front of a very large television and a dizzying array of technology tucked into recycled wooden crates. A bucket full of remotes and controllers was tucked into the coffee table in front of her. "I never thought of a vampire playing video games," she said as she pulled one out.

"Ren is the gamer usually," Stefano confessed. "But I sometimes like something to do on a bright sunny day."

"It really shouldn't surprise me after seeing what Mr. Lambley did with my phone," she muttered.

"I get angry at the new ones. The stupid motion sensors won't work with one of my kind," he complained. "It's like all these hands-free faucets and the damn door at the corner store!"

"I never thought about that," she said as he settled down next to her. "You can't even get into the supermarket?"

"The old one had a pressure pad, but the new one downtown uses an optic sensor. I always end up having to dart in after someone," he said. "I somehow think that this is humanity's way of getting back at us."

"It does only seem fair," Georgia said. "You eat us. We make it so you can't get into a mall on a slow day."

"Totally unfair," he laughed as he started leaning a wee bit closer.

Georgia responded by hopping back to her feet and prancing over to the section of the loft dedicated to the stereo and a vast collection of vinyl, CDs, and an entire shelf of cassette tapes labeled with all sorts of mix volumes . "Wow," she said as she pulled out one called *Songs to Suck By* (*that do not suck*). "I have got to know," she said as she tossed it on the couch next to him.

"I like the physical process of recording a tape," he said. "I know it's easier to use a computer, but there was just something special about sitting there and pressing stop and start and listening to the songs as you stitched them together."

"I want to know what songs you like to listen to when you bite some girl's neck. Call it morbid curiosity."

He just smiled and took the tape to a shiny silver tape deck. "First off," he said as he popped it in the machine and fiddled with some dials, "who ever said I feed like that?"

He beckoned her toward him with a gentle flick of the wrist as the speakers crackled and popped to life. She approached him cautiously, looking to the side as she tried to figure out just what golden oldie was about to start. "Aerosmith?" she asked as a guitar started low and slow.

"Very good," he said, pulling her close. "Local boys."

She pulled back.

"Trust me," he said, raising her hand to his lips. "You're in my home. I invited you in, and you're under my care. You're a guest, not a meal."

"You like to eat with classic rock in the background?"

"A little electric guitar is good for the digestion," he said as he pulled her in again. This time she dared to rest her head on his chest as he swayed back and forth. "See? I know what you see in the movies, but we don't plunge our fangs into pretty young things' necks," he said as he slid his hand slowly down her bare arm.

She listened to the music blending into the distinctive rushing sound of the blood swirling through his chest. As his cold fingers swept down to her wrist, she shuddered.

"It's so much easier," he said softly as he once more lifted her hand up to his lips. This time he turned her hand, and she could suddenly feel the very tips of his teeth dragging their way agonizingly slowly across the papery-thin skin separating her veins from his hungry fangs.

"Dream on," she snapped as she yanked her arm back. "Sorry, but that doesn't turn me on at all."

"Oh really?" he said as he looked at her flushed cheeks and shallow breathing. He swooped back in again.

"Really," she said, pushing him right back. "There is nothing sexy about being a Big Mac."

"That is not what you are to me, I swear!"

Georgia took a deep breath and collected herself. "Look, I am not one of those girls who swooned over Dracula—"

"Well. I can't blame you, he's a lowlife Transylvanian piece of trash. You saw him," Stefano interrupted.

"Wait," Georgia said as the realization crept over his face. "Oh, that's where I heard Tepes before. Somehow I thought a guy known as Vlad the Impaler would be more *mean*-looking, but that is beside the point. What I'm trying to say is that I've never been into the whole romantic, vampire . . . thing. I know what you are. You're a collection of super-duper bacteria wearing a human suit, and that's not what I'm into. I'm not ever going to be any more than your friend, no matter how cute your particular human suit happens to be."

"So you think I'm cute?" he asked with a devilish grin.

"You have an accent *sometimes*. Is English not your first language?" she asked. "I am not going to lead you on. I'm just not into you that way."

"You think I'm a monster then?" he asked, his eyes growing darker by the second.

"I think you're a vampire."

"I see."

She watched him slump back to the couch and gnaw on his lip. As his face grew more and more pensive and his eyes more and more glazed, she finally took a seat a respectable distance from him.

"You are very confusing, Mr. DeMarco," she sighed. "You're not human, so why are you even interested in one if I'm not on the menu? The truth, please."

"The truth?" he asked.

"Should be a pretty straightforward concept," she sighed.

"You know the truth, don't you?" he said. "You just see through every-thing, and it's ridiculously frustrating!"

"Well, it doesn't really help if I just tell you what I already think I know, does it?" she asked as she once more hopped to her feet. He quickly followed suit.

"Fine!" he snapped. "The truth is—the truth is—"

Georgia started for the door. In the blink of an eye, the superhumanly fast Stefano stepped in front of her.

"That's creepy," she said as she jumped back.

"The truth goes back to the same stupid argument that started this all—the one from the party."

Georgia waited for him to continue.

"When a vampire is born, the human dies, and we are supposed to have no more in common with them than a human would have with a—with a—with a cartoon character! We might look alike and sound alike, but that's all just an illusion. That's the conservative view, and that's what I've been taught ever since I was created. The progressive families, they see things completely differently. They *do* think that we're an infection, a disease that attacks humans and transforms them into different creatures, and that your kind and my kind are inexorably connected until the end of time."

"You mean Geoffrey and his family."

"A few families, yes. The Pendragons are just the most powerful of them. This is kind of a big fight. It's our version of the Cold War. Quite honestly, if both our families weren't at war with the Lungs, I think we'd be killing each other. It got so close a century ago that the Jaeger had to . . . Well, Geoffrey and I were supposed to be friends, to show that we could get along. It's complicated, but believe me, my family hoped that Minerva and I could win over just one of those bastards to our cause, but wouldn't you know it . . ."

He slumped against the jamb, letting his now-unkempt hair flop over one eye. He looked up with hangdog puppy eyes. "Come with me," he said. "Please?"

Georgia nodded and let him lead her back down to the blue room, where they found Mr. Lambley cheerfully slurping the remains of a frothy pink and brown shake while Ren was unpacking board games from one of the cupboards. "Oh Stefano!" the ginger-haired vampire cried. "We were just about to break out the Parcheesi!"

"Geoffrey, I was furious at you," Stefano spat out. "I couldn't understand why you just vanished for years and got worse and worse no matter how much Minerva or I wanted to help you. I sent you the invitation to the Solstice Ball in the hopes of humiliating you, because I was humiliated when you didn't show up for the Jaeger one in 1990. I heard from Ren that you had this human who seemed to be fixing you up and bringing you out of your shell, and I was furious that some little girl could make you better when you had turned your back on your own kind."

Geoffrey put down his glass and stared dumbfounded as Stefano continued, "Oh, and then I saw you and I saw her and I saw how much better you looked, and I was determined even then to get back at you and steal her away. After all, how special could one human be? What could possibly be better about her? I wooed her and danced with her and tried to impress her, and in the end . . . in the end . . . Damn it all to hell!"

Stefano stomped over and gave the still-stunned Mr. Lambley a giant hug. As the younger-looking vampire squeezed his friend, all the stunned humans could do was sit back and gawk.

"As always, you and your family win, don't you?" Stefano asked softly. "I meant to show her how foolish your obsession with humans was, and here I am just as entranced as you. I'm sorry, old friend. I really am sorry."

"What did I miss?" Ren hissed in Georgia's ear.

"I'll tell you over breakfast," she whispered back.

"Apology accepted, old friend," Mr. Lambley said as he patted Stefano on the back. "Does this mean that you are still going to try and steal my assistant away, though?"

Stefano looked back at Georgia. "Oh, Gingersnaps, without a doubt," he promised. "But when I steal her away, it will be by her choice . . ."

"Oh my god," Gail squealed. "So he told you that?"

"Stefano told me a lot of things, sweetie," she said with a coy little smile.

"I have to know what happened!" she said. As Georgia remained maddeningly tight-lipped, the young brunette pressed on with, "Come on, you can't just leave me hanging!"

"Well, I wouldn't want to kiss and tell," the blonde teased.

"Oh my god, you kissed!"

Georgia looked slyly off to the side. Gail scooted next to her and banged her fists in adorable drunken fury. "Come on, tell me!" she insisted. "Come on!"

"Well, what do you think happened?" Georgia asked.

"I think that Stefano disagreed with his family and that he secretly wants to care about humans, just like Mr. Lambley! I also think that you . . . that you and Stefano . . . oh please, tell me what happened. I simply have to know."

"It would be nice to tell someone," Georgia said with a wicked grin. "But I can only go on if I'm certain that you are serious about taking the job. Would you ever really consent to be a vampire's assistant, especially after all you've heard so far?"

"Honestly, it sounds like the best job I could hope for," Gail gushed.

Georgia's wicked smile grew even wider. "That's exactly what I wanted to hear," she cooed. "I suppose I should tell you the rest of the story . . ."

11

"Do I even want to know the rest of that story?" Georgia grunted as she tossed another stained and torn cushion into the back of the dumpster set up in the alley between the Intercontinental and the dilapidated warehouse next door.

Next to her Ren groaned as he chucked a partially complete mannequin into the growing pile of random refuse. Even in an old T-shirt and jeans, he managed to look more put together and tidy than the huffing and puffing Georgia, who had unfortunately ended up in the direct path of a blizzard of plaster dust.

"Well, there is a goat coming up," Ren said with a damnably straight face. "A goat and four stewardesses."

Georgia just grumbled and dragged another pair of garbage bags across the pavement. As the sweat dripped down her dirty bare arms and her legs shook with the strain, Ren quickly darted around and helped her hoist the last of the load. Once a particularly filthy mattress made it into the bin, he waved his arms and stood between her and the back door.

Georgia wiped her brow and declared, "Why is it that the man who can spend a hundred dollars on a bottle of wine or box of chocolates can't afford to hire a demolition crew?"

"Oh, you got the chocolates?" Ren asked. "I meant to ask but got lost in the wanton destruction."

"Yeah, and they were even dark chocolate with cinnamon. That Stefano is an excellent stalker, he knows everything I like."

Ren smiled. "Let's go in. The showers work on the third floor," he said. As soon as they were inside, he said, "In answer to your previous question, as much as my master can afford to pay for a crew, this was a vampire establishment for the better part of a century, and there aren't many bondsmen crews who do basic construction."

"Afraid of skeletons in the closet?" she asked as they slowly dragged themselves up the stairs.

"Yes, actually," he said as he swiped open the door.

"As much fun as this has been, I'm not giving up all my days off for this excitement. Eww, I did break my last nail on that trip."

She followed him down some temporary carpet to another fresh and new door. This one led into a part of the Intercontinental that wasn't on the tour—a stark, clean, and relatively small space, with an executive desk on one side and a platform bed on the other. Georgia could see a fridge and stove peeking through one door and the edge of a tub through the other.

"It's exactly the type of apartment I'd expect for a robot," she said as she squinted to hunt for a single piece of dirty laundry or a dish in the sink. She was sorely disappointed, however, to see that the only traces of dirt entering the apartment were coming off their grungy shoes.

Ren popped over to the fridge and came back with two blissfully cold, sweating bottles of water. "Here you go. Don't worry. Once I've finished this initial inspection, it can be turned over to a real crew. I just don't want to have to explain too many bloodstains."

"I'm surprised that your boss doesn't just kiss them all and make them forget," she said after a long drink.

"Well, he could, but it would be just as suspicious to have a whole team come home with amnesia time and time again," he said. "The simplest solution is usually the best. If you'd like, you can use the shower."

"And get back into these?" she said, tugging at her once-white tank top.

Ren slipped over to the drawers and pulled out a T-shirt and shorts. "It's not high fashion, but it should keep you decent until the laundry is done."

"Music to my ears," she said. She slipped into the cramped bathroom and nearly banged her knee on the tub that filled most of the space. After a quick blast of blissfully warm water that sprayed from the showerhead with the force of a category one hurricane, a full bottle of water, and a clean change of clothes, Georgia finally began to feel human again.

As she was yanking her fingers through the hacked-off ends of her hair, she noticed a bit of orange plastic tucked behind a jar of cotton balls and a box of tissues that was tucked in one of those porcelain holders that usually only were found in high-end hotels. She inched the container ever so slightly to read the prescription label, but instead of finding some antibiotics or clandestine painkillers, it was simply carbonyl iron for the treatment of anemia. Next to it, however, was a row of all sorts of other vitamins lined up like neat little soldiers, each one with the expiration date inked on a tiny label with disturbingly neat handwriting.

"So, he's a health nut," she said.

She finally noticed that her borrowed T-shirt had a faded row of letters on it. She smiled at the peeling edges of the U in UCLA and the slight tear along the lower hem. The bright blue and gold shorts looked a bit crinkly and worse for wear as well. "I'm done," she shouted.

"Just leave the laundry on the floor. I'll get it once I'm done."

She found another bottle of water waiting for her on the desk, complete with a coaster and a plate of all sorts of neatly chopped-up fruit. Ren waited patiently for her to clear the door, then disappeared into the bathroom with his ninja speed and silence.

"How does he do it?" she sighed as she settled at the one little table in the room—a two-seat bar in front of his lone window. Her purse and phone had somehow made their way to the table as well, further reinforcing his ninja aura. Before she could really ponder it all, the serene calm of his room was interrupted by a phone vibrating violently on the desk, followed by a second buzz from another phone stashed next to the TV.

She counted the sheer number of electronic devices tucked neatly around the room. Eventually she found a third phone, a tablet charging on the nightstand, and a pair of computers under the desk linked to three rather large monitors—each flashing with "Hit CTRL-ALT-DELETE to Unlock."

"This guy has to disconnect," she sighed.

Before she could poke around too much more, the bathroom door swung open, and a freshly scrubbed Ren came sauntering out in a pressed pair of trousers and a sparkling white T-shirt. His hair was still damp but neatly combed, and his skin positively glowed red from the shower.

"Love the sleeves," she said.

Every inch of his left arm from his wrist to the edge of the shirt looked as if it had been flayed open to reveal wires and sprockets. She noted the pink dots, particularly farther down, and faint traces of adhesive on his wrist.

"My master said it was too obvious," Ren said. "But I wanted a change."

He turned to show off his less-decorated right arm. She tried to make sense of the feathers trailing to his elbow. She peeked back over at the left and saw feathers mixing in with that ink as well.

"My roommate—well, my former roommate—has wings tattooed on her back. Did you do the same?"

"Wouldn't you like to know?" he asked as he grabbed phone number one and flicked through messages.

"Well, yeah, I want to know, that's why I asked," she said.

"Mysteries are meant to be savored, Georgia," he said, still only half paying attention. "*Kuso!*" he snapped, and he darted over to phone number two. "Just give me a minute."

She watched him burst into a flurry of activity, unlocking each screen while he pressed a phone to his ear. She heard him speak something in Chinese into one phone before grabbing the next and sounding completely different in the following conversation. Finally he finished with something hushed and possibly German before turning back to a screen and sending an e-mail or ten.

"Look, if you're busy, I can head out. We can have breakfast some other time—" she started.

"No!" he said surprisingly quickly. "I just need to upload a birth certificate for the third time, and I have to cross-check a few references. Then we can go out. We've earned it after all the manual labor. Ugh, who would have thought that the Cleveland Hall of Records would have decent security?"

"I have never seen you this stressed," she said before popping a grape in her mouth. "It's kind of refreshing."

"There is this one employee who is impossible to crack. She refuses to open any e-mail attachments, and all her machines are so old I can't get in there. I have to arrange a physical drop, and that's just a sink of time and money. I think I've finally got it going, but now I'm trying to finalize the details. Now, I just need a few more photos . . ." He trailed off and stared right at her chest.

"Yes?" she said, putting her hands on her hips.

"Do you mind if I take a picture of your jaw through your chest?" he asked.

"My jaw through my chest? What is this, vampire porn?"

"I promise I'll show you the results. It's just that you have a similar skin tone, and I think I can use it for a selfie."

Georgia just grabbed one of his phones, popped it over to the camera mode, and turned it around. She bent over ever so slightly and got a good shot of her chest. She then adjusted the camera and pouted cheesily for the camera. "This one is a bonus just for you," she said, then snapped another picture.

He reached for the phone. "I could have taken it."

"Then it wouldn't be a selfie, would it?" she teased. "Look, after everything Mr. Lambley has asked me to do, a boob shot is really nothing of note."

She watched him upload the pic and mix it with a few others on some sort of social media page. In a manner of minutes, he changed the background and shaded her jaw ever so slightly to tweak the shape. He then mixed it with pictures of the French Quarter and some dude doing a kegstand.

"She's supposed to have gotten back from spring break recently. It would look odd to not have pictures," he muttered.

"Who?"

"Hanna Broadbeck, well, Hanna Broadbeck von Jaeger now. She needs a new identity here in the states."

"A vampire from Cleveland?" she asked with a raised brow.

"Born in Cleveland to German immigrant parents. She's just settling into Cincinnati and needs a full identity—birth certificate, driver's license, passport, the works. She's been to school at UCLA, which is easy enough for me to fake, and is a bit of a party girl. I have a couple of tickets to Cancun and New Orleans, as well as a record of a brief stay in rehab on Daddy's dime. It's the perfect setup for someone destined to live fast and die young," Ren said as he continued to type away.

"So, this is what you do?" she asked. "Wow, you have dental records and everything. Is that a copy of a library card? Who goes to the library anymore now that we have the Internet?"

Ren eased back in his chair as a new e-mail popped on-screen. He burst into a huge smile. "Yes!" he cheered. "I finally got the fax in there and filed. Hanna was born in 1995, and her original birth certificate was lost in a small recordkeeping glitch last month. The new copy was just sent over from the archive to put her in the system after it was discovered. It was all terribly awkward, but you know civil servants, they'd hate to be accused of incompetence after nearly a decade of service. One of the clerks I bought off just sent me the confirmation. Little does she know that she's done this two times before."

"Oh my god, you bribe government employees and then have your vampire boss cover it up? That's so terrible it's kinda awesome."

"I only use it as a last resort. Once she had to forget seeing a corpse get up, and the other time I needed a marriage certificate refiled for an Azarola. My master buys her dinner and everything. It's all very discreet and civilized."

"How many people do you do this to?"

"A few dozen, and that's only when we have to establish a new identity in the United States. Hanna was our first job in a while, and she's easy since she's on her first modern life. Some of the older ones are a nightmare to process."

"You do so much," she said appreciatively as she eyed the number of screens dedicated to social media.

"You just have to plant the seeds, and the Internet takes care of the rest. If you send out enough friend requests, someone always bites. After all, most people feel bad saying no when you want them to like you. Everyone wants lots of friends even if they don't know them—especially if there are pictures of boobs and booze. It's like when you go to a party and someone says hi and starts talking as if they know you. Even if you have no clue who they are, you'll play along to avoid looking like an ass."

"I don't," she said.

"I think we've already established that you are a unique little snow-flake now, Georgia," he said. He pulled up a few more screens to send out invitations to play little games or join alumni groups. "You see? I use the same principle when I create an identity. Any criminal with a decent printer and the right tools can make a fake ID; the art is getting that ID into the system once. At that point it feeds on the mountain of documents and paperwork you need to survive in society. Once you have a social security number, it snowballs. I even have Hanna's credit report going. She's been late on a car payment—that's going to sting."

"You make your clients deadbeats? Wouldn't all vampires want to be rich and powerful?" she asked.

"The world is too transparent for that anymore. If you look like you have too much, you become a target, and if you look too perfect on paper, you come into question. I've found that parking tickets work really well to help establish an identity. You don't want anything criminal, but a few annoying charges help you look human. Hanna requested a few years of fun, so I'm setting her up to look like Daddy's little estranged princess. That should give her the tools to lure a few accomplices and some easy food."

"Also known as people," she chimed in.

It was Ren's turn to roll his eyes. "You can't have it both ways, Georgia. You do serve a vampire."

"A vampire who eats rats and chickens," she corrected. "I guess I haven't gotten a taste of the criminal life like you. I mean, damn, you must have been popular at college if you can make such great IDs."

"My family takes pride in our service," he said, returning more to his subdued robotic voice. "I am very good at what I do. Our motto is that it takes a human nine months to create a life. We can do it in only four."

"Four months?"

"That's our promise. We can have a new identity established and any old ones removed in four months or less."

"Or the next one is free?" she asked.

Ren's eyes clouded over for a second. "In the old days if we failed, it was expected for the responsible family member to take his or her life. What can I say? We are terribly Japanese."

"Oh my god—"

Ren relaxed a little and locked the screens. "Luckily we don't fail. I can perform miracles in four months—life and death so to speak. It's gotten easier and harder at the same time with the amount of crap I have to produce online, but on the flip side, I can use one identity to generate another even more rapidly than ever, and I simply love the advances in photo-manipulating software. You should see what I was able to do with some splicing and filters." He pulled open a drawer and plopped a Texas license on the desk with a shockingly familiar face with big brown eyes and floppy brown hair.

"That's . . . how did you get a picture of—?" she stammered.

"It's a mix of a few photos of a young aspiring actor who is a distant grandnephew of my master. He went to a makeup test—supposedly for a razor commercial—but never got a callback," Ren said with a sly smile. "I think it's almost impossible to tell the difference and certainly not at a quick glance."

"Stefano goes by Steven Drake?" she asked as she read the license. "And according to this, he's pushing forty now."

"It's an older ID. He was lucky that I had such a close match. Getting doubles for others can be a nightmare."

"And you do this for any vampire that asks?" she asked. "Wow, Steve is a Republican and an organ donor according to this."

"My family does. I've done a few, and I help out whenever it's for the family. Outside of the Jaegers, any vampire has to pay extravagantly to use our service."

"Quite the family business," she said. Ren replied by pulling out a few more IDs, these with his face. She picked up the first one and giggled. "So, you're a doctor?"

"Research pathologist actually," he corrected. "Dr. Yoshida is one I use when I have to transport fluids. He's even published. I did a paper on staphylococcal pneumonia and had to present at a conference in Orlando once. I think I did a little too well on that one."

"So, you do humans too?" she said. She picked up another ID and asked, "Can I call you Jacob Imahara?"

"You wouldn't like him, he's a thug," Ren warned.

She continued to peruse the small pile of personal identification. "I've never seen a Korean passport before," she mused. Before she could pick up one green book with Republic of China on it, he snatched it back and tossed it in the drawer.

"You'll excuse me if I keep a few secrets. I want to make sure I don't compromise too much client confidentiality, and unlike most other visitors, I can't be one hundred percent certain that—"

"That I'll forget this ever happened?"

"Exactly."

"Come on, you crazy criminal, let's go get breakfast before I've really seen too much . . ."

"So why four months?" Gail asked. "Why not ninety days or something like that?"

Georgia shrugged. "They seem to be able to always get it done. There are four laws, so it makes sense with vampire logic, but I don't really know for sure. My one theory is that it's somehow auspicious. Four is the number of death in Japan, and the Matsuoka family is terribly Japanese in all things, and vampires are all backward with the whole death-life thing."

Gail simply answered with a "hmm" noise. She then returned to the hunt and pointed to Georgia's rather glitzy ring. "So? Am I going to get any of the real dirt?" she asked.

Georgia hopped up to her feet and stretched a little. "Hang on, sweetie, just have to take one call."

Gail bounced on the sofa as she watched her interviewer once more creep to the back to have a conversation. This time her normally calm face became animated, and Gail could clearly make out a few four-letter words before Georgia turned to face the wall. Meanwhile the blonde at the bar drifted across the room and watched the little human from her new perch. Finally the staring became too much, and Gail asked, "Can I help you?"

The vampire laughed surprisingly loudly. "No, you're here to see if you can help zee helpless one," she said in a slurry German accent. "Too funny, you are."

"You're Minerva, right? Stefano's sister?" Gail dared to ask.

In a blink the blonde was parked firmly in Georgia's former seat. Gail jumped at the inconceivably close proximity of the inhuman creature. At the new distance, she could finally see just how alien Minerva's bloodshot eyes and skin really were, and as the vampire smiled, it was clear as day that she had long and lovely fangs sprouting from her insanely red gums.

"Yah, I am she," Minerva said as she continued to size up the relatively petite morsel on the sofa. "You keep wanting to know about *mein bruder* and zee little *Berliner* over there."

Gail kept staring until it occurred to her that the vampire was staring at her staring, and she abruptly looked away. "Um, I—" she stammered.

"You should ask her about zee hot tub. I think that was their favorite spot," Minerva said with another wicked giggle. "Oh! Did I do zee spoilers?

Gail's eyes lit up. Minerva took the opportunity to lean in closer and say ever so softly, "Oh, there is nothing like *schtupping* a vampire, dearie. Why do you think your kind writes so much about it? You want to know more, neh?"

Gail looked over her shoulder to make certain that Georgia was still in her conversation before nodding enthusiastically. "So she and Stefano—?"

"What do you think? *Mein bruder* might not be the best-looking of our kind, but he is still Jaeger-born and we Jaegers make zee hunt exciting always."

"Not the best-looking?" Gail muttered.

"Well, he's not my type," Minerva corrected. "You need green eyes to ride this ride, so to speak."

"Oh," Gail said. "I guess we all have a certain type."

The blonde burst into her super villain-worthy laughter again. "Oh, you are so very cute!" she laughed. "You get shaky like those wee little dogs from Mexico when I get too close."

Gail noticed her leg trembling and quickly smoothed her skirt and took a deep breath. The vampire responded my leaning even closer. "I tell you, you have nothing at all to fear"—her ferociously bright red eyes narrowed, and her voice dropped to an especially guttural, conspiratorial tone—"from me."

"Should I be afraid of someone else?" Gail whispered.

The blonde looked over toward the door for just a second. She then slapped the terrified young lady on the knee. "You are too funny!" she cried.

The waiter took this moment to walk over and give the vampire a stern look. "Do we need to remind you, miss, that this is strictly a catered venue?" he asked.

Minerva clutched her hands to her chest and pouted. "Who am I to flaunt such rules?" she asked. "I ask permission to BYOB."

"Just reminding you that this young lady is a guest of the Pendragon tonight," he said. "That is all."

Minerva slid from the sofa to a chair across the table. "This better?" she asked haughtily. "You know that we Jaegers—"

"Oh, what did I miss?" Georgia asked as she walked back into the scene.

Minerva lounged back and shook her head in exasperation. "As always, if I take even zee slightest interest in any little thing, everyone gets so defensive," she snorted. "It's like 1944 all over again."

"Maybe your reputation just precedes you," Georgia sniffed. "You've never been known for your self-control."

"Look who's talking, *Berliner*," Minerva shot right back.

Gail kept looking back and forth as the two blondes stared each other down. Finally Minerva waved her hand dismissively as if to say, "carry on," to the humans. Georgia took a deep drink of her drink before she smiled again.

"Are you German?" Gail finally asked.

Georgia giggled. "No—" She and the vampire both started to laugh as it dawned on them that Gail had made the same mistake as the thirty-fifth US president. "She's comparing me to a jelly doughnut because, after all, what are we to a vampire but sweet treats filled with red goo?"

Gail's eyes grew even wider. Georgia didn't make her suffer long.

"I'm sure she was telling you how I was her brother's girlfriend for a while, a brief while," Georgia sighed.

"You're a human. It's always brief," Minerva added.

"Don't you have anywhere else you need to be?" Georgia asked.

"Oh, I think it's about to get very interesting right here. I always wanted to know. When did you stop rejecting *mein bruder* and start letting him in?" Minerva asked.

"It all started when we began movie night, if you must know. You haven't lived, Gail, until you watch a vampire movie with actual vampires."

"Really?" she asked.

"Oh, we watched a bunch—everything from the classic *Nosferatu* and *Dracula* to modern-day romances and a few gems of comedy from the eighties, but the night that changed it all was when Ren dared to bring in the collection from the nineties . . ."

"Well, that was utter shit," Stefano said flatly as he stared at the credits rolling down the screen. "You've actually had this in our collection, Matsuoka?"

"Why does that Eastern European trash get all this attention?" Geoffrey asked. He quickly stood and sniffed. "Excuse me, but I need some air," he said before tromping toward the terrace outside Stefano's penthouse.

Georgia was busy leaning over to Ren and pointing at the other vampire's hair, which had totally absorbed every bit of static from the sofa. Georgia hopped from her half of the loveseat and tried to shape the wild tangle of curls into humps.

"What do you think, Ren? Think he could pull off the butt hair?" she asked.

Ren looked away for a second but managed to settle back into his robot face before his master could face him. "I don't think the look would suit anyone," he said diplomatically. "Can I get either of you any more refreshments?" the servant asked.

"So, you're sure you can't turn into mist or a bat or anything like that?" Georgia asked. Somehow Stefano's arm had ended up wrapped around her waist, but for once she didn't yank it off.

"No, but that Tepes bastard can't either," Stefano sighed. "It's all his miasma, you know. It's particularly hallucinogenic."

"So he's just a stinky, old Eastern European dictator then?" Georgia asked, still staying next to the vampire. The warm summer night and lack of working AC made the normally clammy companion a pleasant relief to lean against, and Georgia quickly found herself inclined against his chest and listening to the strange whooshing sound that replaced a vampiric heartbeat.

"Stinky!" Stefano said. "I think I shall call him that next time we meet. He is rather fragrant."

"So nothing in that movie was correct?" she asked seriously. "I feel so shocked that Hollywood has lied to me."

Stefano laughed. The sound echoed pleasantly in Georgia's ears.

"Well, they did show his obsession with a certain vampire strumpet in all its glory," Stefano said. "I'm sure Gingersnaps will be sulking for a week or more."

"Lucy?" Georgia asked. "Wait a second . . . Mina Harker—"

"Mina Harker . . . Mina Thakkar," Stefano said in a little singsong voice. "The nineteenth-century Brits certainly wouldn't have a character from their backwater colony as a heroine now, would they? She likes to flaunt their little affair as publicly as possible."

"No wonder he's so upset," she said, looking toward the door.

"Oh it's old news, sweetheart. He's had to put up with all this Dracula nonsense for over a century. His mother's gift is inspiration, and you can always see where she's worked her way in."

"Just give me a minute," she said as she walked to the door. "Hey, Ren, I think Mr. Lambley and I will take another round. Just give us a few."

Stefano's eyes darkened a little as Georgia walked away yet again, but he remained dutifully on the couch, watching her walk out the door. She didn't have to walk far. Her boss was slumped in the first chair next to the hot tub, his hands tugging out what little wisps of bright orange hair were fighting to grow in his forehead.

"Hey," she said as she knelt next to him.

"I really hate that story," he said without looking up. "And I hate the way everyone talks about her sometimes. All the Jaegers, they like to call my mother many undignified names, and sometimes the way the story keeps getting told again and again—"

"Hey, do you want to tell me the real story?" she asked softly.

"My father is not the easiest man to get along with, I know," Geoffrey sniffed. "He constantly has to keep the family in line and deal with the stigma of being what our kind considers a bastard. Pardon my language, Georgia."

She took a turn ruffling his hair. "I think I can take it. So, vampires have bastards?" she prodded.

"The clan founder was dying, killed by his own traitorous son. That much of the human Arthur legend is true. He had no choice but to call out to any of the kind who could hear, and he had to bite a dying soldier on the battlefield, an Irish mercenary who fought on the side of the king. The other vampire was a commoner who, mercifully, happened to not be sterile. Lorcan was born on that battlefield and had to rise up and lead, with no help or support for centuries. It was only when he got the backing of the East and my mother joined forces with him that the Pendragon clan rose to power. It was a political marriage, I know, but I had always hoped somehow . . ." He trailed off to watch the moonlight and the lights from neighboring buildings dance across the bubbling water. The scent of chlorine mixed with the night breeze.

"So your mom basically is giving your dad the finger by encouraging all this Dracula love story. That's really not right," Georgia said.

"Her idea has worked though," Geoffrey sighed. He finally looked at his assistant. "The plan was called Hiding in Plain Sight. She said that by making vampires part of human mythology, we could better hide among you. By encouraging your kind to idolize us, it would make it easier to blend in."

"So we think vampires are fiction," she agreed.

"And you imitate us, so anytime your kind sees one of us—"

"We just think it's a crazy emo kid of a fetish thing," Georgia finished. "Well, I just want to know where the sparkling came from."

"The human imagination knows no limits," Geoffrey said weakly. "You know that my poor brother has been sent a tub of body glitter every deathday for the past three years? It doesn't always get to me, but just sometimes I feel as if flames are going to shoot from my eyes and ears whenever I think of that—"

"Trampsylvanian bastard?" Georgia offered.

Mr. Lambley smiled. "That is rather apropos," he said. "Thank you for coming out here to listen to me simper like a fool."

"Well, I just lost two hours of my life to watch your mom run off with another man and see Keanu Reeves try to do an English accent. I'm honestly not sure which was more disturbing," Georgia said.

The vampire took a moment to chew on his lip. "At least it wasn't Dick Van Dyke trying to be a cockney," Geoffrey said. "Why must that have happened?"

"I'm still sorry I picked that one. I wanted Disney—sue me!"

"I'm certain that Stefano will want us to return," Mr. Lambley said. "And I'm sure you would prefer his company to that of an old sad sack."

"First off, it's about ten degrees cooler out here, so I'm OK with being outside. Second, you're both old to me. It's that funny little thing about vampires. Last, but certainly not least, I work for you, Mr. Lambley. If I can't look out for you first, what good am I?"

Mr. Lambley rubbed the back of her hand. "You are too good to me."

"Let's invite the boys out here, and next week, you pick the movie."

The party ended up moving outside, with cold beer and warmed blood sloshing in big mugs as the stereo was piped onto the deck. Mr. Lambley ended up swaying to some mellow jazz, while Georgia and Stefano ended up lounging side by side on a pile of beach towels. Ren stayed in his corner, sipping his drink and staying half-absorbed with his phone and monitoring the levels of others' beverages.

"Is he OK?" Stefano asked.

"How would you like it if everywhere you looked, you saw your mom running off with another guy?"

"My mother is a raving psychotic."

"Oh."

"Geoffrey whines and cries over Dracula, but that's just a silly sentiment he needs to get over. Look at my folks. When they say that Claudia is a Nazi, it's not just an expression. It means that she actually fought for the Nazi Party. My parents were chosen for breeding purposes, and then she was right back to being the clan founder's number two dame. He's a Pendragon, for Christ's sake. Their entire family line started with one of the greatest stories of adultery in human history."

"You really feel no sympathy for your friend?"

"Sympathy is like fashion, it gets old after a decade or two. You're new, sweetheart, eventually you'll get sick of it too."

"Well, I can think of one thing I'm already getting sick of," she snarled as she rolled to have her back to him. She pulled out her phone. After she spent a few minutes pointedly checking texts and messages, Stefano finally rolled back her shoulders.

"Look, I'm sorry if I'm a little tired of it, but I'll try to do better. You make me try to do better," he confessed. "Let's go out tomorrow. I'm sure I can plan something fabulous—"

Georgia sat up and put her back to him again. "Don't do that," she sighed.

"We can get dinner anywhere you want, or Ren can arrange something here with candles and—"

"Please, you don't have to do that, Steve," she said, rolling her eyes.

"A show? Box seats at Fenway—"

Georgia finally turned to him and took his hand. She looked him squarely in the eyes and tried not to be too drawn in by the puppyish earnestness. Ren took the opportunity to discreetly escort Mr. Lambley inside with promises of Pictionary and a special milkshake.

"I will give you a moment to last a lifetime if you just let me," Stefano pleaded. "I have the means to treat you like you deserve."

Georgia took a deep breath. "Look, Stefano, it's not that I don't like the flowers or the chocolates or the being whisked away to Manhattan—"

"And all this," he said, waving his hands toward the stunning view of the rooftops of downtown Boston. "I will share all of this with you if you just let me."

Georgia squeezed his hands. "I really don't know how to say this—"

He interrupted her by grabbing her roughly and kissing her on the lips. The fresh rush of warm blood mixed with the warm night air had changed him from totally unappealing and clammy to just slightly cool, but she still jerked away from his metallic breath and prominent fangs.

"Hey!" she snapped as she leaped to her feet. "It's not going to happen."

"Wait—why?" he asked. "Don't you see, I . . . I—"

"If the next word out of your lips is 'love,' I'm jumping off the roof," Georgia snapped.

"What if it is?" he taunted. "You're the only—"

"I get it. I'm the only person you've met who can kiss you without forgetting, but, news flash, being the only option doesn't exactly make you feel wanted. It makes me feel like I'm some consolation prize."

"But—" he started.

"Just stop!" she snapped. "You talk about giving me the moments to last a lifetime, but that's not how it works. Love isn't based on moments and money and perfect settings. Love is what happens when you can be boring and just do nothing together." Georgia sighed. "I know you keep trying to find out what I like and you do everything you can to impress me, but that doesn't make *me* want to be with you. I'm only here because it's part of my job, and that's it."

He jumped to his feet and reached for her, but managed to contain himself after the previous outburst. Against the night sky, his features looked particularly striking, with his deep, dark eyes absorbing the lights and his cheeks and jaw chiseled by his movie-star perfect stubble.

"Your job," he finally choked out.

Georgia let her own face soften, and she took his hand again. "Look, Stefano, I know you aren't human, but you once were, even if you don't really remember it. I owe it to you, and to that human you once were, to be honest," she said. "I appreciate all you've tried to do, but it's never going to be anything more than me working for your friend. I don't want to lead you on. OK, Stefano?"

He said nothing. Finally the weight of his stare became too much, and she turned to head for the door.

"It's Steve," he said, his voice suddenly perfectly clear, understandable, and stripped of anything other than a distinctly American twang.

"What did you say?" she asked softly as she turned back to face him again.

"My name . . . it's Steve."

"You're totally American," she said. "I knew that accent was terrible, but I assumed it was a vampire thing."

"I was born in Queens, raised in Italian Harlem," Stefano confessed.

"So what's with the Eurotrash facade?" Georgia asked before shaking her head. "You know what? What does it even matter? I'm going to get Mr. Lambley—"

He pulled her back again, and this time she ended up toppling against his chest. He helped her right herself but refused to let her go.

"Can you please just give me a chance?" he asked, still sticking to the much more natural-sounding American accent. "I have to tell someone, and you are the only person that I can tell that really matters."

"What?"

"I've confessed the truth over and over, but I always chicken out at the end and make them forget. Even Gingersnaps doesn't know the whole truth, but he's probably closer than anyone other than my parents. I want to just say it once and have to live with the consequences. I'm sick of being a coward."

Georgia yanked free but wandered back to their former perch by the hot tub. She settled down on the mound of towels and patted the indentation next to her. "OK, Steve, talk," she said. "Tell me your story."

She raised a brow, as the first thing he did was start unbuttoning his shirt. He stopped, though, at his plain white undershirt and turned to the side to show off a distinctive pattern of round scars on his arm.

"Bullet holes," Georgia said.

"I'm sure you know by now that my kind doesn't scar."

"So you're younger than guns. That only narrows it down by a few centuries."

He then slipped his hand under his shirt and pulled out a jingling string of dog tags. He dropped them right on her lap before settling down next to her and waited for her to pick up and read, "DeMarco, Steven J.," along with his serial number and an address in New York City. The metal was weathered and highlighted by that certain dark staining that only seemed to plague metal that was left unpolished for decades. She ran her finger over the punched-out letters, stopping at the second name on the tag—Ann Marie DeMarco.

230 R E C A R R

"I listed my mom as next of kin," Steve said. "Dad was a traveling salesman, and I never thought they would be able to track him down. I guess I should thank him though. His mistress in California provided me with one hell of a look-alike grandnephew."

She counted back the generations in her head. "So that war you went off to—"

"The war to end all wars—*part two*," Steve sighed. "One grandmother was a German Jew, and Papa was fresh-off-the-boat Italian. Our whole lives my sisters and I were forced to learn a mishmash of both languages and English just to get by. You can imagine how useful the army found a guy that could speak four languages. I picked up French in school to try and get a girl, you see."

"Did it work?"

"*Oui*," he said with a little grin. "You know, I think she's the last dame who even remembered my name before you came along. Look, I'll spare you the nitty-gritty, but let's just say I was assigned to a unit whose job was to go ahead and meet the local troublemakers and give them encouragement, and sometimes weapons. I was the mouth of the group—go figure—and I had made it through my entire tour of duty without ever having to pull the trigger. It became a running gag in my unit. I had two best friends there, both of them crack shots. Leibowitz was a sniper as a hobby, or so he said. He did most of the shooting for us, and Chandler was a good ole boy from Texas. The medic, Stanley Smith, and I were supposed to keep our hands clean according to them, but I think part of them just liked to do all the dirty work. The four of us all became thick as thieves after a while, even as we got farther and farther into the blasted-out hellhole that took the place of France for a few years in the forties. I would have done anything for those guys . . ."

Stefano started chewing on his lip, his fangs glistening in the moonlight. His eyes had drifted off to some faraway place, while his fingertips tugged and toyed with the edge of one of the towels. Finally Georgia dared to rest her fingers gently on top of his and leaned a little bit closer.

"You seem to remember it so well," she said.

"When I close my eyes, I still see their faces. It's like it was yesterday," he said. "We had been a lot luckier than most guys in the war. We seemed to have an almost unnatural ability to avoid getting caught, until one night we ran into a group of totally spooked refugees from Alsace. I thought they were just shell-shocked. There was a father and daughter. The girl couldn't have been more than fourteen, and she kept going on and on about the German monster who killed her mother. We asked around and heard rumors of a Nazi death squad that stole women in the night. I mean at that time in France, the Germans were accused of everything short of eating babies, but there was something about these two that seemed different. They had me question them, but they didn't make any sense. Her father couldn't remember anything really. He heard his wife scream and then found her dead the next day. The little girl, though, said something about a red demon that drank blood and left her mother drained dry. None of the other guys took her seriously. *I* didn't take her seriously."

He fumbled for the remains of his beverage and groaned as it turned out to be nothing more than crusty remains in the bottom of the tankard. As he looked at the red streaks, the lip quiver returned for a moment before he could continue.

"Our CO had gotten cocky. After all, we were the unit that couldn't be touched. He wanted to find out what sort of scary freak show the Nazis were running around this village, especially after we found a bunch of desiccated cattle on the edge of town. Leibowitz thought he spotted a group of enemy soldiers holing up in an abandoned brewery just east of town, so even though we didn't have any hope of backup, we were ordered to check it out."

"This doesn't sound like it ended well," Georgia interjected.

Steve shook his head. "You mean you didn't see the movie about the brave team of soldiers who single-handedly stamped out a Nazi death squad and ended the war?" he snorted. "He hadn't made it within half a click of the brewery when the first shots were fired. Leibowitz managed to peg one before he was hit, but the rest of us were mowed down in seconds. The funny thing was, for a death squad, these Nazis were remarkably bad shots. All of us took hits to legs or arms and were clocked upside the head rather than blown to bits.

"So, yeah, I woke up that last place I expected to after an encounter with a death squad—in a bed with a blonde tending to my wounds. This nurse was the prettiest gal I'd ever seen, a prime specimen of the blonde-haired ice princess that exemplified the Aryan ideal. My bullet holes had been sewn up, and I had even gotten a shot of the good stuff, so there was a moment there where I was convinced that I had died and gone to heaven. Then I looked over and saw all of us strapped in the beds in a neat little row—everyone but Leibowitz.

"I heard them talking in the background. It was muffled, but I knew they wanted to examine us, like we were some kind of experiment. A few hours later, I saw them drag in our sniper and dump him in the one empty bed. He looked like death warmed over and was covered in bruises. They took Stanley next—poor bastard. One by one we were dragged into the next room until I was the only one left. We were a recon unit. I had been told the theory of what to do when tortured, but honestly, all the theory in the world means nothing when you're sweating and bleeding deep inside contested territory. Still, I was so young and stupid that I didn't know any better. I made up my mind to fight even when it was my turn to be dragged into a tiny little room in the basement. I think it used to be a distillery or something because there were all these pipes and barrels still in there and the whole place smelled like a dive bar.

"I'm dragged in and dumped in a chair. They don't strap me down. They actually chained me to the floor. All I can see are streaks of blood and god knows what other fluids running from the base of the chair to a door in the back, and there is this tall, pale man in a black trench coat with eyes so blue that they couldn't be real.

"He starts by testing my German, talking to his friends about the Americans they've captured. At first I tried not to show that I knew exactly what he was saying, but when he mentioned cutting off Stanley's finger, I flinched. He asks me all these questions about who I am and who my parents are, but I only respond with various versions of fuck you. Finally, he has these two goons give me a solid once-over. Never let it be said that the Germans don't know how to throw a punch.

"I dunno, I just got into this stubborn mode, where I found it easier not to talk, no matter how *persuasive* my interrogators became. I knew I was dead meat, so I wanted them to really have to put in some real effort before I was done. After a while I was dragged back to my bed, and once more it was the sweet little princess and her painkillers. This went around and around for a good day or two with no food and only a bit of water to keep me from dying. I heard some cries and screams for the first few hours, then . . . nothing. I figured everyone else had been taken care of, so when they grabbed me again, I just said a little prayer and hoped there would be enough to send something home to my mama."

"But you didn't die," Georgia started. "Well, I mean you didn't stay dead."

"This time when I went in the room, there was another soldier, a much more petite one, who was practically bursting out of her SS uniform. She was like the pinup girl for Adolf's Angels—a spitfire with flaming red hair and lipstick to match. I remember seeing my reflection in her thigh-high boots. I'd never seen leather polished so well. But as cute as she was, something in the pit of my stomach told me to run, to fight to do any-thing in my power to get out of that room. I knew, somehow, that I was in greater danger than I had ever been before in my life."

"Claudia," Georgia whispered.

Steve nodded again. "Claudia von Jaeger had worked her way into the regime. She agreed with their ideals of racial purity and loved having a job where no one seemed to be disturbed by her habit of torturing and killing. She had staffed her team with commoners from across the Third Reich and formed a tight-knit vampire crew to do all manner of wet work for the Nazis."

"Nazi vampires?"

"Oh, you knew they had to be there. Every war has been a good time for our kind. You can get away with so much on the battlefield that can simply be explained away as soldier's trauma, and with so many people dying, who is really going to notice a little missing blood? The problem with this war was that it was spreading from your kind into ours, and several of the families weren't too keen on the Jaegers so openly siding with a human power. It had been nearly a millennium since vampires had tried to go legit and join with a human government, and you can ask Gingersnaps how well that turned out for his grandpa. Claudia may be stubborn, but she's not stupid, and she could already see where the wind was blowing once the boats landed in Normandy."

"Vampires fought in World War II," Georgia said incredulously.

"To be fair, millions of humans fought in World War II, while only a handful of vampires joined in openly. This was nearing the end of 1944, and Lorcan Darcy and his whole family were getting dangerously close to signing a treaty with the Jiangshi and the Azarola to petition to have the entire Jaeger clan exiled, just like the Lungs. No matter how powerful the Jaeger might be, no sane clan would want to be pinched between all the progressive families and the Lung."

"No, that doesn't sound good at all," Georgia said.

"But I didn't know this. I just knew that there was this terrifying creature in the room—something completely inhuman but dressed up like one. She knew I was afraid too. She kept circling me like a vulture until I dared to blink. Next thing I knew, she was in my lap with my wrist in her mouth. I remember crying out, as I could actually feel her sucking the life out of me, but it was only for a second. I blinked again, and she was across the room whispering to the scary man in the coat. All I can remember is them arguing over and over again if I would work, if I would be enough of a symbol.

"You see, I was a good old American boy with—gasp—Jewish roots. What could be a better symbol to show that the Jaegers could change their ways than by welcoming a US mongrel into their ranks and scoffing entirely at the führer's ideals?

"We thought we were hunting them all those weeks in France, but as it turns out, the Jaegers were the ones stalking us. She whispered my name. She knew my favorite color, my brand of cigarettes, and even the name of my first girl—Jeanette. I thought they were going to ask me for troop movements or codes, but instead she asked if I'd ever killed a man. I finally admitted that to her. I was a pretty piss-poor soldier. I mean, my job was translating and getting us cognac half the time. I'd never taken anything I'd done too seriously until then. It was always the other guy's turn to be the hero, that is, until that night—" He stopped again to fidget.

"Go on," Georgia said.

"They dumped us in the basement, all of us pretty beaten and broken. Claudia paced in front of us all, taunting that we were all dead men and that we just didn't know it. She said she had one offer, if there was anyone with the balls to take it. The offer was simple: if one of us would volunteer to be tortured to death, then she would not kill the others. Of course this was in German, so I was the only one who understood it perfectly. The others got bits and pieces, but I heard it loud and clear. For once in my life, I was going to be the hero, so I raised my hand.

"'A promise is a promise,' she swore to me," Steve snorted. "I let her drag me into that little room, while the rest of the boys were taken upstairs to recover. I think you can guess what the manner of my death was."

"You gave your life up for your friends?" Georgia asked.

The vampire closed his eyes. "Claudia kept her promise, yes, but Steve DeMarco had to die that day. I could never go back home and ended up spending time in England and then America with Geoffrey to try and improve relations. My whole existence is nothing more than one big PR stunt, you see. I had to wait until all my war buddies were long gone before I could come back to the East Coast."

"And you don't tell the truth now, why?" Georgia asked.

"The Jaegers are an old-school family, a conservative family. To them what happens after you die is the important part. Being human should have nothing to do with what you are. To admit that they chose a human to appease the progressives is nothing more than an admission of defeat in some vampires' eyes. I'm just a necessary evil, and the further I get away from that truth, the happier my family will be. Don't you see? The fact that I even remember my old life makes me a lesser being in their estimation. Most vampires can only barely recall being human. It's just like a daydream or some hazy early-childhood memory."

"That sounded pretty clear to me," Georgia said.

"Haven't you figured it out yet?" Steve asked. "Vampires exude poisons that make your head fuzzy. They make you forget. No one remembers getting turned into a vampire because the whole process should be too traumatic and they should be too drugged-up from the miasma to know what is happening, but every once in a while, there are special people, people who don't seem to be affected at all by mist—"

"You mean—?" Georgia asked.

"Yes, Georgia, I was just like you."

12

"What does that even mean?" Georgia asked as she lounged back on the sofa. Gail's eyes had grown into adorable little saucers, while the blonde vampire shook her head dismissively.

"It means that *mein bruder* is zee dramatic one in zee family," Minerva snorted. "It also means that he is a freak, like our lovely little *Berliner* here."

"It also puts a pretty big hole in the theory that we humans are nothing more than mindless suits you wear," Georgia snapped.

Minerva burst out laughing. "Oh, yah, yah, wee little Steffan proves all the Pendragons and their soft-sap ilk to be right and zee evil Nazi-*leiben* to be wrong," she said. "And there are freaky little ones of your kind that say they remember being Napoleon or Cleopatra. Those that choose to believe them, do, those that are sane do not. As a newborn, little Steffan vas obsessed with his human shell. He has quite zee imagination too."

"Oh of course, you would never believe him, would you, Minerva? You just sprang forth as a walking, talking, blow job-obsessed little princess, didn't you?" Georgia snapped.

"If you listened to one of our sane scientists, Dr. Schreiber perhaps, then you would know that this so-called human soul is no more than a set of chemicals imprinted on now unused tissues. It's no more than watching one of your videocassettes—" the vampire started.

"First off, the videocassette was a thing when I was in elementary school. Please, get with the century. Second, you're interrupting my interview, so if you wouldn't mind—?"

"Interview?" Minerva laughed. "Just get to zee good parts. I want to hear how *mein bruder* got in those wee wittle *höschen* of yours."

The other human furrowed her brow and cocked her head a little as she pondered exactly what the vampire had claimed. "Wait, if you're saying that there are still memories present in the brains of the humans you inhabit and you can recall them, doesn't that just make them your memories?" Gail finally asked.

"Hah! Does watching *Enter the Dragon* make you the heir to the Shaolin Temple?" Minerva snorted.

"Huh?" Gail asked.

This time Georgia stepped back into the ring. "Don't mind Minerva. She only watches kung fu flicks and porn, so her use of pop culture analogies is a little stunted," she sighed.

"That is because they are zee only films worth watching," Minerva said.

"Yes, I'm fairly certain that the whole trend of all vampires knowing martial arts was completely started by her," Georgia added. "The one time she came to movie night . . . wow, let's just say I learned how to disembowel a man using one finger and chop off a head with a hat."

"Oh, can I show her?" Minerva said, suddenly even giddier. "*Bitte!*"

"I guess it's time for party tricks of the undead," Georgia said before flagging over the waiter and asking, "Do you have anything wooden that you aren't too attached to back there?"

The waiter smiled slyly for a minute but refrained from any comment. He nodded and slipped off to the kitchen, while the blonde vampire continued to bounce in her seat. "Minerva is like the rest of her family, a lightweight after a bit of the drink," Georgia warned. "Do me a favor, sweetie, and grab that pillow and hold it to your chest."

Gail dutifully grabbed a cushion before the waiter came back with an empty fruit box tucked in a thick plastic bag. "For the lady," he said before setting it between the girls. Minerva eyed it carefully and took time to check that the plastic was wrapped completely around before daring to pick it up.

"Now you put this over zee pillow and hold it really tight, little one," Minerva said as she kicked off her heels and started dancing back and forth on the balls of her feet, Bruce Lee-style.

"OK," Gail said and stood up and gripped the box around the cushion. The vampire continued to dance and stared intently at her target before taking a deep breath and moving to less than an inch from the smaller, frailer human. Gail gulped as she was once more face-to-face with the stone-cold face of a vampire.

Suddenly Gale lurched as the box shattered, and she could feel an impact in the depths of her gut. Minerva remained in place, but Gail fell back and was only saved from a full topple by the waiting arms of Georgia Sutherland.

"Is that some vampire power?" Gail gasped as she dropped the bagful of shrapnel to the floor.

"It took me nearly twenty years, but I finally mastered a one-inch punch!" Minerva said. "Isn't it awesome? I love to show it off!"

"That's not all you like to show off, Minnie," Georgia cracked as the vampire shimmied her dress back down her thighs. "You know, one day you aren't going to know your own strength, and you'll end up with wood poisoning again."

Minerva blew Georgia a kiss. "I knew you cared about me, *Berliner*."

"It's not that I care about you, it's that I care about not having to deal with a sheriff's inquiry on a Friday night. It would be very messy to take care of a vampire body here, wouldn't it?" Georgia said as she kicked the remains of the crate under her seat. "Are you done with your little display, Buffy?"

Gail continued to furrow her brow. "That was really dangerous, wasn't it?" she finally asked.

"Oh, what is life without a little risk, *shatzi*?" Minerva said while pinching Miss Filipovic's cheek. "A wee bit of danger stimulates the blood, yah?"

"Twenty years, wow," Gail said.

"It always takes them longer to learn things," Georgia said. "Maybe that's why they have to live so long."

Minerva nodded emphatically as she returned to her seat. "That is sad but true. Zee only thing I envy you humans is how fast you can train your muscles to do what you want. We have to replay what we used to know and practice over and over again to make perfect, but once we do—" She punctuated her sentence by whipping off one of her earrings and hurling it at the humans. Gail jumped as the gold stud pierced the velvet less than an inch from her arm.

"Wow," Gail gasped.

"Stronger than us, faster than us, and tougher too," Georgia muttered. She plopped back on the sofa and tossed the earring back to the vampire. "Can we move on now?"

"That depends," Minerva said, "Are we going to get to hear anything good?"

Gail jumped in. "So, Stefano . . . err, Steve, he can actually remember being human?"

Minerva rolled her eyes. "We all see what we were, but *mein bruder* is just obsessed with his shell. It's because he is a baby still."

"So you remember being human?" Gail asked.

Minerva sighed deeply. "You see this body? It once belonged to a pretty little daughter of a village artist. Zee poor artist lost his wife to zee plague and his son to some noblemen's war, but he managed to keep two daughters around. He was the finest maker of colored glass in zee whole region, but the nobles liked to take from him more than they ever gave. Blah, blah, blah, poverty, suffering, so much sadness. Zee poor wittle family couldn't buy food one winter, so zee artist sold off one of his useless daughters to a fat, ugly, old, rich man because she was so pretty, with hair like gold. Well, long story short, some other humans decided that they wanted what zee artist's village had, and there was raping and pillaging and all zee normal old-time pleasures. Zee merchant didn't want this shell anymore after a dozen pillagers or so had had their way with her, so she was cast off like so much other garbage. Boohoo, rather than die, she made a deal with zee devil, and I have enjoyed my existence ever since. Zee end!"

"But what happened to the artist and his family?" Gail asked, wide-eyed.

Minerva shrugged. "Hell if I know. That was in the past—a place where far too many pathetic people choose to dwell. I am grateful for zee Fenstermacher *tochter* for being strong enough to give her life for me, but that is zee limit of my connection to your kind. You are amusing creatures and you help pass the time, but in zee end, I know you are ultimately one thing—food."

"If there is one virtue Minnie here exemplifies, it's honesty," Georgia said. "In fact, I'm sure the only person she's ever lied to is herself."

Minerva responded with a grin that could freeze hell over.

Gail quickly filled the silence with, "So, what happened after Stef . . . err, Steve confessed to you? Was it . . . were there—"

"I told him that I needed to take Mr. Lambley home, and I left him there in shock," Georgia said.

"No way!" Gail cried.

"It's true," Georgia said. "I left him hanging. What? Do you think we'd end up rolling around the terrace while Ren and Geoffrey were on the other side of a glass door?"

"I would," Minerva offered.

"Are you going to stay and be the peanut gallery for the rest of the night?" Georgia asked.

"Only if it gets interesting," the vampire said.

"Oh, Gail, if you like, I can tell you all about Mr. Lambley's schedule and the best cleaners for all the furniture," Georgia said with a wink.

Minerva gave an exaggerated roll of her eyes and stretched like a cat. Finally she folded her hands neatly and sat like an attentive little school-girl. "I promise to be good," she said sweetly.

"I don't care if you're bad or good, just be quiet!" Georgia said. "I hope you're not drinking anymore tonight. Seriously, do I need to make a call?"

Minerva shook her head. Georgia waited patiently to make certain that the giddy vampire was indeed keeping her promise to be quiet. Gail took over as the energetic one, practically bouncing in her seat as she waited for any further details.

"You sure you don't want to hear about the amazing dry cleaner in Brighton?" Georgia asked. She kept a straight face even as Gail's eyes practically fell out of their sockets. Georgia milked the suspense by taking a drink and checking her phone. After one more sly little look over her screen, she said, "Well, I did head back after tucking Mr. Lambley in. I mean, I had to know more . . ."

Georgia stood frozen in the pool of light from the streetlamp in front of the Intercontinental. The first rays of the August sun were threatening to poke over the buildings but weren't quite enough to flip off the nighttime sentinels. Every time she tried to move a foot closer, she shuffled back toward the curb until she finally gave up and started walking back toward downtown and civilization. She hadn't made it twenty feet down the street before the sight of a rat scurrying from a dumpster to a storm drain made her jump and turn right back around.

"Grow a spine, woman," she muttered. This time she made it within a foot of the door before wheeling back around. This time the door swung open to reveal a tall, slim figure in leather pants and a tight-fitting shirt.

He stared down at her bemusedly from under a perfectly untamed curl and smiled just enough to tease her with a fang. "Well, this is a surprise," Steve said.

"Where is Ren?"

"Cleaning up. He told me that someone was skulking by the door. I was hoping, but I didn't think it would really be you."

"Well, Mr. Lambley passed out early tonight. I think there was a bit too much brandy in his blood. I couldn't sleep so I thought—I dunno, I thought I'd finish the conversation."

"Did you and Gingersnaps have a good laugh at my expense? I am the Jaeger who thinks humans have souls, after all."

"What?" Georgia said. "No! We talked about Dracula in the movies and how he was an oily, home-wrecking sack of undead shit. I'm not really one to comment on existential vampire issues. All I want to know is why you think you're so much like me and to find out the rest of your story."

"Do you want to come in or talk out here by the dumpster?" Steve asked.

She let him lead her back up the stairs. She stared in wonder as he stepped effortlessly into an early-morning dust mote without so much as a flinch. Instead of going into his penthouse by the front door, he led her to a fire escape and pointed toward the roof. "I'm a sucker for a good sunrise. How about you?" he asked.

"This is so weird," she said as they climbed up to meet the sun. The bottles and towels had been dutifully cleaned, so Steve ended up perching on the edge of the hot tub to watch the light creep across the Boston skyline.

She watched the light play against his washed-out face and light up his dark eyes. The warmth of the early-morning glow gave some life to his features and highlighted his sharp jaw and the toned lines of his arms. When he was stripped of his suits and hair gel, Georgia could finally notice Steve's dimples and adorably girly eyelashes, as well as the overall smoothness in his quirky face.

"You were just a baby when you—"

"Died?" he finished. "Well, they say war is a young man's sport. I guess you finally see me as they see me. To them I'm just a baby too."

"Well, you aren't even one, right?" she asked.

Steve shook his head. "I'm getting there fast enough though. I've tried playing their games and being all that they expected me to be, but it hasn't worked yet."

"Here's a novel idea—just be yourself," Georgia offered as she finally sat beside him. Together they watched more of the warm light pour onto the decking.

"That's some solid advice. Did you get it from a fortune cookie?" he asked.

"Probably."

They sat in silence for a few minutes more. Finally Steve started to scratch the back of his hand and sigh at the faint red patches just showing up along his knuckles. Georgia reached in her purse and pulled out a tube of burn ointment.

"I've learned to carry this around," she said softly as she worked it into his joints. "We should probably go inside."

"I don't want to give in. It makes me feel so inhuman," he said softly.

"Well, news flash, you are a vampire," Georgia sighed. "Look, if you don't want to go in, I'll just get Ren. I'm sure he can convince you."

"All right, all right," he sighed.

As they slipped inside, a rather surprised-looking Japanese man nearly dropped the glass he was drying in the kitchen. "So it is a guest," he said. "Is there anything I need to prepare, master?" Ren asked.

"Just go to bed."

"As you wish," Ren said, but he didn't move as quickly as Georgia was used to. Instead, he stared at her for an agonizing few seconds before ducking out the door.

"Claudia picked me not just because I was a good old American Jew-boy, but because I somehow was immune to vampire's mist," he started again.

"I got that much already," she said.

"The mind protects itself from trauma. When a vampire is born, they forget the feelings of being human. They forget the pain of dying. Even the Pendragons don't remember their transition. They just remember waking up," Steve said. "The problem is that all that confusion, all that blissful amnesia, is triggered by the same sort of power that allows vampires to control humans. If you're immune in life, you are in death as well."

Georgia watched closely as his face turned even paler than usual and he sort of staggered until he could steady himself on the counter. As his eyes glazed over, the human drew closer to touch his arm and make sure he was still even conscious. Even the slightest touch made him jump.

"You remember—"

"It's a terrible thing to remember your own death, especially when it was slow and drawn-out and painful. I felt this thing growing inside of me, taking me over, and I remember begging for hours for the agony to end. I felt my last breath, and I remember just how weak it was, and how I was cold and alone. I—I'm sorry, there really aren't quite the right words to describe it."

"So you are like Mr. Sugar?"

"No, he's a stillborn. The vampire never killed him. I don't know how he can stand it. I just remember my human life ending and my vampire one beginning. My family thinks I have an overactive imagination, but I know I lived that life. I know I was once human. I'm sure it helps sell their whole claim that they've changed and become more accepting, but there are those in my family that just wish I could either learn their truth or disappear. I keep thinking that if I'd only been taken by the Pendragons that it somehow would have been different."

"And that's why you're so jealous of Mr. Lambley?" she asked.

"Well, that, and he gets to take you home every night."

"You do know that there is nothing like that between Mr. Lambley and me, right?" Georgia asked. "I'm home with him every night because I work there and that's my whole being-under-his-protection clause. You know, that thing that keeps me from being a late-night snack to other vampires?"

"But I see the way you look at him."

"Oh, come on—" Georgia started.

"No, nothing like that," Steve said quickly. "All I mean is that when you look at him, you aren't afraid."

"He's my boss, and he only tried to attack me once or twice, and he has no fangs to bite me even if he did lose control again. I have to take care of him! You really can't be afraid of someone who needs you that much."

"I just wanted you to know why I could never attack you. I know you have the same curse I did. No matter how much I would want to, I know that if I hurt you, I can never take it away."

"That's the problem, Steve. Don't you get it? In life there shouldn't be a happy magic eraser to make your problems go away. You need to learn that your actions have consequences and do them right the first time, or just learn from your mistakes and make them better. You've had it so easy up until now."

"Easy?" he snapped. "I've been stuck with memories that nobody should have, and if you think I want to just magically erase all my problems, well, I—maybe I used to, but it gets old really fast when you can't be with someone without them forgetting you. Maybe you despise me, sweetheart, but at least it's something real, something that evolves!"

"Steve, we keep going round and round," Georgia said. "I know you're alone and I know you have issues, but can you honestly expect me to take on a relationship with someone with nearly a century of baggage? I mean, what will this even lead to? I'll be dead in doggy years to you and old and wrinkly in a blink of an eye."

"Would you give up on something wonderful just because it's going to end? Everything comes to an end, sweetheart. It's not like it's your problem anyway. Look at it from my point of view. I'm the one falling for the mayfly. It's not like you'll have to go on with the empty gaping hole inside!"

Steve stormed halfway across his apartment and then started pacing furiously around the couch. Georgia's face softened a bit as she saw him gnaw on his lip in that adorably awkward way Mr. Lambley liked to do as well when he was upset.

"You are exhausting to argue with, you know," Georgia finally sighed.

"You are rude and difficult and frustrating . . ." Steve growled. His voice trailed off as Georgia dropped her purse on the floor and sauntered over slowly.

"Keep going," she said as she placed an arm over each of his shoulders. "Tell me how you really feel."

He looked down at her chest, her bare shoulders, and the way one camisole strap had slipped down her arm. His gaze kept dodging hers and instead focused on the little butterfly earrings in her ears and the curve of her backside in her jeans.

"Your hair was in style fifty years ago, and you dress like a hooker on top and a tomboy on the bottom," he said.

"Mmmhmm, you really do know how to sweet-talk," she said as she leaned up to his ear. She then breathed slowly, carefully, all around the delicate curves of cartilage. "And I think you are an entitled, undead, obsessive asshole," she whispered.

He started to protest, but words failed him as she followed her comment by sliding lower and rubbing the bridge of her nose down his neck and nuzzling right into a comfy place along the collarbone. She smiled as she felt his back stiffen and he had to shift his weight to adjust his pants.

"Do you really hate me that much?" he finally choked out as she slid her face back up and started tracing the edge of his jaw with her cheek.

She moved her mouth right next to his. "No, I don't hate you," she started. He held his breath and finally met her gaze. "But it's not like I love you either," she finished.

He closed his eyes, and his shoulders slumped. They snapped back open suddenly as, for the first time, Georgia's lips pressed against his and her tongue forced its way into his mouth. For a second he limply pushed her back, but his arms caved as one of her hands slid off his shoulder and started making its way hungrily down to his waist. He let her mouth explore his thoroughly and come up with air before he dared to start protesting. "What are you doing?" he asked.

"Look, you have two choices here," she said flatly as she yanked the top of his fly and slid her fingers around the button. "You can keep talking, or we can go to your room."

Steve grabbed her by the waist and jerked her forward, quickly covering her mouth with his own and deftly preventing any buzz-killing conversation opportunities. He was rewarded with Georgia swinging both legs up around his hips, facilitating easy transport to his room in the back. Neither of them said a word as they collapsed into his mattress, instead, they focused with near-military precision on the fastest way to unbutton, unbuckle, and undress.

Georgia did smile as she discovered that underneath the designer threads, there was a fairly sculpted chest and the absence of any completely unappealing bodily surprises. She took a moment to run her hands down his back and breathed a sigh of relief that she didn't snag a load of hair. Meanwhile, her undead companion took a fair bit of time scientifically analyzing the exact circumference of her breasts and thoroughly verified that she had neither any unwanted lumps nor silicone underneath her perky little nipples.

Georgia didn't make the poor soul wait as she flipped him over and jumped on top of him. Steve tried his best to stem the tide of excitement, but the whole messy affair ended up lasting only a few violent minutes before both of them were lying exhausted and giggling next to each other.

"Well, that was something," Georgia said as they both stared at the same water stain in the ceiling plaster.

"I've never quite . . . yeah," he stammered out.

"A little excited?" Georgia teased. "Oh come on, I know they don't remember it, but you've had to have gotten some practice."

Steve continued to stare at the ceiling. "What just happened?" he asked incredulously.

Georgia rolled back on top of his chest and started toying with the little wisps of hair there. "I got sick of arguing with you," she said. "I figured I'd try something different."

"That was definitely not what I was expecting," he said as he wrapped his arms around her.

"Are you complaining?"

"No," Steve said quickly.

"Then shut up, and we might even do this again sometime."

She curled up against him and rested her head against his chest. As she listened to his lack of heartbeat, her eyelids grew more and more heavy. Soon the whooshing sound gave way to soothing strains of moody jazz and the faraway voice of some silky-sounding siren.

Georgia snapped her eyes open as she felt something drift over her shoulder. She blinked as a cat jumped from her chest and padded off toward the door. It was a huge ginger thing, with huge luminous eyes and a tail that twitched relentlessly.

She looked next to her, but the buff vampire was gone and the black silk sheets had morphed into white satin. The smell of bacon filled her lungs for a moment, followed by something acrid and metallic.

"Hey, sleepyhead, think the krauts are gonna wait for you to wake up?" a new voice said.

Georgia whirled around to see a man covered in blood from head to toe. He smiled and tipped his iron-bucket helmet her way. Georgia blinked again, and the world spun in circles. Snippets of French, German, Japanese, and other languages chattered in her skull as faces and places blurred together. She raised her hand and screamed as red streaks poured down between her knuckles.

"Bloody hell, pull yourself together!" a big, bold, and British voice commanded.

This time as she blinked, she saw a dashing figure with a barrel chest, slicked-back hair, and a perfectly tailored pin-striped suit. In the dim lights, she could barely see a buxom blonde perched to one side and a mysterious brunette to the other. The stranger licked his lips, his fang tips still glistening and sticky with a tinge of red, but his face remained shadowed by the brim of his fedora.

"What is happening?" Georgia managed to stammer out. She blinked, and the Brando-worthy gangster was gone. She screamed as bullets whizzed by her ears and the ground shook. As she fell to the ground, she could see white spats splattered with blood.

"Georgia! You're late for school."

Georgia's eyes widened as she found herself in a long linoleum hallway with bright blue lockers framing her as far as the eye could see. She looked down and saw a plaid skirt and skinny white crop top.

"Oops, you did it again," a lady with a pink beehive said as she roller-skated by. "You're late for class."

"Class?"

"DeMarco, get your ass down!" someone shouted as the ground shook. The same guy yanked Georgia by the arm and tossed her into the mud, but she ended up landing on a pile of silky pillows.

"Can you really get me into motion pictures, Mr. DeMarco?" a breathy voice asked as Georgia found a perky bottle blonde with terrible roots straddling her.

She blinked again, and the whole world turned. She could see that awful fountain, the mix of cherubs and chintzy mosaic, but the closer she got, the more red liquid she could see dripping down the little statues' faces.

"Help us!" one of the statues begged.

She screamed and took off running down the hall, but everywhere she turned, all she could see was another door marked detention or a cafeteria full of hall monitors. The next time she ran down the corner, she saw a tall, handsome biracial beauty holding a tray full of jelly doughnuts.

"Hey, baby, I was thinking of you," he said as he took one and chomped right through the flaky, buttery pastry. As he pulled it away, the raspberry filling dribbled from the corner of his mouth. One blink later, and the sauce kept pouring down his neck, pooling in his collar as the distant rat-a-tat of gunfire once again filled Georgia's ears.

She tried to run again and had to cover her face as the spotlight shone in her eyes. As she blinked again, she could barely make out a room full of cushy leather banquettes and a cloud of cigar smoke. Light after light flickered from corner to corner as the plumes wafted around shadowy forms. Her eyes locked on the corner table, where the king held court over a bevy of bodacious babes.

"You gonna sing or what, sweetheart?" a dead ringer for Humphrey Bogart asked as Georgia froze on stage. She stared down at her slinky silver dress, and by the time she looked up, the entire room had been replaced by eager parents and cameras waiting to take that perfect shot. Georgia looked down to see a chintzy satin number and a belt made of aluminum foil.

"Come on, honey," she heard a nice lady in a denim skirt and polyester blouse say.

"Miss McConnell?" Georgia choked out. She looked back to see a group of antsy kindergarteners dressed as wise men and shepherds waiting for her line.

"Sing," the teacher hissed.

"Away in a manger . . . No crib for a bed," Georgia sang weakly as everyone stared. Her hands shook as the piano drowned her out.

"Georgia!"

She blinked again and felt the world spin, but this time it was two strong arms that caught her. She looked up into a pair of freakishly green eyes and burst out laughing. "You're Irish, ain't yah?" she giggled as she was dragged out of the hallway and plopped onto a bed.

"Georgia, can you hear me?" the voice said again.

"Said the little lamb to the shepherd boy . . . do you hear what I hear?" she sang sweetly as strange hands wiped the sweat from her brow. Her fully dilated eyes darted frantically around the room as she tried to find something to focus upon with bright lights shining in her eyes. "That's not my line," she protested. "I'm the angel, not the shepherd boy."

"Come on, Georgia, come back to me," a voice pleaded. "Wake up."

Georgia smiled and snuggled into the blanket on the bed. "Here, kitty, kitty," she cooed and waved to the empty floor.

Her benefactor flicked cold water on her face over and over until she finally swatted him away. "You're a bad man," she said with a little pout, but then she smiled wickedly and yanked her friend toward her until he toppled onto one knee next to her. "But I like you bad," she cooed as she leaned up to kiss him.

He pushed her away and left her rolling on the bed. A few minutes later, Georgia was rewarded with a full glass of water poured over her head. She squealed like a little girl and started chain-conjugating expletives until her eyes fluttered fully open.

"Ren?" she asked softly as she could just make out light eyes and dark hair.

He didn't say a word. Instead, he wrapped a towel over her head and shoulders and set a cup of coffee in her hands. She tried to turn her nose up at it, but he carefully eased the beverage toward her lips.

"Caffeine helps," he said.

Georgia sneered but sipped the brown beverage a little. She rubbed her temples and wrapped up in the blanket. "I'm tired," she groaned.

"You're high," Ren sighed.

Georgia looked at his dark pants and white shirt with the collar unbuttoned. His hair, for once, was a bit untamed, and an exasperated smirk filled his face.

"You look like Han Solo," Georgia giggled. "Can I see your lightsaber?"

"Han Solo doesn't use a lightsaber," Ren instinctively corrected.

"Yes, he does," Georgia insisted. "That's how you sliced open the beastie and saved your buddy—"

"Yes, he did use it once, but he's not a Jedi." Ren stopped to face-palm. "And I cannot believe that I am having this argument with you right now. You need to get your system moving. Adrenaline and caffeine will help."

"Asian Han Solo—" she laughed as her eyes grew heavier.

"Just go to sleep," Ren said as he took the cup away and tucked her in. "I'll talk to you when you're lucid again . . ."

"Han Solo?" Gail asked. "The guy from *Star Wars*?"

"Well, apparently I was tripping over *The Empire Strikes Back*, to be more precise. I don't remember everything—more like flashes or flashbacks, if you will," Georgia confessed. "Ren wasn't kidding when he warned me about the more colorful properties of vampiric bodily fluids."

"So you're not immune?" Gail asked, wide-eyed.

"Obviously not," she muttered.

Next to her the blonde didn't bother to contain her giggles.

"I woke up in Ren's room. Somehow in my trip, I had managed to escape, run naked around the hotel, and crash a full floor down, all while managing not to wake up the vampire in the penthouse. Ren threatened to record my ramblings next time if I wasn't careful . . ."

Georgia's eyes snapped open as she found herself in a strange room with the light fading through the curtains. She rolled over to find a perfectly set TV tray with a carafe of coffee, an assortment of energy bars, and a box of condoms. A neatly penned note said simply, "For Next Time."

Gail turned bright pink as she saw her clothes neatly laundered and pressed at the end of the bed as well. "Oh my god," she groaned.

She hopped into her clothes as quickly as she could, chugged the cof-fee, and hunted for her purse, all while she tried desperately to avoid any of the current tenants of the Intercontinental. Just as she had made it to the hall, she felt a tap on her shoulder. She jumped, and the ancient banis-ter simply couldn't take the strain as she crashed into it. Before she could so much as scream, a hand shot out and yanked her back against a now familiar chest.

"Oh come now, it wasn't that bad, was it?" Steve teased as he helped Georgia to her feet.

"Wow, adrenaline does work," she muttered as she grabbed her own chest.

"You OK?" the vampire asked.

"Yeah, about last night—" she started.

"How about, 'about this afternoon'?" he countered. "You look like you've seen a ghost."

"I need to go check on Mr. Lambley," she said quickly. "Have you seen my purse?"

Steve curled his arms around her and rested his chin on top of her head. She couldn't help but sink against him and let her breathing calm down a little.

"I sent Ren off to get him settled."

"Oh god, Ren!" she cried.

"What about him? I'm pretty sure he can handle Gingersnaps, even if the old boy woke up without his usual companion."

It was Georgia's turn to facepalm. "I ended up in his room. I had no clothes. Oh god—"

"Is that all?" Steve asked with his usual grin. "Trust me, Matsuoka has had to deal with worse."

"You're not upset?" Georgia asked incredulously.

Steve laughed and started leading her back up the stairs. "It's Ren!" he laughed. "Trust me, he's not interested in any girl."

"Oh," Georgia said. She furrowed her brow as the information slowly processed in her recovering brain. "Well, I guess that makes sense. But what about the party—"

"He serves the family. What can I say?" Steve sighed. "It might not be his thing, but he does what he's told."

"I see," she said. "Yeah, the pieces are starting to come together. So, are things about to get weird between us then? It's just that whenever I, you know, um, let's just say it tends to get awkward."

"Well, usually at this point in a relationship, my partner has forgotten me, so I'm kind of in awkward territory too," Steve said. "But I'm willing to keep trying if you are."

Georgia finally gave herself the luxury of a real smile. "You know, I think I might just be able to take you up on that, Mr. DeMarco. Why don't we pick up Gingersnaps and head out on the town . . . ?"

"So there you have it," Georgia said with a triumphant little bow from her seat. "You now know how I ended up in a relationship with a vampire."

Gail giggled and gave a little clap as she waited for more. When Georgia remained silent and returned to her drink, the brunette began to pout a little.

"Surely there's more," she prodded.

Georgia shrugged. "What's there to say really? I mean, we had a relationship—went to movies, had some very interesting dinners considering our disparate diets, and generally did all the same things a human couple would do. I mean, most of the time I had to work too, so we weren't alone all that much. Come on, do you really want me to gush about a few sloppy quickies right at dawn or how I'd stay at his place on my night off and Ren would cover my shift back in Brookline?"

Gail's face fell ever so slightly. This time it was the vampire who chimed in. "You have to understand, my dear," Minerva explained. "*Mein bruder* is terribly American. He grew up with zee apple pie and lights off with his one true gal. He's not some super-sexy kinky human fantasy child of zee night. Would you agree, *Berliner?*"

"Like I said, Minerva only lies to herself," Georgia said. Her smile turned slightly toxic. "We don't all get the exotic foreign types, now, do we?" she asked.

"Well, you don't," Minerva countered. "Oh, you can't leave zee poor girl hanging, *Berliner.*"

"I think I've shattered her illusions quite enough tonight," Georgia sighed. "Perhaps we should be going . . ."

"No, I'm not disappointed!" she exclaimed. "It's kind of fun to hear that vampires can be normal."

Minerva snorted in disgust. "*Mein bruder* is abnormal in his normality," she snapped.

"So, was Mr. Lambley excited? Are you leaving to be with Steve?" Gail asked. Her eyes once more darted to the ring on Georgia's finger. "Come on, I have to sweet-talk patients to get info all the time. I can tell when someone is holding out on me."

"Well, Mr. Lambley is a creature of routine. I think he could handle Steve and I being together as long as he was involved and we kept to our schedule. I must say, though, that he had his moments of frustration, and I was surprised to discover that he wasn't the only one getting moody just because Steve and I had taken our relationship to the next level . . ."

13

"You're quiet tonight," Georgia said between slurps of her little plastic cup of miso soup. Across the table Ren continued to check his phone with one hand while toying with a rapidly unraveling sushi roll with the other. The bright orange fish eggs and grains of rice kept falling on the faux wood grain, mixing with the casualties from the three helpless maki that came before.

Ren flicked his screen over again. "Some of my hedge funds are down. I've got to keep an eye on the exchange rates in East Asia," he said in his terminally bland full-on robot voice. "I also have to order new socks for my master and check on the status of a vehicle registration for Lady Claudia."

"Sounds *fascinating*," she said. She turned her attention to her salad until she caught the attention of the little man in the chef's hat behind the counter. He ran over as he saw his masterpieces of fish, vegetables, and rice lying practically untouched on the shared platter between them.

"Everything OK?" he asked. "Something not good tonight?"

"Oh, something is wrong, but it has nothing to do with the food," Georgia muttered. She then looked back to the proprietor. "No worries, Jiro! We're just taking our time."

"You want more tea? Another soup?" he asked, still staring at the untouched spicy tuna. Ren shook his head.

"We're good," Georgia said, but as soon as Jiro had wandered away from their traditional corner table, she dropped the plastic smile and snapped, "What the hell, Matsuoka?"

"I'm busy," he replied curtly.

"Then maybe we should get you a to-go box," she growled right back.

"As you wish."

Georgia took a deep breath and stared intently at her sweet potato sushi. The happy orange dots tucked under sweet dripping streaks of deep brown sauce offered no solace from the utterly stone-faced dinner companion sitting with his back to the door. She finally peeked at the reflection in the glass and noticed that the order page for some sort of argyle hosiery was still on his screen.

"If you didn't want to see me, why did you come out here?" Georgia asked.

"I'm just busy," he said again.

"Really? The connection that slow that it takes you a half hour to order socks?" she asked.

Ren locked his phone and slapped it on the table. "Happy now?" he asked.

"Wow, who pissed in your cornflakes?"

"Maybe if you weren't so loud this morning, I could have gotten a decent night's sleep."

"Sorry, Steve was actually willing to put in a little effort for a change, so you'll excuse me if I was excited," Georgia snapped.

"I'll order soundproof ceiling tiles," Ren said drily. "It's good to see you've taken my advice. I haven't found you wandering the halls and accusing me of being a smuggler as of late."

"I am sorry about that," Georgia said. "I really am."

"It's what I'm trained to do. Usually I'm putting the girls into a cab once they're lucid enough to walk away, but for you, I'm the one who had to leave. Mr. Lambley was concerned about you, to say the least."

"Yes, you've both been as subtle as freight trains in expressing your displeasure as of late," Georgia said. "What gives? Are you jealous that your master is choosing to get a little nooky on the side?"

"No!" Ren said. "That's not why I'm upset at all."

"Then what is it? Are you mad that you have to babysit my boss? Did I steal the last of your not-so-secret cookie stash one too many times? What?"

"You do know that you and my master are not going to last—" Ren started.

"Oh, now that is starting to sound like jealousy. It was all well and good when one-night stands came in and out of the picture, but once Steve actually found someone he could actually try—"

"Try? Try what? No matter what he may look like to you, my master is still not what you think he is!"

Georgia made certain that Jiro had stepped into the kitchen before hissing, "Yeah, I get it, he's a vampire and I'm human. Sing me a new song—"

"Please don't start singing again," Ren muttered.

Georgia narrowed her eyes. "You are so jealous, aren't you? Just because you can't have what you want—"

"You're right!" he snapped. "I can never have what I want. Maybe we should just go back to focusing on helping you actually do your job."

"Well, I'm sorry. I didn't ask for this. I wasn't born into some family of perfect little assistants who can be rich and powerful and know just what to do. I just stumbled in and happened to be just the right kind of freak to step in and make my boss's and your master's lives a little bit better. Sorry!"

"Wait, you think I'm perfect?" he asked.

"You're the great high and mighty Matsuoka boy who knows exactly how to do everything, except maybe talk to another human being without sounding like an ass. You were made for what you do—"

"Are you kidding me?" Ren snapped.

"I'm just waiting for it. I want my next lecture that makes me feel like an idiot while you lord over me your lofty experience as the perfect assistant."

"That's how you see our meetings? I thought you wanted help!"

"I do want help, but I'm sick of your passive-aggressive, subtext-laden bullshit. I get it, you're a Matsuoka and know all—"

"And you know nothing—"

"Yeah, you've made that point a lot," Georgia growled.

Ren shoved back from the table, sending soup and tea sloshing, and he hunched over to glower at the shocked Georgia. All traces of his bland mask had melted away as his freakishly light eyes practically glowed under the fluorescents in the little hole-in-the-wall sushi joint.

"And you know nothing about me," he snapped. "You think I was born for this? That I even wanted my job? You think I like cleaning up the messes of an overgrown child and his toys? You think I want to be used up and thrown away by whatever Jaeger happens to be in town?"

"I—"

He cut her off. "You see this demure little Japanese man who scrapes and bows, don't you?" Ren asked. "I grew up in Irvine! I went to UCLA and Stanford and had job offers from every coke-loaded day-trading start-up before the crash. I was dating a pro snowboarder, for fuck's sake! Trust me, coming here and taking this job was the last thing I wanted."

Georgia sat there, gobsmacked, as cool, calm, and collected Ren kicked his chair and stomped off toward the men's room. She started rifling through her purse, fumbling for any cash to pay the bill, while the terrified chef and waitress peeked out from behind the beaded curtain that marked off the tiny kitchen space.

"I'm so sorry," she mouthed as she finally found her wallet. The waitress dashed out with all possible speed and whisked away the mess. Jiro himself bowed and waved his hands. "It's on the house tonight," he said quickly.

Georgia eyed the empty tables all around and plopped down a fifty-dollar tip. She grabbed her purse and almost made it to the door before Ren reappeared, his hair slightly damp and his face quite pink. Ren bypassed her and instead went to mutter a soft apology to the owner. Georgia took the opportunity to start walking.

She let the first cool breeze of the early fall soothe her burning cheeks. Before she made it to the train station, however, a huffing and puffing Ren jogged up to her and blocked her way.

"I'm sorry I lost my temper," he said.

"I'm sorry I just assumed everything," she muttered back.

"I'm upset because I don't want you to get hurt, Miss Sutherland," he said.

"Oh, it's Miss Sutherland again?" she snapped before the filter took control between the brain and her mouth.

"Georgia," he corrected himself. "And you're right. I am jealous."

She stopped trying to walk any farther. "What have you possibly got to be jealous of? I mean, oh, it's about you and your master, isn't it?"

"It's about you getting a chance to be happy with one of their kind," Ren confessed. "Let's just leave it at that . . . please?"

September had entered Boston with a vengeance, and Georgia found herself shivering as the wind whipped through the streets and had forced most of the sane people into jackets already. She grabbed her bare arms and shuffled back and forth as she waited for Ren to ruin the moment. The sheer number of normal new inhabitants to the Boston area for fall made conversations on the street a little trickier, and Ren joined her fidgeting as words seemed to escape him.

"If you hated it so much, why did you take the job?" she finally asked.

He pulled off his jacket and handed it to her. As she slid into it, he pulled out his phone and opened up a photo gallery for a change. He landed on a shot of a chubby-cheeked young man with bright red spikes of hair falling over his eyes. Even though he was clearly Asian in most features, the stranger's blue eyes and light brown roots told a mixed tale.

"My cousin, Mischa," Ren explained. "Aunt Sachiko married a Russian. It was quite a scandal. Anyway, he dreamed of nothing but becoming a servant since he was five. He was going to be our generation's donation to the family until a drunk driver took him out on the way home from a party."

"Oh god, I'm so sorry," Georgia gasped.

"It was me or consigning my little brother to this fate," Ren said softly. "I studied how to make money. He's writing equations to figure out where the universe came from. It was a no-brainer."

"Equations?" she asked as Ren swiped over to show a picture of a young man in a mortarboard and gown. The stranger with the same high cheekbones and sly smile as Ren on his good days waved his temporary degree proudly in front of the camera while a rather stern-looking man flanked him. The man's impossibly dark brown stare and fixed jaw actually made Georgia shudder.

"As you can see, I got my glib sense of humor from my father," Ren said. "And Rikuto takes more after our mother."

"MIT, not too bad," Georgia said as she squinted to make out the details. She let Ren switch to another shot—this one of him with his arm around the much shorter and slighter Rikuto. She had to smile as she saw a rare glimpse of Ren with his shaggy hair down and a toothy grin.

"He now has degrees in mathematics and physics and is working on his doctorate in astrophysics as we speak," Ren said proudly. "Lady Jaeger was actually one of his tutors when he was stuck on electromagnetism."

"Really? Which one—redhead or glamazon?" she asked.

"Neither. Minerva was a close follower of Nikola Tesla for years. She's always had an interest in theoretical science," he said, looking away as soon as he said her name.

"You mean Miss Kung Fu and Porn Barbie knows physics?" Georgia laughed. "Next thing you'll tell me that Steve studies philosophy."

Ren started leading her toward the subway. "While the Jaeger clan doesn't prize academics as some of the other families do, there are a few of them who choose to study fields other than stalking and martial arts."

"So you took the bullet for your little bro?" she said. "And if you ever want to change jobs?"

"My contract isn't exactly as short-term as yours," Ren said. "My master wanted to plan something special for you, you know—"

"You really like to change subjects on me," Georgia said. "Just tell me, did you sign a lifetime contract?"

All Ren had to do was look to the side for Georgia to get her answer. She shuffled beside him in silence all the way to the subway platform. Ren pulled his phone out and started flipping idly through his photo gallery while Georgia tried her best not to stare too much. A picture of a very pretty Japanese woman in a blue kimono couldn't help but catch her eye. She stood next to the super-stern man from Rikuto's graduation photo, while the two little boys posed demurely in front of her. Georgia had to giggle at the much taller, older-looking one who was stuck with an unfortunate bowl cut that only drew attention to his distinctly unexpected green eyes, while the smaller boy showed off the same almost-black irises as the father in the photo.

Ren closed the app the second he noticed Georgia's lashes flutter. She gave him a cheesy thumbs-up as the train roared by. "Loved that hair," she snickered before crowding into the car and leaving Ren to shuffle into the next one down. As she crammed into a tiny space in the back of the green line, she took a moment to pull up her own phone and search for "genetics of eye color . . ."

"Wait! Did you say that Ren's mother had brown eyes too?" Gail interrupted as the three of them started on a fresh round of various beverages.

Georgia nodded. "You caught that too, huh?" she asked with a little wink to the blonde vampire.

"Maybe she does pick up on zee little details too," Minerva said. She wrinkled her nose at the first taste of the thick red liquid in her snifter. "Ugh, this is old," she complained. "Ren does look ever so much like his cousin, no?"

Gail smiled knowingly. "Oh, I think I get it. So there was more than one reason why he ended up having to be a servant. Poor Ren—no wonder he has anger issues."

"You have no idea," Georgia sighed. "Well, actually you do get the idea. Ren had his moods, and Mr. Lambley wasn't much better. Finally, one movie night after a fairly uneventful showing of *Casablanca*, Mr. Lambley finally decided that enough was enough after he caught Steve and me sneaking a kiss in the kitchen . . ."

"You know I think I'm just going to take a morning stroll," Geoffrey growled as he found his way to the fridge blocked by a pair of snogging young lovebirds.

Georgia pushed away from her partner and opened the fridge for her boss. As she handed him a carafe marked G. L., he turned up his nose.

"Geoffrey," she sighed.

"There was a time when a man could get a glass and ice for his blood," Geoffrey sniffed.

His assistant just smiled and untangled herself further to grab him a glass. Before she could even start pouring, the elder vampire pointed to an infinitesimal spot on the rim. "It's filthy."

"Mr. Lambley, you drank rat puree out of a blender last cleaned in the seventies, and you're worried about a little spot?" she snapped. Steve took this opportunity to make a hasty retreat toward the living room.

Geoffrey continued to hold his nose until she took the time to find a new glass, carefully fill it with three perfect ice cubes, and then decant the pig's blood neatly over the rocks and top with a sprig of fresh mint. "Better?" she asked. "You know we do have the movie you requested coming up next."

"I don't want that one anymore," he pouted. "I want you to find the one where you-know-who gets stabbed on a pike and dies slowly on-screen like the rotten sack of murderous shite he really is."

"Well, I haven't found too many gory retellings of the Arthurian legend, but I'm sure we can find something where Mor—where you-know-who—bites it in a graphic fashion," Georgia offered. "Just give me a minute . . ."

Geoffrey sniffed again and continued to tap his feet impatiently in the kitchen. "Oh, you have time for Stefano always, but when I want something—"

"Mr. Lambley!" Georgia snapped.

"Well, he's not the one paying you, is he?" Geoffrey snapped.

"What is wrong with you tonight? I thought we were having a good time—"

Geoffrey leaned in and took a deep, long smell. "Oh, you've been having a good time, haven't you?"

"There is nothing in my contract about dating your friends, Geoffrey."

"It's just that you smell very Jaeger now," he said, still making the patented Pendragon poo-smelling face.

"Are you jealous?" she hissed.

"Certainly not!" he said, puffing up his chest and summoning a full-on aristocratic glare down the tip of his stubby little nose. "Now I want to see my family's disgrace die over and over, and if you can find anything where that . . . what did you call him?"

"Trampsylvanian," Georgia, Ren, and Steve all chimed in at once.

"—bastard dies a terrible death too, then I will be most pleased," Mr. Lambley finished. "Oh, and I want fizzy blood. This pig was slaughtered days ago and tastes all stale and flat."

"Yes, sir," she said with an exaggerated bow. After the third attempt to make his drink properly, she gritted her teeth, looked him right in the eye, and growled very slowly, "You better like this one, or you're going to end up wearing it."

Mr. Lambley puffed in his chest for a second more but decided that discretion was the better part of valor as he found himself burning in the full blue-hot fire of Georgia Sutherland's glare.

"Thank you," he huffed before wandering off toward the sofa. Georgia quickly texted Ren the next movie request and let herself cool off in the kitchen for a few before daring to pop some popcorn and return to the boys. As the aroma of crispy snacking goodness mixed with artificial butter wafted toward the sofa, Steve groaned and licked his lips. She clutched the warm paper bag to her chest and gave a withering look as both vampires eyed the dangerous bag of plant-based foodstuffs.

"Oh, that smell reminds me of the ballpark," Steve said. "I've missed it."

"Sorry, Steve-o, this isn't bloodsucker-approved," she said before popping a handful in her mouth. She offered the bag toward Ren as he fiddled with the remote, but he seemed far too focused on scrolling through the thousands of titles online for just the right selection to pay her any mind.

Steve grabbed her by the waist and ended up tickling her as she toppled on the sofa. Geoffrey shot them both dirty looks again, but they were
too focused on fumbling and fondling to pay the elder any mind. Finally
Ren cleared his throat as the screen went dark.

"Are you sure this was what you wanted?" he asked.

"Oh yeah," Georgia said as the screen faded back into an image of the
Magic Kingdom.

"Oh, not a cartoon!" Geoffrey whined. "Only one of us is a child
around here," he said with a pointed look toward the other vampire in the
room.

"Really?" Steve said. "Can't we watch—?"

"No," Georgia said flatly.

"But I wanted to see Mordred get disemboweled," Geoffrey whined.

"No! We are going to make it through one night with no family history,
no World War II, and no bloodsucking on the screen," Georgia snapped.
"For once we are going to watch something lighthearted and fun and perfectly pleasant, and you are going to deal with it."

"But—" both vampires stammered.

"No! I'm picking the movie, so shut up and deal."

Ren started to speak up but quickly shut up as he saw Georgia crack-
ing her knuckles. Instead, he reached for the popcorn as the screen turned
into a lovely scene of an African savannah.

"It's got animals in it—" Steve muttered. "This is going to be stupid."

"Really, Georgia. It's called *The Lion King*—" Geoffrey tried to protest.

"Hush, both of you, or I'll stab you with toothpicks!"

The vampires relented and rolled their eyes but acquiesced to sitting
quietly and watching the lovely tale of an adorable lion cub coming of age.
Twenty minutes later Georgia found herself passing tissues as both big,
bad creatures of the night were sniffling.

"The tragedy of it all," Mr. Lambley whimpered.

By the time the final credits rolled, Georgia had a head resting on each
of her shoulders as Steve and Geoff struggled to pull themselves back together. She gently patted the trembling older vampire as he blew his nose.

"You said this was happy!" he choked out.

"Well, he won in the end," she said. "Aww, let it out. I cried the first time I saw it too."

She looked slyly to her left, where Steven tried his best to put on a brave face, but he had to rub the corners of his eyes a few times. She gave Ren a little wink across the room.

"So, isn't it nicer to not be snapping at each other?" she said.

"Do you have any more of these movies?" Geoffrey asked.

"I think we can manage it for next week. We need to be getting you back well before dawn, Mr. Lambley."

Steve gave a little pout. "Can't you stay the night?"

"I think we do need to be heading back. I have work to do around the house, and I know Geoffrey hasn't had a good solid day's sleep at home all week," she said before giving Steve a kiss on the cheek.

"But—"

"I'll be back," she said in a fake deep Austrian accent.

Steve pouted the whole time she packed up her purse and got ready to go. He kept pawing at her arms and waist to tease her into giving up her crazy scheme. She just rolled her eyes and kept playfully pushing him back.

Mr. Lambley smiled like the cat that landed the canary as they drifted down to the first floor well before sunrise. Once they were safely tucked in the cab Ren had so graciously called for them, Mr. Lambley rested his head gently on Georgia's shoulder one more time.

"Thank you, Miss Sutherland," he said.

"I had housecleaning to do," she said.

"I know I shouldn't give in to the green-eyed monster, but I am sometimes vexed to see him get so very much of your attention," Geoffrey said.

"It's apples and pears—"

"Stairs?" Geoffrey asked, confused.

"You and your weird British slang. Apples and pears . . . apples and oranges—pick a fruit," Georgia sighed. "You are my boss, and I do my best to take care of you. Steve is my . . . friend, with a decided amount of benefits, that's all. Why is it suddenly bothering you so much?"

"It's my deathday coming up in less than a month's time. It got me thinking about time and how quickly it passes," he said softly.

"Oh, Geoffrey, don't be silly, I'm not—"

"Please, indulge a weak old man. What seems like forever to you isn't so long to someone like me," Mr. Lambley said as he looked out the window.

She squeezed his hand. "You can be rather sweet sometimes, Geoff—morbid, maybe, but still sweet. I'll try to balance my time better," she said.

Geoffrey continued to be lost in thought. "I can't help but worry since he is, you know, a Jaeger."

"And what is that supposed to mean?"

He waited till they were safely dropped off at the brownstone and out of prying earshot before daring to answer. As Georgia fumbled with the keys, the vampire took the time to pet the little concrete bunny statues tucked in the new fall mums in the window box.

"You know that the Jaegers aren't like my family. Stefano may be my friend, but he's still one of them. They are all, to their very core, hunters born and bred."

"Well, Steve isn't like the rest of the family. You know that," she said. "Did you want a shake before bed?"

"I just want you to listen to me, please. I know it's easy to get lost in the fog of young love—"

"Love?" Georgia laughed. "It's not really like that. He's fun and he's sweet, but we're still just, well, not that."

Geoffrey started gnawing on his lip again. Georgia chose to tuck him back in his room and get the TV going. The vampire did manage to get lost in his soap opera enough for Georgia to start puttering away at laundry and dusting. Just as she finished the last pair of silk pajamas, her phone vibrated in her pocket.

"Hey, you still awake?" Steve asked on the other end.

"Obviously," she laughed.

"You got time for me?"

She smiled. "Sure, what's up?"

"Look out back."

She nearly dropped her phone as one glance out the window revealed the young vampire perched on her fence. He waved before hopping over the raised bed and sauntering to her back door.

"What the hell are you doing here?" she asked.

"Well, you said you wouldn't stay, so I decided to drop by," he said, leaning ever so suavely on the doorjamb.

"You know, this is dangerously close to stalker territory, Mr. DeMarco," Georgia warned. "Remember that talk we had about the distinct difference between interesting and creepy?"

He tipped up her chin and kissed her on the lips as sweetly as an undead stalker possibly could. He gave a little bow and took a few steps back to say, "I am sorry. You know, sneaking over seemed far more romantic when I first conceived the plan, but, yeah, creepy."

"At least you don't watch me when I sleep and stare all bug-eyed when you think I'm not looking or any of those other stereotypical broody vampire things," she said.

"You really ditched me to clean?" he asked as he sniffed the traces of laundry detergent on her fingers.

She kissed him back. "I ditched you to keep my boss from getting too much more jealous and upset. He's a creature of habit, and he's just gotten a little more comfortable with going out and being seen. It's a lot for someone like him to share his toys with anyone else."

"Well, sometimes he needs to suck up and deal with things a little more," Steve said. "He's my friend, but—"

"You know, for guys who are supposed to be friends, you use a lot of conditionals," Georgia said.

"Gingersnaps is my friend, but that won't stop me from seeing you," Steve warned.

"Um, really, you're going back into the creepy possessive zone. You and Geoff being friends is completely independent of anything we have, OK? There is no kinky undead love triangle going on *at all*. We clear?"

Steven nodded. "What can I say? You are the only person who knows me this way. I don't want you to see me like humans see the rest of my family. I don't want you to fear me," he said softly. "It would break my heart if you ever—"

She wrapped her arms around him, gave him a solid hug, and buried her head against him. "Stop worrying so much, Steve. I know you're different."

He squeezed her tight. "It's just, Georgia, I've had this whole stigma of being a Jaeger all my—"

"You became a vampire to save other people. You may be a Jaeger, but—"

"To save people," he choked out as he buried his face in her soft golden hair. "I wanted to save them, so much. You have no idea what it's like when you're backed in a corner. People do the most terrible things when they have their backs against the wall, Georgia."

She squeezed him tighter. "People also do the most wonderful things when they have their backs against the wall. You're proof of that, silly thing. Come on, kiss me good morning and get out of here before the sun comes up."

He leaned down and stared right into her eyes. In the late moonlight, his face positively glowed. "You are amazing," he whispered before kissing her.

She did stumble slightly as he let her go. He smiled at her as she tried to recover and give him a more come-hither look rather than look like a lovesick schoolgirl. For a moment he paused as if to say one more thing, but he ended up just shaking his head.

"I have a big surprise for you and Geoffrey both. I'll send Ren around tomorrow with the details."

"What sort of trouble are you causing now?" she asked.

"Just wait for Ren tomorrow," he said before blowing her one more kiss. He hopped back on the fence and gave her a little salute. "Oh, you do have a passport, don't you?"

"What?" she asked, but the vampire was already long gone . . .

"Ahh, you are getting to zee best part of the story—zee part where you meet me," Minerva chimed in.

"I thought we covered your intro already, Miss Hoover?" Georgia asked.

Minerva chose to focus her attention on the enraptured Gail and waved her hand dismissively toward the other blonde. "You simply must hear all about their little trip, the one where *mein bruder* takes his sweet young thing home to meet zee family," she said.

"Oh, I have got to hear this," Gail said eagerly. "So, did you go to Europe? Do vampires there have castles or stay in apartments or what?"

"No, dearie," Georgia corrected. "Steve didn't take me to meet *his* family. I got to meet *the* family. If I was really going to date one of their kind as well as serve a member of a rival clan, it was probably for the best that I got a little training and once-over by none other than the premier family of vampire service . . ."

"Tokyo? Are you serious?" Georgia cried as she waited in line at the post office, passport application in hand. She was rewarded with Ren's normal lack of public expression. "Oh, I forgot. You're always serious."

"I told you that my master had big plans for you and for Mr. Lambley," Ren said. "Did you get the photos?"

"I've got everything. Trust me," she said before giving her folder of forms another once-over. "Are you going to tell me what we'll be doing in Japan?"

"You? I'm not entirely sure," Ren said. "My master and I have business, and we've arranged for Mr. Lambley to get an appointment with a doctor who is normally booked a few decades in advance."

"You mean about his, um, teeth?" she asked softly as she scanned the line for any eavesdroppers.

Ren nodded. "My master and his sister cashed in a few favors to get the time opened, and we, err, my master, thought that you would enjoy a trip."

"Well, I am a little curious, but I've never really thought about going to Asia. I don't speak a lick of Japanese either."

"One of my family members will always be with you to interpret. If you get stuck, just learn the phrase '*Watashi-wa atama-ga warui gaijin desu. Biru ippon, kudasai,*' and you'll be all set."

"Water ski atom bomb—what?" she asked,

"*Watashi-wa,*" he said slowly.

"Watasheeee-wa," she repeated.

"*Atama-ga-*"

"Atom bomb." She stopped as he gave her a stern look and correctly mimicked him with "A-ta-ma-ga."

"*Warui gaijin desu.*"

"Worried *gaijin* days," she said quickly.

"Close enough," Ren sighed. "*Biru ippon, kudasai.*"

"Bee-rude, eep-on, koooo-da-sai!" she finished triumphantly. "So, what did I just say?"

"I'm a stupid foreigner. May I please have a beer?" Ren said with a wicked little grin.

She whacked him with her folder a good few times as he burst out laughing. Before she could finish his thorough beatdown, he was saved by the postal worker calling her forward to finally process her paperwork. Ten minutes later he was still smiling as they wandered out into the bright autumn sun.

"You are such a dick," she said as he continued to snicker.

"Your Japanese was pretty bad," he said.

She pulled out her phone and searched furiously for a few minutes before taunting him with, "You know how I said you were an Asian Han Solo? Well, you're actually Chew-*Baka*!"

He peeked over to see the page with lists of Japanese insults still showing on her phone. "That was truly terrible, you know," he said flatly.

"*Baka* means jackass, right?" she asked.

"More or less, but it's all in the delivery. If you really want to insult someone, you need to do it in Russian," Ren said.

"You know Russian?"

"Of course I know Russian. I have to work with various families," he said. "Anyway, my family will be able to help you. They are eager to meet someone who can help bridge the gap between the Pendragons and the Jaeger—"

"Bridge the gap? With the way those two have been lately, I think I'm more driving a wedge," Georgia muttered. "So this doctor—"

"Dr. Pang," Ren offered.

"His name is Pang? Does that hurt?" Georgia asked.

"The puns . . . so . . . terrible," Ren said, clutching his chest. "Why are you doing this to me?"

"You started it," Georgia teased. "Come on, don't you have some amazing Russian insult for me?"

"*Ya znayu chto ty gadkaya smes' kozla, osla i barana!*" he said without missing a beat.

"Do I even want to know?"

"Bear in mind that the beautiful thing about Russian insults is that they completely depend on context," Ren said. "I said that I know that you're a nasty mixture of goat, donkey, and sheep."

"You called me a farm animal?"

"It's a Russian thing."

Georgia burst out laughing as they made their way down the street. She dragged him in for a quick bite of pizza and cold beer before they finally noticed the sunset.

"So, how many languages can you insult me in?" she asked.

Ren rubbed his chin thoughtfully. "Insult you? Probably eleven."

"You speak eleven languages?"

"I speak five actually, but I've learned to swear in many more."

"And here I was proud that I made it through seventh-grade Spanish," Georgia sighed. "Well, I've figured out Russian and Japanese. What are the other three?"

"English—"

"Duh!"

"Mandarin, and I'm learning German."

"You really know how to make a gal feel inadequate," she said. After picking at the last bit of crust, she dared to ask, "I can only guess who taught you German."

"Both my master and mistress thought it was best that I speak their parents' native tongue," Ren said as diplomatically as he could.

"You really serve both of them?"

"I stay predominantly with Master Jaeger, but, technically, yes, I belong to both Stefano and Minerva."

"You don't belong to anyone," Georgia countered. "Last I checked, the United States outlawed slavery a while back."

"Like I've said, my contract is much more long-term than the one you were able to get from Mr. Lambley. It doesn't matter, though. I don't have anything to go back to anymore."

"Come on, Ren," Georgia sighed. "There has got to be more that you want to do than be the fake ID man for a bunch of undying creeps."

"Don't forget being a sustainable food source," he added drily. "Speaking of which, Lady Minerva will be in Boston in a few days. She will be staying until we go to Tokyo for Mr. Lambley's treatment."

"Oh, I bet she will love seeing me around. I didn't see much of her, but she had the same snooty attitude as the other Jaeger ladies. No offense."

"She's more traditional than my master," Ren said. "But I know she will want to see Mr. Lambley and perhaps be over for a formal dinner. If you need help arranging it—"

"The Jaeger bombshell wants to come over for dinner?" Georgia said, shaking her head. "How *nice*."

"I can handle the arrangements."

"No, I'm Mr. Lambley's assistant, aren't I? How about you tell me what we need to do, and I'll take a stab at it. If I get stuck, then I'll call in the cavalry."

He reached out to shake her hand. "Fair enough," he said with another smile . . .

"Needless to say, I was completely unprepared for a formal vampire house call," Georgia mused. She waited for Minerva to make a quip, but the blonde vampire only snickered under her breath. Georgia continued, "Ren told me to check Higgins's old notes first because Mr. Lambley used to be quite the entertainer and it had a number for catering in there. You can imagine my surprise when it turned out to be an escort service! Still, I scrubbed the brownstone from stem to stern and managed to get

Mr. Lambley's suit cleaned, all while brushing off my vampire beau. I thought I had it under control until it was finally time to start dinner prep . . ."

"Georgia!" Mr. Lambley whined as the front doorbell rang. She set down the block of chocolate she was grating to run and grab the door, all while keeping the phone to her ear to get an updated ETA on their expected dinner guests. She stumbled over her shoes littering the hall, while her boss continued to grumble from upstairs that his pants had disappeared.

"Delivery for Miss Sutherland," the courier said as Georgia signed on the dotted line. The packing slip simply read, "Ingredients," and was postmarked from one of the exotic bondsmen vendors Ren had put her in touch with.

She raised a brow as she saw a row of airholes on either side of the rather unwieldy box. "What the hell is a deluxe amuse bouche set for a vampire?" she dared to ask as she schlepped the parcel toward the kitchen table.

"Georgia!" Mr. Lambley whined again.

She ran upstairs and found his pants hanging from the banister. Without looking she tossed them on his bed and reminded him to brush his hair and teeth. "I've got too much to do right now!" she called back. This time as she darted down the stairs, she scooped all the remaining undergarments that her boss had decided to decorate with and hid them quickly in a convenient linen closet. Much to her surprise, Mr. Lambley had also chosen that closet as the perfect place to hide his illicit stash of tomato juice and liquid candy. "He's going to kill himself," she growled as she dragged the contraband back to the sink. As she was pouring the toxic neon-colored sugar water down the drain, a distinctive mewing sound came from the table.

"Oh . . . no . . ." she gasped as she heard more adorable little noises coming from the box. "A vampire amuse bouche."

Her phone lit up with a thirty-minute warning. She rushed back to the fridge to check on all the little dessert cups chilling between plastic bottles of plasma and various pig fluids.

The mewling grew louder until Georgia finally dared to grab some scissors and snip at the tape on the sides. She actually squeaked as she pulled away the lid to see pairs of little green and gold eyes staring plaintively back at her . . .

"No!" Gail cried. "You had kittens for dinner?"

"The young ones have an exquisite, nutty flavor and lack zee funk that older felines get," Minerva added. "It's always a delight, even if they never last long."

Gail's jaw continued to quiver. "You didn't—"

"Oh, zee *Berliner* gave us a night we would never forget, didn't she?" Minerva said. "Tell her just what sort of sacrifices you have to make if you want to serve us."

Georgia drained the rest of her drink. "It wasn't my finest night, but it taught me so much about the vampires around me."

"But . . . kittens?" Gail said.

"You do realize that vampires' primary food source is blood, don't you, sweetie?" Georgia asked. "What do you think I had to do? If I can serve a freshly slaughtered hog to my guests, what is the difference if I serve a live appetizer? These were animals that would have been used for animal research anyways or put to death at the pound, not some local kids' pets . . ."

Georgia continued to stare dumbfounded at the fluffy balls of fur writhing around in the towels that served as temporary packing. One of the little creatures had dared to put its paws on the lip, while the other two huddled at the bottom, crying out for some unfathomable kitty desire. The curious ginger beast ended up toppling over the side and staring in amazement at his huge white paws before his tail commanded his interest and he started rolling on the place mat.

Georgia picked up this largest and fluffiest of the kittens and plopped it in the box. A second later the same orange one jumped right back out and started meowing as he saw the edge of the table and realized that he was a touch higher up than his little legs were used to.

Just as Georgia was picking up the fluffball once more, her vampire host chose that moment to waddle into the kitchen and clap his hands with delight. "My favorite!" he exclaimed. "Can you blend one for me?"

Georgia turned as ghastly white as her companion. He stared at her in confusion as she shook her head slowly.

"Well, I can't very well sink my teeth in one!" he blustered. "Seriously, woman, you are balmy on the crumpet sometimes."

Her phone alarm chimed in with a fifteen-minute warning. She took that moment to text a desperate, "Help!" to Ren's direct line before running upstairs, kitten in tow. She ended up plopping the plump orange furball in the bathtub while she frantically finished shoving herself into a dress and hose.

"You stay here," she hissed before locking him in her special room and darting down the stairs. She then popped the lid on the box and shoved it under the table before she plugged in a baby bottle warmer so she could get the freshly pressed duck's blood up to an appropriate aperitif temperature.

She ran to the dining room to light candles, the lounge to start a record, and the parlor to fluff each and every newly cleaned pillow. The once dark and dusty home had been transformed into a dark and spotless cavern, with fresh silk flowers on every table and the rich scent of vampire-approved bacon air fresheners tucked in each formerly musty corner.

Just as the ten-minute warning buzzed, Georgia jumped as the doorbell rang again. She snatched her phone from the mantel and double-checked the time, and the bell rang again.

"Oh, Lady Jaeger is notorious for showing up early," Geoffrey called from the landing. "Did I tell you that?"

"No, as usual," she muttered as she straightened her hem and ran her fingers through her hair. She swung open the door to find a tall, leggy blonde in an impeccably tailored suit. Next to her an apologetic-looking Ren Matsuoka held out a wine bottle and gave a curt little bow.

"So, you *schtupp mein bruder*," Minerva said. "He must like tiny American tits, after all."

"Well, hi, why don't you just come on in?" Georgia replied without missing a beat. She looked over Ren's shoulder, but his other master was nowhere to be seen.

"He is responsible for family business tonight," Minerva said. She waited patiently for Ren to slip off her outer coat and take her handbag. Once more he was in ninja mode, slipping away to attend to her things while Georgia was left to entertain. Minerva leaned in and sniffed. "You've seen him recently enough."

"I'll get you a cocktail. Geoffrey, your guest is here!"

Much to her surprise, Mr. Lambley was right around the corner, cowering behind the china cabinet. Georgia gave him a pointed look as he was trembling and resembling a little lost child rather than a lordly creature of the night. "It's just her," she whispered. "I thought we'd at least have Steve as a buffer."

"Come, come, my little *rotkopf* darling!" Minerva cooed from the parlor. "We have so much to catch up on."

"I think I feel ill," Geoffrey said. "You can handle her—"

"Oh, no, you're not," she snapped. "She came here to see you, and I have dinner to get done."

She had to literally drag the vampire across the hall and plop him awkwardly on the sofa, while Minerva decided to perch on the chaise. Before she addressed her peer, she flagged over Ren from his hiding spot in the corner and made him whisper something in her ear before he carefully wiped the corner of her mouth with a tissue and helped her reapply some lipstick.

"You'll have to excuse me," Minerva said. "I was starving, so I had a little Japanese takeout on the way."

"Yeah, let me get dinner ready," Georgia said quickly as she left her master to deal with the awkward silence in the room. No sooner had she made it to the kitchen when Ren wandered in after her and grabbed a glass of water.

"So, is your mistress going to eat at all, or did she get her fill?" Georgia asked brusquely as she started pouring freshly warmed bird juices into highball glasses.

"It's traditionally served in a balloon goblet," Ren said.

Georgia yanked open the cupboard door and pulled out a different pair of glassware and re-poured the drinks. Ren grabbed a towel and helped her clean the rims.

"So, my boss and your mistress have history?" Georgia asked.

"Vampires always have history, remember?" he said. "She just wants her old rival back, that's all."

"I can't imagine Mr. Lambley being anyone's rival," she said as she readied the drinks on a tray. "They like art and stuff, right?"

"I've heard as much," Ren sighed. "I'm sure if we give them enough time, it will quickly turn into what vampires love most—a bunch of reminiscing."

Instead, they returned to an awkward silence. Georgia walked over and offered the tray, but Minerva waved it away. Georgia let Mr. Lambley greedily chug both before taking them away. She waited a few minutes before setting the dining room with two bowls of consommé.

"Dinner is served," she said to the still, silent room.

"How delightfully human," Minerva said as she settled to her bowl. She twirled the spoon and let the candlelight dance on the polished silver. "I haven't used one of these in years!"

This time before Georgia could escape, Minerva motioned to the empty chair. "Let zee Matsuoka take a course," she said. "I'd like to get to know you."

"Really?" Georgia asked. "I'm pretty sure humans aren't that interesting to someone like you."

"Usually you would be right, but I must say I am fascinated by any little pastry *mein bruder* would rather be inside than have inside him," she said before slurping a bit of soup. She wrinkled her nose and didn't take another sip. "Why doesn't he feed on you, little *Berliner*?" she asked.

"I serve Mr. Lambley and am under his protection."

"Oh, are you zee only one that gets to taste this crumpet then?" Minerva asked sweetly as she stared across the table. "No, you gave that up, didn't you?"

"I'm sure you can talk to your brother—"

Minerva burst into a throaty laugh. "*Mein bruder* and I do not talk if we don't have to. It's obvious what is going on here. He wants to shame his house as always and is rebelling by playing with his food. It's a phase that he has been in for far too long."

"A rebellious phase?" Georgia snorted.

"Oh yes, it is zee latest plague of zee young," she said. "They keep seeing all those Pendragon lies and human fantasies and think that they are supposed to be all tortured and brooding and love zee little human girls. It really doesn't matter to me so long as you know zee truth."

"Really? Why do you even care if your brother is stringing me along? Aren't I just food?"

Minerva's smile broadened a bit. "Yes, you have a wee bit of sense, little *Berliner.* That is exactly why I came—to tell you this! If you want to play your little human fantasy and have your fun, do it. Do it every way you can, because I'm sure that few breathers will ever give you zee kind of pleasure one of us can, but *mein bruder* is just a baby, and I don't want him getting crazy ideas from his friends," she said, giving a pointed look to Mr. Lambley. "I like everyone to know where they stand before they too stupid and lost up their own asses."

"Well, that's very *kind* of you," Georgia said. "Anything else?"

"No, zee rest of my business is with your master, little *Berliner.* You can go now."

Georgia gave her a little curtsy and ran off to the kitchen. She served up two more courses of various animal liquids, each of which only ended up serving Mr. Lambley, while Minerva continued to babble away. Georgia caught a few snippets about frescoes and missing Impressionist works until the guest began rattling off in nothing but German while Mr. Lambley sort of nodded and enjoyed his full belly.

Ren looked at the last course in the fridge and raised his brow. "That smells like—"

"I checked with Steve already. He says she can have it," Georgia said as she pulled out the dishes and started topping them with faintly pink whipped cream. "Ours are in the back."

She peeked into the dining room. "Wow, does she ever stop talking?" she muttered back to Ren.

"It's been a few years for them. I know she wanted to catch up."

Georgia slid a delicate little dish of pudding and cream in front of each vampire. The blonde immediately stopped talking to breathe in the rich sweet aroma of the Italian delicacy.

"Is this—?" she asked.

"It's Mr. Higgins's recipe for sanguinaccio," Georgia said proudly. "And the cream is flavored with kirsch and type O-negative, just like you remember."

This time Minerva grabbed her spoon and plunged it in eagerly. She closed her eyes as the mix of pig's blood and chocolate slid into her mouth, and for a few blissful moments, she remained utterly silent.

"It is Higgins's recipe!" Mr. Lambley exclaimed. "He got it from a lovely Italian lady from the Lower East Side. I haven't had this in years."

"Thank goodness I am not as intolerant as Steffan," Minerva said. "This is quite a pleasant surprise, *Berliner*. I guess you can cook something after all."

"You're welcome."

She let the vampires finish their dessert in peace and could even smile as she heard Mr. Lambley start a story about some rare-book vendor in London. Meanwhile Ren pulled out two puddings covered with foil and notes that said "vegetarian." He handed her a spoon and tipped his glass.

"Chocolate and coconut milk," she explained. "I practiced a lot of pudding this week. I think I gained ten pounds."

"This is so good," he said as he gulped it down.

"Well, two years of working with desserts was good for something," she said. "I, um, my last job was making and selling doughnuts, but we had to do the fillings too."

"I couldn't make pudding that is this good," he said.

"Wow, something I am actually better at than you," she said. "I'm going to have to write this down for posterity."

They enjoyed their little moment until both of them could hear the vampires calling out for drinks. Once blood was warmed and poured and the guests of honor moved to the lounge, the humans tried to make an escape, but Minerva clearly had other plans.

"Matsuoka, sit here," she said, patting the cushion beside her.

"As you wish," he said before dutifully perching next to her.

"And you, you stay too, *Berliner*," she said. "So, do you only sleep with *mein bruder*, or do you serve your master too?" she asked.

"Mr. Lambley is just my boss," Georgia said as neutrally as possible.

"Oh, that is such a shame," Minerva said. "You really are missing something. Geoffrey's mother had him trained by zee very best. You learned zee oral pleasures from those French lesbians, didn't you, darling?"

"There is really no way for me to answer that," Georgia said. "Thanks for the info."

Mr. Lambley looked helplessly around the room. "Please, Lady Fenstermacher, she is from a different world than us," he said.

"You've been around zee Americans for too long," Minerva sighed. "I am so happy that you agreed to come with us. You will have such a good time in Tokyo. It's not as repressed as it is over here. A few days in Chimachi will have you sprouting fangs again, I promise you. I bet we can have you right as rain before Dr. Pang even sees you."

"Chimachi?" Georgia asked.

"It's a hidden district within a district in Tokyo," Ren offered. "It's where my family does business primarily."

"It's vampire Disneyland," Minerva said cheerfully. "It's one of zee few places where we are allowed to simply feed as nature intended, among other things."

Georgia looked away as the vampire started toying with Ren's hair and running her hands slowly down the side of his neck. Minerva smiled and inched closer as she noticed the sour expression slowly crossing Georgia's face.

"I'm not sure that I can fly—" Geoffrey started to fret.

"You can and you will," Minerva snapped. "You owe me that after all I did to get you seen, but know this, little Pendragon, this trip—no matter what zee outcome—it isn't charity. This makes us even. Are we clear?"

Geoffrey nodded. Minerva started nuzzling the side of Ren's throat hungrily. Georgia took this as an opportunity to excuse herself. She darted to the kitchen and made sure every dish was cleaned and put away. As she put the last fork in the drawer, she could feel cold, inhuman breath against the back of her neck.

"Jesus!" she shouted as she whirled around.

"Guess again," Minerva said with a little giggle. "You are a jealous little thing, aren't you, *Berliner*?"

"What?"

The vampire licked her lips hungrily. "Do you think that you can have it both ways—that you can be *mein bruder*'s little toy and that you can play with mine?" she asked in a dangerously low voice.

Georgia took a step back. The blonde vampire continued to stare right through her. "Do you know what a Jaeger is?" she asked.

"A vampire family," Georgia said, still stepping back.

Minerva shook her head. "A Jaeger is a hunter," she said. "We are born to catch our prey. Zee more difficult the hunt, zee greater our pleasure."

Georgia took off running back to the lounge, where Mr. Lambley immediately stood up as he saw just how flushed and terrified his assistant was as she burst into the room. Ren hopped to his feet as well.

"Georgia?" both of them asked at once.

"What is the meaning of this, Minerva?" Mr. Lambley asked with a surprising amount of force as the blonde vampire came sauntering back into the room, smacking her lips and licking her fingers.

"Oh, don't worry, *shatzi*," she said. "Your little human was good enough to give me a snack."

Both Ren and Mr. Lambley looked on in alarm. Georgia looked at the vampire in confusion until a horrible realization came over the stunned young woman. She clutched hands to her mouth and barely let out a squeal before running back to the kitchen. She only needed to see the box back on the table to burst into tears.

"Georgia, are you all right? Did she bite you?" Ren asked as he grabbed her shoulder. She turned and sobbed against his arm as the box remained terribly silent.

"What is the meaning of this?" Geoffrey asked as he came barreling in too. His righteous indignation turned to confusion as he saw an unmolested human and a pair of fuzzy corpses in a cardboard box.

"She killed them," Georgia choked out.

"They were food. Come on, Matsuoka. I am bored now," Minerva said flatly. She gave him a venomous look as he had to untangle himself from the sniffling Miss Sutherland. "See you in Tokyo, darling."

Georgia tried not to look in the box, but her eyes kept focusing at the streaks of red until the vampire finally found the lid and covered the scene of the crime. The two of them stood and stared for a good long time.

"I should have known. I should have expected it," Georgia sniffled. "I thought I was ready—"

"They were food, Georgia," Mr. Lambley said.

"I'm food, aren't I? The way she looked at me—"

"Come now, let's go," he said softly.

"The way she looked at me—" Georgia stammered again.

"What you have to realize is that she is a Jaeger," Geoffrey said. "Every Jaeger is expected to be a hunter. It's in their blood, for lack of a better word."

Georgia leaned against her master for a change. He awkwardly put his arm around her. "It is said that every Jaeger-born is given a test to prove their worth to the clan. Those that can hunt are welcomed with open arms. Those that can't, never see another sunset."

"That means . . . Steve . . ."

"My friend has always been different from the rest of his family," Geoffrey said weakly. "Come now; you go to bed, and I will clean this mess up for a change."

Georgia nodded and started padding toward the stairs. Her tears started anew as she realized that as soon as she was on the landing, she could hear the blender whirring to life.

14

Gail stared in horror at Minerva, and the blonde vampire laughed it off. She gave another exaggerated cat stretch. "Mmm, all this talk is making me hungry."

Gail stood up and made a beeline for the bathroom. After a quick pit stop, she splashed her face over and over. "This is crazy," she muttered as she examined her now blotchy complexion. "What are you still doing here?"

"Pretty crazy, right?" Georgia said as she exited the other stall. "You know, I've probably dropped in too much of the nitty-gritty, and we've both had a few too many. Do you want me to get you a cab?"

Gail shook her head. "It's so bizarre and exciting. Did you really all go to Tokyo? Was the doctor able to help Mr. Lambley? Was it totally romantic?" she gushed.

Georgia washed her hands. As she was flicking her wrists, the little cleaning woman came rushing over to give her a towel and offer a mint. Gail followed suit and left a five-dollar tip in the basket as the woman gave them both huge smiles.

"I never know what to do with bathroom attendants," Gail said as they snuck out.

"Think about the poor guys," Georgia said with a little laugh. "At least we don't have someone watching us.

"She's gone," Gail said as they came back to an empty set of tables.

"That's Minerva for you. She comes and goes whenever she wants. It should help my headache though. Minnie is as strong as some of the older ones, and it can get overbearing really fast."

"Is she going to be your sister-in-law?" Gail asked innocently.

It was Georgia's turn to laugh. "There is so much that happened. I mean, it's really complicated," she said with a sly grin. "Oh, here I am babbling about me! I should probably get to know you better, Gail."

"I'm really not that interesting," she sighed. "You've seen my resume. I want to know what happened in Japan. Come on, we've gotten this far!"

"Japan is amazing. I'll give you that. If I even started talking about the shopping, we'd be here for a week."

"Will I get to go? If I get the job, that is?" Gail asked.

"I honestly can't say. The Jaeger family and their servants do all their business out of Japan, but Mr. Lambley would only be going back for his follow-up appointment, which isn't scheduled until 2036."

"Twenty-thirty—!" Gail gasped.

"Vampire time, dearie," Georgia chided. "I did put it in the calendar already though. It would be part of your start-up package. Honestly, no matter what Minnie claims, Chimachi is far more her kind of place rather than Mr. Lambley's. It caters to the, um, more *traditional* type of vamp, and he's just not ready for that kind of excitement, you know?"

Gail nodded. "I guess, but what did the doctor say?"

"I keep forgetting you were a nurse," Georgia said. "Vampire doctors aren't exactly like your good old primary care physician around here, you know, and Dr. Pang is unique even for a vampire doctor."

Gail looked at her in wide-eyed anticipation. Georgia motioned to the sofa again. "So much happened in Japan, you know. It was a total blur. Getting Mr. Lambley on a plane probably shortened my life for a few years."

Gail scratched her head. "I didn't even think of that. How did it even work?"

"We packed him in a coffin and had him shipped."

"What?"

"Oh, it's the easiest way to fly a vampire," Georgia said. "They only need like one tenth the oxygen we do, so you pack them up with a little tank, pay a certain set of fees, and slip them by. That way you can un-pack them only when you are ready. Steve, on the other hand, likes to fly first-class since he's not as bothered by the sun. The only hiccup is get-ting through the new security scanners. I think he enjoyed the pat down though."

"You put him in a coffin," Gail said, still rolling around the details in her mind.

"It's been the travel method of choice for centuries. Even if someone opened it up, they'd just find a cold body lying still. Mr. Lambley was a terror getting ready, but I know for a fact he slept the whole way there and found it rather soothing. We've had to keep it in the basement since he found it so comfortable!"

"I guess that makes sense."

"I've added to Higgins's notes. Ren helped me digitize the lot," Georgia said. "It's really not too bad if you just know where to look, and of course, there is always the Internet."

"And you've been to Japan," Gail sighed. "I can't even imagine."

"Yeah, nothing can really prepare you for Asia if you've spent your whole life in the States. It's very loud, very bright, and you quickly need to get over the concept of personal space. The first time I saw a subway packed up like a sardine can, I was certain that either Mr. Lambley or I or both of us would be a gibbering idiot within a week, but it was the strang-est thing. The same shy little vampire who a few months ago could barely walk down the street actually rode the wave of people and just crammed in there with me."

"Really?"

"And to make it worse, everyone stared at us. Neither Mr. Lambley nor I have ever been the tallest in our class, but in Tokyo we might as well have been Godzilla. There aren't that many pasty, flabby, tall gingers in Japan, so we were practically a tour stop in the outlying areas where we went to meet the doctor."

"How did he manage then?"

"Well, the funny thing is, when you know everyone is staring at you openly, you don't ever have to wonder who's looking at you. You're just different, and it's kind of liberating. It's hard to explain, but after a while, you just get used to it, and the attention can even be nice. Once we got over the flight and the jet lag, the first few days were one nonstop party, at least for Mr. Lambley and me. Ren, Minnie, and Steve were all off on business until I finally got this message that they were ready for us. Mr. Lambley was taken to a spa, where he was supposed to detox and purify before Dr. Pang would see him, while I was given instructions to meet the guys for our first evening out all together . . ."

Georgia checked her phone twice as she found herself smack-dab in front of a tower of glowing musical notes in the heart of Shinjuku on a crushingly busy Saturday night. A quick glance to the right confirmed a convenience store to one side and a girl in a miniskirt and heels handing out flyers to the other.

"Um, excuse me," she said. "Um, soomi-maasin," she tried to choke out in Japanese to the girl, but rather than embarrass herself further, she flipped her phone around to show off a string of kanji characters that Steve had conveniently just sent her. The girl burst into giggles and pointed to the neon-ringed door behind her.

With an evil smile, she said, "Have good time!" and gave a little wink.

Georgia eyed her text message suspiciously. "I have got to learn more Japanese," she muttered as she darted through the crowd and managed to slip into the Red Room Music Haven Club, where yet another cheerful young woman in a miniskirt and heels bowed deeply to her.

"Room Three, this way please, Miss Georgia!" she said.

"I guess I stand out," Georgia muttered as she was led to a frightfully narrow set of stairs lined with rainbow metallic wallpaper. Her overstuffed pile from shopping made it tough to inch by until she reached the relative spaciousness of a hall lined with English-named rooms. Her tiny guide pointed to the third one down, the "Rose Palace Suite."

"He is waiting for you. Do you need me to take bags? Get you anything?" her guide asked.

Georgia closed her eyes as she took in the cacophony of various musi-
cal styles and faint voices drifting from all around. "Surprise me," she said.
"Just bring me something to drink that I don't normally get in the United
States."

"Very good, miss," she said before sliding open the pink door.

"Wow," Georgia gasped as she found herself in a room full of white
leather cushions, mirrors, and flowers sculpted out of neon. A tower of
fabulously fake roses formed an arbor-like frame around a flat-screen TV,
while each microphone was wrapped in floral-printed ribbons. In the corner of the room, a decidedly different-than-normal Ren Matsuoka leaned
back against a pile of pillows—bobbing his head to the nineties' grunge
rock pouring out of the speakers.

"Never would have pegged you as a Nirvana fan," Georgia said as
she tossed her pile of shopping conquests onto another banquette. She
stretched out her arms and admired her new rows of brightly colored
charm bracelets in the trippy lights. "Have you been singing alone in here,
Ren?"

"No, I've been drinking alone," he sighed as he tipped back his beer.
"I take it that my master's directions were clear enough? He's still across
the street having dinner."

Georgia wrinkled her nose at the thought of Steve's preferred variety
of Tokyo supper. As she caught Ren looking her way in the reflections,
she quickly flicked her fingers through the freshly cut ends of her hair
to transform her normal pixie cut into a golden halo around her brightly
made-up face.

"I see you didn't keep the blue in there," Ren noticed. "It's a shame."

"That's the advantage of hacking it all off," she said cheerfully. "You
can try anything crazy and make it gone in an instant. Oh, why didn't you
tell me that such a thing as curry doughnuts exist? I feel like my life has
been incomplete until now!"

After one more tousle for good measure, she yanked open her largest
shopping bag and pulled out a puffy white coat with a brilliant light blue
collar of luxurious faux fur. "Can you believe this, Ren? I managed to find
a Muppet-skin jacket!" she exclaimed with glee as she slipped it on over

her T-shirt. She then popped her hands on her hips and struck an appropriately haughty pose worthy of her American height.

"So, what do you think?" she asked.

"I think the Cookie Monster is going to be found dead in a ditch," he deadpanned before taking another slow sip of his beer. He picked up his phone for a moment. As she scowled, he finally relented, tossed the device on the leather, and added, "At least it brings out the color of your eyes."

"You are especially cranky tonight, Mr. Matsuoka," Georgia teased. She looked at the dark circles under his eyes suspiciously. "Jet lag hitting you still?"

Ren plopped down his now-empty bottle. "I've had to spend three days with my family," he muttered. "I had two presentations to give and a client to meet. Sleep was considered *optional*."

Georgia checked her phone. "Have Steve and Minnie been with you?"

Ren shook his head. "Both of them have been guests of the main family. They had business to handle."

"The kind of business that keeps them out of touch?" she asked.

Ren nodded. "The kind of business that even I don't know about," he said as the next round of drinks came into the room. "Did you have any trouble getting Mr. Lambley to Hanada?"

"No, the car was there and everything," she said, distracted by her champagne flute full of chartreuse liquid that had a thick vapor rolling over the rim. Ren grabbed yet another beer and returned to his spot in the corner. "Um, what did I order?" Georgia asked.

"I don't know, what *did* you order?" he asked in uncharacteristically animated sarcasm.

"I asked for something you could only get in Japan," she said before taking a sniff. "Oh well, everything else has been bizarrely delicious. *Kampai!*"

"*Kampai,*" Ren echoed. He watched her closely as she took a long sip and sloshed the insanely bright beverage around her mouth.

"Oh thank god, it's green tea-flavored and not wasabi," she said as she put the fancy drink down. She cocked her head and let out a woof. "That tastes really strong."

Ren changed the music to something else broody and alternative while Georgia started ruffling through her bags again. He took his time, rolling another bottle in his hands while his unusually product-deficient hair flopped over his eyes.

"So, other than a ridiculous amount of shopping, what have you been up to in Tokyo?" he asked.

"Well, the girl you sent, Mitzi—Mishu—?"

"Mitsuko, my cousin," he offered.

"Yeah, Mitsuko, she showed us around a temple and got us to the hotel and stuff, and there was this ramen place she recommended that was out of this world. Then last night we ended up in this club show-type thing, where there were giant dancing robots and tanks and about a million different things that must have been dreamed by people on acid, but it was amazing," she gushed. "Half the time I have absolutely no idea where I'm going or what I'm going to see next, but I haven't had this much fun in . . . yeah . . . it's been a while."

"I'm glad you like it," Ren said softly, staring off into space.

Georgia took a moment to really look at her companion. His shirt-tail flaunted itself—wild and untucked—and he had left his collar unbuttoned. He slouched in a decidedly un-Ren like fashion, with wild hair and slightly bloodshot eyes, as if some younger, wilder, more haunted version of himself had taken possession of his body.

"Hey, are you OK?" she asked.

"I've just had a rough day," he said.

"Want to talk about it?"

"No."

"Well you're really not being yourself—"

"How can you even say that? It's not like you know me," he snapped.

"Of course, I don't know you," she said. "How could anyone know you when you put in so much time and effort in keeping others away?"

Ren snorted and focused on his drinking again. Georgia started to play with her phone but ended up tossing it onto the leather in a huff. "What is your damage, Ren?" she asked. "I mean, I get that you're upset because your life hasn't quite turned out as expected, but guess what, no one's ever does, so why are you suddenly all mopey?"

"What is *your* damage, Georgia?" he asked, finally looking at her and not staring off into space. "I mean, what happened to make you such an expert on disappointment? Enlighten me, please."

She wandered over to look at Ren's playlist full of songs about longing and loneliness. "You couldn't mix it up with a little "Don't Stop Believing," could you?" After a few seconds of his painfully bright green stare, she took a seat next to him and started rolling her own drink between her palms. Just as Ren grew impatient and began picking at a hairline fracture in the paint, Georgia finally took a deep breath but ended up choking up before any real words formed.

"You can't think of anything, can you?" Ren said, venom dripping from his voice.

"I wish I could say it was one thing, something tragic," she finally spat out. "Something to rationalize just how little I've done with my life, but I can't."

Ren leaned forward to listen but didn't dare say a word. She continued.

"It's just—it's like—" she stammered. "It's like my dreams were worn away by paper cuts, and at some point I woke up and realized that, 'Hey, you aren't going to be in a music video, land on the moon, cure cancer, or win Olympic gold.' It's like you spend your whole youth being told just how awesome and special you are, but then you take one step outside and that bubble bursts. The cold truth sinks in that you're average and that you're destined for middle management, at best."

"Says the girl dating a vampire and jet-setting in Tokyo," Ren said softly.

Georgia laughed sadly. "Hey, you asked. Don't blame me if you don't like the answer."

The soft mix of neon and shadow played beautifully with the lines on his face. Georgia reached over and pushed the hair out of his freakish eyes. She froze in place as she found herself so close to him that she could smell the alcohol on his breath. Gravity began to weave its spell as her face grew heavy and leaned in closer to his.

"You are such a disaster," he said as his lips pressed against hers for the briefest of moments.

Georgia broke free and jerked away. "A disaster, huh?" she snapped.

"Wait! That—" Ren stumbled.

"That's what you think of me, really?" She stomped over to her bags and pulled out a rather tiny cocktail dress. She gave him one more glare, one more chance, but his tongue remained tied. "I've got to get ready. Steve is on his way," she choked out before nearly ripping open the door.

The startled attendant pointed the way to the ladies' room. Georgia stomped there and found a way to twist her body sufficiently to slip out of one outfit and into her teeny white number in a stall that couldn't be more than a foot and a half wide. As she looked in the mirror to check her makeup, Georgia finally realized that tears were streaming down her cheeks.

"What the hell, Georgia?" she admonished herself. "He's always an asshole."

She splashed water and reapplied mascara and lipstick. By the time she was done, nary a trace of any emotion was left on her pretty little face. "Wouldn't Ren be proud now?" she hissed at her repaired reflection.

This time when she returned to the room, she was greeted by the smiling face of one Stefano DeMarco. Without missing a beat, she wrapped her arms around him and gave him a long, passionate kiss. "Missed you," she said while looking right over his shoulder at the still slouching and silent Ren.

"Well, hello to you too," Steve said, swinging her around playfully. "I hope we have a big night of plans . . ."

"We did have a big night," Georgia said. "It was dancing, sushi, and way too much karaoke. We took this long, beautiful walk that ended up right near the Tokyo Tower. It was like Steve had been given a list of all my favorite things and checked them off one by one."

Gail nearly squealed, not noticing the faraway look rapidly taking over her interviewer's eyes. Georgia looked down and caught her breath for just a moment before her face settled back down and she dared to look Gail in the eyes again.

"It was simply perfect, and for just a moment, everything was right. Steve looked me right in the eyes and told me that he loved me, and we went back to his hotel room for the rest of the night."

Georgia let the now-bouncing Gail have her moment as she absorbed the wonder of a vampire confessing his feelings in the moonlight. The interviewer pulled out her phone and started flicking through her pictures until she found one of her in said white dress, posing awkwardly for a self-ie, as if there was someone next to her that didn't make it onto the screen.

"I look pretty happy, don't I?" Georgia mused. "I can only imagine how happy I would have stayed if I hadn't grabbed the wrong phone at the karaoke bar that night . . ."

Georgia padded out of the bathroom as she heard a buzz coming from her purse. She squeezed the last bits of moisture into her makeshift turban and gave her ears a good shake before letting the towel fall so she could pay attention to other things. As she noticed the plain black case instead of her purple leopard-print one, she sighed.

"Great, now I'll have to talk to him," she muttered. She picked up the phone to see the text "Great ideas. What next?" from Stefano on his screen.

"Great ideas?" she asked. On a lark she swiped her fingers across the screen but was stymied by a PIN prompt. She went back to finish getting ready, but just as she was stepping into her shoes, there was a knock on the door.

She opened it to find a very neat and tidy Ren in his typical dark suit and tie. In one hand was her phone, in the other a box with a beautiful aqua-colored bow.

"My master wanted to send his apologies for having to leave before you awoke," Ren said, eyes lowered. "And I wanted to apologize for last night. I was drunk."

Georgia let him pass and went to grab his phone. "So, what were the great ideas?" she asked.

Ren froze. She sauntered over and took the box. Inside were delicate little pastries all lined in a row, with the faint aroma of fenugreek and cumin wafting from the filling.

"Curry doughnuts—how thoughtful," Georgia said. "Steve is always so very thoughtful. It's like he knows exactly what I want every time I want it."

"My master—"

Georgia paced a bit and touched her finger to her lower lip, lost in thought. "In fact, if I didn't already know that he was some superhuman creature, I would be sure he had magic powers."

"He tries his best," Ren said. "We should be going soon. We need to take your boss to Dr. Pang—"

"Did he ask you to get these delicious-looking curry doughnuts?" she asked pointedly.

"He simply asked for me to get you a gift," Ren said evasively.

"Holy Cyrano De Bergerac, Batman! You really plan everything he does, don't you? All the dates and the romantic dinners—it's always you."

"I make arrangements, yes."

"You know, I teased Steve about him nearly veering into creepy stalker territory from time to time because he always had this great attention to detail and a perfect sense of timing about some things. I guess I was so swept up on that whole vampire romance shtick that I was stupidly blind to the real stalker. Go ahead, insult me now," Georgia dared. "Say something to make me furious so we can just storm off and ignore everything that's happened in this conversation. That is how we communicate, isn't it? Isn't it?"

"We should be going to get Mr. Lamb—"

"You're both in on it!" she snapped. "You feed him all my information, every little thing I like—"

"Yes," Ren said softly. "Yes, it is my job to watch you, learn about you, and predict exactly what will make you happy."

Georgia shook her head in disgust. "I am such an idiot."

"I'm the idiot," Ren muttered.

"What was that?"

"I said I'm the idiot. I'm the one who does everything in his power to get to know you, to learn just how smart and fun and crazy you are, just so that you can sleep with my master over and over again," Ren said in his most flat, cold, and borderline robotic voice. "Now, can we please go to get Mr. Lambley, as Dr. Pang is not one to be kept waiting?"

Georgia grabbed her purse and made sure to switch phones. As she got near Ren, she could actually see the veins pulsing on the side of his neck as he strained to keep his face damnably calm.

"And that bothers you?" she asked.

He whirled to face her. "Of course, that bothers me!" he barked.

She didn't budge. "Why?"

"Why do you think?" he asked.

"You're right, we should get Mr. Lambley now," she said before storming out the door. They walked in silence from the hotel to their car. Ren went for the passenger seat, but the driver waved him to the back. He tried to protest but was ultimately forced to sit uncomfortably close to the still-fuming Georgia as the car rolled slowly toward the garage gate.

"Does he ever plan anything?" Georgia finally sighed.

"My master just wants to please you."

"He wanted you to figure out how to seduce me. Does that make sense to a vampire? I mean, is that one of their things?" she said, still staring out the window rather than looking at him.

"Like I said, he just wanted to please you."

"Oh, if he wants to keep pleasing me, he's going to keep you out of the equation. Maybe I'm just being *dreadfully* American, but I'm not into three-ways," she spat. "And you, what did you want?"

"It never mattered what I wanted," Ren said.

"That's your problem right there. You let them walk all over you—"

"I have to."

"I know, I know, you have your contract—"

"My life depends on it," Ren said softly.

Georgia turned to him. "Are you being literal or having one of your dramatic episodes?" she asked.

"Literal."

She waited for him to continue. Ren looked around uncomfortably for a few minutes as the car slowed to match the thick traffic of downtown Tokyo. He started rolling his lip between his teeth and fidgeting as words escaped him over and over.

"My family is different," he finally said.

"You're a Japanese genius with green eyes, I figured that out already," Georgia deadpanned. She cringed as she saw Ren still struggling for words.

"They say that the first servants of the Caesars sent emissaries across the entire empire to look for fresh blood, so to speak. One group ended up trapped in the Far East until they encountered a group of women who were born and bred to serve the other great clan at the time. To make a long story short, one family of these women decided to leave the service of their old masters and took in these strangers from the West. My family came from this special clan. When war broke out between the Lung and the Caesars, my family fled from China to Japan and have been there ever since, carefully expanding the interests of the Western families."

"So that explains where the green eyes came from, but what aren't you telling me?"

"Each branch of my family is carefully bred for whatever traits the particular vampire family needs to complement it. The Matsuoka line serve the Jaeger—"

"So you are bred to be smart then, since they are mostly the brawn, am I right?"

Ren nodded ever so slightly, but said, "We are chosen to work well with them—to be subservient." He paused and took a deep breath before finishing with, "And we are also carefully, selectively bred to have a rare genetic disease."

"A disease?"

"Every little Matsuoka girl is a carrier, every boy is born without the ability to make antibodies. We're missing certain white blood cells, so what would be a day off school for you could be a death sentence for us."

"Oh my god," she said. "But—"

"The main family has it. If for some reason you aren't a carrier, you get moved to the outer reaches of the family and slowly excluded or married off to one of the branches that serves a more progressive clan. You don't get to serve the lofty house of Jaeger unless they are absolutely sure that they can control you."

"You mean—?"

"For centuries the only hope we had was being adopted by our bene-factors. Any Matsuoka boy was raised from birth to serve his betters, or he took his chances and died the first time cholera broke out in town. Yes, we're nothing more than glorified bondsmen, usually bondsmen from birth."

"So you do need vampire blood to live."

"Oh it's worse. Most bondsmen get an immunity over time to the controlling effects, but for some reason, our years of unnatural selection actually make us more susceptible to vampiric control."

"But something changed. You said you weren't going to serve a vam-pire. You were going to be a Wall Street tycoon," Georgia said.

"The twentieth century happened," Ren said. "You suddenly had a choice as a Matsuoka mother. Now you have antibiotics and clean rooms and movies about boys in plastic bubbles. By the time Rikuto and I came along, you could get transfusions. We were given the choice between the pain and risk of human medicine or the tried-and-true method of drink-ing a vampire's blood. It wasn't like there was a shortage of Matsuokas to vampires at the time, so we were indulged."

"So you—?" Georgia dared to ask.

"Once a year I get a very special birthday present from Minerva Fenstermacher," Ren said. "My contract is always in blood, her blood, and if I don't take it, I'll die."

"But can't you just go back to your treatments?"

"I've been dependent on Minerva's blood for nearly a decade, Georgia. The transfusions contain other human plasma that could be contaminat-ed, and the reaction would be catastrophic. Anyway, what does it matter? Not only would I be condemning someone else to take my place, but what do I even have to go to? I've spent a decade doing . . . questionable things, and without the blessing of my family, I'm sure I'd be left out to dry."

"Wow, it does suck to be you," Georgia said. It was her turn to bite her lip before she apologized with, "Poor choice of words—sorry."

Ren smiled a little. "Minerva orders me to obey her and her brother, but she could be far worse. All she wants from me is food, and Stefano just wants a glorified butler."

"Well, I've seen the way she likes to eat. You're right, it could have been much worse."

"I'm just food to her," he said again.

"Why do you keep . . . ?" She trailed off. "Well, I'm not just food to Steve. He may be a bit of a jackass for using you, but we're not like you and Minnie."

They rode the rest of the way in silence until Mr. Lambley joined them. He eyed them both suspiciously as Georgia and Ren made it a point to look out opposite windows.

"Is there something you're not telling me about this doctor?" he asked, worried.

"Oh no, just bored from traffic," Georgia said quickly. "Now tell me all about your day. Did they feed you well?"

As Geoffrey started blabbing about the high-quality freshly drawn blood and silk sheets at the spa, Georgia continued to watch Ren. The Matsuoka toyed idly with his collar, rubbing the scars that ringed his neck.

The car pulled into a rather nondescript-looking beige office building at the edge of Tokyo proper. They were escorted by a pair of identical twin girls in lovely pink kimonos, who walked silently along a red carpet that had been rolled from the door right to the limo's side.

Although the garage door was plain putty-colored metal, what lay beyond it was an entirely different world altogether. Georgia and Ren both coughed as puffs of rich incense filled their lungs, and they had to squint to see anything in the candlelit room with dark paneling. Every nook and cranny was carved with ornate images of dragons and covered with red lacquer or gold leaf—a far cry from the usual simple and sleek design of a Japanese office.

The girls said nothing, but motioned to three red floor cushions lined neatly against the wall. The visitors took the hint and kneeled down on them, waiting in silence until a very tall, handsome man in a tailored suit and slicked-back hair came from behind a curtain to greet them.

"Ah, you must be Geoffrey Lambley, scion of House Pendragon," he said in perfectly clear, crisp English. "Miss Fenstermacher was just telling me all about you."

"Minerva is here?" Geoffrey asked.

"She is already inside with the doctor," their greeter said. "If you would all be so kind as to remove your shoes and wait here a moment, you will escorted to your proper waiting chambers."

They did as they were told, with Georgia having to help the woefully inflexible vampire in removing his loafers. She wrinkled her nose at the distinct and incredible funk of his bare feet.

"Mr. Lambley, if you would please come through first and head to the right, humans to the left."

Georgia squeezed his hand. "You'll be all right, Geoff," she said. "You're looking better already."

The vampire nodded weakly and gave a little gulp before waddling off inside. Ren and Georgia followed the polite greeter to a small locker room, with the twins on either side of a wooden screen—each one holding a neatly folded white robe and pair of sandals.

"If you would," he said. "Dr. Pang is very sensitive to the aroma of animals, and you need to be bathed and dressed appropriately before going forward."

"Animals?" Georgia mouthed, but she still dutifully stripped down and changed into her robe. "I did take a shower this morning," she sighed before getting into another one. All of her groaning and moaning subsided as she walked into a gorgeous bubbling hot spring bath and was offered luxurious Egyptian cotton towels and steaming green tea. She eased into the tub and let the soak sooth every inch of her as she could see a spectacular view of the night skyline from the window nearby.

A few moments later, Ren was escorted in, also wearing nothing but a towel. She made a point to look away as he had to drop it to step into the tub, but did cheat by sneaking a peek at the slight bit of reflection in the water. "Nice moon," she muttered under her breath.

She made it a point to keep herself as covered as possible under the water, not a difficult feat considering how warm and soothing the bath was, while Ren stuck to one corner with his hands folded over his lap.

"I didn't think we were going to see Dr. Pang too," she said.

"He probably just wants to observe you since you stay with him. Dr. Pang is a homeopathic doctor and is very concerned with the mind-body connection in his patients. Why I'm here, I don't know, unless I'm expected to serve as payment."

"The doctor will be ready for you soon, please try your best to relax and enjoy yourselves," the greeter said.

"I can certainly do that," Georgia said as she eased back under the water. They two of them ended up lounging for what seemed like an eternity in the dimly lit steamy bathroom. "I thought he said he'd be here soon."

"The greeter was probably answering in vampire time," Ren offered. Georgia took the opportunity to see more of the ink nestled under Ren's skin. In the bath she could finally make out talons carving their way into his chest, right where his heart should be.

He turned for her to let her see that it wasn't an eagle swooping down to claw out his heart, but rather a great snowy owl. One arm looked like it had been flayed to reveal circuitry, while the other had German text. In the small of his back, he had the male equivalent of a tramp stamp—a big black rune that looked like a badly written letter M with two extra lines inside.

"M?" she asked.

"It's Mannaz, the Norse rune for mankind," he said. "I'm not showing you the other tattoo though."

"Oh, where could that one be?" she teased. "So, what's with the bird?"

"The owl is the traditional animal of Athena. I had it done a few years back," he said. Before she could press for more details, the greeter chose that moment to clear his throat and request them both to get dressed.

Georgia slipped back into her robe, keeping her back to Ren until he said, "All clear."

"You didn't peek, did you?" she asked softly as they walked toward the other door in the bathroom.

"Of course not," Ren said. As they got to the door, he leaned over and whispered, "Nice bunnies."

Before she could get her arm back far enough to slap him, the door swung open. She blinked as they found themselves looking into a room full of ornate wall scrolls and more gilded paneling. Off to one side, a still-as-a-corpse redhead lay on a beautiful silk cushion while wearing nothing but what looked like a diaper. On the other side, a slim blonde lay stiff as a board, her modesty only maintained by what looked like cotton balls on knotted strings.

"Mr. Lambley!" Georgia exclaimed at the same time as Ren gasped, "Mistress!"

At the head of the room, a mysterious, huddled figure swayed back and forth in front of two pots of thick, heady incense. Each coil of smoke seemed to make a beeline for each vampire, drifting into his or her nose with unnatural precision.

"Oh, the young ones are here," a very crackly, nasal singsong voice said from the hunched figure. He turned around to reveal a face so cut and folded with wrinkles that it was difficult to make out individual features other than a stringy white Fu Man Chu mustache and a pair of thick black lenses covering his eyes. He wandered over slowly, teeter-tottering under an array of layered robes of all different patterns and colors. He made a tittering giggle as he saw Georgia's shapely bare leg peeking out from under her robe. As he looked her up and down, he made a giddy sucking sound through his teeth.

"Oh, very nice," he said before giving a little giggle. "And what is this? Is this a Matsuoka boy?" he asked as he sized up Ren. "Very nice indeed."

The wizened creature pulled a walking stick out from one of his voluminous sleeves and used it to help him pace around the pair. He even tapped both of them in random places, prompting several "Ow!" noises before he finally stopped.

"What did you do to them?" Georgia dared to ask.

"Better that they sleep," Dr. Pang said with a rapid nod. "It's always better to examine if they sleep. The fat one squirms, and the woman never shuts up, no?"

Georgia and Ren both clamped their mouths shut as they let the old man continue his walk-around. He once more zeroed in on Georgia and raised a crinkled hand up to grab her chin. Her eyes widened as she felt warmth radiating through his fingers.

Dr. Pang smiled widely to show off his bright and shiny gold-plated fangs. "You've seen one of me before, haven't you, little missy?" he asked. "Yes, you've seen one of the other two. You know what kind of monster we are!"

"You're still alive," she said.

"Indeed!" he squealed. "You must have met Mr. Sugar, yes? He's the only one of us who gets out much. Very interesting. You care for the toothless Pendragon, no?"

Georgia nodded.

The half-vampire took a deep breath before poking her in the chest. "Sit!" he commanded.

"What?" Georgia asked.

Dr. Pang actually squealed with delight. "You are one of *those* people!" he cried. "The Jaeger wasn't lying."

"I get that a lot."

"Oh, I wish I had more time to study you. When you die would you consider giving your body over to me for research—well, refreshments and research?"

She just shook her head. "Not really thinking about that now."

"Pity," he said. "You know I can have one of the girls give you some very good acupuncture. It will help with the headaches you get from my kind."

"Acupuncture?" Georgia asked incredulously. "Does that even work?"

"You are standing in the presence of a two-thousand-year-old living vampire, and you question whether or not our needles really work?" Dr. Pang asked.

"Good point," Georgia said.

"Your face is very English, very Pendragon," he said, looking over her again. "I think it might be what is helping inspire your master's recovery. I've prepared many supplements for him to take, and he must continue the best diet. His humors must be balanced between cooling blood from waterfowl and the hot blood of woodland creatures, like deer. If you fail to balance these temperatures within, he will simply not recover. I have prepared these schedules, and you must keep to them as his handler."

Georgia's eyes widened as she was handed a pile of paper all in Chinese. "I can't—" she started.

"You have eyes. You have a brain. Use the Internet, little one! I cannot be bothered with you not learning a proper language," he said as he foraged around for something in one of his robes. "Open wide."

She stared dubiously at the tongue depressor he had yanked from some unknown nether region, but she reluctantly went "Ahh!" anyway. The vampire peered deep within until he fished out a little light and made his job easier. He then looked in her ears and eyes and made many obnoxious little grunts before stopping to sniff her neck like she was a fresh-baked loaf of bread.

"You smell faintly of Jaeger . . . interesting," he said before moving on to examine Ren. He clucked his tongue a few times before sniffing him in much the same manner. "You smell like Jaeger too. My, my, these young ones certainly like to warm themselves up at night, don't they?"

Ren and Georgia both started studying the floor. "I recommend more iron for you, Matsuoka boy. Also, you need to adjust your energies to focus more on the self this year. You are born in the year of the Monkey and need to realign your emotions if you want to avoid being unwell."

"You're a monkey, really?" Georgia asked.

Dr. Pang turned back to her. "Even beautiful women should learn the allure of silence," he warned her. "You, Matsuoka, should take the Jaeger back to her waiting room and see that she gets fed and dressed. I wish to finish my consultation with the patient and his keeper alone."

Georgia watched Ren carefully scoop up Minerva and take her dutifully back to the bath area. Dr. Pang puttered about mixing little bottles into a bowl and creating something that looked nasty even by vampire standards.

"Is that to help Mr. Lambley regrow his fangs?" she asked as the half-vampire poured the liquid into Geoffrey's mouth.

"Oh, no, no, no," Dr. Pang said. "There is no medicine on earth that can treat the slow death once it gets this far."

"What?" Georgia cried.

"There is no medicine, but that does not mean his case is hopeless. There have been Pendragons who have recovered. The key is to awaken their inner strength so they can heal themselves. The Pendragons are not strong . . . but they are resilient," Dr. Pang said with a little nod.

"We came all the way out here to find out what we already know?" Georgia snapped. "Really?"

"Oh, little one, you should know by now it's not what you know but what you *believe* that matters. I have given your master a little snake oil and tiger's blood, and I will tell him that it will cure him and then it will. It may take time, but I think it will work."

"Really?" Georgia asked.

"Indeed!" he said cheerfully. "Now, I sense you have questions. You had better ask now before your time is up because I cannot be sure we will ever meet again."

"Do you know about the Matsuokas and their condition?"

Dr. Pang burst out laughing. "Oh, little one, you can say I know them all too well." He slowly lowered his glasses to reveal two perfectly bright, perfectly green eyes. "You want to know if they can stop being bondsmen now that there is new treatment, yes? In fact, you want to know if it will work for that pretty young one, yes?"

Georgia nodded.

"Difficult to say, really. There is a chance the other blood would contain some trace of something incompatible and kill him instantly, but there is also a good chance that he would be fine. The real question is why? Vampire blood is much safer and kills every disease. The human treatment is only a stopgap."

"Just curious."

"Curiosity killed the cat," Dr. Pang said with a little giggle.

"Too late for that," Georgia muttered as she started rousing the sleeping vampire.

Just as she was almost ready to walk out with him, the old half-breed tottered over and handed her a little vial wrapped in pretty red silk. "In case of emergency," he said. "One dose will cure almost any human disease, but you must use it all in one dose."

"Why are you giving me this?" she asked suspiciously.

"Because you asked about the Matsuoka boy rather than yourself. You go with your Pendragon. I will have Walter set up a follow-up for a decade or two from now. You follow that routine, and the medicine will do its job, yes?"

"And that was how we got Mr. Lambley on the right track," Georgia said as she futzed with her phone again. "It's very important, however, that he continues to believe that he got a slow-working cure from Dr. Pang. Mind over matter, always. Dr. Pang's people also gave each of us complimentary acupuncture and a full numerology workup. It did really help with the headaches, and they put me in touch with someone local if you ever need them."

"And the schedule?" Gail asked.

"Ren helped me get it on my phone. I've really learned a lot about Eastern medicine this past year. I suggest that you brush up on it too."

"And you and Stefano, err, Steve?" she asked hopefully.

"I did what any normal person would do. I didn't rock the boat until we were back from vacation."

"But did something happen? You and Ren—"

"It's complicated. I just wanted to separate the two. I asked Ren to cool off on the perfect date nights because I needed to see just what Steve would do."

"And?"

"We watched a lot of movies and had some pretty good sex," Georgia said drily. "I mean, there's not much to tell. Sometimes you get in a rut and do what is convenient. I had my hands full learning a diet, meditation, and exercise routine for a cranky English vampire who still tried to grind up crisps and mix them in his blood. The last thing I had time to worry about was my relationship with his friend. Everything was . . . fine, but—"

"Oh no, not a 'but,'" Gail said. "I have a bad feeling suddenly."

"You know that sinking feeling you get in the pit of your stomach when you know something is wrong but you can't quite put your finger on it?" Georgia asked. "It's that sort of dread that reminds you that you're putting your head in the sand."

"I hate that feeling when you know something isn't quite right—" Gail started.

"But you don't know what to do about it," Georgia finished. "Minerva went back to New York straight from Tokyo, and I thought that would make things better, but it's so weird, even though she was gone, something both she and Geoffrey had said kept gnawing at me . . ."

"A Jaeger is a hunter," Georgia whispered as she sat at one of the laptops she had borrowed from Ren.

Across the bed Steve rolled over and blinked a few times. "What was that, sweetheart?" he asked.

"Sorry, just thinking about something your sister said," she confessed.

Steve opened his eyes fully and looked at the alarm clock. "It's after dawn, what has gotten into you?" he yawned.

"Your sister is a killer," she said, furrowing her brows.

Steve responded by wrapping his arms around her and trying to pull her toward him. "You're not having nightmares about the kittens again, are you?" he asked.

"Would you?" she asked.

"Would I what?" he asked as he started nuzzling her side.

"Would you have eaten them?" she asked.

"Any vampire would eat them if they were hungry enough," Steve said sleepily. "But I wouldn't tear apart helpless animals in front of you. I'm not like that."

"In front of me?" she asked.

Steve looked up at her. "I am not my sister, now come on and curl up. If you're not going to sleep, we might as well do something more interesting," he said as his hand started to slide up her leg.

"You know I need to check on Geoffrey's duck carcass order. It's time to start the cooling phase of his diet," she said.

Steven reached over and snapped the laptop screen closed. "Ren is over there. The man is so detail-oriented that he makes spreadsheets to document his toast. This is your one night over here, so can we leave Gingersnaps out of it? Pang gave him some magic juju, it'll work."

Georgia continued to stare at the ceiling and refused to answer any of Steve's advances until he finally sat up and started twiddling his thumbs in annoyance. "Is this one of those moments where I'm going to have to talk?" he sighed.

"People in relationships usually talk," Georgia muttered.

"What do you want to talk about?" he asked.

"Nothing," she sighed before sliding down and rolling over as if to sleep.

"Fine by me," he sighed.

No sooner had he closed his eyes than Georgia asked, "Steve, what is the Jaeger test?"

"The what?"

"The test. Geoffrey said that every Jaeger had to pass a test to prove their worth to the family."

Steve wrapped his arm around her and hugged her tight. "Every Jaeger has to show their courage, that they have what it takes," he said. "You know what happened to me. I had to volunteer to die a horrible death so that Claudia and Klaus wouldn't slaughter the entire unit. It's not the traditional Jaeger test, but I'm not your traditional Jaeger. Am I missing something here? What is going on in that pretty little head of yours, sweetheart?"

"You saved all those people," she whispered as she curled against him.

"Yeah," he said softly before kissing her goodnight.

As soon as she was sure he was out and snoring, she lifted his arm up and snuck back on the laptop.

By the time she had managed to get a tiny bit of sleep, a mix of thunder and the door opening snapped her awake. She could see sheets of water pouring down the windows and hear droplets plopping into the bucket left over from the previous nor'easter.

"Hey, sleepyhead," Steve said as he came wandering in shirtless but in leather pants. "Matsuoka is back if you want coffee."

"Just give me a minute," she said before checking that the laptop was still on her side of the bed. She quickly got dressed and sent messages to both Mr. Lambley and to Nicolette.

Steve eyed her as she walked into the room with a computer in hand. "You've got your shoes on already," he complained.

"I don't think I'll be staying long," she said.

Ren paused in the kitchen as he saw her hands shaking as she set the computer on the breakfast bar.

"It's awful out there," he warned. "I made certain that Nicolette made it over before I dared leave."

"Yeah, he's got a babysitter and it's awful out. You should stay," Steve said playfully.

"I have some things to do before it's too late," she said, staring at the door.

"Baby, what is it?" he asked.

She looked him right in the eyes and said, "Steve, we really need to talk . . . alone."

"I'll be in my apartment should you need me, sir," Ren said, but he continued to look at Georgia.

As soon as the door shut, Georgia walked the vampire over to the couch and gently took both of his hands. "Steve, I'm just going to say this and not sugarcoat it," she said. "I think we need to not see each other anymore."

"What?" he said.

"I need to focus on Mr. Lambley right now—"

"Bullshit!" he snapped. "What is going on here?"

"I need to focus on my job," she said weakly.

Steve hopped to his feet and started to pace frantically. "Georgia, you can't . . . I mean, just tell me the truth."

Georgia let out a strained laugh. "The truth?" she asked. 'Do you even know what the truth is, *Stefano* DeMarco?"

"Yeah, I lied about my name. You knew that already. I came clean!"

"Then tell me, what was your test?"

"I told you!"

"What happened to your unit back in France? What really happened to them?"

"I told you, I turned myself over to Claudia—"

Georgia flipped open the laptop and showed him the very same webpage she had left open last night. "Joshua Leibowitz—killed in action in 1944; Stanley R. Smith—killed in action in 1944; Robert Chandler, guess what, he was also killed in action in 1944. Can you guess the only member of that entire unit who wasn't confirmed killed in France in 1944?" She clicked a link to show a small and faded portrait of a cute and familiar curly-haired boy in a uniform. "News flash, Steve: everything ends up on the Internet eventually."

"They weren't there," he said, staggering back. "They don't know the whole story."

"They were found in a mass grave . . . by a brewery."

Steve all but stumbled over his own feet as he looked at a picture of his old unit uploaded on some site called WWII Stories Online. Georgia didn't wait to pounce.

"Did you think I wouldn't be curious? Did you think I'd never find out the truth?" she snapped.

"That isn't the truth," he said.

"Then tell me the truth, please," she begged. "Tell me what really happened."

"Everything I told you was true, I swear," he said, reaching for her. "I did turn myself over to Claudia and Klaus. They promised that if I gave myself to them that they wouldn't kill the guys. They promised!" He closed his eyes and started tugging the ends of his hair. "A vampire always keeps a promise."

"I know that. You all keep saying that over and over and over again! So if a vampire always keeps a promise, how did they all end up dead? Convenient Nazis?"

Steve turned his back to her. She saw his shoulders shake.

"They killed me. Klaus and Claudia took their turns with my dying corpse, and then they left me. They left me locked in the basement with Leibowitz and Smith and Chandler. As they promised, they didn't lift a finger to harm the boys."

Georgia covered her mouth with her hand in horror. Steve whirled around, his eyes welling up and his fangs bared.

"You—"

"You would have done the same thing," he said even as she shook her head violently. "It's easy to say that you'll be noble and good until you're really, truly backed in a corner and you know it's you or them. I mean, do you even know what it's like to be starving? You sit there on your high and mighty horse, woman, but you have no idea . . . no clue . . . no inkling of what I had to go through!"

"Every Jaeger is a hunter," she said softly. "Every Jaeger is a killer."

"You're right. You know in those vampire movies when you hear all that crap about how you're only really a vampire when you make your first kill?" he growled. "Well, guess what? That little bit of lore did come from my family. We are all killers."

"You should have just told me," she said as she started backing toward the door.

"Why? So you could look at me with disgust like you're doing right now?" he growled.

"I'm gonna go."

Before she could even blink, she felt the full body weight of the vampire crashing into her chest. She screamed as he dashed across the room until she was jammed against the wall. Posters came crashing down, sending glass shards across the floor, as she continued to struggle.

"Let me go," she screamed.

"Listen to me!" he yelled in her ear. "Look at me!"

"Let me go!"

He grabbed her jaw and forced her to face him. "I am not like the rest of them, Georgia," he snarled. "I may have killed, but I never enjoyed it. I'm not like them!"

She stared at him. His rage had turned his once puppyish brown eyes fierce and red. She could feel every inch of him forced against her, leaving her completely trapped. No amount of effort from her arms or legs could seem to force the inhuman creature back.

"You're acting like them," she spat.

"Oh really?" he snarled. "You want a vampire? You want to meet a real Jaeger? Then fine!"

She started to whimper as he tilted her neck and let his breath tickle her trembling skin. She felt the very tips of his fangs scraping the very top layer of skin, teasing and probing for her now-exposed vein. "Please stop," she begged.

He pulled his head back for a second and closed his eyes. "I need to make you understand," he said. "You need to have me inside you. You need the real me inside you."

He rolled his lip back and bit into it violently until a large dot of blood welled up on the surface. She froze in abject horror as he changed to caressing her cheek gently, teasing her lip and urging her to kiss him.

"Just let me show you," he whispered as he swooped in. Before he reached her mouth, he roared in pain and staggered back. The vampire grabbed the back of his neck, where a bright yellow pencil had been jammed into the gap behind his collarbone. Georgia wiped the drops of blood from her face, leaving a crimson streak across her cheek as the vampire began to shake.

"Run!" Ren yelled as he rammed his shoulder into his master's chest.

Steve retaliated with a solid punch and sent his servant reeling.

"Ren," she gasped as she watched him take another blow. Rather than wait, she grabbed one of the fallen frames and cracked it over her knee. She brandished the splintered wood and tried to get between Steve and the now-bleeding Ren.

"You dared to—" he said, still staring as Ren. "You—"

"Georgia, run! Run back to Lambley," Ren shouted.

"I'm not leaving you with a monster," she said, still pointing her little stick at Steve even as her hands shook.

The vampire pulled the remaining pencil shard out of his back and dropped to his knees. "What have I done?" he asked. "Georgia, Ren, I'm so sorry."

"Georgia, go. I'm under the protection of Minerva. He can't do anything to me without her permission," Ren said. "Please, go to safety. Please!"

Steve wiped his lip and reached for her. "Sweetheart, please. Listen to me, that wasn't me. I'm so—I'm so sorry."

She grabbed her jacket and purse and ran out the door. Despite the torrential rain, she started walking from the relatively deserted waterfront area straight for downtown. She saw the bright black and white of the T, and a few taxis slowed down to stalk her as she started to soak through, but nothing slowed her steps.

Minute after minute she walked forward. She felt her phone vibrating against her hip every few seconds, but it only served to spur her onward. The cold autumn rain tried its best, but she could still feel his breath creeping down her throat. As she got closer and closer to home, she clutched the pit of her stomach. She looked over her shoulder, but there was only the rain.

She nearly got blindsided as she dared to cross Commonwealth Avenue. The car honked, and she flipped the bird. As she reached the corner where she could have turned to head toward Brookline, she instead chose to keep walking straight into her old neighborhood of Allston.

By that point the rain had run out of nooks and crannies to seep into, and instead flowed off of her in glistening sheets. She muttered a quick thank you to the weather gods as the torrents thoroughly drowned out her tears, no matter how many seemed to come out. She thought she heard her name but didn't look back. Instead, she picked up the pace and hustled to a familiar convenience store and a door with a V-shaped crack in the vestibule glass . . .

"Oh my god," Gail gasped as she now squeezed Georgia's shaking hand. "I'm so sorry."

Georgia smiled weakly. "It's funny," she said. "I used to hate the rain, but now it's all I ever dream about."

"What happened next?" Gail dared to ask.

"The beginning of the end . . ."

15

"Look what the cat dragged in," Alice gasped as she opened her front door.

"What a perfect choice of words," Georgia said with a bitter little laugh.

"Georgie, what happened to you?" she asked. "You look like shit."

"Gee, thanks," Georgia said. "Look, I'm sorry to just show up, but I, um, I had a fight with my boyfriend, and I was wondering if I could crash here just for a night or two. My key to the front worked, but—"

"Baby, who is it?" a male voice asked from the back.

"Hang on, honey," she said. "It's Georgia! Silly thing, you get in here before you melt."

She swung open the door to reveal a far cleaner apartment than Georgia remembered, with pizza boxes replaced by potpourri bowls and laundry substituted with tasteful throw pillows.

A very tall, pale gent with a green Mohawk and a dog collar waved cheerfully from the sofa. He put down his game controller to say, "Hey! Long time, no see, Georgie-Porgie. What happened to you?"

"Boyfriend fight," Alice said matter-of-factly. "That sucks donkey balls, Georgie. Don't worry about the key thing. I had to change them because there was a break-in a couple weeks back. Paul's been here since then, but you've still got a paid-for room, and I was kinda hoping you'd slum it with us sometime and see how nice the place has gotten."

"It does look pretty great," she said as she shivered and dripped on the kitchen floor. She jumped as she heard a banging from the vestibule door.

"Georgia!" someone cried.

"Wait, don't invite them in," she said instinctively.

"Is that the douche?" Paul said as he took command and left the sofa to go defend the home.

"Just don't let him in," she said softly. "Don't try to—"

"It's some Asian dude," he called back. "I think I can take him."

"Ren?" she gasped as she sloshed out into the hall. Both sets of neighbors banged on the wall as Ren continued to shout for her from the porch. She shoved past the giant with the Mohawk and yanked open the door. "What are you doing here?"

"He sent me after you," Ren said between shivers. "He ordered me to make sure you were safe."

"Um—" Alice started.

Georgia moved to the side. "Alice, Paul, this is Ren. He, um, worked for my boyfriend," she said.

"The old guy?" Alice asked.

"Different boyfriend," Georgia confessed.

"You've been getting around! Both of you get in here, and I want to hear everything—" She stopped as Paul cleared his throat. "Shit, we were gonna go out and get a movie tonight, but it's not—"

"No, you guys should go," Georgia said. "I really need to just get a shower and some dry clothes. Ren is here, so I'll be all right until you are done."

Alice eyed both of them. "I'm sure you will be. Get your asses in here."

The soaking pair stayed in the kitchen until towels and T-shirts were handed to them.

Alice reluctantly grabbed her sparkling purple raincoat and umbrella with little skulls on it. "It's the only night we both have off," she said guiltily.

"I'm the one who crashed the party. I'm fine! I do still have a bed in my room, right?" she asked.

"Yeah, Paul's D&D stuff is in there, but you can just put it on the floor. We'll be back by midnight. Help yourself to the fridge, but the vodka is spoken for," Alice said before heading for the door.

Paul stopped to get a good look at Ren's rapidly darkening eye socket. "The boyfriend gave you that, right?" he asked with a rather menacing snarl.

"Yes," Georgia hissed. "He's just my friend, and he's here to help."

Ren waited for the couple to be out of the door for a good minute before he dared to speak. "Are you OK?"

"Hell, no," she snapped. "What kind of question is that?"

"I meant, are you hurt?' he said, looking at a small bruise already welling along her jaw. "Vampires never know their own strength."

"I've got a few bumps and I have blisters on my feet, but I'll live. We're both gonna catch a cold if we don't get dry though."

She reached for the corner of her still heavy and soaking jacket and tried to peel the drenched corduroy off her shaking shoulders. The more she struggled to twist and wrench, the more doggedly determined the fabric became to stick to her skin. "Ugh," she moaned as it refused to budge.

"Here, let me," Ren said softly as he slid his fingers gently around her collar and under the sodden fabric. He managed to pull both sides back and peel away the sleeves. His hand instinctively wandered back to slide up the bra strap that had wandered out from under her tank top and crept down her arm. "Do you ever wear sleeves?" he asked even as his hand remained on her arm.

"Well, if you had inherited the shoulders of a linebacker, you'd have trouble with them too," she said, now looking at his hand.

"I was terrified when I found you—" he said as the hand squeezed the shoulder. The motion made her other bra strap slide into view. This time Georgia took the initiative to work it back into place, looking at him for the first time since he had been yelling her name at the front door.

"You're the idiot who scared me. You attacked a vampire. What were you thinking?" she asked.

"I was thinking that he couldn't hurt you, that I couldn't let him hurt you, no matter what he did to me," Ren said.

Georgia dropped her hands across her waist and slowly pulled her tank top over her head. She unbuttoned her jeans fly and slid her thumbs around the band until the top of her little rabbit tattoo could just peek over her hipbone. They stood there, frozen for a minute, listening to each other's breath and chattering teeth until Ren's hands slid over hers and finished loosening the band. The damp jeans started creeping toward the floor, tangling in her feet as she ungracefully tried to yank them off. Finally she ended up on the kitchen table until her knight in soaking armor was able to rip them away—taking her socks along with them. From this new angle, she was able to pull apart his already damaged shirt and fling it on the floor next to the growing pile of clothes.

He tried to pull off his T-shirt but found himself as tangled as Georgia had once been. He held his breath as he felt her hands slide from his waist to his shoulders, stopping on each and every line of muscle to fully feel the smooth contours of his brightly tattooed back. As he became twisted and tangled with his arms overhead and the tight collar of his T-shirt trapped under his nose, Georgia chose this moment to strike.

She grabbed his neck and pulled his mouth down to her level. He froze awkwardly as her lips pressed fiercely against his until he was finally able to jerk free of both her and his antagonistic clothing.

"Now's our one chance to say something stupid and ruin this moment," she dared him.

Ren grabbed her by the hips and dragged her into the hall. She barely managed to fumble over her old bedroom door as he was struggling with his belt. They both frantically shoved a pile of binders and gaming books off the bed with such force that the comforter ended up on the floor with them. She laughed as she had to help him get off his pants, and his socks too ended up flying to parts unknown.

He remained deathly silent as he kissed her neck, her shoulders, and the top of her breasts. Anytime she so much as threatened to speak, he covered her mouth with his own, all the while fighting with a bra clasp that seemed as impenetrable as Fort Knox.

Finally he gave up on top and focused his attention to removing any remaining clothing. He beamed with delight as Georgia finally managed to bend her arms around and free herself from her final remaining garment. He tossed her down on the bed, prompting her to yelp as she landed on a handful of pointy and awkward dice that had slipped under the covers. After another desperate sweep for rogue objects in the sheets and a Hail Mary dive into the still extant condom drawer, they finally managed to crash into each other and make all manner of random noise as they worked out months and months of pent-up frustration. After they finally both yowled and made ridiculous faces, Georgia collapsed into a pillow and shuddered for a solid minute.

Next to her Ren stared at the ceiling, still not making a coherent sound. Georgia handed him some tissues with a sheepish grin. After a quick cleanup and a plunge to the floor for the comforter, he wrapped them both up in tacky striped polyester and pulled her next to him.

"I'd forgotten what it was like to be this warm," she said as she listened to an actual heartbeat thumping and pumping inside a chest.

"Me too," he said. "Me too."

They stayed interlocked together until Ren kissed the top of her head and snuck out to gather the incriminating laundry and hide it closer to the scene of the crime. She watched him sneak back in and started to giggle. "I feel like I'm back in college and I need to put a sock on the door," she said.

"You did that too?" Ren asked.

"Things just got a whole lot more complicated, didn't they?" Georgia asked.

"They were already complicated," Ren said. "I think this actually made things simpler."

"How so?"

"I used to beat myself up, wondering if I was in love with you," Ren said. "Now I just know I am."

Georgia raised a brow. "Well, I guess I could see that, but don't you remember? I'm a disaster."

She waited for the ire to rise, for the moment to shatter, and for Ren to get up and walk away. Instead, he leaned over, kissed her, and looked into her eyes.

"If there is one thing I'm terrible at, it's analogies," he said, staying right in her face. "Don't you get it? You *are* a disaster to me. I thought I had everything in place, everything calm, but then you came along, and it was like a tsunami hitting me. I knew there was nowhere I could run, but I tried to. I really tried, but you just came crashing into me, and I'll never be the same."

"You are . . . so . . . ridiculously . . . utterly . . . wonderfully terrible with analogies," she said before kissing him until she couldn't even breathe anymore. But what can I say? I love you too."

"I'm going to shut up now before I ruin things."

"Good call," she said before curling in his arms and falling asleep.

Georgia woke up to the now-strange feeling of warm morning sunshine after a long and restful sleep. She could smell coffee and something toast-like and found a neatly folded T-shirt and shorts at the end of the bed. "Ren," she muttered as she rubbed her sleep-crusted eyes and thoroughly insane hair.

She moseyed out to the hall once she was dressed and yawned heartily. As expected, Ren was in the kitchen, preparing plates for both of them. Once properly bribed with toast and coffee, she settled at the kitchen table and gave him an incredibly bright smile. "Hey, you," she said.

"Hey, you," he said.

"Oh, hi," Alice said as she too wandered in for the siren's song of freshly brewed French roast. Even though Ren was horribly mismatched in a Sisters of Mercy T-shirt and Bermuda shorts, he still tried to stand perfectly straight and dignified and even gave a little bow as he handed Alice a plate and cup.

"Great contacts, dude," she muttered as she wandered by him and plopped at the table. "You look a little better, kiddo," she said as she saw her friend finally smiling.

"Just needed a good night's sleep, I guess."

"Damn, this is good coffee," Alice said before tipping her cup to Ren. She smiled as she saw the matching red marks on his and Georgia's necks. "Looks like someone had a run-in with a vampire," she said in a delightfully singsong voice.

Both Ren and Georgia fumbled their cups and looked over in utter shock. Alice snickered.

"What—what do you mean?" Georgia finally choked out.

"I mean you'd better get some concealer if either of you have work today. Friends don't let friends go out with hickies. You crazy kids, you."

Ren reached for his neck in alarm. Alice didn't miss a beat. "Hey, I get it. What happens here stays here, lovebirds. I've got to get to work, but I've got a spare key in case you need to crash for a few. Don't have too much fun without me, and we are totally drinking and catching up tonight."

"You have to go back to work tonight, don't you?" Georgia asked Ren. "You look like you're beaten-up pretty bad. I hope you can hide that," she said as she pointed to his neck.

He nodded. "The bigger worry is when I'm going to see you again," he said softly.

"We're smart people, right? We just have to be careful . . ."

"Famous last words, right?" Georgia snorted. "See, that's the problem when you're in love with someone, I don't think you ever realize just how obvious you are until it's too late. Have you ever had that problem, dearie?"

Gail shook her head. "But did Steve? Did he?"

"Steve wrote me an apology. He sent flowers too, and this time I'm pretty damn sure they didn't come from Ren. I told him that I wouldn't see him for a while and certainly not alone. I told him that if he had any messages for me that he should send Ren, which served my purposes just fine. The two of us had this code. He'd text me every morning before he went to bed with the words *mada ikite iru*."

"Is that 'I love you' in Japanese?" Gail asked.

"No, it means 'I'm still alive' actually. We always knew we were on borrowed time. That was part of the excitement of it all . . ."

"So, if you could be anyone in the world, who would you be?" Ren asked as he toyed with the chopped-off ends of Georgia's hair. The two of them lounged in Georgia's old bedroom, surrounded by empty take-out containers. Ren would occasionally poke at a laptop for a few minutes but quickly get distracted by the woman curled up beside him, who was half-heartedly doodling and taking notes on the highest protein contents in various foods while trying not to get caught watching funny pictures of cats on her own screen.

"That question is a wee bit heavy for a Sunday afternoon," she said. "I'm pretty happy with being Georgia Sutherland right now."

She punctuated her statement by tipping her head up and kissing him on the jaw. She scrunched up her nose. "You need to shave, boy."

He kissed her back before pulling up some sort of spreadsheet. "I'm looking for ideas. I was working on some new identities," he said.

Georgia read off the physical details column. "Blue eyes, blonde hair, five foot ten? Now, doesn't that sound familiar?" she said. "Has Minerva looked eighteen for a little too long to even pass in Hollywood? Hey, what's that look for?"

"Come on, answer the question," he said, now totally lost in thought.

"I dunno, maybe I'd be like a personal assistant to a rap singer instead of a vampire. I hear they are lower-maintenance. Hey, what is really going on here?"

"Indulge me," he said. "You'd *really* want to be that if you could be anyone?"

Georgia put her distractions on the nightstand and turned her full attention to the new woman taking shape in digital form. "Maybe I'd be a botanist," she said.

"A botanist?"

"You know, a person who makes new kinds of flowers. My grandparents bred champion roses, and I always thought they were beautiful," she said softly. "Plus flowers don't complain if you take care of them wrong, and it sounds like the kind of job that people would just go 'oh, that's nice' and not ask any more questions about. Wouldn't that be great for a vampire?"

"Hmm, a job with lots of vegetable matter and artificial sunlamps? I'm sure that would go over well," Ren said with a little laugh.

"No plan is without its flaws. Now, are you going to tell me what is really going on in that pretty little head of yours, or am I going to have to tickle you until you are plaid?" Georgia asked, readying her fingers to strike at a moment's notice.

"I look terrible in plaid," Ren deadpanned as he clicked open another window to show a scanned image of a US passport with Georgia's face on it.

She squinted to read the slightly blurry text. "Jennifer . . . Lee?" she read. "I never knew my birthday was in August. Here I was thinking I was an Aries all this time," she said. "Ren, why is there a passport with my face and a different name on it?"

He snapped the laptop closed. "I was just being stupid—" he started to say.

"Ren, you are many things, but you are never stupid. Just spit it out!"

He scooted up against the headboard and kept fidgeting with the edge of the comforter. Georgia pushed up on her hands and knees to meet him face-to-face. His furrowed brow and tight-set jaw made Georgia pause.

"It's my birthday in a little more than a month," Ren said.

"Well, if you are worried about your age, try to remember that my last boyfriend was nearly a hundred," she teased. Ren's face fell farther. "OK, now I'm getting really worried."

"On my birthday Minerva will give me the gift of her blood. She also likes to have a special meal beforehand," he said.

"Let me guess, Japanese takeout," Georgia growled. Her face softened as she watched Ren bury his face in his hands. "Come on, I know it sucks, and while I don't really *like* the thought of a pretty blonde doing god knows what with you, I know that you need it to survive. I signed on for this after you saved me from Steve."

"You don't know what it's like, to have one of them inside you," Ren said. He shook his head as Georgia started to protest. "I mean really inside you—in your system, in your blood. I will do anything, say anything while under her control. I also know that once I'm with her again—"

"What are you saying, Ren?"

"For nine years she has been the sick, twisted love of my life. You asked me what happened to my snowboarder? I couldn't stand to be around her after Minerva. I didn't even think it was possible to care about anyone else."

"I see," Georgia said, turning away from him. She jerked away as he tried to grab her shoulder. "Is he putting you up to this? Did he find out why you've been sneaking away during the day?"

"What? No!" Ren said, crawling around to look her in the eyes. "I'm sure he knows I'm seeing you, but not that—"

"Are you sure?" she asked.

"He'll know for sure as soon as Minerva makes me tell him everything. She does it every year. She tells me that confession is good for the soul, and I will give her every secret in a heartbeat. She already asked me about you once, but I was still able to control myself back then."

"Jesus, Ren!" Georgia said. "So are you just trying to let me down easy? Why would you even—?"

He grabbed her shoulders and pulled her close. "I am an idiot sometimes, but when you're faced with an unstoppable force like you, what was I supposed to do?"

"Then this is my fault?" she snapped.

"It's both our faults. Maybe it's because we're human. What do humans love more than a good tale of star-crossed lovers?" he asked. "For the first time in years, I found something that I want, to hell with what the Jaeger family thinks. I just thought . . . I just hoped—"

"Hoped you'd finish a train of thought?" she asked.

He got up and rooted through his coat until he found a little green booklet. He tossed it in Georgia's lap. She opened it slowly and saw his face staring back at her.

"What would you do if you knew your boss was taken care of and there was a place where my masters couldn't find us?" he started as Georgia's eyes widened and her jaw dropped. "What I'm about to say is so crazy that I know you are going to say no—"

"Yes," Georgia said softy.

"It's ridiculous, I know. There is only one place on earth where—wait a second, did you just say yes?"

"Yes," she said again, this time a little louder.

"Just listen to me. We would have to disappear entirely and go halfway around the world—"

"I said . . .yes."

"I don't think you realize just what I'm asking. The only place the Jaegers can't go is Hong Kong—"

"Ren, in all those months you watched me, did you ever see me change my mind once it was made up?" she asked. She looked back at the passport. "Lee, huh?"

"It's the kind of name that could be Asian, could be not," he said weakly. "It was easier to forge an identity if it was already connected to one that I'd faked, but I realize now that it was terribly presumptuous of me—"

She silenced him with a kiss and kept kissing him until his protests stopped. "Ren," she said, brushing the hair out of his eyes, "I don't make the best decisions. I make them fast, but I never, ever regret them. I said, *yes . . .*"

Gail broke into a huge smile as the pieces fell into place at last. She pounced on Georgia and gave her a huge hug. "I understand now," she said while squeezing tight. "I finally understand what you've been doing this whole time. It was a test, right? You needed a replacement so that you and Ren could run off together!"

Georgia patted the young girl on the back and eased out of the hug. Gail cocked her head as her once-bubbly interviewer was suddenly stone-faced. The blonde was staring angrily toward the door. Gail looked back, but no one was there.

"Georgia?" Gail asked. "That is what's happening, right? You need someone to take care of Mr. Lambley—oh no, is Minerva—?"

Georgia stood up and stretched before moving over to their original seats. She dug into her purse and pulled out a pair of plane tickets. Gail clutched her skirt and squealed in delight as she saw the letters HKG in the corner.

"You're right," Georgia said. "It's always been a test."

"When are you leaving?" Gail asked. She quickly lowered her voice. "Can you tell me? Should I shut up in case she comes back?"

"Oh, I have one more story I need to tell you, you know," Georgia said. "Earlier tonight, I told you about the second-worst Saturday of my life, didn't I?"

Gail nodded.

"It's time I told you about the worst. It's important that you know before any decisions are made," Georgia sighed.

Both women froze as the other blonde drifted in. Georgia put her mask back on and waved to Gail. "So, you were telling me that you were a nurse, right? Did you just work at home, or did you ever fill in at clinics or hospitals?"

Gail nodded and all but gave a wink to Georgia. "Um, I mostly worked at home. I did do Fridays and Saturdays at Mass General, usually the outpatient clinics, sometimes for the geriatrics department. A girl's gotta eat, you know," she said as she eyed the vampire.

"True words," Minerva said as she drifted by. Her cheeks were pinker than before, and she picked her teeth a few times as she slid into a seat next to them. "So, have I missed anything interesting?"

"No," Gail said quickly. "I was just telling her about my work experience. I, um, am familiar with chronic care. I usually work with the elderly, but I'm familiar with blood, you could say. I mean, I've worked with a lot of it—transfusions, blood work . . ."

The vampire rolled her eyes. "Are we still at zee boring part? I want to know something juicy, something truly, terribly interesting," she said.

"I still have to tell her about Mr. Lambley's schedule and about the final plans for transition," Georgia started.

"Don't you have a few months more on your contract? You have loads of time for a human!" Minerva whined. "*Mein bruder* has been calling too. He wants to know when you'll see him again."

"I want to make sure this transition goes smoothly, Minnie. Now we have at least a half hour more of boring details."

"I need dessert then. Maybe I'll get a jelly doughnut," she said with a pointed look at Georgia. She waved and said, "I'll be back."

Gail darted over to Georgia as soon as the vampire was gone. "So?" she asked.

"So?"

"When are you leaving with Ren?" Gail hissed.

"These things take time to plan. I needed to make sure that someone would be able to take my place before I could leave, and we had so many details to take care of. You're a nurse, so you know what it's like to account for a medical condition. As good as Ren can be, it takes time to fake a medical record," Georgia said.

"But couldn't you just take care of that in you know where?" Gail asked. "It's not like it's a third-world country."

"Don't you remember what Dr. Pang said? There's a chance that trying the old treatment could kill him. It's the problem all bondsmen face, that the antibodies of one strain of vampire could react badly with the one in their system. The last thing Ren wanted was for me to be stuck, alone, in a foreign country. I'd never be able to come back because of *them*."

"Don't you see? I can help you," Gail offered. "I've worked the hospitals around here. I could help slip in his chart."

"You would really do that for me?" Georgia asked.

"It's not every day you find true love, right?" Gail gushed. She looked down. "You know, there is something I should tell you since you've been so honest with me."

Georgia led her new confidant back to the sofa. Both of them did one more sweep for prying eyes before daring to speak.

Georgia started, "You don't have to say anything . . ."

Gail let out a deep breath. "You've looked up so much about me. I'm sure you know that I'm from a family that can be a little organized.

Sometimes they have me spy for them at the hospital. You never know when it's useful to know when someone has a drug allergy or a habit, and of course, they want me to tell them if anyone they know is seriously ill."

She sank back into her seat. "I've never told anyone what I've had to do," Gail said. "But I guess you know what it's like to have to keep secrets."

Georgia smiled and snuck out the tickets again. "That I do," she muttered. "You really want to help now, don't you?"

"Vampires can't be worse than the people I've dealt with," Gail offered.

Georgia set the tickets on her lap. Gail looked on quizzically.

"He already went in to get his treatment. Everything was already set in motion long before tonight," Georgia said.

"But that would mean . . ." Gail said, shaking her head. "Wait, what does it mean?"

"Sometimes you have to take a leap of faith, Miss Filipovic," Georgia said. "If you love someone, you'd do anything, wouldn't you?"

Gail looked down at the tickets. "Wait a second, these are from November."

"Like I said, he already got his treatment. We had everything so *perfectly* planned. Ren was always great at making plans. My bags were packed, and I wrote this great letter to Mr. Lambley explaining to him how lucky I was to have met him, but that I was going to have to end our contract a little early. Ren gave me cash to get the tickets. That was my job while he got worked into a clinic. Do you know how many days it took for him to build that whole damn health record?"

"I don't understand," Gail said.

"He had gone in on a Friday to get his infusion. I got his text. Everything was fine until I got a call at eight in the morning on a Saturday. Now, even before I started working nights, I never got up that early on a weekend. But he told me that we had to meet before our flight. I could hear something different in his voice, so I got my keys and I rushed over to our special meeting spot. Lucky for us, Alice and Paul were heading to his hometown for Thanksgiving already . . ."

Georgia fumbled with her key as she tried to balance a travel mug of Joe, her purse, and her phone in the crook of her arm. The wind ruffled her Muppet fur collar around her neck, and the rare-in-New-England late-autumn sun made her squint. She finally got in both sets of doors and dumped her stuff on the counter. "Hey, you here?" she called as she saw the water still running in the sink and an open bottle of ibuprofen on the counter. "Ren?" she called again.

The door was open to her bedroom, but there was no light coming into the hall. She approached it cautiously as she heard heavy breathing from inside her room.

"Ren?" she asked.

He was lying half-dressed and facedown on the bed. The tattoos across his back didn't quite conceal all of the deep red lines running from shoulder to spine, and two large welts stood out on the base of his neck.

"Ren!" she cried as she ran to him. As she rolled him over, all of the blood rushed from her head, and she let out a choked cry, "Ren!"

His eyes opened slowly, and he reached for her face. "Hey, you," he said.

"Ren, what's going on? You said you were fine," she said as she felt his ice-cold hands.

"It will be . . . it will be fine," he whispered. "I made her . . . I made her promise."

"Ren!"

He closed his eyes for a moment. Georgia started shaking him awake.

"We need to call the hospital. Something is wrong," she said. "Ren, baby, please—Ren, wake up. Wake up!"

He cracked his eyelids open again and pointed to the nightstand. Georgia looked over to see a folded-up piece of paper that was spotted in red. "Georgia—" he said.

"No, no, no," she repeated as his eyes closed again and the terrible rattling breathing started all over. "Ren? Ren, please?"

The rattle stopped.

"You mean . . . ?" Gail choked.

Georgia looked away as she put the tickets back in her purse. Slowly, deliberately, she pulled out a wrinkled, nasty scrap of paper. Gail looked on in horror as she could see a few faded words.

"It's funny. When you watch people cry in movies, it's so quiet really. People's eyes well up, and there is sad music," Georgia said. "I remember crying until I threw up. Believe me, there was nothing pretty about those tears, Miss Filipovic."

"I don't understand—"

"This letter is a promise of protection, a contract of loyalty," Georgia read. "May the bearer of this be granted pardon and immunity from all harm from the Jaeger clan."

"A promise made is a promise kept," a thickly German-accented voice finished.

Gail whirled around to see Minerva standing right behind them. She jumped to her feet but ended up tripping and landing on the floor next to Georgia. Her interviewer neatly tucked the paper back in her purse, stood up, and straightened her skirt. The blonde vampire smiled widely to reveal all of her now-bright pink fangs.

"I don't understand. What kind of test is this?" Gail cried.

"Oh, sweetie," Georgia said, her voice suddenly as cold and biting as Minerva's. "Did you really think that this was a test . . . for you?"

Gail scrambled backward along the carpet until she ran into another chair. In the blink of an eye, the vampire was next to her. Minerva scooped up her prey with one hand and plopped her unceremoniously in a velvet armchair. "You, stay," the undead blonde commanded.

Gail looked around desperately and tried to push her arms down, but her strength failed her. Minerva continued to stare at her. "You, stay," she said again, this time much more calmly.

"I don't understand," Gail whimpered.

"I told you how sometimes the three of us—Steve, Geoffrey, and I— would have these bullshit conversations, didn't I? We'd ask each other what we'd do in certain scenarios, as if we were still a bunch of pricks in college.

Here's one for you," Georgia said. "If it came down to a choice between saving yourself and saving a complete stranger, what would you do?"

Georgia didn't wait for the flush-faced little pixie to respond. "How about a better one?" she asked. "Would you sacrifice one innocent life to save a bunch of others?"

"What kind of question is that?" Gail asked, still eyeing the vampire next to her.

"It's supposed to be difficult, but it's not. It's easy to be noble and say you wouldn't sacrifice one to save the many if you're talking about an innocent," Georgia said. "But what happens when you slide that moral scale just a touch? What would you do if you were given the choice between saving yourself or someone who hurt you so badly that you'll never, ever recover?"

Gail just shook her head. "I don't understand. I've never even met you before today—" she stammered out.

"We had everything planned," Georgia said, wiping the corner of her eye. "All we had to do was take a cab to the airport on Sunday morning. We only needed one more day."

"I don't—" Gail started to say. Her eyes widened with horror. "The tattoos. You said Ren was covered in tattoos, didn't you?"

Georgia nodded. Now it was Gail's turn to tear up.

"No—no, that guy didn't have green eyes," she said quickly. "There was a guy who seemed suspicious—really tall, with scars and tattoos. He had this name that sounded vaguely familiar, like one of the triads my uncle worked with. All I did was make one call, but that guy was Taiwanese, not Japanese, and he didn't have green eyes—I swear!"

"Are you sure?" Georgia asked.

"I'm sure I'd remember an Asian guy with green eyes," Gail said. "This guy's name was weird—Ty something, not Ren!"

"Tyrone Lee, perhaps?"

"That was it!" Gail said. "All I did was tell my uncle that he was in the hospital. How? What happened?"

"I tried to warn zee little *Berliner* that I didn't like it when other girls played with my toys," Minerva said. "But she didn't listen."

"At first I didn't know exactly what happened, how Minnie ever found out about our plan to run away," Georgia said. "Frankly I didn't care, but I was given a choice."

"Georgia?" Gail whimpered. She then dared to address Minerva. "You killed him? You killed Ren? Why?"

Minerva paused for a moment with an unusually thoughtful look filling her sanguine eyes. She crouched next to the trembling girl and set her ice-cold hands on Gail's shuddering shoulders. "It was never my intention to kill zee boy," she said. "I just couldn't have him leave. Zee scandal, zee shame that would fall on our house if we let zee help run off with some Pendragon's little crumpet would be so dreadfully annoying."

"So she forced him to drink her blood," Georgia said.

Minerva clucked her tongue and waved her finger in shame. "Oh no, little *Berliner*, I didn't have to force him," she corrected. "I simply made him a better offer than you ever could, but your stupid human *sheisse* science had to go and ruin everything!"

"You knew something was wrong when you fed off him, Minerva!" Georgia snapped. "You knew it was wrong, and you gave him your blood anyway."

The vampire whirled around and started cursing in German. Gail took the brief distraction to try to run for the door. Their waiter took this inopportune moment to walk into the room. Gail grabbed his arm and looked up into his big brown eyes with a face of pure desperation.

"Help me!"

The waiter smiled, finally revealing his own fangs. Gail suddenly felt the cold radiating from his arm. She stumbled back and found Minerva waiting. "You're—you're—" Gail sputtered.

"Is there anything I can get you?" he asked. "You've done so much for me already."

She took in the pretty face, the big brown eyes, and the floppy waves of chestnut brown hair. For the first time all night, Gail was able to notice just how pale her waiter really was. He gave a neat little bow to her.

"Such zee showman, *mein bruder*," Minerva said, rolling her eyes. "Why don't you tell her about your little connection with zee Filipovic family?"

"I've never met you before in my life," Gail said.

"True," Steve said. "That's why it took me a while to find you. Your uncle, on the other hand, has been a good friend for a long time, and I found a way to convince him that it was in his best interests to tell me all about his sweet little *bratanica*. It's been enough time, and I think my little sweetheart here is ready for some closure, so I figured it was a good opportunity to introduce you two."

Gail looked desperately to Georgia. "What is going on? Please, just tell me what is going on," she begged. "I swear—"

"Vampire society has four laws," Georgia said softly. "Law number one is that vampires can't kill one another."

Gail whimpered as both Minerva and Steve drew closer. Georgia stayed perfectly still off to the side. She gave the poor girl an apologetic look at last.

"Law number two is the law of secrecy," Georgia continued. "So you can guess which one I'm in violation of right now, but you see, the law of hospitality says that I can't be hurt as long as I was under Mr. Lambley's protection—"

"Which didn't apply when you were sneaking off to screw my servant," Steve added. "You were also planning to run away with him, leaving the Pendragon protection. That was really not your smartest moment, sweetheart."

"So that leaves the fourth law, which is that a vampire's word is his bond," Georgia countered. "That's why Ren got you to sign that contract, isn't it, Minnie?"

"So true, neither *mein bruder* nor I can touch you," the blonde vampire said. She turned back to face Gail. "But there is nothing to stop us from taking care of you, is there, little one?"

Gail dashed over and threw herself at Georgia's feet. She stared at her with big, desperate brown eyes and clutched at Georgia's leg. "I swear, that guy didn't have green eyes," she whimpered. "He must have been someone else. He didn't—"

Georgia crouched down and wrapped her arms gently around the poor shaking little girl. Slowly she leaned down and whispered ever so sweetly, "He wore contacts, you little bitch," before pushing her back.

Gail screamed as a Jaeger grabbed each arm and swung her against the wall. She slumped over like a broken doll, begging and crying as the twin predators took their time working their way over. Georgia looked away.

The misery on Georgia's face was too sweet a bait not to attract the male vampire. He darted back to his former lover and smiled. "You thought you were so much better than me, didn't you?" he asked. "I told you, when given a choice between saving yourself and saving someone else, you're always gonna pick the home team."

"Please help me," Gail begged as Minerva picked her up and tilted back the poor girl's neck. "I promise I won't tell anyone, I swear."

The blonde vampire rolled her head back to give Georgia just one moment to grit her teeth before the blonde human dove for the floor. Both vampires watched in shock as Georgia jumped back to her feet and brandished one of the splintered sides of the crate Minerva had smashed earlier in the evening.

"I can't believe I'm saying this, but let her go!" Georgia barked.

Minerva dropped the girl and took one threatening step toward Georgia. "You realize that if you attack us, zee contract will no longer protect you, Georgia darling," she said. "And you know what else—"

Meanwhile Gail scrambled to her feet and started inching for the door, watching in horror as Georgia was now the targeted prey of two young vampires. Her interviewer took a bold step toward Steve, making certain he could see each and every splinter in perfect clarity.

"You also realize that Ren told me just how long it took Steve to recover from one incident with a pencil. I'd love to know what some nasty old pine would do to him," she snapped.

"Why?" Gail said. "Why are you doing this?"

"Because every Jaeger must pass zee test," Minerva spat. "To be one of us, you must be a hunter, be a killer."

Gail watched in confusion as Georgia shoved a manky piece of wood into her hands. For a moment the tiny brunette actually had to feel the warmth radiating from the girl next to her and watch just how heavy the other blonde's breathing was.

"I don't understand. Georgia, you aren't a vamp—"

It was Steve, the cocky vampire's, turn to speak. He kept a close eye on the pair of makeshift shivs and maneuvered to stand just behind his sister before he opened his mouth.

"Oh, did you think that the Jaeger rules only applied to the fangs?" he asked with a little smirk. "Everyone has to play their part. It's not just the family that has to prove their virtue. The help has to show that they are hunters too."

Gail looked at Georgia in horror. "Wait—you wanted to be a—a Jaeger?" she asked in disbelief. "But, but they killed—but Ren?"

Minerva burst into laughter. "Oh, you confused little thing! Don't you know that this was the *Berliner*'s one last chance?"

"Seriously, we all but handed it to you on a platter, sweetheart, but in the end, you were only human," Steven sighed.

"What is going on?" Gail cried.

Georgia didn't bother wiping the tear out of the corner of her eye. "It was my one last chance," she choked out.

"To what?" Gail asked.

"To be with him!" Georgia spit out at last. "It was my last chance to be with him."

Both girls felt the hairs on the back of their necks stand on end as they heard the door by the bar swing open. Instead of a waiter, a man in a sleekly tailored gray suit walked to the bar, grabbed a pair of glasses, and started plopping in ice ever so methodically. Gail's jaw dropped as she saw near-shoulder-length jet-black hair and a pair of mirrored sunglasses on a chiseled, distinctly Asian set of features.

Everything grew shockingly quiet as he dropped in the last ice cube before grabbing a dark bottle from the bar fridge and pouring two cups of thick red liquid. He smiled before pulling off his shades to reveal pale green eyes.

He nodded genially to the terrified Serbian with a shiv. "Nice to see you again, Miss Filipovic."

"You're alive!" she squawked. She then looked accusatorily at Georgia. "But you said—"

"I said he stopped breathing," she snapped. "Do you think I'm such an idiot that I wouldn't try to revive him, that I would just sit there and cry?"

Ren dutifully handed a drink to each Jaeger and then stood protectively in front of them both. "Can we please be civilized?" he asked. "I think we've heard enough drama for tonight."

"Georgia—" Gail said. She looked over and saw her interviewer still holding up her sliver of wood, but her hands were shaking violently.

"So, you finally decided to show your face," Georgia said as she took in the sight of her former lover walking among the Jaegers. "Minnie let you off her leash."

"Ooh, I should tie you up again tonight, *mein shatzi*," Minerva cooed as she wrapped around the servant and gave a little wink to Georgia. "Hey, *Berliner*, if you get this over with quickly, I'll let your first duty be warming him up."

"You were going to serve *Minerva*?" Gail gasped.

"It's the only way she'd let us be together," Georgia said. "A Matsuoka can only serve a Jaeger, right? Because, heaven forbid, you ever think for yourself, Ren."

"We tried it your way," Ren snapped. He yanked a little silk-wrapped bottle out of his pocket and brandished it in front of a now red-faced Georgia. "And instead of being free—"

"I didn't know what would happen. You think I wanted you to be more dependent on her?" Georgia snapped.

"I certainly don't mind zee extra attention," Minerva cooed. She leaned around Ren and motioned to the still-dumbstruck Gail. "Dr. Pang's little potion stopped zee reaction that was killing my poor toy, but now he needs my gift every month, or else, well, let's just say it's not very pleasant, no?"

"The vial? Oh my god, you tried to cure him with that thing from the scary guy in Japan?" Gail asked. "What were you thinking?"

"You're questioning *my* judgment?" Georgia asked. "You're the girl who followed me into a bar the first day we met after I warned you that I worked for vampires."

"But—" Gail started to stammer.

"Look, dawn is coming," Steve sighed to Georgia. "Can we just kill her and go home? If you don't give us permission, it won't count, sweetheart."

"What?" Gail squawked. "You can't—Georgia, please!"

Ren reached his hand toward Georgia and said gently, "Come on, Georgia. We can be together. Just put down the pointy thing and let my masters take care of the rest. You know that it's too late. She knows too much, and if you let her live, the sheriff will be coming for you. Come on . . . be logical. Be reasonable for once."

Gail whimpered as she saw Georgia's hand start to lower. Ren smiled and took a step toward them. His smile faded in the split second it took for Georgia to shove him right back into the two vampires, sending a spray of blood over both their sets of designer clothing. "Go to hell!" she snapped.

"You little—" Minerva growled.

Steve shoved Ren right back at the human, sending her toppling and the splinter flying out of her hand. Gail gasped as the vampire's hand snapped around her wrist, and in her surprise her weapon also ended up maddeningly out of reach.

"I'm tired of these games. You know, I think it's about time I taught you a proper lesson, sweetheart," Steve said. "You need to know exactly whose emotions you've been messing with."

Gail screamed as Steve jerked her against him and tilted her neck.

Minerva helped Ren to his feet and then grabbed Georgia. "You know, I am thinking that this one time, I may just have to break a rule to be rid of this little pest," she hissed as she held Georgia's hands behind her back. "You OK with that, little Matsuoka?"

Ren looked pleadingly at Georgia. "Just for once, be reasonable, Georgia. She isn't worth this," he said.

"I won't play the game anymore," Georgia snapped. "Ren, we will find another way, a better way, but we don't have to keep playing their little vampire games!"

"Talk, talk, talk, blah, blah, blah!" Steve sighed. He rolled back his lips to bare his fangs. "I think you're right, sis. Maybe she is worth breaking the rules just once. I mean, I didn't see any piece of paper. Did you?"

"*Nein,*" Minerva said.

"And pretty soon you won't see anything," Steve cooed in Gail's ear. "And you, servant, you aren't getting any ideas, are you? I forgave you once, but if you come at me with so much as a toothpick, I will snap your neck and use your skull as my next punch bowl. We clear, Renny-boy?"

Gail whimpered and cried as she struggled desperately against the wild-eyed vampire, but he didn't so much as budge no matter how much she squirmed. After a few seconds of delicious agitation, Steve used one arm to gently stroke her neck and push the hair off her throat.

"Isn't this that romantic fantasy you human girls have?" Steve whispered in her ear. "You act all scared and innocent, but isn't this what you really want? Just relax, and I will make this the most gentle and pleasurable experience of the rest of your short little life."

"Help, please!" Georgia cried as Gail screamed again.

"Oh, be quiet!" Steve snapped. "Who the hell is going to come save you from the secret little trap that you set up, sweetheart?"

"I will, you Jaeger brat!" a new booming and decidedly British voice said as the back door flew open. Both girls squinted as a tall, dashing figure stood in the blinding floodlights pouring in from the alley. The only feature Gail could make out was a glowing halo of bright ginger hair.

Georgia took advantage of the second's surprise and wrenched free of Minerva. Gail remained frozen in abject terror.

"Take your hands off the girl, Stefano," their hero said. "And if you so much as look at Miss Sutherland in a manner I do not like, I shall be most cross with you."

"Gingersnaps, is that you?" Steve asked incredulously. "Are you threatening me or something?"

"I said, take your hands off the lady," Geoffrey Lambley said as he strode into the room. Minerva tried to stave off a giggle when she saw the pudgy little man walk in with a puffed-out chest and his hands raised in adorable little fisticuffs.

"Oh, this is rich," Minerva said. "What are you doing here, Geoffrey?"

"I said, let her go," he said, still advancing. Minerva's grin faded a little as she saw a new resolution in his firm brow and grim set jaw. Steve tossed the girl to the side, where Georgia picked her up and dragged her to the far side of the bar. Both of them peeked over the edge to see a terrified Ren scrambling to join them, while one Mr. Geoffrey Lambley stood face-to-face with the taller, younger, more muscular hunter and his Kung Fu master of a sister.

"That's Mr. Lambley?" Gail gasped.

"Shh!" both Ren and Georgia said at once as the three vampires began to circle each other and size one another up.

"You really need to butt out of this, Gingersnaps. If you could have just kept your assistant in line in the first place—"

Geoffrey responded with a satisfying bitch slap right across Steve's face. "You? You dare to talk to me about control? You come to my city, come into my home, and you try to steal the one person of importance in my life and you expect that challenge to go unanswered? I knew you couldn't stand that Miss Sutherland saw right through your dizzying array of lies and poppycock and preferred the company of your far more capable and, from what I've heard, far more satisfying servant to yours."

Minerva giggled. She stopped as the violent redhead turned to her. "And you, how can you indulge your younger brother and his obsessive schemes? I thought you knew better than that. You disappoint me greatly," he said in a voice so withering that the blonde actually retreated.

Steve rolled his eyes. "Stop your blustering, Gingersnaps!" he said. "Step aside and let me drain the outsider, and then if you want, you can help me take care of the little tramp—"

This time Geoffrey's slap turned the younger vampire's head. Steve once more made a move for the girls, but to his utter shock, the scrappy shorter vampire decked him. Steve tried to swing back, but the Pendragon easily dodged and gave him a solid round of body blows.

"These girls are under Pendragon watch, so unless you want to face not only me but the entire wrath of my family, I strongly suggest you take your skinny little Jaeger bottom and get out of my sight!"

Steve snapped his hands out and grabbed the redhead by the collar. All the witnesses watched in wonder as Geoffrey didn't so much as flinch. He continued to stare right through the Jaeger with a glare more like two pure green daggers rather than his normal dewy eyes.

"There is something different about you, old friend," Steve said as he let go.

"You know better than anyone who I was and who I will be again soon enough," Mr. Lambley growled. "Do you really want to cross me?"

"This is your mess then, Gingersnaps. You have to clean it up, or your little minx will end up at the bottom of the Charles," Steve warned.

"Get out of here, both of you," Geoffrey snarled. The two Jaegers took a moment to straighten their clothes and wipe up the blood.

Minerva motioned to the shocked Ren. "Let's go," she barked.

Georgia grabbed Ren's hand and looked pleadingly in his eyes. "Please, just stay with me. Mr. Lambley—"

Ren brushed her away. "The only thing you ever wanted to do was run away. I should have known you wouldn't have what it takes to survive in our world," he said coldly.

"Ren!" Georgia begged.

"I guess I wasn't worth it," Ren snapped bitterly. "I should have known better."

Gail watched as Georgia was left wiping away tears as Ren walked out the back door with his Jaeger masters. As soon as they were out of sight, Mr. Lambley let out a deep sigh and flopped onto the sofa.

"Oh my, that was intense, wasn't it?" he said. "Dear Georgia, are you all right?"

The other girl finally came out from behind the bar. Gail threw herself at the vampire's feet. "Thank you!" she gasped.

Georgia pulled out her phone and finally hit the end-call button. Mr. Lambley responded by pulling a Bluetooth earpiece out from under his tangle of hair. He let out a weak little wave. "You must be the mysterious Miss Gail I've heard about all night."

"You were listening all along?" Gail gasped.

The redhead smiled as his assistant settled down next to him. His smile faded as he saw just how red her eyes were even in the dim light.

"Oh, Georgia, we'll find another way to reach him, I promise," he said gently.

Georgia shook her head and leaned it on his shoulder. "No, no, Mr. Lambley, Ren Matsuoka is dead to me. I couldn't—I just—"

He squeezed her shoulder. "Don't give up hope, dear Georgia."

Gail slumped pitifully on the floor. "What the hell is going on here?" she asked.

"I thought I would do anything to get Ren back, but I was wrong," Georgia said. "And now I've gotten you stuck in this mess."

"Oh, pishposh," Mr. Lambley said. "There is nothing done yet that cannot be made right. I promise to you both, the Pendragon family will fix this."

Gail looked at him and smiled with genuine gratitude. "Does that mean I'm under your protection too?" she asked.

Mr. Lambley pulled out a handkerchief and dabbed at her eyes. "Oh, dear heart, you look a mess. Why don't you go freshen up before we leave?"

Gail nodded and struggled to her feet. She let Georgia gingerly help her smooth her hair and her blouse. As they finally looked each other in the eyes again, the little brunette gushed, "I'm so sorry for what happened. I never meant for anyone to get hurt, I swear."

Georgia turned away. "Let's not get into that now. You've got a bit of blood on your shirt. You should probably take care of that."

Gail acquiesced and went to wash her face and blow her nose. As she rooted through the empty attendant's stand, she heard a flush coming from the handicapped stall.

"Oh my, are you OK?" a sweet little voice said as an old lady in a violet tracksuit came wandering toward the sinks.

Gail sniffled. "I'm fine."

The old lady's hands shook as she tried to pass them under the sink, but the water refused to run. She motioned to Gail. "Would you mind? This one is broken, dearie," she asked.

As Gail passed her hands in front of the sensor, she felt a slight pang in the pit of her stomach. She looked past the doddering, tiny old thing to see the edge of a blue apron and a limp hand hanging down from the handicapped toilet. Gail looked up slowly to see only one reflection looking back in the mirror. She tried to scream, but the old woman's talons snapped around her throat with shocking force.

"I would be very, very quiet, if I were you," the old lady said. "Now I want you to tell me absolutely everything you think you know about vampires."

Meanwhile, out in the alley, one Georgia Sutherland opened the door to the stately old vehicle and let a few more tears fall. Once inside, an extremely concerned-looking man with thick ginger hair wrapped an arm around her. The driver, a butch Barbie doll of a woman with a prominent Adam's apple, let out a deep sigh of relief.

"I told you that she'd come back, Mr. Lambley," Nicolette Tesla said. She shut up quickly as she saw the poor girl sob. "Should we head back to the house?"

"Wait, what about Gail?" Georgia asked. "You didn't—"

Mr. Lambley held up a hand and motioned her to wait. He squeezed his assistant once more for good measure before there was a tap on the glass. He rolled it down to reveal none other than a concerned-looking Mr. Sugar.

Georgia's eyes widened. "What is he—?"

"I promise you, all will be explained. You have to know that the sheriff was involved. The Jaegers would never be so flagrant with the rules, even a couple of young idiots like those two," Geoffrey said.

"The sheriff has it all taken care of. Mr. DeMarco has just gone in," Mr. Sugar said in hush-hush tones. "Now, you should take her home."

"Wait—Steve?" Georgia asked weakly as she looked up from the damp spot on Mr. Lambley's neatly tailored lapel. "Is he going to—?"

"Now, Georgia—" the vampire started.

"Don't you worry, sweetie," Mr. Sugar said. "He's only being asked to kiss her good night."

"Just a kiss?" she asked again.

"Take her home, Mr. Lambley."

Georgia and her boss rode in silence through the streets of Boston until they arrived at a quaint little brownstone in the busy restaurant district of Brookline. She ran her fingers slowly over the little bunny statues while Nicolette took care of the door. The moment she stepped inside, a shambling mass of orange fluffiness bolted toward her, purring as he twisted and coiled around the young woman's leg.

"Schrodinger is certainly glad to see you," Mr. Lambley said in forced cheerfulness. "Come now, we'll have a little tea, and I can put on a movie."

Georgia gave the pudgy old vampire a quick kiss on the cheek. Her eyes widened. "Something is *different* about you," she said.

The vampire smiled weakly. Georgia pounced on the opportunity to run her finger under his lip. He pulled away, but not before she could just feel a tiny bump growing where once there had only been a gap.

He blushed. "So, movie?" he asked weakly.

"I think I'm tired and am just going to go upstairs." She looked over at the drag queen futzing with the mail. "Nicolette, are you OK with staying another night? Are you paid up?"

"Sure thing," she said. "Are you sure I can't get you anything?"

Georgia shook her head before shambling up the stairs. Much to her surprise, a pair of puffy gingers followed her.

"I said I was tired, Mr. Lambley," she said.

"You know what happened to that Matsuoka boy wasn't your fault. You couldn't have known what would happen when you gave him that vial," the vampire offered.

"I should have known, and I should have come to you and Mina and Lorcan rather than trying to run away. You were right. I do belong here."

"But it's not over. You could still—" he said.

"Good night, Mr. Lambley," Georgia said. "Don't stay up too late with Nicolette."

The vampire hung his head but turned and walked back down the stairs, leaving only the oversize kitten to follow Georgia to her bedroom. Once inside she took her time peeling away the layers of clothing until she was left only in her bra and panties. She pulled a clean tank top over her head and cracked her neck a few times. Finally she yanked off her diamond ring and placed it carefully on her dressing table on top of a pair of passports—one green, one blue.

"Every Jaeger has to pass a test to prove his worth to the clan. Every Jaeger has to be a killer," she said softly. "And I couldn't do it. I'm not like them," she told her reflection.

Just as she had calmed down and managed to settle into bed without any more tears, a buzzing sound lured her back to the land of consciousness. Her hands shook as she pulled out her phone in its snazzy leopard-print case, and a single text splashed across the screen.

It read, "Meet us tomorrow."

16

Georgia struggled to open the door to Little Jiro's Sushi Hut with her arms full of a bright blue box topped with a floppy silver bow. After a solid minute of struggling, she finally managed to wedge her toes between the frame and the jamb and kicked it open enough to hop inside.

Georgia let out a sigh of exasperation as a tall, leggy blonde continued to lounge in her chair rather than offer even the slightest inkling of help. Instead, she flipped through a fashion magazine and ogled a bright pink and white striped sun hat.

"I don't think it will do you much good," Georgia snapped as she set the box on the table.

"Ooh, you took zee time to wrap it up with a pretty little bow." She squealed in delight as she took a deep sniff. "You really shouldn't have."

"You're right about that," Georgia muttered. "I got up early for this."

Minerva pulled the bow with the giddiness of a schoolgirl at Christmas. She giggled and pulled out a little plastic container full of rich reddish brown pudding. She looked in frustration at the chopsticks littering the table until Georgia came to the rescue and produced a spoon from the bowels of her purse.

"What? No gift for me?" Steve asked as he wandered to the table and snagged the chair next to the blonde. "After all, I was the one who had to take a beating."

"That was hardly a beating, *mein bruder.* Georgia here has hit you harder," Minerva sighed.

"Well, she's certainly hit more below the belt," Steve laughed. "Seriously, sweetheart, you should move to Hollywood because those were some of the greatest crocodile tears that I've ever seen."

"Well, it had to be convincing. That's what Dr. Pang said," Georgia said, looking off anxiously toward the sushi counter.

"I still think it would have been quicker to just take him to a nice farm in Bolivia and let him discover his roots there," Minerva sighed.

"There you are, still thinking like a Jaeger," a new, lilting voice said. Georgia turned to see a striking brunette drifting across the plastic tiles without making so much as a click even in her five-inch heels. She tossed her long braid of inky hair over her shoulder and found a way to ease into her chair that perfectly displayed her sizable assets, which were barely contained by her silk blouse. "My Geoffrey is a Pendragon boy, and you have to think like a Pendragon to save him, dearie."

Georgia half bowed, half curtsied to the final vampire joining them at the table before she too took a seat. Lady Mina leaned over and kissed the blushing girl on each cheek.

"I am so glad he found you, Georgia darling. I knew you had spunk from the moment I met you. I just knew you'd be the key to his recovery!" the Pendragon continued. She leaned across the table and gave the younger vampire a knowing smile. "You see, we just had to make our Geoffrey a hero and give him a little quest."

"Why did I have to be the villain though?" Steve whined. "You could have let someone else—"

"You're a Jaeger, darling. It's what you do," Mina sighed. She rustled around her purse and pulled out a few little velvet boxes. She handed a small one to each of the Jaegers and a larger one to the surprised Georgia.

Once more Minerva was all smiles as she pulled out a pair of glittering pearl and diamond earrings. Mina smiled and said, "I'd give you a pearl necklace, but I know you've had so many of those in the past."

Minerva laughed and replied, "You and me both!"

Steve pulled out a pair of cuff links and jumped out of his seat as he read the inscription. "How did you . . . ?" he asked.

"You weren't the only vampire sleeping with half of Hollywood. I just happened to land a few costume designers, and yes, those are from *Casablanca*," Mina said.

"I really can't accept anything—" Georgia said as she looked at the blue velvet box in her hands. The elder vampire smiled and brushed a little bit of hair off of Georgia's forehead to reveal a substantial bruise.

"Steve, you are a Jaeger brute. You play too rough always!" She turned back to Georgia. "I am a woman of honor, Miss Sutherland. You had the most dangerous part to play in this little game, and I will see you rewarded."

"Why reward her? We don't even know—" Minerva started.

"They were growing back. I felt them!" Georgia said.

"Oh, I'm sure you did," Mina said with a little wink.

Georgia decided to diffuse the situation by opening up the box. It contained a familiar house key, mounted on a beautiful new chain, as well as a very old-looking key mottled with rust and pits.

"You are welcome both in the house of Pendragon here and in our main estate, Miss Sutherland. You are under my protection as well," Mina said with a pointed look at Steve. "Now, I'd say that my work here is done. I think I should leave town with the sheriff before my little lamb gets wind that I messed with his affairs again. *Auf wiedersehen*, Minerva. Good-bye, Stefano."

"*Auf wiedersehen*, Mina. As always, it was a pleasure doing business with you," Minerva sighed.

Georgia rose as soon as the elder Pendragon drifted out the door. "So we're done, right?" she asked.

"I suppose," Minerva said. "Dear Steffan, could you get zee car? I want a moment here."

Steve reluctantly got to his feet. He did stop right in front of Georgia. "You know, now that Gingersnaps is on the mend, maybe you and me could—"

"Remember what I said last time? You know the never, ever, ever getting back together part? Was it somehow unclear?" she asked.

"Well, I was pretty sure it was all pretend, for Geoff's sake. I was hoping that—"

"It wasn't all pretend, Steve," Georgia said.

"Well, I guess I won't be seeing you for a while."

"I guess not," she said with a sarcastic little wave. "Bye, Steve!"

"Seriously, Minnie, what is with your brother?" Georgia asked as she settled back at the table. She got distracted as she saw another figure lurking just around the bend at the counter.

"Yes, he's here," Minerva sighed. "Matsuoka, come!"

Georgia stiffened as Ren once more drifted into her life. He made a point to sit right next to Minerva and kept his head lowered. The vampire lifted his wrist and inspected where a few fresh welts had appeared.

"I do love Japanese food," the vampire said with a wicked little grin. "Don't you, *Berliner*?"

"I really should be getting back to Mr. Lambley. It's a key point in his recovery—"

"If there is one thing I know about Geoffrey, it's that he likes to sleep in," Minerva said. "Stay a moment. I have questions."

"I don't have anything to say to you right now, Minnie," Georgia snapped. "Did you really let that girl go?"

"Yah. She has a headache that will last for days, but as far as she knows, she got drunk and had an amazing one-night stand with zee waiter from a club downtown."

"I won't see her in the papers?" Georgia asked.

"*Nein, nein,*" Minerva said. "Zee sheriff was there with Lady Pendragon. Nothing bad will happen. Plus it would be bad for zee business if one of our Serbian friends were to disappear. Are you satisfied?"

Georgia nodded.

Minerva looked over at her stiff, blank-faced servant and raised a brow.

"You know, when you were telling zee story, I almost thought you really cared for him," the vampire said.

"Like I said, I had to be convincing. Mina thought it would only work if there were humans in danger."

"I mean, I really don't mind if you want to use my toy from time to time. A little passion makes zee blood flow," she sighed. "But you have to know that he belongs to me and I only share when I want to."

"Of course," Georgia said, looking at Ren rather than the vampire. "Look, we're done, right? Mr. Lambley will get stronger, and maybe at some point, you guys can all be back to your good old frenemy selves."

"Perhaps," Minerva said, standing up. "I guess we should go."

Georgia did finally look back at the vampire. "You know, there is one thing. I know that Steve and Mr. Lambley were buddies, but why did you agree to help? Why get him to see Dr. Pang in the first place? I know that can't have been cheap or easy for you."

"It wasn't," she said. "And let's just say that Mr. Lambley once helped me and never knew about it, and I wanted to return that same favor. He is never to know of my part of this arrangement, am I clear?"

"Crystal," Georgia said.

Before she could turn for the door, Ren said quietly, "I have the business arrangements to take care of with Miss Sutherland, mistress. I'll take her to get a cab."

"I don't know. Can I trust you two alone?" the vampire asked warily.

Ren bowed submissively to his master. "I assure you, mistress, that I only carried out my orders exactly as requested. We had to be convincing. That is all."

Minerva waved him away. "Do what you have to. You know, I wonder what would have happened if you had really fallen for this girl? We could have used another servant and a nice live meal. Oh well, *que sera sera!*"

"I'll be but a moment, mistress," he said as he led Georgia back out the front door. They shuffled together until they reached the corner, where he pulled out an envelope marked with Georgia's name. "It's your portion of the fee for your part in this charade," he said.

She grabbed the envelope but didn't pull it out of his hands. Instead, she let her fingers rest against his for as long as she dared. She looked over her shoulder, as did Ren.

"I'm going to find a way," she said.

Ren closed his eyes and let the tiny touch fill every inch of his senses. He then let go and turned away. "It's too late for me. The treatment didn't work."

"But there have to be other treatments—"

Ren shook his head. "Not known to human medical science."

"Then we'll find another vampire doc—"

"I can't go to any other vampire doctors," Ren hissed. "You know what is happening to me. I can feel it. We've both seen the signs."

"Ren, please. Just have a little faith. Mr. Lambley promised me that he will find a way to save you."

Ren shook his head. "You have an awful lot of faith in a vampire who lost his fangs, you know."

She darted around to face him again. "No, I have a lot of faith in a really smart man and his desperate would-be sweetheart," she whispered. "Next time we will find a way to escape."

He leaned his forehead against hers and squeezed her hands as tightly as he dared. "Georgia," he hissed, "the only way you'll be safe is to forget about me. They have to think . . . no, they have to *know* that what we had was a lie, or one of us will end up dead . . . again."

She pressed against him. "We already got past that once," she offered weakly.

"You don't understand. Minerva can feel my emotions when she feeds off me, and she keeps feeding me over and over again. She's inside me all the time, and it's getting harder and harder to resist—"

Georgia looked up at him. "Please, you have to keep fighting," she begged. "You aren't that monster they want you to be."

Ren shook his head. "That's the problem. I can feel a new monster welling up deep inside the pit of my stomach. Something is wrong, Georgia. I can feel it. It's not just Minerva. Something changed that night. I don't know what, but there is someone else in here," he said, pointing over and over to his temple. "There is something seriously wrong with me."

"Of course, there is something wrong with you. You fell in love with an idiot like me," Georgia hissed. "You just have to hang on, OK? Just find a way to think of me wherever you are, whatever you're doing, and I'll be there with you. We will fight this, OK, Ren? Promise me that you'll fight."

Ren fought between shaking his head and nodding. "You have to go," he said. He gave in and grabbed her, kissing her within an inch of her life right on a public street corner. He ignored the wolf whistles from some college kids and the honking from an appreciative cabbie.

"Make sure you tell her that I attacked you in a fit of human emotion," Georgia said as she pulled away.

"Of course."

She embraced him one last time. "Be strong and think of me," she whispered once more.

"You should just forget about me, Georgia. I'm a lost cause," Ren said sadly.

She gave him a little salute before flagging down a cab. "Don't you know, Ren? Lost causes are my favorite kind."

She took the ride back to Brookline in relative silence. When she arrived at the brownstone, she was greeted with the aroma of curry and the sounds of swelling music coming from the TV room. She peeked in the lounge to see Mr. Lambley curled up in a blanket watching his soaps while sipping on a steaming mug of blood and milk.

"That better be duck blood. Dr. Pang would tell you that you need some cooling influence after all your recent excitement," she warned.

"It is, darling," Nicolette said as she plopped down another TV tray and her microwaved meal. "Want me to heat you something up too? We're about to watch a marathon of nineties soap operas."

"No, I think I'm still a little worn-out. Mind if I head upstairs?" she asked.

"We'll be fine!" both of the drama junkies said as they snuggled into the sofa.

She gave them a little wave before checking the fridge. Sure enough, there were neat little rows of bottles and baggies full of various Eastern remedies, each marked with the appropriate amounts and day of the week. She noticed the bottle warmer with a rack of pink-tinged bottles next to it, and the row of bar blenders just waiting for something nasty from the freezer.

She smiled at her new normal and took comfort in the sole surviving kitten winding his way around her legs as she wandered up to her room. Once there she slipped on her new necklace and smiled at her reflection with the keys resting squarely over her heart. "Come on," she whispered pleadingly to her phone.

She ended up curling in bed, petting the kitty for a while until she started dozing off. Just as she entered the first hazy edges of dreamland, a buzzing from her nightstand snapped her back. Her heart skipped a beat as she read three little words painted across her notification screen.

"Mada ikite iru."

ACKNOWLEDGEMENTS

Thanks to Cheri Madison for her tireless efforts editing *Four* and for trying her best to teach an old writer how to use a comma consistently.

The author would also like to thank Reginald Atkins for his brilliant cover. If you're going to be judged by something, it might as well be awesome.

Sincerest thanks to the Kindle Press Team for making *Four* possible, but, above all, thanks to all the Scouts out there who believed in a crazy little story about vampires.